PRAISE *for* BARBARA WOOD

for *The Prophetess*

"Here is yet another winner by Wood . . . A fun, exciting novel."
—*Library Journal*

"The action, bolstered by a clever if trendy use of the Internet, comes fast. . . . [Readers] will relish Wood's passionate New Age message."
—*Publishers Weekly*

"An entertaining suspense thriller."
—*Kirkus Reviews*

"The plot and pacing are masterful, and there is enough sex, betrayal, murder, and intrigue to keep the most skeptical readers breathlessly turning pages. Wood skillfully envisions a society set in biblical times, with people-trading, marrying, and scheming in a thriving coastal town at the center of ancient trade routes, rendered in soft focus but with marvelous clarity and complexity."
—*Publishers Weekly*, for *The Serpent and the Staff*

"Wood crafts vivid sketches of women who triumph over destiny.
—*Washington Post Book World*

"Absolutely splendid."
—Cynthia Freeman, *New York Times* bestselling author of
A World Full of Strangers and *Come Pour the Wine*

THE
PROPHETESS

OTHER BOOKS *by* BARBARA WOOD

Rainbows on the Moon
The Serpent and the Staff
The Divining
Virgins of Paradise
The Dreaming
Green City in the Sun
This Golden Land
Soul Flame
Vital Signs
Domina
The Watch Gods
Childsong
Night Trains
Yesterday's Child
Curse This House
Hounds and Jackals

Books By Kathryn Harvey
Butterfly
Stars
Private Entrance

THE PROPHETESS

A NOVEL

Barbara Wood

TURNER

Turner Publishing Company

424 Church Street · Suite 2240
Nashville, Tennessee 37219

445 Park Avenue · 9th Floor
New York, NY 10022

www.turnerpublishing.com

The Prophetess

The Prophetess is a work of historical fiction. Although some events and people in this book
are based on historical fact, others are the products of the author's imagination.

Cover by Susan Olinsky
Interior design by Kym Whitley
Cover image: © Serg Myshkovsky/iStockimages

Library of Congress Cataloging-in-Publication Data
ISBN 978-1-63026-767-4 (paperback), 978-1-63026-877-0 (hardcover)

Printed in the United States of America
13 14 15 16 17 18 19 20—0 9 8 7 6 5 4 3 2 1

For Carlos

"It is now the hour for you to wake from sleep,
for our salvation is closer than when we
first accepted the faith."
—THE LITURGY OF THE HOURS

"A baby is born believing."
—KATHRYN LINDSKOOG

"Information wants to be free."
—UNIVERSAL HACKER CREDO

THE
PROPHETESS

PROLOGUE

She knew they were following her.

But there was no time to hide. Catherine was in a race against time. She had to get to the seventh scroll before the others did—the scroll that contained the formula for unlocking the most powerful ancient secrets. A priceless document for which so many had risked—and in some cases lost—their lives.

When Catherine felt the 747 shudder, she looked out the window at the cloud cover below, and decided she was somewhere over New York. Faster, she silently urged the aircraft. Go faster, faster. . . .

A magazine lay in her lap, dated December 1999. The headline on the cover read: IS THE WORLD ABOUT TO END? We face the New Millennium, Catherine thought. Was she also facing her own personal Armageddon? She certainly hadn't thought so three weeks ago, when she had been minding her own business, an archaeologist following the trail of an ancient legend—until she had accidentally stumbled upon an astounding discovery that had forced her to change her identity and her looks, and go into hiding, run for her life.

Her own Armageddon . . . or that of the human race?

The answer was locked in the seventh scroll.

As she felt the 747 start its descent, Catherine's heart began to race with fear and excitement. Soon now, she told herself, it was all going to be over, this nightmare that had begun twenty-two days ago, literally with a bang. . . .

DAY ONE

The explosion occurred at dawn.

It rocked the region, shattering the morning silence and setting off avalanches down the barren cliffs; birds perched in the date palms suddenly flew up and winged out over the blue water of the gulf.

Dr. Catherine Alexander, startled awake, burst out of her tent. Shielding her eyes from the glare of the rising sun, she squinted at the operation going on two hundred yards from her encampment. And when she saw the massive machinery tearing up the earth, she almost screamed. They had promised they would warn her before they blasted; they were excavating too close to the dig, and the dynamiting could ruin her delicate work.

Hastily lacing up her boots, she shouted to members of her crew who were emerging sleepily from their tents. "Check the trenches! Make sure the supports are still holding. I'm going to have a little chat with our neighbor." As Catherine sprinted across the sand, she saw bulldozers move into the newly demolished area. And she swore under her breath.

They were building yet another resort, just like all the fancy, air-conditioned playgrounds that were sprouting up along this eastern shore of the Sinai Peninsula. Up and down the curving coastline, for as far as she could see, hotels and high-rises, white monoliths against the stark blue sky, were turning this barren wilderness into another Miami. Before too long, Catherine knew, there wasn't going to be anywhere left for archaeologists to dig, which was what she had tried to explain to the bureaucrats back in Cairo, when she had begged in vain for a stop-work order while she completed her excavations. But no one in Cairo wanted to listen to a woman, especially one to whom they had only reluctantly granted permission to dig in the first place.

"Hungerford!" she shouted as she neared the compound where the engineers were housed in pre-fab shacks. "You *promised!*"

Catherine did not need this right now. The Department of Antiquities was already breathing down her neck, taking too keen an interest in her dig. It was only a matter of time before they discovered the real reason she was out here and, worse, that she had lied to them. On top of that was the letter that had arrived last week from the foundation, informing her that unless she produced some positive results from the dig soon, her grant would not be renewed, the funds would stop.

But I'm so close, she thought as she went from shack to shack, pounding on doors. I just know I am going to find the well soon! All I need is to be allowed to do my work without these infernal interruptions.

"Hungerford! Where *are* you!"

As Catherine neared the trailer that served as the construction office, she suddenly heard a commotion behind her. Turning, she saw, in the sunlight breaking over the gulf, Hungerford's Arab workers running toward the blast site.

Catherine watched for a moment as the men gathered in a knot at the base of a cliff where the dust was just settling, and when she saw how they gestured and shouted to one another, exclaiming over something one of the workers had found, Catherine felt her stomach tighten. She had witnessed this same excitement before—at digs in Israel and Lebanon.

When something *Big* had been uncovered.

Suddenly she, too, was running, jumping over rocks and around boulders, arriving at the group just as their boss, Hungerford, was pushing his way through, saying, "Awright, awright, who said you all could stop working?" The stout Texan removed his bright yellow hard hat and raked his hand through reddish hair. "Mornin', Doc," he said when he saw Catherine. "Awright, boys, what's going on?"

The Arabs all began talking at once as one of them held out what looked like an old yellowed newspaper. "What the blazes?" Hungerford said with a frown.

"May I?" Catherine said, taking it from him. As the men fell silent, she turned the paper over to inspect it. Her eyes widened.

It was a fragment of papyrus.

Pulling a small magnifying glass out of the pocket of her khaki blouse, Catherine examined the fragment closely. "Jesus!" she said suddenly.

Hungerford grinned. "Blaspheming, Doc?"

"No, it's written here. See? It says Jesus, in Greek."

Hungerford narrowed his eyes at the spot where she was pointing. *Iesous.* "What's it mean?"

Catherine looked at the papyrus—honey-gold with neat black writing, the letters predating modern Greek. Had she stumbled upon what every archaeologist dreamed of? No, it was just too good, too far-fetched to be true.

"It's probably the work of some fourth-century mystic," she murmured, brushing back a long strand of auburn hair that had escaped from the clip at the nape of her neck. "These hills were full of ascetic hermits in those days. And Greek was the common tongue at the end of the Roman Empire."

Hungerford scanned the barren region to their left, jagged cliffs emerging stark and raw in the light of the rising sun. The wind that always blew along this shore seemed to pick up; the two Americans and the Arab workers thought they heard a strange whistling in the air, like steam or vapor escaping. Hungerford brought himself back to the fragment. "Is it worth anything?"

Catherine shrugged. "It depends on its age, and"—she raised her eyes to his—"what it says."

"Can you read it?"

"I would need to take it into my tent for a closer look. The writing is faded and the papyrus is rotted away in places. And this last part here . . . the bottom of the fragment is torn off at this point. It would help if we found the rest of it."

"Awright!" Hungerford boomed as he stepped back and replaced his hard hat. "Let's see where this came from. Five Egyptian pounds to the first man who finds more papyrus. *Tallah,* boys!"

They began to search the blast site, an area of rubble consisting mostly of limestone and shale, and when one of the workers saw something sticking out from under a rock, they all fell upon it.

But it turned out only to be the front page of the *International Times,* dated two days ago, most likely carried here on the wind from one of the nearby tourist hotels. Catherine saw the headline: MILLENNIUM FEVER. And the sub-headline: "Is the World Going to End in Twenty Days?" Beneath was a photograph of St. Peter's Square in Rome, where people were already gathering to hold round-the-clock vigils as they waited for the world clock to tick over from 1999 to 2000, in less than three weeks.

Finally the Arab workers started to recover fragments of hemp rope and rotted cloth from the rubble, and as Catherine inspected the weave of the fabric, the knot in her stomach tightened: *This is old.*

She looked at the scroll fragment again. The word leaped out at her: *Iesous.*

What had they found?

"We need to clear this area," Catherine said quickly, her pulse beginning to race. She glanced at the workers clustered around her, studied their faces, and she thought: *They know.* She felt her nerves stretch to their limit. She and Hungerford were going to have to keep a lid on these men. If word got out, in less than twenty-four hours every Bedouin within fifty miles would be setting up a tent over the demolition site and picking it clean of artifacts. She had seen it happen before.

"Dr. Alexander!"

She turned to see her site supervisor, an Egyptian named Samir, come running up. "I am sorry, Doctor," he said in the English he had perfected while doing graduate studies in London, "some of the walls have sustained damage, and trench six has collapsed."

"That's a whole month's work!" She turned to glare at Hungerford, who grinned sheepishly and said, "Sorry, honey, but you've gotta make way for progress. Can't let the past stand in the way of the future."

Catherine didn't like Hungerford—from the minute he had arrived two months ago with his equipment and crew, saying, "What's a pretty little gal like you doin' out here all on your own?"

4

Catherine had politely explained that, with a staff of fifteen plus locally hired workers, she was hardly on her own.

But Hungerford had countered: "Well now, you know what I mean. A lovely little gal like you needs the company of a man." Wink, wink.

When she had pointed out that she had come here to work, he had said, "Shoot, we're all here to work. But that doesn't mean you can't take some time off now and then for a little relaxation."

The "relaxation" turned out to be trying to get her to have a drink with him at the nearby Isis Hotel, a small seedy establishment where Catherine occasionally liked to unwind with some of her crew in the smoky bar. But she never joined Hungerford. She didn't like the way he grinned all the time or frequently rubbed his stomach that hung over an enormous silver buckle. He was forever trying to draw her into a discussion about her dig, asking her questions like "So, you lookin' for the tablets of the Ten Commandments or somethin'?" Catherine would answer evasively, not telling him the real reason she was out here.

In fact, Catherine hadn't even told the authorities in Cairo the real object of her excavating. "Searching for Moses," was all anyone knew.

She could imagine the reaction if she divulged the truth: that it was not Moses at all she was searching for but his *sister*, Miriam the Prophetess.

"So," Hungerford said now with a grin and pointing a nicotine-stained finger at the papyrus, "do you think this might have something to do with what you're out here digging for?"

Catherine looked at the brittle fragment in her hands, felt its coarseness between her fingers, saw the deeply aged color of the paper, the carefully inscribed letters. *Was* this startling document somehow connected to her search for the prophetess Miriam?

Catherine lifted her face to the wind, cold and bracing and laced with the ancient, salty tang of the gulf and the aromas of progress: diesel exhaust and smoke from a nearby mound of burning trash. Catherine tried to imagine what the air had smelled like over three thousand years ago, when the Israelites had come this way; she tried to recapture a taste of how the sky must have felt, how the wind might have tugged at veils and cloaks on that fateful day when Miriam had had the audacity to stand up to her powerful brother and demand of him: "Has the Lord spoken only through Moses?"

5

Catherine brought herself back to the present, and when she saw where Hungerford's eyes were, she looked down and discovered that in her haste, having been startled awake, she had left the top buttons of her blouse undone.

"I'll need to take a closer look at this papyrus," she said, turning away. "In the meantime, tell your men to keep looking."

"Yes *suh!*" Hungerford said, and she heard his laughter echo off the hills.

She turned back to face him. "Hungerford," she said, "I'll bet your lips move when you read a stop sign."

He laughed louder and walked away.

When Catherine reached her camp, she found her crew, made up of American students and volunteers, already at work shoring up the trenches damaged by Hungerford's dynamiting. She had a good crew this season, but unfortunately most of them were going home for Christmas in a few days, and some had not yet committed definitely to coming back. It worried her. The New Year that was approaching was no ordinary New Year. A new decade was going to flip over, as well as a new century and a new millennium. Catherine feared that she might be forced to close the dig.

The world needs what I'm searching for.

Why couldn't she make her bosses back at the foundation understand that? People were soul-hungry, they were yearning for spirit-food, a Message that would put purpose back into their lives. *If I find the well, and proof that Miriam was who I think she was, then there will be an era of fresh, new empowerment from a book that some people are beginning to consider outdated—the Bible.*

Going inside her tent to examine the papyrus fragment, she went first to splash cold water on her face, and she caught her reflection in the mirror over the washbasin.

Although only thirty-six, years of laboring beneath the harsh sun of Israel and Egypt had etched tiny wrinkles at her eyes—premature crow's feet due to "archaeologist's squint." The permanent tan, ironically, made her look wealthy—a woman whose life revolved around tennis and the poolside. Catherine was reminded of the old joke about how an archaeologist knew she was in trouble when a visitor entered a tomb and said, "Which one of you is the mummy?"

6

"Cathy, my girl," she murmured as she pat-dried her face and massaged in moisturizer, "ten years from now you are going to be putting some plastic surgeon's kid through college."

Now for the papyrus.

After clearing a space on her cluttered workbench, Catherine raised the flap over one of the screened windows to let in the natural morning light. The first sun's ray fell across a photograph taped above the workbench, and she saw Julius smiling at her, as if he had just reported for work.

Very handsome with black hair, neatly cropped black beard, and penetrating dark eyes, Dr. Julius Voss had entered her life two years ago at an archaeological conference in Oakland, where Catherine had presented a paper. Julius, a medical doctor who specialized in diseases of the ancient world, had read his paper on the high incidence of broken forearms in Egyptian skeletons, particularly among women, his hypothesis being that the fractures occurred when the arm was raised in self-defense. He and Catherine had made each other's acquaintance during the lunch break, and the mutual attraction had been instantaneous.

"Why, Cathy?" she heard him asking again, as though he were suddenly there in the tent with her. "Why won't you marry me? It can't be because you're not Jewish. That's not the reason. And you know I'm not asking you to convert."

Catherine had already told him that as far as religion was concerned she had had enough Catholicism to last a lifetime. But there were other reasons why she couldn't marry Julius, as much as she loved him.

Gently putting Julius from her mind, she returned to the papyrus.

Scanning the lines of Greek letters, she found no other mention of Jesus. But it was enough.

Could there be some link, she wondered, between this Christian document and the Old Testament prophetess she had come to the Sinai to search for? Might this be the sign she had been looking for, to tell her that she had indeed located the ancient oasis where Miriam and her brother had engaged in a power struggle?

Catherine reached up to a shelf and brought down a book, published in 1764, the English translation of the memoirs of a tenth-century

7

Arab whose ship had been blown off course in 976 c.e., casting him away on an ancient, unidentified shore. When Catherine had first read the book and had come across the phrase "marooned in the Land of Sin," she had wondered: Sinai? Putting together obscure clues in the Arab's story with further clues found in the Old Testament, and then throwing in astrology and celestial navigation—the Arab mentioned seeing "Aldebaran rising over my homeland"—and piecing them together with legends and traditions among the Bedouin of this region, Catherine had reached the conclusion that it must have been on this very shore—where resorts were now sprouting up—that Ibn Hassan had been stranded. That was when Catherine's lifelong quest had finally found focus, because the Arab castaway, Ibn Hassan, had written: "I spent my lonely days in a place where the local Bedu water their flocks at *Bir Maryam*. . . ."

The Well of Miriam.

Catherine's personal quest had actually begun when she was fourteen years old and the nuns of Our Lady of Grace School had run a series of movies during pre-Easter Week for the eighth- and ninth-grade classes: biblical epics from the forties and fifties, culminating in the 1956 de Mille classic, *The Ten Commandments*. While most of the kids, raised on the special effects of *Star Trek* and *Star Wars,* had giggled and shifted restlessly through the movie—although they did cheer for the spectacular parting of the Red Sea—Catherine had been puzzled. The films had been dominated by larger-than-life male heroes: Samson, Moses, Solomon—all good and pure and noble men. The women, on the other hand, seemed to fall into two categories: evil temptress or patiently suffering mother/virgin.

This simple bemusement—that there must have been *female* heroes in Bible times—had spawned an adolescent obsession that had ultimately led Catherine to her life's work: biblical archaeology. For surely, she believed, these ancient sands that had yielded such rich treasures as Tutankhamon's tomb and the Dead Sea Scrolls concealed many more wondrous secrets. If the Bible heroines couldn't be found in scripture, then Catherine was determined to find them in the earth.

She had soon discovered, however, that the male-dominated fields of archaeology and Bible scholarship were defended by a staunch bastion of Old Guard who not only just barely tolerated women in their ranks but deeply resented any assault on their most entrenched beliefs. When Catherine had first applied for a permit to dig in this region five years ago, telling the male officials in the Department of Antiquities in Cairo that she wanted to search for the Well of Miriam in the hope of finding evidence to support her theory that Miriam had shared her brother's leadership of the Israelites, as his equal, it had taken months of red tape, bribes, delays, lost documents, and being shuttled from office to office before her request had been denied.

So Catherine had retreated, regrouped, and returned a year later to apply for permission to search for the Well of *Moses*. She got the permit.

Opening Ibn Hassan's book now, she read, not the clues that had triggered her search for the Exodus route, but another passage, one that Catherine had paid little attention to before but that now caught her keenest interest: "I awakened in the night," the tenth- century Arab had written, "and beheld a most wondrous apparition of such beauty and whiteness that I was blinded. The vision spoke to me in the voice of a young woman. She led me to a well, and asked me to fill it, first with soft earth, and then with stones, and afterward to fashion an anchor made of reeds and place it on the well. If you do this for me, Ibn Hassan, the angel said to me, I will tell you the secret to living forever."

Catherine went back to the words: *an anchor made of reeds.*

They had meant nothing to her before—what good was an anchor made of reeds? But now . . .

The anchor of reeds was not meant to be a real anchor at all but a symbol!

And one anchor-symbol that sprang immediately to her mind was the anchor of very early Christianity, predating the cross. . . .

She frowned. Here again was the unexpected Christian link.

Turning to the beginning of Hassan's book, another section she had paid little attention to before but which she now studied in rising excitement, she read, "To me, therefore, was granted the key to living forever. I, Ibn Hassan Abu Mohammed Omar Abbas Ali, having been rescued from that shore and restored to my family, speak to you from my age of six score and nine, in robust health and in the certain belief that I will live forever, because of the gift the angel bestowed to me."

Catherine had originally tossed off these words as the idle boasts of an old yarn-spinning sailor—claiming to be 129 years old! But *now . . .*

She looked at the Jesus fragment Hungerford's men had found, and as she scanned it, two words jumped out at her: *zoe aionios.*

Life eternal.

Was there a connection between this fragment, which she tentatively placed at two hundred years after Christ, and the hallucinations of a shipwrecked sailor, seven centuries or so later? But if so, then what did this fragment, with its Jesus reference, have to do with the Well of Miriam?

Outside of Ibn Hassan's memoirs, Catherine had not been able to find any other references to a Well of Miriam. But in her search she had come across a book written by a German Egyptologist in 1883 in which he described an expedition into the Sinai wilderness, setting up camp on the coast of the Sinai east of St. Catherine's monastery, at the base of an escarpment near a well called *Bir Umma*—Well of the Mother. And there, during the night, the Egyptologist's men had experienced bad dreams. What had intrigued Catherine when she had first read the book was that the dreams were like those of Ibn Hassan. In fact, the German's wife had used nearly the same words to describe a beautiful, ghostly apparition that had appeared to her. And so Catherine had wondered at the time: Could the similarity in the dreams indicate that Professor Kruger's party had camped near the same spot where Ibn Hassan was shipwrecked?

The final clue that had led her to excavate in this spot was found in the Old Testament itself—Exodus 13:21, "And the Lord went before them by day in a pillar of cloud to lead them the way, and by night in a pillar of fire to give them light to go by day and night. He took not away the pillar of the cloud by day nor the pillar of the fire by night from before the people." Catherine wasn't the first to notice that this could be a description of a volcano. She knew there were no volcanic mountains on the Sinai peninsula, but that there were on the eastern side of the Gulf of Aqaba, in Saudi Arabia, in an area called the Land of Midian. It would make sense, Catherine had reasoned, that if Mount Sinai were on the *western* shore of Arabia, the Israelites would have followed the fire and smoke of the eruption to this place on the *eastern* shore of the Sinai across the gulf, from where they could see continually this cloud by day and fire by night.

But she had come here expecting to find evidence of the Exodus and of Miriam the Prophetess, not a papyrus with the name Jesus written on it!

What did this fragment of papyrus, she wondered, with its words "eternal life," have to do with Ibn Hassan's angel, the nightmares experienced by the Egyptologist's party, and the local Bedouin legends that this area was haunted?

Catherine listened to the sounds beyond the tent wall: the morning wind picking up, whistling off the aquamarine gulf to mingle with the shouts and yells of Hungerford's men as they combed the rubble for more papyrus. Catherine thought: *I, too, had a strange dream last night.* No, not a dream. An old memory, which she had worked hard to suppress, coming back now, inexplicably, to haunt her. *Filthy little girl! Ton will be punished for this. . . .*"

As she picked up the magnifying glass to begin translating the ancient Greek, she suddenly heard shouting outside.

They had found something.

NEAR THE BLASTING site, the men had unearthed what looked like the opening to a tunnel. Catherine dropped to her knees to inspect it, and then, her heart suddenly pounding, she ran back to her own site.

Before starting to excavate, Catherine had first explored the area using the latest geological engineering technology and had determined that there was an unusual subterranean tunnel formation here. So she had laid out a grid and started digging. But although after a year she had yet to find any evidence of human habitation below the second level, at the third level, where they had struck a layer of limestone, they had found the beginning of a curious tunnel.

As Catherine stood now at the entrance to that tunnel, in one of the trenches of her dig, she noticed how the tunnel ran horizontally underground in the direction of where Hungerford had been dynamiting, toward the section of tunnel his men had just unearthed. It didn't end there but appeared to continue in the direction of the jagged escarpment. Where did it lead to?

There was only one way to find out.

CATHERINE TIED A rope around her waist, lay down on one of the wheeled pallets her crew used for moving rubble, and went in with a flashlight.

She paused. The tunnel was dark and narrow, with dust and debris sifting down. Since they couldn't be sure of the stability of the rock, or how much the dynamiting had weakened it, they had devised a signal: One yank on the rope and they would pull her out.

Before going in, Catherine had cautioned Hungerford to account for all his men and make sure they stayed close by—the fortunes that local Arabs had made in the black market sales of Dead Sea Scrolls and the Nag Hammadi cache were legendary. Still, she was worried. It had been three hours since the early dawn blasting had tossed up the Jesus fragment; the hue and cry could already be up and down the peninsula.

Going slowly into the tunnel, Catherine pulled herself along by her elbows, keeping the flashlight pointed ahead at the seemingly endless void. She had to stop several times when sand rained down on her and she feared that the tunnel was about to collapse. She fought to keep her nerves in check. The tunnel was so narrow that she had to hold her head down and shoulders in, and still she bumped the sides. And when she felt her bare knees scrape on the limestone floor, she wished belatedly that she had changed from khaki shorts into blue jeans. She kept going, determined to find what lay at the end.

Although the tunnel bored through dense magmatic rock, Catherine decided as she inspected it with her flashlight that this was not a manmade phenomenon but a natural fissure in the limestone. Perhaps created by an earthquake, or water gushing from an underground source. A well?

Despite the coldness of the limestone, she began to perspire. One of the nightmares that Ibn Hassan had shared with Kruger's party was a vision of being buried alive. Some sort of ghost-memory? Catherine wondered now as she felt her neck crawl with fear and a cold shiver run down her spine. Or was the dream a warning . . .

She suddenly came upon a blockage.

She estimated that she had traveled fifty feet from where Hungerford and his men were slowly feeding her safety rope into the tunnel. Then she examined the blockage and found, to her astonishment, that it appeared to be a basket of some sort, lodged partway in the passage, partially imbedded in the rock. She reached up and tried to move it; it came away easily, bringing a shower of sand onto her head. She screwed her eyes shut tight and held her breath, and when the dust cleared, she focused the flashlight beam up ahead.

The tunnel continued.

Tucking the basket between her arms and under her chin, she resumed pulling herself forward on the wheeled pallet.

Finally she came to the end, where the tunnel suddenly opened out upon a circular shaft rising up to the surface. The shaft, about twenty feet in diameter, was blocked overhead and the walls were lined with large, undressed flint slabs, typical of Bronze Age masonry.

Had she found the Well of Miriam ?

Catherine shined her light down and peered over the edge, praying she didn't fall in. She saw rubble at the bottom, some of it fresh, as if the blasting had caused part of the circular wall to cave in. And then her flashlight caught something white at the bottom. She shifted her weight and scooted forward for a better look.

The trembling beam swept over rock and shale and finally illuminated—a human skull.

The Magus pulled the purple robe from around the young woman's shoulders, exposing her nakedness in the moonlight.

His men gasped, and then fell silent in the presence of her beauty, thinking how she resembled the statues in the marketplace, so white and cold and perfect. But that rich black hair cascading down her back and the way she trembled was proof too, that she was a living woman.

Her hands and feet bound, she stood with a dignity that made some of the men shift nervously and cast their eyes downward. Their leader, the one who now clutched the young woman's purple robe in his fist, was not impressed by the proud way she stood. He had tried all means of getting her to talk, back in the city. He had threatened her, locked her away, starved her, everything short of physically marring her beauty. He couldn't have done that, for then the Emperor would have been outraged.

But they weren't in the city now. He had brought her to

this desolate place at the end of the earth so that he could finally extract the secret from her with only the snakes and scorpions as witnesses, and then let the desert sands swallow up the evidence of his deed.

They had ridden long and hard to reach this place, six men on horseback, racing across the moonlit desert as if demons pursued them, leaving the Emperor's legions far behind, and coming to a halt at a place on an ancient shore where ragged cliffs stood against the star- splashed sky—a barren, forsaken spot inhabited only by ghosts and spirits.

The men had read of the well in Holy Scripture—a deep well that, according to legend, had once sustained the Israelites during their forty years of wandering in the wilderness. The men first tied the specially prepared basket to a rope and gently lowered it down while one of them murmured a prayer. When the basket reached the bottom of the well, the men had turned to the woman and brought her to the edge of the well to stand before their leader.

"Tell me," the Magus said now in a low voice, as he drew his sword from its scabbard, "where is the seventh scroll?"

She still did not speak. But when her green eyes met his, he saw in them the glint of challenge.

Like her, he trembled, not from the cold but from a barely contained fury. The last of a long line of magi, he knew his days of power were coming to an end. But, with the final scroll he knew he could work miracles, stop the inexorable process of the world coming to an end, and seize eternal life for himself and for those who followed him. This woman possessed the key to that mystery. For years he had pursued the trail of the final scroll; it had ended with her.

The desert silence stretched on until finally he said, "So be it." He gestured to the men.

They turned to the young woman, laying coarse, rough hands on her white, flawless skin, greed and lust illuminating their faces as they threaded a rope under her arms and breasts, to lower her as gently as possible into the well.

"I do not want you to be injured and therefore die

quickly," the Magus said to her. "I want you to know this dark prison for a long time. You will memorize every stone, every texture, every shade of darkness. When the sun rises high and beats down on you, you will be baked, and at night the freezing wind will make your bones contract and snap. You will know a thirst that is beyond human comprehension, you will experience a loneliness that is emptier and more terrifying than the aloneness of death. You will call out, but no one will hear, only the vultures as they wait to pick the flesh from your bones." He stepped closer to her, holding the staff of his religious office, a staff that had once inspired awe in hundreds of thousands but which now had little effect except upon these men and a few left back in the city.

aOne last time," he said softly. "Where is the scroll? If you tell me I will let you go free."

She didn't speak.

"Then tell me only this: Does the seventh scroll indeed contain the magic formula for living forever?"

And she spoke, for the first time since her captivity. It came out as a sigh: "Yes. . . ."

Believing in immortal life, the Magus cried out and raised a fist toward heaven. "If I cannot have the secret, then no man shall!"

His companions picked her up and lowered her into the well, inch by inch, the rough stones scraping her tender back, and as the darkness swallowed up her freshness and beauty, the Magus struck the stone rim of the well with his gold staff and cried to the stars, "By the power of this rod, which was handed down to me by my father and his father before him, all the way back to when the Immortal Ones walked the earth, I place a curse on this woman and the six books I have buried with her, so that the secrets will remain forever hidden. Let no man find them and read them and learn the secrets. And cursed be he who does."

A lone rider on a black horse appeared on the shore, stopping a distance from the encampment so as not to be heard. He *jumped down and, running swiftly and silently, with a single knife slit the throats of the sleeping men, one by one, so that they never even cried out. Then he went into the tent of the Magus, and he searched for his betrothed. But she was not here. He straddled the Magus and held the knife to his throat. When the Magus awoke, his eyes were full of sudden comprehension and resignation. He said, "You will never find her and you will never save her. For if I cannot have the secret, no one will."*

In his anguish, the young man slit the Magus's throat and watched the blood run crimson on the satin pillow.

Then he left the camp to look for his beloved. He searched along the shore, and the deep, dry wadis that came out of the jagged escarpment; he even threw back his head and looked up at the stars, searching for her there.

And then he heard a sound in the night.

Stumbling through the darkness, he found the well. He listened. He called down to her. He heard a whimper. Running back to the camp, he found a rope. He returned to the well, secured the rope around a boulder, and lowered himself down.

Then he felt in the darkness for his beloved. She was there, and he cried out.

Then he felt at her breast that there was no heartbeat. But she was still warm, and only moments ago she had whimpered.

He bellowed his outrage, the cry echoing up the stone shaft and out into the cosmos. Sobbing, he climbed back out of the well and went back to the camp. In the High Priest's tent he found the rich purple robe embroidered with gold threads that had been hers.

Returning to the well, he lowered himself down and stopped a short distance from the bottom; bracing himself, he reached up and severed the rope with his knife. He fell the rest of the way, the rope dangling overhead, beyond his reach. Draping the robe over his beloved's body that was now growing cold, he curled himself alongside her, wrapping his arms around her, his tears dampening her hair.

"You will not have died in vain, my love," he wept. "As the gods bear witness to my oath, I promise you that someday the scrolls will be brought out to the light of day once again, and the world will receive their message."

"SO, JUST HOW big a find do you think this might be?" Hungerford said with a grin. "In dollars and cents, I mean. Like, how much would a museum pay for that piece of papyrus?"

"Five million, at least," Catherine said, brushing the dirt from her clothes.

"Five million!"

"Sure. Maybe even five hundred million. Maybe even a gazillion."

"Okay, okay. I was just asking."

"Hungerford," she said in exasperation, "I have no idea what this is worth. We don't even know what it is yet." She looked back at the tunnel. *That skull*... "I'd like to go back in one more time, take another look...."

"So what do you make of *this* thing?" he said, prodding the bundle she had brought out of the tunnel.

"Seventh, eighth century is my guess," Catherine said, as everyone crowded around to get a look. She was covered with grit and sand, her auburn hair dusted with fine powder, and despite being out in the sunlight and refreshing sea breeze once more, she couldn't shake the terror of the narrow tunnel and the deep, dark well. "Judging by the weave of this linen, and the look of this string . . . definitely post-Byzantine."

"Let's open it."

But Catherine stepped back from the Texan's reaching hands. "No, good science dictates that it be opened in front of credentialed witnesses. I'll call Cairo, inform the Department of Antiquities. They'll send someone out. In the meantime, you'd better not work this area until the government has inspected it."

"Sure, yeah. I can move my boys to that section over there. We have to clear it for tennis courts anyway. You be sure and let me know soon's you've found something out, okay?"

"Hungerford, you can believe me when I say that at this moment you are foremost in my thoughts."

He grinned and walked off.

Catherine hurried back to her tent, zipped up the doorway, and turned on a light. She had to wait a minute to compose herself.

Had Hungerford and the others bought her story? She hoped so. There was no way she was going to let on that this could be an even bigger find than they had all been envisioning. If she did, the plunder would be obscene. This find was *hers,* and the sooner she contacted the authorities in Cairo the better.

But, as she searched for the keys to her Land Rover, she paused.

The bureaucrats in Cairo were notorious for dragging their feet. She needed to get them out here right away. But how? She looked at the papyrus fragment, which she had yet to read. If she could report that the papyrus was definitely third or second century, or even older, the authorities would be here in a flash.

She knew what she had to do. Situating the fragment under a high-intensity lamp, she reached for the magnifying glass and started to read.

IT APPEARED TO be the beginning of a letter. *"From Perpetua your sister, I send greetings to the community of sisters in the house of dear Aemelia, revered . . .* Catherine frowned. What was that next word?

8lOiKOVO(X

Diakonos!

It had to be an error. Catherine had come across the title of *diakonos*—deacon—before, but only in reference to men. A woman was *diakonissa*—deaconess. She read the sentence again. No, it was quite clear: Perpetua was addressing Aemelia, a woman, as *diakonos*—deacon.

With a puzzled frown, she continued reading: *"What I am about to tell you, dear sisters, is a message of such astonishing proportion that my hand trembles even as I write. But know first that it is not my voice which speaks to you but that of a blessed woman named Sabina, who came to me through the most miraculous circumstance. Here I add a warning: read this letter in secrecy, in fear for your safety and for your lives."*

Catherine's eyebrows arched. Read this in secrecy? In fear for their *lives?* Going back to the beginning of the letter, she read again: *"Aemelia, revered diakonos."*

Beyond the nylon walls of her tent she heard the sounds of business as usual in her camp—Samir calling for a trowel, one of the students laughing at something, a portable radio playing a Jerusalem station—but these barely registered in Catherine's mind as she hastily searched among her books.

When she found what she was looking for she quickly turned to the glossary at the back and read: *"Diakonos* (Strong's Number: 1249-GSN) Greek: 'servant' Translated today as deacon. In the early Church the *diakonai* ('those who carry out the king's orders') baptized, preached, and presided over the Eucharist, so that a closer translation in New Testament context would be read as 'priest.'"

Catherine drew in a sharp breath. *"Aemelia . . . diakonos."* A female priest? In a letter invoking the name of Jesus?

Impossible!

Quickly turning to a chart in the center of the text, she picked up the magnifying glass and closely examined the handwriting in Perpetua's letter, comparing the script to the alphabet illustrated in the book. It was a near perfect match. According to the textbook, Perpetua's letter, Catherine realized in astonishment, was almost without doubt written in the second century. When women serving in the Church were definitely *not* addressed as *diakonos*.

She closed the textbook, trying to absorb the staggering implication, and when she saw the author's photograph on the back cover, she suddenly heard Danno's voice from long ago: "You can't go on blaming the Church forever."

She had said, "Yes I can. The way my mother died is the Church's fault and no one else's."

Gazing now at the picture on the back of the *Handbook for New Testament Greek*—Dr. Nina Alexander when she was young, her large green eyes smiling out at the reader with a lively intelligence—Catherine heard again her mother's voice, frail at the end of her rich and controversial life, all alone in a cold hospital room, whispering, "They were right, Cathy, I shouldn't have done what I did, because I had no proof. If only I had had proof. . . ."

Catherine brought herself away from that painful day, when she had seen how the Church had won in the end, finally getting her mother to recant, her spirit beaten, and she returned to the papyrus and its explosive word: *diakonos.* And she thought, Have I found the proof my mother needed?

Catherine acted quickly now, hurriedly securing the fragment in a lockbox and stowing it, along with the ancient basket, under her cot. As she grabbed the keys to the Rover, she checked the time and calculated that it was just past midnight in California. She made a quick mental list: first, get Samir to guard her tent; then, call Julius from the Isis Hotel; call Daniel next, in Mexico; and lastly, get a schedule of the earliest flights out of Egypt.

And then make one last foray into the tunnel.

"SHE'S FOUND SOMETHING, awright," Hungerford said to his foreman as he searched through the shovels and axes stacked up against the back of his trailer. "I could see by the way she held on to that ol' basket, like it contained jewels."

"So what are you going to do?" the foreman asked as Hungerford selected a large pickax.

"The Doc says she wants to go into the tunnel one more time." He hefted the ax and grinned. "But funny thing about that ground out there. It's about to get real unstable all of a sudden. Next time the Doc goes in—well, she oughta know that archaeology can be hazardous bidness."

"ERICA! ERICA, COME quickly!"

Havers took his wife's hand and nearly yanked her out of the chair. "Miles! I was in the middle of—"

"You have to see this, darling. Hurry!"

He walked with such long strides as he drew her outside, through a *portal* furnished with antique Spanish chests and wicker furniture, that Erica had to run to keep up. "You're going to be *astounded!*" he said, his voice rising up to the *latilla* ceiling and echoing off the white adobe walls of their sprawling 20,000-square-foot Santa Fe house.

Erica laughed. She had no idea what exciting new thing her husband was about to show her—with Miles it could be anything from an unusual cloud formation to a new super-fast microchip—but she was instantly and breathlessly caught up, as she always was, in his excitement and passion. In thirty years of being Miles Havers's wife, she could not recall a single dull moment.

They dashed across an expansive courtyard, startling a chauffeur polishing a maroon Corvette ZR-1, part of Havers's collection of twenty-three vintage 'Vettes, and then down another long *portal* where ceremonial artifacts from Zuni Pueblo were showcased; out into the open again, and skirting the edge of the private eighteen-hole golf course where groundskeepers were carefully removing the recently fallen snow to clear the course for use.

Havers's sandals made sharp slapping sounds on the *saltillo* tiles, a familiar sound heard around the estate—Miles Havers, fifty-two years old and expensively fit, was an avid jogger and known to run at all hours. Erica, on the other hand, a slender, ethereal woman also in her early fifties, was so light on her feet that her footsteps hardly caused a whisper as she followed her husband around the fifteenth-century Spanish fountain that had been brought over from Madrid, stone by stone.

Finally Erica realized where he was leading her: to the greenhouse.

As they arrived at the locked entrance, where Miles had to punch in a security code on the keypad, Erica looked off to the west toward the Sangre de Cristo Mountains, snow-covered now on this biting December day. After living here for nearly ten years, Erica still wasn't used to the stunning blue of the New Mexican sky, an effect, she had been told, that was caused by the lack of moisture in the air. And she thought: Sangre de Cristo—*blood of Christ*—a strange name for mountains.

As a cold breeze suddenly came up and swept through her short, ash-blond hair, causing her to shiver, she scanned the periphery of the golf course. She couldn't see them but she knew they were there, the extra security guards Miles had placed around the sixty- acre compound that was the heart of their 5,000-acre estate; it was because of the recent influx of visitors to the Santa Fe area. The Millennium was approaching and Santa Fe was considered one of the earth's sacred spots.

Although people the world over, in anticipation of the year 2000 less than three weeks away, were preparing for earthquakes and cataclysms, or angelic hosts and satanic armies—even Hollywood was rumored to be a ghost town as celebrities, terrified of the expected Big

One, had retreated to the more stable geology of Wyoming, Montana, and Manhattan—Erica Havers welcomed the Millennium. In eager expectation of a major religious epiphany, both personal and global, she had spent the past year planning the "Party of the Century," with over a thousand guests on hand to witness what she hoped would be the Great Convergence.

The electric doors of the greenhouse whispered open and Erica felt a sudden breath of hot, moist air rush out. Miles took her by the hand into this minitropics he had created in the desert two thousand feet above sea level, and he led her among rows of seedlings and cuttings, buds and full blossoms, lush ferns, vines, and creepers. When they reached the place where Miles raised his prize orchids, he stopped anti whispered, "There . . ." as if afraid to disturb the delicately balanced biosphere.

When Erica saw the flower, with midnight-purple petals and shimmering green leaves, she pressed her hand to her chest. "Oh, Miles!" she breathed. "It's stunning. . . ."

"Zygopetalum Blue Lake," he said with pride. "It was a struggle, but it has survived."

Erica knew what an effort Miles had put into bringing this particular orchid to bloom, from the day he had purchased it as a bulb from a California grower; he had even slept here in the greenhouse, to nurture his "baby."

"They told me it couldn't be done," he said. "And yet I have done it! Here is proof, Erica, that with a combined conscientious effort we can *stop* the obscene pillage of the rain forests perpetuated by the greed of certain collectors who have no conscience and no morals. We can raise healthy plants under controlled conditions, right here in the United States, and leave the jungles in peace." Erica watched him as he spoke, felt his passion in the sultry air, and then she wrapped her arms around him and gave him a hug. This was what she most adored about Miles, his courage to fight for what he believed was right.

Sometimes it astonished her to think how far she and Miles had come since their days as college dropouts roaming the United States in a psychedelic VW bus, ending up dancing naked in the rain at Woodstock. Miles was now a computer mogul whose net worth *Forbes* had pegged at $10.5 billion. Although no one knew exactly how extensively Havers's electronic empire stretched, *Time* magazine had recently referred to him as "the human Internet." His personal network was that global.

The pager on his belt suddenly went off. Havers pressed the intercom on the wall. "Yes?"

"You have a telephone call, sir. Urgent."

"Who is it?"

"They didn't say, sir. The call is from Cairo."

Havers's eyes flickered. "All right, I'll take it here." He turned to Erica. "I'm sorry, my dear, but I shall have to take this. Do you mind?"

"Not at all. I need to get back to tonight's menu anyway." She kissed him on the cheek. "I love the orchid."

After the doors closed behind her, automatically locking, Havers picked up the wall phone, punched in a coded number, and when the other party answered, said, "Speak."

He listened for a moment. "A fragment?" he said. "And you're sure it says 'Jesus.' Have any other fragments or scrolls been found?"

As he listened to the reply, his hands slowly curled into fists, and he felt a familiar, dizzying rush. It had been such a long time. . . .

The call from Taiwan, six months ago: "I have found an orchid for you, Mr. Havers—Zygopetalum Blue Lake—very rare, very difficult to get to. Illegal to take out, risky to harvest. It will cost a great deal." Miles hadn't slept for days afterward. And then the precious bulb had arrived, from "a grower in Santa Barbara." And now he had his prize, glowing and shimmering in his private tropical world, a breathtaking rare flower for his sole personal pleasure.

"A basket?" he said into the phone, speaking softly, even though the thickness of the greenhouse glass prevented anyone from overhearing. "Do the authorities know about it yet? I see. . . . What is in this basket? Find out and report back." His instincts were kicking in now, the way they had six months ago, and he thought: This was the real high of being a collector—not in the acquisition, but in the anticipation. And the danger. There always had to be danger.

He hung up and quickly punched in a code on the intercom. "Get me Athens. Tell Zeke I need to talk to him right away."

The wait was less than five minutes. The intercom buzzed: "Zeke is on the line, sir."

Havers briefed him, then said, "Drop the Athens assignment and get over to Sharm el Sheikh. Leave immediately. Find out if the basket is related to the papyrus fragment and if there are scrolls. If there are, *I want them.* Be discreet, but get them by whatever means necessary. And Zeke, don't leave any witnesses."

"HELLO? *SEÑOR?*" CATHERINE shouted into the phone. "I'm *still* trying to get through to Dr. Daniel Stevenson. I keep getting cut off. His camp is at—Hello? *Hello!*" She glared at the dead phone in her hand. "Not again!"

When she returned to the front desk, Mr. Mylonas, the manager of the Isis Hotel, gave her an inquisitive look. "No luck," she said. "I can't get through." She had been trying for the past three hours to contact Daniel in Mexico, but to no avail.

She stood for a moment with her hands on her hips, gnawing her lip as she tried to decide what to do next.

It had been only ten hours since the dynamiting had unearthed the papyrus, but Catherine envisioned news of its discovery speeding around the globe like electrons around a proton. And now, as she scanned the lobby, she imagined spies everywhere, lounging in the rattan chairs, murmuring over cups of Turkish coffee, reading Arabic and French newspapers behind the potted palms—even the sportsmen carting scuba gear through the lobby and out to the hotel's private pier looked suspicious.

"Making phone calls, Doc?"

She spun around. Hungerford's bulk and toothy grin blocked her view of the hotel verandah and, beyond, the emerald swimming pool sparkling in the last rays of the westering sun. "The Department of Antiquities is sending someone out," she lied.

Hungerford's pale brown eyes roamed her face. Then he winked. "Sure bet. Say, how about a drink to celebrate our find?"

"I'm waiting for a phone call."

His eyes seemed to linger on her face for a moment longer. Then he said, "Yeah, sure." And he turned, laughing, to continue on into the bar where a belly dance show was just beginning.

Catherine didn't like the way he was acting. Had he already called someone, maybe even already had a deal in the works? She couldn't waste any more time. She had to get the papyrus and the basket out of Egypt tonight. Unfortunately, she required help.

And there was only one person she could call.

During the drive from the camp to the hotel, Catherine had reconsidered her intention to contact Julius. What she was planning was illegal and unethical; at the least it would tarnish her reputation, at the most it could land her in an Egyptian prison. She couldn't ask Julius to get involved.

Which left Daniel.

Catherine knew that Daniel loved taking risks and could always be counted on to do the outrageous—even that first day she had met him, twenty-six years ago when, as a terrified ten-year-old, she had been cornered on the school yard by a gang of bullies chanting that her mother was going to burn in hell. A shrimp of a kid had burst through with fists flying, rescuing her like a prince on a charger— Daniel Stevenson.

He had been there for her always after that, and she for him, through the loss of his mother, and then the loss of her parents. It was Daniel who, one dark night before her twenty-third birthday, had brought her back from the abyss.

And Daniel, too, who truly understood why she had left the Church and could never return.

Daniel had also been in the dream last night, because he was part of the memory. Danno—the only kid in the class who hadn't laughed at her as she had stood on the stool with a sign around her neck.

She looked at her watch. It was nearly eight a.m. in Mexico. She was familiar with Daniel's work habits: he would be leaving the camp soon and heading for the dig, where he would be completely out of touch, she knew, for the next ten or so hours. Catherine didn't have those hours. She had to get word to him.

But *how?*

"THERE IT IS!" Daniel shouted, his voice echoing in the stone burial chamber. He quickly typed on his keyboard: *Do you see it, Dallas? Have you got the image?*

An instant later, the reply appeared on the laptop monitor: *We see it, Dr. Stevenson. Congratulations.*

25

Daniel turned down the Coleman lantern and increased the brightness on his computer monitor to get a sharper image. There was no doubt about it. He had done it. He had his proof at last. The ancient Maya *were* the descendants of survivors of the lost continent of Atlantis.

If only Cathy were here to share this moment with him!

As Daniel gazed at the superimposed images on the monitor, the result of years of work, he laughed aloud, and the sound ricocheted off the damp, flaking walls of the ancient tomb. And then it died.

Cathy.

In the whole world, Cathy was the only one who *hadn't* laughed when he had first posited his theory that the Maya were descended from ancient Minoans who had washed up on the Yucatan shore after the destruction of Atlantis—Cathy, who had given him moral support by letter and phone during the long, lonely weeks he had worked in the hot, cramped rooms of the Maya king's tomb, nearly deafened by the roar of the generator that provided light—Cathy, who had reminded him that, with a B.S. degree in physics and a brilliant doctoral dissertation that had challenged the accuracy of thermoluminescence in dating Bronze Age pottery, he had as much right to be taken seriously as anyone. And it was Cathy who had taught him to thumb his nose at his detractors. "Push the envelope,

Danno," she would say. "Bring down their idols. But bring them down with *proof.'*"

Years of search and exploration, poring over aerial photographs, feeding data into computers, and a single-minded focus that bordered on obsession had turned up a curious mound in the Mexican jungle that, after two years of painstaking excavation, had revealed itself to be the final resting place of a heretofore unknown Maya king.

For this, Daniel had received a grudging tip of the hat from his colleagues. But when he had uncovered a mural unlike any seen before—instead of portly figures with flabby arms and sagging bellies like the ones found at Bonampak, these were lithe and willowy, narrow-waisted, long black hair trailing over their shoulders, but already showing the flattened foreheads and elongated skulls that would later mark Mayan art—when Daniel had declared that here was proof to support his Atlantis theory, the scoffers had resumed scoffing.

But there was more telling evidence. After removing the layers of calcite from a second wall, Daniel had exposed something else not found anywhere in Mexico or Central or South America: a mural devoted to snakes, the precursor to the Plumed Serpent that had evolved into a major god throughout the Toltec, Aztec, and Maya empires. In the newly discovered mural, people were shown holding a snake in each hand, a theme common to Minoan art.

Finally, on a third wall in the burial chamber, Daniel had exposed a mural that astonished even him. Resembling Aztec artwork that would not appear until centuries later, it showed humans either crouching or lying on their backs with mysterious swirls emanating from their mouths—ribbon-like curls that, in Aztec art, had been variously explained by archaeologists as symbolizing speech or breathing; some even went so far as to say the swirls represented the breathing apparatus of ancient astronauts. But Daniel interpreted them as indicating that these people were *underwater* and drowning, and that this mural told the story of the great catastrophe that had swallowed their ancestors when Atlantis plunged into the sea.

His critics still unconvinced, Daniel had then pointed to the murals at Bonampak, dating centuries after these. How, he had challenged, did one explain the theme of sea life running through those eighth-century murals? Priests and nobles wearing lobster costumes, headdresses resembling octopi, fishtails, and seaweed? Why would a jungle society evoke the imagery of the *ocean?*

Setting up camp at his newly found tomb, Daniel had gotten to work. Using his old IBM ThinkPad with a Xircom PCMCIA V.34 modem and Motorola cellular phone, he had set up a cyberspace laboratory with colleagues in Dallas and Santa Barbara, remote- accessing art databanks at one and an art reconstruction program at the other. Transmitting images of his new Maya murals to both locations via a satellite link-up in Cozumel, Daniel had carefully orchestrated the superimposing of selected samples of Minoan art over one of his murals, matching specific points such as noses, knees, and fingertips, and using the reconstruction program to fill in missing places.

They were nearly exact.

"Mazel tov!" the guys at the Santa Barbara lab now said, their message scrolling in the chat box on the screen. *"Break a bottle of*

champagne over your head for us!" And from Dallas: *"Where's our money?"* A running joke, since Daniel was notorious for always being broke.

When a warning beeper sounded, indicating that his laptop battery was about to die, Daniel turned down the screen brightness and messaged to his friends, *"Thanks, guys. The caviar's on me."*

He fell silent then and listened to the incessant rain beyond the tomb's entrance. He felt his elation begin to shrivel, and his spirits dampen. He really did wish Cathy were here to celebrate with him.

All he had was her photograph, taped to the inside of his laptop case. He had put it there so that he could see her face whenever he worked.

It was an old photo, taken at their graduation from Immaculate Heart High, Cathy laughing, holding her hand up to the camera. As he gazed at the picture now, wishing she were sharing the musty, dank chamber with him, he recalled the day that had been his personal turning point.

He was sixteen and Cathy had found him behind the bleachers, weeping his heart out. She had put her arms around him and told him everything was going to be all right; he had inhaled her perfume, felt the warmth of her supple body, and in that instant had gone from being her best pal to being desperately in love with her. Catherine hadn't known it at the time, and Daniel had taken care that, twenty' years later, she still didn't know.

"Julius has asked me to marry him," she had written in her last letter. It hadn't come as a surprise to Daniel, but it had cut him to the core all the same. Daniel had no illusions about their relationship—best friends, even soul mates, but never lovers. Julius, in Danno's opinion, was forty-six going on seventy. Other people thought Catherine and Julius an odd pair, but Daniel had his own secret suspicions about why Catherine was drawn to him.

So, let her marry Julius and find happiness as "Mrs. Voss." There were worse things to endure. Although, as Daniel gazed at the picture on his laptop screen, trying to recapture his ecstasy of a few moments ago, he couldn't think what.

IT CAME TO her. How to reach Daniel.

Catherine had spent a summer helping him map a region in

Chiapas, where he suspected a tomb was hidden. His daily routine at the camp had rarely varied: up at dawn, coffee before anything and lots of it, a review of the previous day's findings, and then—Now she remembered! Daniel always spent an hour on the Internet before going to work, to catch up on news and mail.

She quickly returned to the front desk. Over the past year, Catherine had become a familiar figure at the Isis Hotel; she came every day to collect her mail and frequently to purchase supplies when she didn't have time to go into Sharm el Sheikh. She had even, on occasion, joined Mr. Mylonas, a widower in his seventies, for tea. "Mr. Mylonas," she said to him now, "I would like to ask a favor. Do you think I could use the hotel's computer for just a few minutes? I'll gladly pay for the time I'm on it."

"Blessed St. Andrew!" he said, laughing. "Four years ago Mr. Papadopoulos says to me, 'Mylonas, it is time to modernize the hotel.' So he sends to Athens for a computer. But Mr. Papadopoulos does not know how to use a computer. *I* do not know how to operate a computer, Miss Hassan does not know how, and Ramesh only knows how to write letters on it. In four years, I can show you, Dr. Alexander, with one hand how many guests have used the computer. For the last five months, no one. And today? Suddenly the machine is the most popular machine in the world!"

"Others have used it?"

"Mr. Hungerford, your American friend."

She gave Mr. Mylonas a wry look. "Who else?"

"A guest who checked in this afternoon. He is using it at this moment."

"You mean the computer's in use right now?"

He offered her an apologetic shrug. "Perhaps you can try at the Sheraton or the Gulf Hilton."

But there wasn't time to go elsewhere. Daniel never stayed online for more than an hour, and it was now eight-thirty in Mexico. She might only just catch him before he left camp.

"I am sorry," the manager said, and he turned his attention to a guest who had come to exchange money.

Catherine thought for a moment, then she went around to the office at the back; the door ajar, she looked in and found a small room cluttered with outdated furniture, old-fashioned rotary dial telephones, a manual typewriter, both Islamic and Western calendars on the wall, and corkscrews of sticky flypaper hanging from the ceiling fans. The reservations secretary wasn't there, nor was Ramesh, but Catherine saw someone standing before the computer terminal, his back to her as he typed on the keyboard. Tall and broad shouldered with an almost military bearing, he wore a black short-sleeved shirt tucked into blue jeans that fit snugly, Catherine couldn't help noticing, over a very nice, tight rear end.

"Pardon me," she said from the doorway. "I was wondering if—"

He turned. She saw a rugged face, blue eyes set in tan skin, and a very attractive smile. And then she saw that the black shirt was no ordinary black shirt, and that he was wearing a Roman collar. She stopped. Mr. Mylonas had failed to mention that the guest was a priest.

She cleared her throat. "I was wondering if the computer was free."

"I just started downloading my e-mail and I'm afraid it's going to tie up the computer for a while."

"How long?"

"A couple of hours."

"Hours! Why is it taking so long?"

"I think it's operating on a 300 bps modem!" he said with a laugh.

Catherine looked at her watch, then at the computer, and lastly at the priest. She started to say something, changed her mind, and abruptly left.

Back at the desk she asked Mr. Mylonas to please contact the Sheraton and see if they had a computer available. While she waited, she drummed her fingers on the guest register book and glared toward the office. As much as she had wanted to, she couldn't bring herself to ask a favor of a priest.

"I am sorry, Dr. Alexander," Mr. Mylonas said as he hung up, "but their lines, too, are tied up. Please, feel free to use the telephone in our office. Perhaps you will have better luck this time."

Deciding that she might indeed have better luck with the hotel's line than with the pay phones, she went back into the office, and when she saw that the priest wasn't there, she glanced at the computer, wondering if he had finished downloading. But there was a message on the screen, seeming to mock her:

Expected download time: 1 hr 27 min.

As she tried again to reach the radio link-up in Cancun, it briefly crossed her mind to abort the downloading while no one was looking, transmit her message to Daniel and deal with the priest afterward.

"Come on, Danno," she murmured as she listened to the outmoded telephone signals connecting snail-like around the world. "Please be there." She looked at her watch again. Had he already left for the tomb?

Through the partly open door of the office she heard a sudden explosion of applause in the bar, Hungerford's recognizable guffaw rising above it. Why was he still here? Why hadn't he gone back to his job site?

She pictured Samir back at her own camp. She had asked him to guard her tent, but she knew he couldn't be there every single second. She thought of the papyrus and the basket, hidden and yet vulnerable. She knew she shouldn't leave them alone for much longer. What would she do if she didn't get through to Danno?

I'll leave tonight, she thought. There was no other choice.

"Hello?" she shouted into the phone. "Yes, I'm trying to reach Dr. Stevenson. He's at—Hello?"

The line went dead.

"Dammit," she said.

"What's wrong?"

She turned to see the priest in the doorway, a masculine silhouette against a backdrop of hotel lobby and, beyond, through the glass doors at the entrance, a scarlet and gold sunset. He came all the way in, filling the office with his presence, making the room suddenly seem smaller than it was. Catherine guessed he was around six-feet-two, and the slight gray in the dark brown crewcut placed him around forty. But his body, Catherine noted, showed no hint of approaching midlife.

She hung up the phone. "What's wrong is I urgently need to use that computer to get in touch with someone."

"Why didn't you say so?"

"I don't like being at the mercy of a priest."

He gave her a surprised look. "You're hardly at my mercy." He went to the terminal, sat at the keyboard, typed quickly, and then shot to his feet. "It's all yours," he said abruptly, not looking at her, and walked out.

Catherine stared after him for a moment, then she sat down, consulted the slip of paper on which she had written Daniel's electronic address, and began to type.

DANIEL HAD JUST finished sending his electronic signature line— *"I'm the Cat!"*—when he thought he heard something outside in the rain.

He turned toward the tomb's entrance just as his assistant burst in, shouting, "We gotta get outa here! *Now!"*

"What—"

"The rebels have overrun the camp! I barely got away in the Jeep!"

Daniel slammed the lid down on his computer, stuffed it under his plastic poncho, and plunged out into the rain just as gunfire cracked like thunder over their heads.

THE BLACK INFLATABLE boat skimmed over the water, reaching the shore before the moon could start its rise over the gulf and thus shed light on the night landscape. The two occupants, clad in black wet suits, cut the outboard engine and then went swiftly and noiselessly over the side. When they touched sandy bottom, they towed the boat the rest of the way, dragging it up onto the beach.

They paused to look around for signs of life. But all was dark and deserted at this cold midnight hour; the first in the line of tourist hotels, glowing against the night sky, was enough of a distance to the south that the men were certain they had not been seen. Nonetheless, as they quickly unloaded their gear, they kept a sharp lookout. Because of the nature of their assignment, they had entered the country illegally.

The leader of the team frequently checked his watch: they had one hour in which to locate their target and report to their employer.

AS THE NIGHT wind howled around her tent, sounding like evil desert *jinni* trying to get in, Catherine gazed at the basket on the workbench. She planned to open it as soon as she was certain her camp had settled down for the night.

She had finally heard from Daniel, calling from a military outpost while an uprising raged about him. He had shouted four beautiful words: "I'm on my way!"

But it would take him nearly a day to reach her. In the meantime, Catherine was so constantly on her guard that she thought her nerves would snap. As the wind whistled around her tent, she regarded the basket on the work table.

It wasn't very big, roughly the size and shape of a picnic hamper, smelling of soil and decay. The outer wrappings were already falling apart, and some of the rope had disintegrated since being exposed to sunlight. But Catherine had an idea that whatever had been so carefully wrapped inside was still intact and quite possibly well preserved.

"Aemelia, revered diakonos . . . "

She went to the screened window and looked out across the dark plain. In the distance, lights glowed in Hungerford's camp.

In her own camp, lamps continued to burn in two tents, and she could hear several of her people talking. She desperately wanted to open the basket, but she dared not risk the chance of someone walking in on her. Returning to the workbench, she examined the outer wrappings of the basket with a magnifying glass, and when she came upon a minute specimen of flora, she frowned.

Because Catherine believed that the Hebrews would have carried seeds and cuttings with them when they left Egypt, and then planted and cultivated them wherever they rested in their wanderings, part of her work involved the gathering and identifying of ancient botanical specimens. Since some plants are endemic to certain regions and not found in others, it followed that evidence of Nile plants among ancient Israelite pottery could support her hypothesis that Moses and Miriam had brought their people this way. Unfortunately, Catherine had so far found only plant life common to the southern Sinai.

This specimen, however, was unfamiliar.

While she concentrated on her work, going through a book on paleobotany, the moon rose in the night sky, shedding silver light across the wilderness and illuminating, a short distance from Catherine's camp, two men walking along the beach.

"Origanum ramonense," Catherine murmured a moment later, as she satisfied herself that there was no mistaking the leaf shape, the fine hairs on stem and calyx, the perfectly preserved corolla. She read the data in the book which ended with: *endemic to the Central Negev Highlands.*

Israel! Nearly two hundred miles away!

She looked over at the mysterious basket again and felt her pulse quicken. Why had the people who had taken such care to wrap this bundle then traveled such a great distance to bury it? Where did they come from? Who were they? And what about the skull? Had someone purposely been buried with the basket? If so, why?

"Read this letter in secret, in fear for your safety and for your lives."

She couldn't wait any longer.

Picking up scissors and tweezers, Catherine set to work painstakingly trimming away the basket's outer linen wrapping, cutting away the rope, dissecting through the layers as precisely as a surgeon delving a wound.

The wind moaned and shook the tent, sending rainfalls of sand and gravel against its walls. As the moon continued to rise, casting the encampment in a supernatural light, Catherine lifted away the last of the inner wrappings.

She stared in disbelief.

THE BELLY DANCE show was just winding down as the dancer, a woman named Yasmina and touted by the management of the Isis Hotel as "The Honey of the East"—but who was in fact Shirley Milewski from Bismarck, North Dakota—shimmied among the tables and encouraged the guests to tuck dollar bills and Egyptian pound notes into her costume. Out in the lobby, one of the two newly arrived Americans, now changed into tourist gear, secured a room for the night—cash handed directly to the clerk, with an extra fee to cover the inconvenience of their lack of passports—while his partner was on the phone next to the elevators.

He spoke only one sentence, quietly, making sure there was no one around to see or hear: "We have reached the accident site."

CATHERINE FOUND HERSELF staring at a set of papyrus "books," perfectly preserved between leather covers. They had been wrapped in fine linen and bound with string and packed in this basket. With the sensitive, delicate touch cultivated over years of handling fragile, perishable objects, Catherine opened the first of them.

THE AMERICANS TIPPED the porter who had led them up to their room, then they locked the door and got busy setting up their temporary center of operations.

The tools of their trade came out of the luggage they had brought: Russian-made NV-100 night vision scopes; waterproof Diver Tech flashlights; Navy SEAL Team 2000 knives; a Swarovski laser range finder; stun guns capable of delivering 200,000 volts of stun power; and a Scout GPS navigational instrument for locating their precise position anywhere on the globe. Finally, out came detailed maps of the shorelines along the Gulf of Aqaba and Saudi Arabia, LANDSAT photos of the southern Sinai, the Suez Canal, and the Red Sea. The two men had not packed airline tickets or passports. They knew how to slip in and out of countries unseen.

The Glock 17 handgun with nineteen-round option and laser sight, and the Benelli shotgun M3 with folding stock, had already been fitted snugly into shoulder holsters hidden beneath jackets, back at the place on the beach where they had landed.

They were ready to go to work.

CATHERINE PRESSED A button on her microcassette recorder. "The first book," she dictated, "consists of typical papyrus sheets pasted end to end with slight overlaps. It is folded like an accordion rather than being bound on one edge. Opened out, it is a standard length, twenty sheets, with writing on each panel. The writing is on the recto, the side showing horizontal fibers."

As she gently unfolded the brittle papyrus, the wind picked up, rushing across the alluvial plain, creating the strange howling sound the local Bedouin called the Cries of the Lost. Catherine brought out the big magnifying glass, and drew the lantern closer to the papyrus. Hooking her long auburn hair behind her ears, she had started to read the ancient words when she heard a sound outside the tent.

She turned and listened. "Hello?" she called. "Who's there?" She went to the tent flap and, raising it, looked out into the dark, violent night.

The camp was silent, her crew asleep, no lights glowed in the tents. When the wind shifted, she heard the tinkling of goats' bells and the occasional nervous bleating of a kid. The wilderness was cast in a strange, preternatural light.

She listened again and heard another, more familiar sound: footsteps crunching over rubble.

Grabbing her flashlight, she stepped out and swept the beam over the excavation site. At first she saw only the trenches and the ropes being whipped by the wind, and sand skimming over ancient stones. Then she saw him, a prowler.

"What are you doing here?" she demanded, marching up to him. And when she shined the light on his face, she saw that it was the priest from the Isis Hotel.

"Hey!" he said, holding an arm up to his eyes.

"You're trespassing," she said, lowering the beam.

"I'm sorry. I didn't think it would hurt if I looked around." When he saw her face, he said, "You! The computer hijacker! Were you able to get through to your friend?"

Feeling the biting wind slice across her bare arms and legs, Catherine was suddenly aware that she wore only shorts and a blouse. "Yes," she said. She had to use her free hand to keep her long hair from flying into her face.

"Michael Garibaldi," he said, offering his hand.

"What are you doing here?" she asked again, ignoring the hand.

"They told me at the hotel there was a dig out here. I was curious. Do you work here?"

"This is my dig. Isn't it rather late to be visiting ruins?"

"I couldn't sleep. Neither could you, I see." He looked past her toward her tent glowing against the black sky. When he turned away to scan the dark trenches and mounds of displaced rubble, Catherine noticed how the wind whipped his shirt, pressing the black fabric against a strong, well-muscled back. "I take it you're Dr. Alexander," he said. "They said at the hotel that you'd found something."

"We aren't sure yet," Catherine said cautiously. "I'm waiting for a representative from the Egyptian government before I proceed."

He nodded. "If this were my dig I'd be careful, too. I remember reading about that find up near Bir el Dam. Word got out, the next day there were tents everywhere, and within a week the place had been picked clean."

For an instant she was held by his blue eyes. They reminded her of when she was little and how she had believed that when a priest looked at you he could see into your soul. She had outgrown that illusion on discovering that priests were merely men. But now, meeting Michael Garibaldi's open gaze, she had the strangest feeling once again that he could see into her soul.

And she didn't like it.

"The ground is unstable here," she said. She aimed the flashlight beam down and, like a theater usher, led him around the trenches and back toward the camp.

"I just came down from Jerusalem," he said as he followed her, talking softly as they neared the dark tents. "I decided to stretch out my vacation a little and see something of the Sinai. I'm actually on my way home." He paused, then he added, "Home is Chicago, in case you were wondering."

When she still didn't respond, he said, "Why do I get the feeling you don't like me?"

"Father Michael—"

"Please," he said with a smile. "Just plain Mike."

But she refused to be taken in. "I was raised to address priests respectfully, by their title. I am not comfortable with 'just plain Mike.'"

"I see," he said, and she thought for a moment that his expression turned dark. "And *I* was raised to say thank you if someone did me a favor, like giving up a computer he was using."

Because they were standing in the small pool of light cast by the lantern outside her tent, Catherine was able to see more details about him: the creases at the corners of his eyes, as if he were out in the sun a lot, or laughed a lot, or both. When he lifted a hand to brush a moth away from his face, she saw the sculptured muscles of his forearm, evidence of an athletic life. He was from Chicago he said; she suspected that underneath the white collar lay a blue one.

"I'm sorry," she said. "I do appreciate it. I went looking for you afterward to thank you. Mr. Mylonas said you had gone into town. Were you able to download your e-mail?"

The attractive smile returned. "After a couple of hours."

Catherine listened to the wind whistling through the nearby canyons. And she thought of the papyrus books, lying exposed and vulnerable on the workbench in her tent. "It's late," she said. "Good night."

"May I ask you something?" he said. "Back at the hotel you said you don't like being at the mercy of a priest."

"It was nothing personal."

He regarded her for a moment, then said, "I was curious because sometimes people who aren't familiar with Catholicism—"

"I was raised in the Catholic faith, Father. I attended twelve years of Catholic school. And then I left the Church."

"I see," he said quietly. "Good night then." He held out his hand. This time she took it, and she felt a firm grasp close over her fingers. When she looked up and her eyes met his, Catherine experienced a quick, sudden connection with him that both startled and excited her.

He seemed to regard her for a moment longer, then he said quietly, "Dr. Alexander, I hope that whatever you are looking for, you find it."

She watched him go, bewildered by the strange effect he had just had on her, and angry with herself for allowing it.

As she turned to go into her tent, her eye caught something at the edge of the excavation that she hadn't noticed before—an ugly, bulky, squat shape blocking out the stars. And she realized in horror that it was a Bedouin tent.

It hadn't been there at sunset.

"WE HAVE REACHED the accident site, Mr. Havers."

"Excellent," Miles replied into the cellular phone, walking out of the hearing of the others. The call had come while the family was in the middle of decorating the Christmas tree.

As Miles listened to Zeke's brief report, he watched Erica supervise the grandchildren with the placement of ornaments on the twelve-foot Douglas fir dominating the living room. The littlest ones were arranging the nativity scene at the base of the tree, and when three-year-old Jessica said, "But where is Baby Jesus?" Erica laughed, hugged her granddaughter, and said, "He'll appear on Christmas morning!"

Miles smiled at them and then turned his back as he said quietly into the phone, "When you meet with the contact, make it quick. No bargaining. Either cut a deal or get rid of him. Take possession of the goods and be out of there within twenty-four hours."

Miles felt the tiger stir within him—a beast that had been born years ago on a day that had changed his life. The tiger was Miles's intuition, and it was growling softly now, eager.

"Change that," Miles said quietly into the phone. "Whether you cut a deal or not, get rid of him. I don't want anyone else to know about this."

And the tiger flicked its tail. . . .

DAY TWO

*H*oly saints! thought Danno as the Land Rover neared Catherine's dig. *What the hell is going on?*

She hadn't told him over the phone why she needed him, and Samir, the man who had met him at the Sharm el Sheikh airport, hadn't offered any information. But now, as they raced across the plain in Samir's open-topped Rover, Daniel saw a circus of tents, cars, buses, donkeys, tourists, and local Arabs milling around the excavation site.

"Lafayette, we are here!" he shouted when he saw Catherine emerge from her tent, squinting into the setting sun.

"Danno!" she called out, running to him.

He jumped down and drew her into a tight embrace.

"Thank God you came," she murmured.

He held her for a long moment, savoring the feel of her in his arms. Then he quickly released her. "You look like hell," he said quietly, feasting his eyes on her.

She laughed and raked her fingers through his blond hair, which had been whipped into a fright wig. He was covered in dust and his T-shirt that read "An Archaeologist's Career Is in Ruins from the

41

Start" was wrinkled and stained. "So do you!" she said.

She took him by the hand. "Leave your things in the car and come inside, quickly. As you can see, word has spread that we found something."

"The Well of Miriam?"

"Something bigger," she said as she took him into the tent.

"Judging by that carnival outside, it must be gold!"

She regarded him with shining green eyes. "Better than gold, Danno! *Scrolls*. And they're old, my God, they're old—" She stopped and listened. Then she went to the tent flap and looked out.

"What is it?" he said.

"I thought I heard someone right outside." She held up a cautioning hand, then, resecuring the tent opening, went to a table cluttered with bottles and glasses. When he started to say something, she placed a finger to her lips.

As Catherine poured two glasses of Evian, Daniel noticed the workbench mysteriously covered with a sheet. Then he saw the suitcase opened out on the cot. "Are you going somewhere?"

Handing him a glass, she said in a low voice, "I'm leaving right away. I was only waiting for you to get here."

"What's going on?"

"Brace yourself, Danno, because you are not going to believe what I am about to show you."

AS ZEKE STOOD on the balcony of his hotel room, his gaze set on the gulf, growing dark now as the westering sun dipped behind the mountains of Sinai, he heard voices drifting up from the terrace restaurant below. There was a buzz in the air about the nearby archaeological site, that something had been found.

He heard a knock at the door. Their contact had arrived.

AS CATHERINE HASTILY packed her suitcase, she filled Daniel in on the events of the past thirty-six hours, from the moment she had been wakened by the dynamiting. "No one knows I've opened the basket," she said. "But it's only a matter of time before I'm found out. You saw those ropes and the warning signs I placed around the dig. They've held the curiosity seekers off until now, but I don't know for how much longer." Daniel noticed that she wasn't folding things neatly but tossing them into the suitcase—a woman in a hurry. "I think Hungerford leaked something," she said. "I got a message from the manager of the Isis Hotel, who said the Department of Antiquities called to inform me that a representative is on the way. He's due to arrive tonight, but I intend to be gone before he gets here. Hopefully I can sneak out while everyone's having dinner. Hungerford's Arab crew always have some kind of campfire entertainment. It will provide the distraction I need."

"Cath, what are you talking about?"

She stopped what she was doing, went to the covered workbench and drew back the sheet. "These!"

She had separated the papyri into neat piles, with the first one unfolded and laid out. As Daniel approached the table, Catherine explained how she had matched the Jesus fragment to the first page of what appeared to be the first "book," lining up the jagged edges so that the writing fitted together almost seamlessly She had then placed a glass plate over it.

Daniel bent low to inspect them, his expression one of awe. "Why are you calling them scrolls?"

Returning to her packing, she picked up a pair of slippers, knocked them together to get the sand off them, then tucked them into the suitcase. "Look at the ends; they appear to have once been fastened to rollers. But at some point the rollers were removed and the scroll was folded accordion-like, to resemble a book."

"It was around the second century, wasn't it, that the roll began to be replaced by the codex? Sheets of writing material folded and fastened at one edge?"

"Yes, but those aren't fastened at one edge, you'll notice, and they aren't separate sheets. But they do resemble a book. So I asked myself: Why were the rollers removed and then the scroll folded?"

He looked at her. "What's your theory?"

"For easier transport," she said, pulling toiletries off the shelf over the wash basin and hastily tossing them into the case. "Scrolls are cumbersome and difficult to carry in secret. But a flat book can be concealed under clothing."

"You mean, to hide them from people who were persecuting the owners of these scrolls?"

"Possibly. Now," she said as she returned to the workbench, "I believe I've set the scrolls out in the order they are supposed to be read, judging by this first page, which appears to be a cover letter. The rest of that particular scroll seems to be the beginning of the story of a woman's life. The other five," she pointed to the neatly folded papyrus packages, still in their original accordion state so that they did indeed resemble books, "are probably the rest of it."

Daniel gazed spellbound at the laid-out scroll, which stretched about four feet, each folded section a "page" covered with writing in black ink. "Was anything else wrapped in with the books?"

"No."

"Have you translated them yet?"

"Only the first page."

"And?"

She handed him a sheet of notepaper, covered in her own neat handwriting. He saw the first words, *"From Perpetua. . . ."*

"Read the passage highlighted in yellow."

HUNGERFORD SIZED UP the two strangers as he settled his bulk into a chair and said, "I gotta admit, I didn't expect such a fast response. And I certainly didn't expect a coupla fellow Americans."

After Dr. Alexander brought the basket out of the tunnel and secreted it away in her tent, Hungerford had got to thinking that the archaeologist might be beautiful but she was a lousy liar. A quick trip to the Isis Hotel and a private conversation with a desk clerk had produced the name of a man in Cairo, a dealer in "private antiquities," as the clerk had discreetly put it. Hungerford had contacted the dealer right away, not telling too much, certainly making no mention of Catherine Alexander, but just enough—"A papyrus fragment that says Jesus on it"—to whet appetites. The dealer had said he would get back to him. Hungerford had been surprised, and then impressed, when he had received a call from the Isis Hotel and heard an American on the other end of the line saying he was interested.

"So," he said now, "you boys buyin' for yourselves or"—his grin widened—"am I right in guessin' that you work for someone?" The other guy didn't say much, but the one who introduced himself as Zeke had "mercenary" written all over him. Not too tall, but lean and densely packed, with strange white hair cut very short, flat, gray eyes, and a scar streaking one side of his face, from hairline to jaw, puckering his right brow, right eye, and corner of his mouth. Hungerford wondered how he had got it.

Zeke smiled. "Our employer prefers to remain anonymous."

Hungerford shrugged. "Makes no difference to me. So, dollars and cents, gentleman. What's your boss offering?"

DANIEL READ OUT loud: ". . . *for to Sabina was revealed the hour of the Second Coming, the hour of the End of Things.*"

He looked in astonishment at Catherine. "Are you sure this is what it says? I mean, my God! The *hour* of the Second Coming?"

"See for yourself." She pointed to a line on the first papyrus fragment.

Daniel squinted at the word: *parousia.* . . . "If it gets out," he said, "that a Jesus scroll has been found, one that might tell us exactly when . . ." His voice died.

"That's one reason why I haven't told anyone about them."

"What does the rest of the letter say?"

Catherine read directly from the papyrus, translating as she went: "*Before I begin Sabina's story, dear sister, I remind you again of my warning. I have told Sabina of the great tribulations of our sisters, that, after all these years of enjoying equality with men in the Community, we are being relegated to silence and sequestration. Sabina implores me, she does not want her sisters to suffer persecution on her account. If this message is met with indignation by the men, and they seek to persecute you because of it, then take these books to King—*"

Daniel looked at her. "Why did you stop?"

"It ends here, at the bottom of the page." She moved the magnifying glass up to the top of the next column and resumed reading. "*— Tymbos, to keep it safe.*"

"King Tymbos! Who's he?"

"I have no idea."

Daniel ran his hands through his hair and started to pace. As he passed the screened window, he heard voices on the wind: someone shouting at the gawkers prowling the edge of the site to keep back. He stopped and looked at Catherine. "The Community," he said. "The early Church, do you think?"

She went back to her suitcase and shut it with a decisive click. "I expect to find that out when I've translated the scrolls."

"What do you suppose they are? Lost Gospels?"

"I don't know, but I think there's a book missing."

"Why do you say that?"

She returned to the workbench. "They came bundled together in that basket, and I've found no evidence of other books having been buried with them. Now look at the final page of book number six—here," she unfolded it carefully, "at the bottom, read it."

"My Greek's rusty," he said. "But I think it says, 'And I was afraid.'"

"Not quite. This word derives from the root *phobos,* so that it more precisely translates as *'I was afraid of.'*"

"Of?"

"Afraid *of* something. This word has to be followed by another word. Which means this isn't the end. There should be another page after this one."

"What do you suppose they were afraid of?" he murmured.

Catherine pulled a jacket off a hook and draped it over the suitcase. "The first thing I want to do is run some tests on the papyrus—x-ray fluorescence spectrometry and infrared absorption. I've already shipped a sample off to Switzerland for radiocarbon testing."

"Hans Schuller?"

"He can be counted on to be discreet. But in the meantime, I've been analyzing the handwriting."

"And?"

"So far, on gross inspection, it's second century."

"The skull you mentioned, do you think it's related?"

"If it is, then he was either thrown in or he fell in."

"He?"

"Or she. . . . "

As Daniel absorbed this, he heard in the far distance the call of a muezzin from a minaret: *"Allahu akbar. . . ."* The sunset prayer meant that meals were under way; already, the aromas of roast lamb and coffee were starting to permeate the tent.

"I still don't understand something, Cath. Why haven't you reported this find to the authorities? And why are you leaving?"

"That page you just read, my translation, look again at the greeting."

"To Aemelia, revered *diakonos.*" He looked at her. "Okay, she was a deaconess. So? That's not unusual."

"Except that the Greek word for deaconess is *diakonissa.* But the word there means deacon."

"Is it a mistake?"

"I don't think so. There is one other instance in which a woman is addressed by the male title—Romans, chapter sixteen, where Paul refers to Phoebe as *diakonon.* It's the only example we have of a woman holding such a high title, when the *diakonos* presided at the altar. After that, the term was feminized and the deaconess's duties were restricted to taking care of the sick and the elderly."

"And if you prove that these scrolls are first century . . ." He suddenly knew why Catherine hadn't informed the Department of Antiquities.

It was because of her mother.

Although Dr. Nina Alexander had been a paleographer, an expert in the science of dating manuscripts by the way the letters arc- drawn, what she was most famous for was a volatile book titled *Mary Magdalene, The First Apostle,* in which she had claimed that the authority of the current Pope, based upon the apostolic succession begun when Saint Peter had supposedly been the first to witness the resurrection, was groundless. All four gospels, Nina had declared, depicted women as having been the first to witness the empty tomb, and in two of the gospels Jesus first appears after the resurrection to Mary Magdalene, not to Peter, who was away in hiding. Based on New Testament evidence, Dr. Alexander concluded, it was Mary, not Peter who should have been Jesus' successor.

It was the work that had destroyed her.

"And you think that these scrolls," Daniel said now, cautiously, "might contain proof of your mother's theory?"

Catherine spoke quickly. "My mother's critics pointed out the fact that the account of the resurrection in Paul's first letter to the Corinthians makes no mention of Mary Magdalene, or of *any* women in Jesus' entourage, or even of the empty tomb itself. Since we know that Paul's letter to the Corinthians was written at least twenty years *before* the gospels appeared in written form, then his work is the more authoritative, being closer in time to the source. But what if *these* scrolls, Danno," she said as she carefully gathered the papyrus books into a pile, "are *earlier* than Paul? What if they contain a reference to women at the tomb and possibly to Mary Magdalene herself, *before anything Paul wrote?*"

His gold-lashed eyes widened. "Then the entire authority-base of the Catholic Church and the papacy would be blown out of the water! Cath, this is hot! Did you know that Nostradamus predicted that the year 1999 would mark the end of the papacy and the fall of Catholicism? Wouldn't it be a gas if these scrolls contained evidence that your mother was right, that Peter had no rightful claim to succeed Jesus and that the subsequent two-thousand-year succession of popes has been based on an error? It would throw the Church into a *tailspin!* My God, no wonder you want to get these scrolls out of here. If the authorities get hold of them, we'll never see them again!"

"And these scrolls might be my only chance to restore my mother's reputation. Will you help me?"

He smiled. "Such a question."

"I only need to get a few more things together, then we watch for when everyone outside is distracted and we make our break."

Daniel stood over the first papyrus again, still opened out on the workbench. "'The Righteous One,'" he murmured. "That *is* what it says here?"

Catherine looked out the window, her face catching the lantern's glow. She saw that her crew had joined a Bedouin campfire. "Yes," she said softly.

"Isn't there a Righteous One referred to in the Dead Sea Scrolls?"

She turned to look at him. "These aren't the work of Essenes."

"That's not what I'm getting at. The Essenes were believed to be healers, weren't they? The word *Essene* derives from the Greek *essenoi*—healer, right? And those mystical healers were believed to be guardians of many ancient secrets. Just consider the rules of their sect." He enumerated them on one hand. "It was hard to get into, the initiation took forever and was excruciating, and if you broke even the smallest rule, punishment was severe. Why? Because of what you pointed out here: *zoe aionios*. Living forever."

She carefully folded the opened out scroll back into an accordion. "What are you getting at?"

"What if one of the Essenes' secrets was the formula for living forever? Maybe that's why they were so afraid of outsiders, and members leaving the community. The Essenic sect is believed to have been wiped out when Rome destroyed Jerusalem and then Masada in 74 c.e. Right? But what if their secrets weren't wiped out with them? What if the *final* scroll was smuggled out, the scroll that tells us when the world is going to end and maybe even the formula for living forever?"

The words of Ibn Hassan came to Catherine's mind: *"To me therefore was granted the key to living forever."*

"Why couldn't the Righteous One be Jesus?" Daniel continued, hopped up now on his own excitement. "Plenty of scholars claim that Jesus was an Essene, which is why he is portrayed as a healer in the New Testament. So suppose his message of eternal life wasn't referring to the life that comes after death, but *the one right here on earth,* living forever in our flesh-and-blood bodies! He did raise people from the dead. What if those were demonstrations that he knew the formula for living forever? Cath, if we can find out who Tymbos was and what city he was king of, we might be able to find the seventh scroll and find out for ourselves the formula for living forever!"

"MR. HUNGERFORD," ZEKE said, as he paced in and out of the circle of light created by the lamp on the night table. The sun had finally set, casting the hotel room in darkness. "Let me give you a little lesson on the illegal antiquities trade. There is a law, instituted under the auspices of UNESCO, stipulating that any antiquities smuggled out of a country must be returned to their point of origin. When this law came out, it was made retroactive, which meant that collectors who had invested a lot of money in ancient papyrus could no longer allow their collections to be known publicly. This had an interesting domino effect. What it did was to cause prices to rise, and the underground traffic in these materials to go even farther underground. Are you getting my drift?"

Hungerford frowned. "I'm not sure—"

Zeke stepped closer, so that Hungerford could now actually see little white dots around the puckers in the scar bisecting Zeke's face, as though the slash had been stitched with a large needle. "Well, sir,"

Zeke continued amiably, "the underground scroll trade became too hot for a lot of dealers to handle, so it eventually became the purview of a select list of families. These families have incredible intelligence networks, Mr. Hungerford, you would be amazed. They keep abreast of all rumors, whispers, legends, and suspected discoveries involving scrolls and papyrus fragments. Did you know, Mr. Hungerford, that in Jerusalem, if there's a rumor of antiquities buried in a certain area, that interested parties will buy the house that stands on the site and dig straight through the cellar and into the ground, and the authorities never know? Sometimes, they'll even *build* a house on the spot if there isn't one there, and when they've dug all the antiquities out, they tear the house down and move on."

"I still don't—"

"What I am saying, Mr. Hungerford, is that you have chosen to enter a very big game in which the stakes are a lot higher than you can imagine. And your fellow players, Mr. Hungerford, that is, your *opponents,* are not stupid men."

Hungerford started to sweat. "Oh, but I didn't think—"

"You called a certain dealer in Cairo and you told him that a fragment of papyrus had been found, as well as the basket that you thought the fragment had come from."

Zeke bent down, as if to scratch his ankle, but when he straightened, Hungerford saw the flash of a stiletto knife.

"WHAT DO YOU see?" Erica Havers said as she anxiously watched Coyote Man read the sacred smoke.

When the Indian shaman didn't respond, she turned her attention to the action going on around the pool, where the whole family was gathered—her three grown children and their spouses, and the grandchildren, ranging from age twelve down to infant, all here to celebrate Christmas and the New Year. The pool was heated against the biting December day; steam rose up to the sharp New Mexico sky, just as the smoke from the mesquite burning in the sacred bowl was spiraling up and around Coyote Man's head.

He was reading the future.

Erica brought her attention back to the shaman, wondering what he saw in the smoke.

Lately, she had begun to sense a hollowness inside her, as though she were missing a vital piece. She had explored meditation, and astrology, and anchoring with angels, but in the end it was still "new." The hunger inside Erica seemed to be calling for an *ancient* food, a spiritual nourishment that had withstood the test of time.

And then she had met a Native American shaman at a local art show. His Christian name, forced upon his people over a hundred years ago by white man's laws, was Luke Pineda. But his tribal name was Itsaqa, which meant Coyote Man. A Pueblo Indian, he was the head of the Antelope clan and therefore a spiritual and political leader in his village, which included being the caretaker of the sacred kachinas. From Coyote Man Erica had learned about Latiku, the mother-creator of the world, and how the human race had been formed when the ancestors, dwelling in the nether regions below, had pushed their way up to the surface to dwell in the sunshine.

"What do you see?" she asked him again.

This time Coyote Man shook his head, long white braids brushing the front of his shirt. "It is very bad, Mrs. Havers. The world is definitely coming to an end."

She gave him a dismayed look. "You see that in the smoke?"

He lifted eyes that were so washed out they were nearly colorless. People said that the sun had bleached the pigment from the old man's eyes. "No. It is not in the smoke. The smoke is empty."

Then she knew: it was because of the kachina that had vanished from Acoma Pueblo. The police were saying it was theft, but the medicine man declared that the kachina spirit had gone on its own down into the ground because the world was going to end soon.

"He is Soyal, the Solstice Kachina," Coyote Man had explained. "Soyal appears at the winter solstice to signal the beginning of kachina season. He is the first to come out of the kiva and go through the village, preparing the way for the rest of the kachinas to return from the spirit world." Coyote Man had gone down into the kiva in preparation for the kachina's appearance at the solstice, a week from now, but saw that Soyal was not there. "It is the first time in the memory of my clan that Return Kachina will not appear. And so the others cannot come out of the kivas and bless my people. This is very, very bad."

Erica started to ask another question, when she saw a houseboy appear on the terrace and approach Miles, who was turning steaks on the barbecue. She thought of the Christmas gift she had bought for him.

She had wanted to make his present this year unique, for the final Christmas of the second millennium. And so when she had read that approximately twenty thousand manorial titles in England were for sale, she had looked into it. Although ownership of the title did not mean ownership of land or that the new lord could collect taxes, people who bought such a title, even Americans, had the right to call themselves Lord or Lady of the Manor. But even as attractive as it sounded, Erica knew she couldn't settle for just any title.

There was only one she wanted.

Back in 1990, when Miles had read an item about the lordship title of Stratford-upon-Avon being sold for a record $228,000, he had commented about how *he* would like to own that. And Erica kept it in mind, hoping the lordship would come up for sale again.

And it had. But as she thought now about the impressive document that had arrived from London, she thought how blithely she had come to regard money. It was hard to keep in mind that there had been a time when she had had to scrape together thirty-three cents for a quart of milk.

Suddenly she was overwhelmed by an almost insupportable longing. For a simpler life. For the old days. For the time before Miles had converted a revolutionary computer operating system into a staggering fortune.

A phrase went through her mind—Coyote Man had spoken it that morning: "Do you not seek a light, you who are surrounded by darkness? Do you not seek the way home?" And as she considered all her material wealth, she silently said: Yes, I seek the way home.

And in the next moment Erica understood something: I *do* seek the way home, she thought, amazed at the revelation, at its simplicity but also at its profound truth. Amazed, too, that it should come to her now, just like that.

But where was home?

Not here, among all this materialism.

Then where?

Home is in the past, years ago, back before . . .

Before what?

Erica experienced a second revelation that was so clear and so staggering, that she drew in a sharp breath.

Back before the war . . .

And there it was, out in the open. The seed of her recent discontent.

Recognizing it now, Erica realized that this was nothing new, that it had in fact been with her all this time, through three decades of raising a family and being the wife of the nearly mythical Miles Havers: a truth that she had known all along but had buried.

That the man she had married in 1968, on the day before he shipped out to Vietnam, was not the same man who came home.

Erica knew that thousands of lives had been disrupted by the war. But she had sensed that somehow, in her case, it was different. Miles's experience in Vietnam hadn't damaged him the way it had others; he hadn't even come home with a bruise. There had been no post-war nightmares, no waking up screaming, as she had heard other wives reporting. Miles had slept like a baby afterward. He hadn't needed counseling, didn't seek out support groups; there were no psychotic flashbacks, no depression or guilt. In fact, Miles had come back imbued with a strange new ambition that he hadn't possessed before, and a curious optimism that had vaguely unsettled her.

He wouldn't speak of his war experiences, but would only smile and say that he had come back with the power of the tiger. But now, after thirty years of trying to ignore it, Erica forced herself to face the fact that Miles had changed in a disturbing way—he had come home *cheerful.* For the first time since the end of the war, she found herself asking: What did happen to change him so . . . ?

THE CALL WAS from the Sinai.

When Zeke was finished, Miles put him on hold, then punched into the intercom. A masculine voice responded: "Yes, Mr. Havers?"

"Mr. Yamaguchi, get me everything you can on an archaeologist named Catherine Alexander. Where she lives, who her colleagues are, her friends, lovers—everything. And hurry."

He returned to Zeke, his orders brief: "Bypass Hungerford, get the scrolls, and make sure Dr. Alexander isn't around to talk afterward."

Before rejoining the family, Miles decided to go downstairs to his private subterranean domain, a soothing setting of desert pastels and indirect lighting, soundproofed against the outside world. It was a museum, housing his treasures in sealed glass cases and protected in a humidity- and light-controlled environment, with earthquake sensors and a state-of-the-art security system.

Although Havers had never set out on purpose to acquire religious items, it seemed that they made up the majority of his collection anyway. He had discovered that it didn't matter how ancient or rare or how encrusted with jewels a piece might be, if there was added religious significance, then the price became inestimable. People seemed to place so much value on the unseen.

He thought of Erica, lately searching for answers. She wasn't the only one. The news these days was full of reports on religious hysteria and unexplained religious phenomena: Mary sightings, saint statues that wept, the face of Jesus on a garage door. The Shroud of Turin was on display and had been viewed by recordbreaking crowds, many people swearing that the eyes of the image on the shroud, heretofore closed, were now open. In Britain, the army had been called out to control the hordes descending with tents and trailers and RVs upon Stonehenge, in anticipation of a millennial cataclysm two weeks from now. And the plans! Parties on the *QE2* and in the Seattle Space Needle, monster rallies in the Carlsbad Caverns and at Machu Pichu, people chartering planes to the South Pacific so they could fly between two islands that straddled the International Date Line and therefore be able to celebrate New Year's twice. There was a madness in the air, and Miles loved it. Because there was profit in madness. Especially religious madness.

He had once even toyed with the idea of engineering the "kidnapping" of St. Peter's bones from beneath the basilica in Rome and holding them for ransom. What, he liked to speculate, would the Catholic Church, the wealthiest institution on the face of the earth, pay for their return?

Miles now opened the locked cabinet that contained his latest acquisition. No one, not even Erica, knew about this one and he was particularly proud of it.

Standing nearly two feet tall and carved of cottonwood, the

figure was painted a ghostly white; it carried an eagle feather in its left hand, and a white plume rose from the crown of its eerie mask. Miles regarded it with reverence: Soyal, the Solstice Kachina, rumored to be the rarest and most priceless of all the Pueblo kachina dolls.

And it was his.

"WHAT THE HELL is all *this?*" Zeke's partner said.

Zeke didn't reply as he brought the rented car to a swerving halt at the edge of the encampment, the headlights illuminating what appeared to be a commotion going on at the excavation site.

Jumping out, the two Americans tried to push through the agitated crowd that had gathered around some sort of fracas. The shouting and cheering, they noticed, was mostly in Arabic, and Zeke saw that the few Westerners in the crowd—part of Dr. Alexander's crew, he deduced, as well as tourists who had wandered over from the hotels—watched in detached curiosity.

Because the mob was moving, following whatever was happening, Zeke was able to insinuate himself into the fray, and he saw at the center of the mob an Arab in Western dress dragging a woman wrapped in the black veils of the Bedouin. The man was shouting at her as she tried to pull away, while others, mostly Arab men, bellowed in anger, or laughed and jeered.

Zeke tried to muscle his way through to the other side, where Catherine Alexander's tent was, but the mob was too thick. He swore under his breath. He couldn't afford this delay. Back at the hotel he had hung out a Do Not Disturb sign to make sure it would be morning before the maids found Hungerford's body in the bathtub. But a Do Not Disturb sign was no guarantee that someone might not for some reason enter the room tonight anyway. Perhaps they already had.

"What's going on?" he asked one of the bystanders, who looked American.

"That's her brother," the young woman said. "He's accusing her of dishonoring the family."

Zeke eyed the Bedouin woman, who was trying to break free. The black robe, billowing around her body like a stormy cloud, concealed every part of her. But when she tried to twist out of her brother's grasp, it quickly became apparent that she was pregnant.

The crowd was suddenly startled by a man bursting through, loudly protesting in English the harsh treatment of the woman. Because he was wearing a clerical shirt and Roman collar, half the crowd roared its approval, while the other half yelled its disapproval. "This is none of your business!" the affronted brother shouted at the American priest. And the crowd, sensing a good fight, burst into cheers.

Zeke searched the onlookers, wondering if Dr. Alexander was among them watching the commotion. But only a few faces were illuminated by the lights strung up around the camp; everyone else stood in night darkness. He looked across at her tent; there was a light on, and a silhouette of someone moving about inside.

Trying once again to push through, and this time successful because the crowd was moving on, away from the dig, following the unfortunate woman and her brother, Zeke dashed across the camp and reached Catherine Alexander's tent at the same time his partner did. Slipping their hands inside their jackets, ready to draw weapons, they barged in.

HUMPHREY BOGART TOOK Erica Havers into his arms, looked deeply into her eyes, and said, "We'll always have Paris," and then he kissed her hard on the mouth.

The screen went dark and the red velvet curtain whispered closed. As the house lights in his private thirty-seat movie theater came back on, Miles smiled to himself. It was perfect, better than he had hoped. And Erica didn't suspect a thing. He could hardly wait to see her face on Christmas morning.

Even Miles himself, although he had been developing this project for nearly a year, was in awe of what he had achieved. The movie was the result of his newest brainchild, a software program that made the latest in special-effects film technology available to the average person for home movie use.

The idea had been born at a time when Miles's company was starting to buy up the digital rights to famous works of art to be digitally reproduced and put online for people tapping into the World Wide Web. When Dianuba Technologies had then begun gobbling up the rights to literature and movies that had gone past their copyright, transferring them onto glossy, coffee-table type CD-ROMs, Miles targeted old-time movie stars, seizing exclusive rights to Rudolph Valentino, W. C. Fields, and hundreds of others, digitizing their images, and manipulating tiny pixels of information to place the deceased stars in brand-new films. Now, using a home PC and an ordinary video camera, anyone could create a movie starring himself opposite famous actors.

As he poured himself a chilled Perrier, he heard a discreet signal announcing someone at the door. He pressed a button and the door swung silently open.

A slender Asian with long black hair in a ponytail down to his waist, and two earrings in one ear, came in and placed a file folder on the enormous black granite desk that had nothing on it except for a single, stunning yellow orchid. "Here's the file you wanted, Mr. Havers."

The file was thick and, Miles saw as he scanned the first pages, quite comprehensive. Although Teddy Yamaguchi had a degree in biochemistry, the twenty-eight-year-old's true area of expertise was in computers. It seemed to Miles that there wasn't a byte of information in the whole world Teddy could not access.

Everything on Catherine Alexander was here, starting with the hospital where she was born. In the category of friends, the name Daniel Stevenson headed the list.

When his private telephone line beeped, Miles dismissed Teddy and then picked it up after the door swung shut. It was Zeke, and the news wasn't good.

"What do you mean she got away?" Havers said. He listened, then nodded. "Wherever her Arab friends took her, you can be sure they aren't going to let you find her. My dealer in Cairo assures me I am the only one he contacted after Hungerford's call. My guess is Alexander doesn't know yet that we know about the scrolls. This gives us the advantage."

He looked at the file photo Yamaguchi had downloaded from UPI. Alexander was a beautiful woman, Miles conceded, although not his type. The hint of obstinacy in the jaw indicated a strong will. And there was a challenging look in her eyes. The government profile described her as a loner with no relatives, never married, only a few close friends. Perhaps that explained the look in her eyes. There seemed to be something in them that said, "Dare me."

What, he wondered, had put the chip on her shoulder?

Zeke went on to report that an official from the Egyptian Department of Antiquities had shown up at the camp and, when he found that Dr. Alexander had vanished, had confiscated items from her tent: a fragment of papyrus and a basket. But no scrolls.

So, Havers thought, if she sneaked out, in disguise, without letting anyone know, not even her crew, it could mean only one thing: that she was smuggling out something valuable.

"Hungerford said he heard her tell someone the scrolls are very old."

"Okay, Zeke," he said. "Return to Athens and finish your assignment there. I'm putting someone else on this." He hung up and dialed a number in Seattle. It was a private line; Miles didn't have to go through a secretary. "Titus," he said quietly. "It's me. Yes, it has been a while. I'm fine, and yourself) Titus, I am in need of your company's services." After a quick summary, he said, "I'll fax Dr. Alexander's file to you. She's most likely on her way back to the U.S. We need to anticipate every possible location she might return to. See if you can find out where this Stevenson guy is at the moment. He's a field archaeologist, so he might not be in this country." Miles listened for a moment. "Dr. Alexander? She's trouble. Once your men take possession of what she's carrying, get rid of her."

DAY THREE

Catherine kept a watchful eye on the customs agents up ahead. If she got past them, she would be home free.

Getting out of Egypt had been easier than she had expected; Cairo International Airport had been a madhouse, with people streaming into the country to be near the pyramids for the Millennium. And because security had been focused on the crowds coming in, only cursory attention had been paid to those departing. Catherine's luggage, checked through X-ray for weapons, had not been manually searched.

She still had the scrolls.

She looked out through the large plate-glass windows at the dark, snowy evening that enveloped JFK Airport. Winter in the Sinai could be cold, but she had forgotten it was December in New York. She wasn't dressed for *weather.* And over the noise of so many arriving passengers—cranky holiday travelers burdened with Christmas presents and in a hurry to get to destinations—she could almost make out the strains of "Silent Night" over the public address system.

The customs agent at the nearest station was making a family of four not only open their luggage but unwrap their Christmas gifts as well. Why were they being so thorough? Were they looking for something in particular? Another bomb threat, perhaps? Her flight *had* come from the Middle East. What, she wondered with a stab of fear, was the penalty for smuggling illegal antiquities into the country? She had hidden the scrolls but, she wondered now as she saw in horror another customs agent remove the lining of a man's suitcase, what if she hadn't hidden them well enough?

And everything had gone so smoothly until now!

Back at the Sinai, while Catherine had been waiting for Daniel to arrive, she had photographed the scrolls, developing them in the tent she had outfitted as a darkroom, something she always did on a dig. By the time Daniel had arrived at the camp, she had finished photographing all the scrolls. The pictures had gone into Daniel's duffel bag, a precaution should anything happen to the scrolls themselves.

As an added safety' measure, Catherine had left the Jesus fragment behind, as well as the basket, which she had stuffed with stones and rewrapped. Anyone searching her tent would find exactly what eyewitnesses had seen. Finally, at the Isis Hotel, she had told Mr. Mylonas that, should anyone inquire, she had been called home on a family emergency.

As she eyed the customs agents and tried to determine which might let her pass without opening her luggage—the one with red hair seemed to be going easy on the women travelers—she recalled again with a chill the one terrifying moment during their escape when she had thought they were going to be found out—when she had looked back and had seen Father Garibaldi plunge through the crowd to save the "sister." His gallantry could have blown Daniel's cover and destroyed their chances of getting away.

She hated to admit it, but Father Garibaldi's gesture impressed her. It took courage to step into a family fight, especially if it was a family of very different ethnicity and tradition. He could have got hurt. In a strange way, he was like Daniel, another champion of the underdog and lost causes. It made her recall how Daniel had once planned to enter the priesthood, he had even picked out the seminary. But he had abruptly changed his mind, and never explained why. It seemed to Catherine to date back to the day when they were both sixteen and she had found him crying behind the bleachers. She never did learn why he had been crying, but it was after that day that he had announced his decision not to take Holy Orders.

The line moved up, and she moved with it, nudging her suitcases along with her knee. There were fewer passengers now, and only three customs stations open. The agents looked haggard, and they had stopped saying, "Merry Christmas." But they were still inspecting luggage.

Catherine felt her nerves start to dance like live wires. Part of it, she knew, was due to fear—to be pulled out of line, handcuffed, taken away with everyone watching. But another part of her live-wire tension was an urgency to start translating the scrolls. Because they had been tucked away in a suitcase for twenty-four hours, she hadn't had a chance to look at them. But she had felt them all the same, sensed their tug at her, as if they emanated some sort of magnetic force. *"Aemelia diakonos . . . the Righteous One . . . the hour of the end of the world . . .*

Had Sabina met Jesus? And had she learned something from him that did not appear in the New Testament or in any of the apocrypha? Something that was going to alter the face of Christianity forever?

Finally it was her turn. "Open your suitcases, please, ma'am." And her heart sank.

Trying to keep calm despite a racing pulse and a mouth suddenly gone dry, Catherine carefully unlocked the two bags. The first contained only clothes and personal items, the second held tools of archaeology and, underneath, books. As the agent peered down at the texts, Catherine quickly picked one up, Diseases in Egyptian Mummies—a text she had bought for Julius in Cairo—and handed it to him, helpfully opening it out for him.

She purposely turned to a page containing color photographs, and when the agent's eyes took in the shocking images of desiccated bodies with hollow eyes and jawless faces, he thrust the book back at her, glanced down at the other texts—*Handbook of Field Archaeology; Pottery of the Late Bronze Age*—and waved her through. Catherine quickly closed her suitcases and hurried away.

She slipped into the nearest ladies' room and leaned against the sinks. She felt faint. It had been too close. Underneath the book on mummies was a text titled *The Body in the Bog,* with a dust jacket showing a partially preserved man, his face twisted in death agony. It was one look at that horrific image that had prompted the agent to pass her through, an effect she had been counting on.

The author of the book was Julius Voss, M.D., and before she and Daniel made their escape, she had decided to use the dust jacket of Julius's book to smuggle the scrolls out, carefully removing all the pages from an old botany text and replacing them with the six papyrus bundles. They were such a neat fit that when the book was closed the papyrus edges looked like old, yellowed pages. She could now keep the scrolls thus protected and hidden between the hard covers of the book until she got them home.

Anxious to catch the connecting flight to L.A., she headed out through the chaotic main terminal to the exit where the shuttles that picked up passengers for domestic terminals waited in the snowy night. But as she reached the glass doors, an announcement came over the loudspeakers: "Your attention, please! Your attention, please! Due to the snowstorm, all flights will be temporarily delayed. Passengers requesting further information should contact their ticket agent."

"I'VE FOUND HER, Mr. Havers."

Miles quickly clicked on the intercom. "Where is she?"

Teddy Yamaguchi was reporting from Havers's private computer center, housed next to the subterranean museum beneath the Santa Fe ranch. "She caught a flight out of Cairo to Amman and connected to a flight to New York. She passed through customs at JFK two hours ago."

Miles looked at his watch. Ten p.m. Which meant it was midnight back East. "Is she on her way to the West Coast?"

"All flights are temporarily grounded due to a snowstorm, so Dr. Alexander is either waiting in a terminal or has checked into one of the airport hotels."

Havers signed off and reached for the phone.

DAY FOUR

FRIDAY
DECEMBER 17, 1999

"Judging by the look of terror on his face, we can deduce that he did not see the cataclysm coming. The state of preservation of the body—"

Julius clicked the recorder into silence. It was no use. He couldn't concentrate. Ever since Catherine's phone call last night, with the unexpected news that she was in New York and would be home as soon as the snowstorm passed, he hadn't been able to think of anything except that he was going to see her again.

Rising from his cluttered desk, he went to the sliding glass doors that looked out onto a rain-beaten deck, and the turbulent gray ocean beyond. Another storm to punish Malibu. Julius loved rain, but he wished for Catherine's sake that the sun were shining.

He was glad she had changed her mind and decided to come home for the holidays. But something baffled him. Why had she left the Sinai so abruptly? And why had she called him from New York, instead of from Egypt? She had sounded excited on the phone. Julius wondered if he dared allow himself the hope that she had decided to marry him.

This time, he told himself, it was going to work.

Julius had become a doctor because it was family tradition—his father was a physician, and his grandfather and great-grandfather had

63

been medical men. However, when he had completed residency and opened his practice, Julius had found that what he really yearned for was the peaceful life of scholarly pursuit. Since he had always had a passion for ancient history, he had switched to a new specialty, paleo-pathology, the study of ancient diseases.

That was when Rachel, his first wife, had filed for divorce. She was now married to a Beverly Hills plastic surgeon who made four times what Julius made at the institute, and everyone was happy. Julius got to see their two teenage kids on weekends and holidays, and occasionally even took them on archaeological digs.

He looked at his watch, and then at the storm outside, mercilessly battering the coastline and the vulnerable homes perched on the cliff facing the ocean. As each mammoth wave broke on the sand, he could feel his house shudder.

After Rachel took the kids and left, Julius had wondered if he would ever marry again. And then he had met Catherine Alexander, working in a discipline related to his own, a woman who understood how he could get excited about a specimen of bone or a fossilized leaf—*and* she was beautiful on top of it. Julius often marveled that someone like Catherine, so active and alive, found a quiet man like himself exciting.

Turning away from the storm, he consulted the clock over the fireplace. Where was she?

AS CATHERINE DREW up to the weathered clapboard house on the beach, she felt her heart race. It had not been easy keeping her news from Julius when they were on the phone the night before, but she had to tell him about the scrolls in person, she wanted to see his reaction when she showed him the papyrus.

As she waited for a break in the busy Pacific Coast Highway traffic, she looked at the homely little house—so plain and unassuming, like the rest of the modest residences along this stretch in Malibu, that one wouldn't know it was a million-dollar property—she decided that she wouldn't go home to her condo in Santa Monica but would stay here, in Julius's peaceful cottage on the beach, and translate the scrolls.

Carefully guiding the rental car across the traffic and pulling into the small space that separated the house from the busy highway, she saw the front door standing open, and Julius there, waiting.

"Catherine!" he called. "Thank God you made it!"

He took her into his arms right out there in the downpour and kissed her long and hard on the mouth.

"We're getting wet!" she said, laughing.

"Inside, go on. Get by the fire. I'll bring your suitcases in."

As Catherine entered the cozy living room, two fat cats materialized, rubbing themselves on her legs—Radius and Ulna, a tortoiseshell and a Manx whom Julius indulged and who always remembered Catherine because she indulged them as well.

"Oh Julius, it's so good to be with you!" she said when he came inside, shutting the door against the turbulent day. It had been ten weeks since they were last together; she filled her eyes with the sight of him.

Forty-two, with ink-black hair worn longish over his collar and a black, closely cropped beard only just starting to show silver, Dr. Julius Voss, director of the prestigious Freers Institute in West Los Angeles, was a very striking man. Although no athlete—a Stair-Master gathering dust in the bedroom attested to that—there was nonetheless an irresistible sexiness about the rumpled sweater with frayed elbow patches, the comfortable moccasins, and the Meerschaum pipe that was always at hand. Gentle mannered and soft-spoken, Julius possessed one of those quiet personalities that Catherine always thought of as radiating an inner strength.

"Over here, by the fire," he said. "Come on. Get warm." He took her jacket, shook it out, and draped it near the hearth. Then he held out his arms and she slipped into them, wrapping her arms around his waist and resting her head on his shoulder. "You must be tired," he murmured, holding her tight, touching her hair. Catherine clung to him for a long moment as she listened to the rain and the comforting sound of the fire. No, she wasn't a bit tired, and she wondered if she would ever feel tired again. The scrolls were beckoning, with their promise of mysteries and ancient secrets. She drew away, kissed Julius lightly on the lips, and said, "I need to make a phone call."

In New York, and then after landing at LAX, Catherine had tried to call Daniel at his place in Santa Barbara. He had left the Sinai when she did, but by a different route, and since she had been held up by the snowstorm she had expected Daniel to get home before she did.

But she had gotten no answer. Now, standing at the kitchen counter with Radius and Ulna purring in and out of her legs, she dialed Daniel's number and waited anxiously. But there was no answer. Had he run into trouble?

When she returned to the living room, where the roaring fire and Mozart on the stereo created a seductive ambience, Julius said, "Any luck?"

She frowned. "No. I thought Daniel would be home by now." Pressing a glass of wine into her hand and settling her into the most comfortable chair by the hearth, he said, "Cabernet Sauvignon, for a special occasion. Now, tell me right off, don't keep me in suspense. Did you find the Well of Miriam?"

"I might have, yes!"

As she told him about the morning of three days ago, stopping short of mentioning the scrolls, Catherine looked around the living room, so homey and wonderfully familiar, and so welcome after a tent in the field. There were cat toys scattered about; family photographs everywhere; many plants, all healthy and flourishing; and an aquarium filled with tropical fish. Signs of life, Catherine thought, as if Julius were trying to counteract his daily involvement with disease and death.

But then she saw something else. Although Hanukkah had ended six days ago, the evidence was still there. Catherine saw the silver menorah, the dreidel Julius had had since childhood, a Hebrew and English translation of the Book of the Maccabees given to him by his grandfather. But the fringed prayer shawl was new; Catherine had never seen that before.

"Julius, you said on the phone last night that *you* had news."

He took a seat opposite her, his dark eyes reflecting the dancing flames in the fireplace. "Catherine," he said, excitement in his voice, "I've been able to get you on staff at the institute. Our paleographer left, and we desperately need someone who's good. It pays well and it's a secure position. What do you say?"

Before she could react, he quickly added, "I know what you're thinking. Don't worry, you can continue your work at Sharm el Sheikh. The lab job doesn't have to be done at the institute. You can take photocopies of the manuscripts with you when you go back to the Sinai, work on them in your leisure. But this way, Catherine, you won't have to spend *all* your time in the Sinai. You would live here, you'd have roots, *we'd* have roots."

"Julius," she said breathlessly. "You've taken me by surprise! I wasn't expecting this."

He grinned. "I know. What do you say?"

She rose from the sofa and went to the sliding glass doors, and looked out. The storm clouds were black and hung so low to the ocean that it seemed as if Malibu were about to be swallowed up by the sea. "The job at the lab sounds great, but I have to concentrate on my work at Sharm el Sheikh, especially now that I might have found the Well of Miriam. I can't take on anything else."

"And marriage?" he said quietly.

She turned to face him. "I love you, Julius, but I'm just not ready to get married."

He shook his head. "Catherine, I don't know how long our relationship can stand the strain of eight thousand miles of separation. It gets more painful each time we part."

"We don't have to live apart," she said, returning to the sofa, speaking rapidly. "I haven't told you the whole story yet. I saw a skull at the bottom of the well. I believe the rest of the skeleton is buried under a part of the wall that collapsed after the dynamiting. It will need to be excavated out, dated, and identified. Come back with me. This is a chance for us to work together on a dig, and we won't have to be apart!"

"Catherine, I'm the director of the institute. I can't just go off."

"And I can't stay," she said softly.

Silence rushed in between their words as they regarded each other in the fire's glow, both aware that it was out in the open at last, the issue that had remained unspoken between them for two years. Although Catherine's clothes hung in Julius's bedroom closet and her toiletries were in his bathroom, she didn't live here. She came home only for brief visits, to raise funds for another dig, sometimes to go on the lecture circuit. She never stayed long, was always gone again.

Julius rose, went to the fireplace, and gazed into the flames. "I don't know if I can keep on going like this, Catherine. I want us to settle down, maybe start a family. At least put down roots."

"Julius, I can't settle down. I have to keep looking, I need to find answers."

He turned to regard her. "There are answers to be found at the institute. We have hundreds of untranslated and undated manuscripts and documents. They would keep you busy for years."

"I don't want to be kept busy!" she said, startling one of the cats who was trying to claim her lap.

"You've been saying you want to write a book on your theories about Old Testament prophetesses. Why not start it now?"

"I'm not done with my field research yet."

"I see." He picked up his pipe, turned it around in his hands for a moment, then said, "You've spent fourteen years searching for Miriam. Do you really think you'll ever find her?"

"Oh yes! I know I will. Julius, I can *feel* it. When I'm out there in the wilderness—" She grew animated. "I don't know how to explain it. I feel as if the past isn't gone at all, but still there, unseen maybe, but I sense it, Julius. And lately, when I've been digging, sifting the sand, searching for a vital clue, I'm sometimes overcome with the strongest feeling that *I'm about to find it.*"

When he didn't say anything, she said quietly, "Do you believe in what I'm doing? Or do you think I'm chasing phantoms? My search for Miriam isn't a lark, Julius. I want to find a way to empower women."

"I know that, Catherine."

"Julius, men have always used Holy Scripture, and still do, as their authority' for their dominance over women. But it's clear to me that, in Scripture, women had power in the days of the patriarchs and kings, they were prophetesses and priestesses and wise women. But all that has gotten lost through time and I intend to restore it."

"I know," he said, "and that's part of what I love about you." He set the pipe down. "I believe there is validity to your theories, Catherine, but I don't think that after all this time you are going to find evidence of the women you're looking for. We don't have physical evidence of the *men.* Outside of scripture, we have nothing to prove that Moses even existed. How much harder to find something on the *women?*"

She became energized again, her excitement returning. "Ah, but I might just *have* found something." Opening her suitcase, she brought out the book on paleobotany. "Don't worry," she said as she set it on the coffee table, "I didn't use your book, only the dust jacket. The picture is so horrific of this unfortunate Bog Man, I thought it might deter anyone from opening it, particularly when I went through customs. And it worked!"

When Catherine lifted out the bundles of papyrus and laid them carefully on the table, his eyes widened. "Where on earth did you get these?"

She quickly filled him in on what she found after the dynamiting, and as he listened in astonishment, with the flames in the fireplace crackling behind him, Julius very gently folded back the first "page" of the first book, his eyes riveted to the brittle, golden paper.

"I'll need to run some tests first," she said. "Gas phase chromatography, ultraviolet emission, whatever can give us a date and authenticity."

Julius stared at the papyrus books, speechless. Then he looked at her. "Are you saying that you took these? You removed them from a dig and then you smuggled them out without reporting the find?"

"I had to, to keep them from being taken by the authorities. You know what happened to the Dead Sea Scrolls and the Nag Hammadi Gospels. They were hidden away, jealously guarded by a handful of scholars."

"What's special about *these* scrolls?"

She showed him her translation of Perpetua's letter. "Look at this word, Julius—*diakonos*. When Justin Martyr in the second century described the Mass, he said that during the Eucharist the *deacons* handed out the bread and the wine, which is what priests do today. Therefore, in the early Church, Julius, the *diakonos* was more like today's priest than a deacon. And Aemelia is addressed as *diakonos!*"

"A female priest?"

"A *priestess*, Julius, of the Christian Church! Think of it, we might have here the find of the century, of the millennium!"

"Okay," he said guardedly. "I see why you're so excited about these books. But, Catherine, to steal them, to smuggle them out of Egypt? Was that wise?"

She had known Julius was a cautious scientist. Even so, his reaction came as a disappointment. "No, it wasn't wise," she said, "but necessary. Julius, if I turn these scrolls over to the authorities, I'll never see them again. I'm only going to keep them long enough to translate them, and then I'll turn them over to the proper people and publish my translation."

"All right, you translate them and publish your findings, supporting your thesis with material that was obtained by questionable methods. Who's going to listen to you? You'll be attacked from all sides, Catherine. You and I both know how cutthroat the world of biblical scholarship can be and how jealous various factions are of their theories, how quick to attack others—you saw that yourself in the case of your mother. And *she* was dealing strictly with canon! You have 'found something' but you haven't even yet published what you've found, or your methods of archaeology, or how the scrolls came into your possession. And you're going to rush into a translation? You'll be laughed at or labeled a crackpot, and that's the mildest thing that will happen."

He joined her on the sofa, taking her hands between his. "Catherine, listen to me. I understand what this means to you. But this isn't going to restore your mother's reputation; instead, it will only get you crucified. You'll lose everything you've worked hard for, you'll no longer have credibility, you won't be respected, to say nothing of never getting another dig, or getting published! How is that going to help your mother? Catherine, please, turn the scrolls over to the Egyptian consulate in San Francisco. You can tell them you thought the scrolls were going to be stolen or destroyed, that you took them out of Egypt to protect them. You can still save yourself, Catherine."

When she shook her head, he said grimly, "It will mean career suicide. You'll be bringing into question your own integrity, they'll attack your character, and no one will want to be associated with you afterward."

"And what about you?" she said softly.

"I'll always stand by you, Catherine, you know that. But I have to tell you, this frightens me."

"It frightens me, too, but I have to do it, Julius, because if I don't do it now while I have the chance, if I pass this up, then how can I live with myself, knowing that I might have restored my mother's name?"

"At the expense of your own?"

"If necessary. Because I might still have a chance to redeem myself later, but my mother is dead, there's nothing she can do in her own defense."

"Are you sure this isn't some sort of personal vendetta? An attack on the Church for what happened in the past? Catherine, that wasn't the fault of the Church but of one man."

She withdrew her hands from his. "You might see it that way but I don't. Father McKinney was a Catholic priest, and priests are the instrument through which the Church works."

"Priests are also men."

"Whose first allegiance is to the Church."

"So you're saying that all priests are alike?"

To her surprise, Father Michael Garibaldi sprang into her mind, and she pictured him again, pushing his way through the mob to help the Bedouin "woman."

"Catherine," Julius said. "You're letting the past run your life. There's a bitterness inside you that you have to let go, before it destroys you."

"It's a chance I'll have to take."

He stared at her for a moment longer, then he stood, retrieved his jacket from the back of a chair. "I have to go to the lab. Some skeletal remains were found in the hills behind Bel-Air. We think they might be part of an old Indian burial ground, but the coroner's office has asked us to run benzidine-acetic acid tests on them to determine their age." He opened a drawer, rummaged for car keys. "If the bones are over a hundred years old, then they fall into the area of archaeology and the police won't be involved. But if they are less than a hundred years old, then by law it becomes a matter for the police."

Catherine stood. "Julius, do you always have to go by the rules? Haven't you ever done something simply because your heart told you to?"

"Of course I have, and I'm doing it right now. It's precisely because I do love you that I'm trying to talk you out of this foolishness."

"That's not what I'm talking about. You're not listening to me. I know that what I'm doing is wrong, that it's illegal and unethical. My head tells me that you're right, but my heart says I have to follow through with this course I've chosen."

He solemnly shook his head. "Catherine, I have a bad feeling about this. I think you've placed yourself, and us, in a dangerous situation."

"No one knows about the scrolls, Julius. I was very careful." He picked up the car keys. "I was supposed to run the benzidine tests this morning but I wanted to be here when you got home. The coroner is waiting for the results. I made reservations at Moon- shadows for us at eight o'clock. I'll be back by then."

She watched him go, out into the torrential rain, taking the heat and the coziness of the living room with him.

This was not how things were supposed to have gone.

The rumble of distant thunder brought her back to herself. She looked at the time. It was after four. Feeling numb, she went into the kitchen and tried Daniel's number again. This time he answered.

"Catherine! Thank God you called! I just got home a few minutes ago. Listen to me, we're in big trouble."

"What is it?"

"Someone's after us."

"What?"

"Someone else knows about the scrolls."

"That's impossible!"

"I think I know who it is. I'll drive down with the photographs—"

"No, wait," she said. She tried to think. How could anyone know? *I thought I heard someone right outside my tent. . . .* "Oh God," she whispered, closing her eyes. "Danno, listen, don't drive down here. If someone is after me then they'll be watching my house. I'll come up to you. Don't answer your phone and make sure your door is locked. I'll be there as fast as I can."

Quickly searching the house, she found a nylon gym bag tucked away in a closet. She threw in some toiletries, underwear, and a change of clothing. And the book of scrolls, carefully wrapped in a pillow case and a plastic bag.

Then she went into the kitchen and wrote Julius a note, saying that she had to go somewhere on an urgent matter and would be in touch in a few days. Adding, "I love you," she left the note in a conspicuous place.

As Catherine got into her car and joined the northbound traffic on the slick highway, she prayed that Danno was mistaken. Because if someone else did know about the scrolls, then they were in big trouble.

THE YOUNG PRIEST'S footsteps echoed in the corridor as he ran through the Palace of the Congregation on Holy Office Square in Rome. He was bearing an urgent dispatch for His Eminence Cardinal

Lefevre who, at that moment, was in his office, standing at the window, and thinking that the color of the sky this morning was unlike any he had seen before.

What could be causing it?

He turned his gaze toward St. Peter's Square, where a record-breaking crowd was putting a strain on the already overtaxed Vatican security. City police had been called in to help. Everyone was saying the end of the world was coming, and what safer place to be when Satan's army arrives than at the site of Blessed St. Peter's martyrdom? So for the past year Rome had been preparing for an extra ten million visitors to attend this bimillennial birthday of Christ. But the reports were that the numbers had greatly swelled beyond that. There wasn't a room to be had in the city, he had heard, and there was talk of calling in the army for crowd control.

Lefevre looked up again at the sky. *Was* there an ominous meaning to that strange color? He shook his head. Nonsense. The sky was the sky, that was all. It was winter. Rain was predicted. Perhaps he needed to have his eyes checked. A man of seventy had to accept the fact that his senses were no longer as reliable as they once were.

As he pulled himself away from the view—there was too much work demanding his time to waste it debating the hue of the sky!—he heard a knock at his door and the young priest came in, slightly out of breath. "Pardon me, Your Eminence. This just came for you. It's marked urgent."

Breaking the seal, Lefevre unfolded the single sheet of paper, and when he read the contents, his bushy white eyebrows rose. *"Incredibile!"*

"Eminence?"

Quickly refolding the note and slipping it into the pocket of his red cassock, the Cardinal said, "Contact Dr. Fuchs at the University of Rome, in the Department of Archaeology. Tell him I must see him at once on a matter of utmost urgency. In the meantime, I shall be with His Holiness."

As Lefevre hurried out of his office, thinking of the shocking news he had just received, he thought again of the strange color of the sky and wondered if perhaps it was a sign. *Was* there going to be an apocalyptic event when 1999 ticked over to 2000?

CATHERINE TOOK THE stairs two at a time as she rushed up to Daniel's third-floor apartment, praying that he was still there and that he was all right.

The journey northward to Santa Barbara, normally an hour and a half from Malibu, had taken on this stormy night nearly four hours. "We're in big trouble," Daniel had said on the phone. "Someone's after us."

But who? she wondered as she rang his doorbell. The Egyptian authorities? Hungerford? She had racked her brain trying to think of suspects. Recalling her paranoia of three days ago, when she had stood in the lobby of the Isis Hotel and imagined a spy in every person she saw, she tried to conjure up those faces again—was it one of *them?*

She saw movement on the other side of the peephole, and then the door opened. "Cath! Thank God! Come in, hurry."

As she slipped inside, Daniel briefly looked up and down the hall, then quickly closed and locked the door behind her. "Who's after us, Danno?" she asked, as she shrugged out of her raincoat and swept the plastic bonnet off her head. "And how do you know?"

"Hold on." He went to the window, parted the curtain slightly and peered out. "Just making sure you weren't followed."

"I wasn't. If anyone had been watching Julius's house, I would have seen them. His house is right on the PCH, it's impossible to park there without being noticed. Danno, are you *sure* someone is after the scrolls?"

Letting the curtain fall, he turned to regard her across the room, his rumpled hair, baggy pants, and wrinkled T-shirt testimony to his long flight from Egypt. But his golden-lashed eyes, Catherine noticed, were alert. "I'm sure, all right," he said, "and I don't think they're after you out of idle curiosity. I'll show you how I know." He went to the small dinette table where his laptop computer sat in its open case, the screen glowing. "As soon I got home I logged onto the Internet. I wanted to scan the Web, see if maybe there are other papyri that sound similar to yours."

"Don't tell me you found some!"

"I think I did. Here," he said, handing her a sheet of paper. "I downloaded the information onto my hard drive and printed it out for you. There aren't many. The one at the top of the list is in the British Museum."

Catherine read the printout: *"P245 (4th cent.) Written on the back of an Epitome of Livy. Two leaves of a single quire. First person account of a journey to Britain. Ref: 'midwife' indicates possible female authorship. N.T. ref: Lk. 16:5-13."*

Daniel raked his fingers through his floppy blond hair. "Think there's a connection?"

"I don't know," she murmured. "What is this reference from Luke?"

"I looked it up. Chapter sixteen is the Parable of the Rich Man." She stared at Daniel in amazement. "Jesus' words."

His eyes met hers. "Sabina's Righteous One?"

Catherine contemplated the printout in her hand. "It's possible," she said quietly, "that Sabina's scrolls were copied over and over the way the gospels and the letters of the apostles were. There are fragments of New Testament books scattered around the world, so there could very well be copies of Perpetua's letter and Sabina's story. Danno, I'd like to track them all down. We might turn up part of the seventh scroll!"

"That's what I was trying to do before you got here. But I jumped on the wrong links. 'Papyrus' directed me to over a thousand Web sites!"

"Tell me about these people you say are after us—"

"Here," Daniel said, handing her another printout, "This is what made me think that we're in big trouble. I checked the Web for news from the Sinai, just in case, and I came across this."

Catherine quickly read it, a small item about a dig near Sharm el Sheikh that was perplexing local officials. The archaeologist appeared to have vanished, the report said, and in a nearby hotel, an American construction engineer had been found murdered.

"Hungerford!" Catherine whispered.

Daniel shifted anxiously. "I think he knew about the scrolls, Cath. And I think he decided to cut a deal on the side. I also think that the guys who killed him are now after you. It says there that witnesses reported that the engineer had earlier found a papyrus fragment that might have come from an early Christian gospel. So word is definitely out."

"Danno, you said on the phone that you know who it is."

Catherine noticed how nervously he removed his glasses, wiped them on his sleeve and replaced them, slightly askew, as he said, "When Samir was dragging me through the camp, I thought I saw a familiar face in the crowd. An American. The whole time I was on my way home it kept bugging me. Where had I seen him before? It was when I sat down to write an entry in my journal that it came to me—"

A scream suddenly tore the air, followed by running footsteps out in the hall. Catherine spun around. "What was that!"

"My neighbors, they're always fighting," Daniel said, shutting down his computer and closing the laptop case. "I guess we shouldn't stick around here. I'm starting to get a really bad feeling."

Catherine went to the window, parted the curtain, and looked out. As she peered up and down the street, which was glistening with rain but dark and quiet except for a few Christmas lights winking in doorways, she felt her pulse thump in her throat. Hungerford . . . murdered.

"Yes," she said, turning away from the window. "Time to go."

Daniel picked up an enormous canvas tote bag that said *USS Enterprise* on the side and began gathering up charts and files and stuffing them into it. "A friend of mine owns a cabin up in Washington. He's always telling me I can use it during off season—"

"I'm going alone, Danno," Catherine said, as she picked up her blue nylon bag and slung it over her shoulder.

"Hey, no way," he said. "We're in this together."

"Danno, Hungerford's murder is no coincidence. Whoever killed him is after the scrolls, which means they're now after me. Which also means that anyone who is with me is not safe. I'm not going to risk your life, Danno."

"No choice. Listen, you need me. You want to find King What's His Name, right? See if maybe he got the seventh scroll? Without anyone finding you? The best way to do that is to hole up someplace and let your electronic fingers do the walking."

When she gave him a puzzled look, he said, "The Internet, Cath! You can explore the world and never leave the safety of your home. Or, in this case, my friend's cabin."

When she didn't say anything, he quickly added, "When have we never been there for each other, Cath?"

"Filthy little girl," Sister Immaculata said, dragging Catherine out of the classroom. And Danno sitting there, tears running down his cheeks, the only kid who hadn't laughed at her.

"Idiot," Catherine said, and she kissed him on the cheek. "All right, let's go."

"Oh wait," he said as he snatched up a manila envelope. "The photographs."

"I'll take them."

"Shouldn't I continue to hold on to them? In case something happens to the scrolls?"

"Nothing's going to happen to the scrolls. I've got them right here," she said, resecuring the gym bag snugly over her shoulder. "And I'm not letting them out of my sight."

"Then we should be okay, if no one else knows about them."

"Wait, there is someone else. Hans Schuller at the radiological lab in Zurich. I sent him a papyrus sample for carbon dating. I'll have to contact him and let him know where I—"

There was a sudden, loud knock at the door. "Now what?" Daniel said as he went to answer it. "Who is it?" he said through the door.

"Sorry to bother you. I'm from downstairs. I was wonnerin' if you could help me with somethin'?"

"What's your name?"

"Martinez. I'm in 2A. It's real important, man."

Just as Daniel drew the chain back, the door flew open. "Hey!" Daniel said as two teenagers rushed in. They were skinny and hopped up and holding knives. "Give us your money, man!"

Daniel held out his hands, palms up. "Hey guys," he said, backing away. "Let's all be cool, okay? There's nothing of value here—"

"Shut up and give us the money, man!"

"Look, take what you want, okay? Just take it and go."

The taller one lunged at Daniel. "Gimme your watch."

As Daniel fumbled with his watch, saying, "Let's just be cool," the other punk made a grab for Catherine's blue gym bag. "What's in here?"

Catherine jumped back, evaded his grasp. But he sidestepped her and managed to grab the strap. Catherine tried to pull away, but he caught her arm. They struggled for a moment, with the other guy shouting, "Get the bag, man!" and then she drove her knee up into the punk's groin. As he reeled back, she swung around in time to sec the other guy plunge his knife into Daniel's abdomen. The envelope fell from Daniel's grip, black-and-white glossy photographs of the scrolls tumbling out.

Catherine flew at the assailant. And then she saw the gun. He had whipped it out of his waistband and was waving it at her. "Gimme the bag, bitch."

And then the other guy was recovering and making a move toward her.

Danno, on his knees and clutching his stomach, said, "Cathy, get out of here. Run!"

The kid fired, missing her.

"Danno—"

"Go!"

Catherine spun around, ran for the door. She fell over the laptop Daniel had placed there. Blindly grabbing for it, she jumped to her feet and turned around. She saw Danno, the blood seeping through his fingers. And then the two guys were coming after her.

Flinging herself into the hall, Catherine collided with a neighbor carrying a grocery sack. "Hey!" the woman cried as cranberries and oranges went flying. Catherine continued to run, footsteps pounding down the hall behind her, the kid with the gun ordering her to stop.

She heard a deafening crack, like a car backfiring. Looking up, she saw the wall above her head explode in a rain of paint and plaster.

With her feet barely touching the stairs as she flew down the two flights, she reached the front entrance and burst out into the rainy night just as another shot rang out. Racing along the rain-slicked walkway, her sandals slapping the wet concrete, she tossed a quick glance back and saw her pursuers emerge from the stairwell and into the foyer. In another second they were going to be outside.

And then suddenly she slammed against someone, knocking her off her feet, sending the laptop case flying.

"Whoa!" he said, catching her. Catherine whipped her hair out of her eyes and stared in astonishment. It was Father Michael Garibaldi. "Are you all—" he began.

Another loud crack shattered the night. "Run!" she screamed. Bullets whizzed past her head as she snatched the laptop up from the wet lawn.

"What the hell!" Garibaldi shouted.

"Run!"

They fled through the rain, Catherine in the lead, Garibaldi on her heels. When they rounded the corner, she saw her car. "Oh no!" she cried. The tires had been slashed.

The punks came around the corner, weapons aimed; Garibaldi grabbed Catherine's hand and they tore down the sidewalk, shots thundering in the night. Slipping and sliding on wet concrete and grass, they ducked down a narrow breezeway between two apartment buildings. Catherine's foot landed in a pothole; she crashed against empty trash cans. Garibaldi hoisted her by her arm and she stumbled away, her breath ragged, her heart feeling as if it were going to burst.

When they reached a blue Mustang parked on the next street, Father Garibaldi flung open the driver's door. "Get in!" he shouted.

Catherine hurled herself into the passenger seat just as a bullet ricocheted off the hood in a burst of sparks. As Garibaldi got the engine started, they heard another motor start up. And when the Mustang pulled away from the curb, the other car pulled out, tires squealing.

As the priest's car tore down the quiet residential street, a dark Buick in hot pursuit, Catherine held her breath; homes and apartment houses zipped by in a blur, Christmas lights came and went in a flash. She looked back. "They're still shooting at us!"

Garibaldi floored the gas, squealing around a corner, the right rear wheel hitting the curb; the Mustang flew into the air and landed with a crash.

"Faster!" Catherine cried. "They're getting closer!" The headlights of the second car loomed larger, flooding the Mustang with blinding light.

"Get down!" Garibaldi shouted as another shot rang off the roof of his car. He yanked the wheel to the left, spinning the car through a red light, barely missing a pickup truck. Catherine dug her fingers into the dashboard; she looked back. "They're gaining!"

"Uh oh!" the priest suddenly said.

Catherine looked up ahead, her eyes widening in horror. They were heading into a blind alley.

"If you remember any prayers, Doctor," Garibaldi shouted, "now's the time to say them!"

THE SCAR IN the center of his forehead, the size and shape of a large coin, was the result of years of prayer, a testimony to the thousands of times he had tapped his head to the ground, in the direction of Mecca.

People called him a holy man. However, as he prayed on this sultry morning in his palace on the outskirts of Cairo, his thoughts were not upon spiritual matters. He was thinking of money: dollars, francs, marks, dinar, yen. And he was praying for this money to return to Egypt.

Ever since the devastating hostage crisis at the Ali Khan Hotel two years ago, in which five American tourists were killed, tourism in Egypt had dried up. And since tourism was Egypt's second largest source of income, the results were bankrupting the country

Finishing the prayer with, "There is no God but Allah, and Mohammed is His prophet," he rose from his knees, his tall, lean frame stretching to six feet, the long white *jja la bey* a giving him the look of a humble man. But the drink he poured—Chivas Regal in a cut crystal glass—and the way his personal secretary addressed him, when she came in to announce the arrival of a visitor, belied the studied humility.

"We have finished interrogating everyone, Mr. President," his visitor reported. He was Mr. Sayeed, Culture Minister for the Egyptian Antiquities Department, a sour faced man with thousands of employees under him and no money to pay them. "Hungerford's team, Dr. Alexander's crew. Although there is no proof that she found scrolls, the rumors indicate that she did."

"Christian scrolls?"

"It would seem so."

The President of Egypt went to the balcony and gazed at a collection of triangles standing on the dusty horizon: the pyramids, where millions of pilgrims were gathering for the turn of the millennium. Money was pouring into Egypt at the moment, but in January the pilgrims would leave and the source would dry up again. And the pilgrims would not be back for another thousand years.

The President was not only a holy man, he was also a man of vision. And what he was envisioning now was a new building, occupying a garden-park at the north end of Gezirah Island in the middle of the Nile—a museum, housing Christian scrolls. For *these,* he had no doubt, the tourists would return to Egypt.

"Get me Mr. Dawud, in Washington," he said to his secretary. "And then put a call through to the President of the United States."

"WE GOT THE license plate of the guy she drove off with, Miles. I'm running a check on it right now. We'll have an ID in a few minutes." Miles regarded the face on the video screen, his old friend Titus— president and founder of Security Consultants, Inc. in Seattle. White teeth flashing in a swarthy face, chubby cheeks that gave him an inno- cence he did not possess—Titus recruited from among hardened ranks; innocence was not part of his business. "The photographs we managed to take from Stevenson's apartment are coming over right now," Titus said. "I'm forwarding them to you."

"And the tape?" Titus's men had placed listening devices in Daniel's apartment and recorded his conversation with Dr. Alexander.

"Transmitting as we speak." And in the next instant, every word spoken between Catherine and Daniel was coming loud and clear over Miles's phone. As he listened, two things about the conversation stood out: that Stevenson had identified an American at the Sinai camp, and that he had recorded it in a journal.

"Miles," Titus said. "The American Stevenson spotted. Your man?"

"It could be."

"And can Stevenson connect your man to you?"

Havers didn't reply as he watched the first of the photographs that were being downloaded start to appear on his screen, pixels dropping down, forming an image. "These are most likely photographs of the scrolls," he said to Titus. "They're probably for backup in case some- thing happens to the actual scrolls. Did your men get all of them?"

"I'm afraid not. They said some of the photographs slipped out of the envelope. They had to be left behind."

"What about the man Alexander ran with?" Havers asked.

"My agents didn't get a good look at him. We don't know if she knew him or if he was just a stranger."

"And your men are certain she ran with the scrolls?"

"They were in a bag she was carrying."

"What about the journal Stevenson mentions?"

"Our search didn't turn up any journal." Titus smiled. "But don't worry, my friend. I've already put more men on it. We'll get her."

"WHAT IS GOING on!" Father Garibaldi said as he forced himself to bring the Mustang down to a saner speed. They were traveling on State Street, having blended in with the late-night Christmas shopping traffic. "Who were those men? Why were they shooting at you?"

Catherine looked back over her shoulder. The headlights behind them resembled strings of white holiday lights. "Some guys broke in—" She couldn't believe how badly she was shaking. Even her teeth were chattering.

"What guys?"

"That was no ordinary robbery!" she cried. "Those punks were hired!"

"Wait a minute. Slow down. What are you talking about—they were *hired?*"

"The ones who chased after us weren't the ones who broke in." She kept looking over her shoulder, headlights blinding her. "I got a good look at them—two white guys with Republican haircuts. And there was no license plate on their car."

"Clue me in, please," he said, checking the rearview mirror. "I'm saying," she nearly shouted, "that the whole thing was staged to look like it was just a couple of junkies looking for money! But what they were really after were the scrolls!"

"Whoa, hey, wait a minute. Scrolls?"

"Turn the car around," she said.

"Turn it around? You mean go back?"

"Danno was hurt."

"Look, I don't think going back is a good idea, okay?"

"Danno needs me!"

"And what if the Republicans are there, waiting for you?"

They had come to 101. Across the highway was the marina, where boats merrily decorated with Christmas lights bobbed on the black water. "Which way?" Garibaldi said.

Catherine tried to think. The cars behind them were honking. "I need to get to a phone."

"Okay, but which way?"

"Turn right," she said. "Go north."

As he pulled out into the northbound traffic, the Mustang fishtailed violently, causing a Camaro to jam on its brakes and a Cadillac to honk. "Sorry!" Garibaldi said.

Catherine saw that he was driving with only one hand. "What's wrong?"

He had been gripping his left shoulder with his right hand; when he brought it away, his fingers were bloody.

"You were hit!"

"I think it's just a graze. . . ."

But she saw how pale he was, perspiration sprouting on his forehead. "Pull over. Up there, on the shoulder."

"I don't think—"

"Pull over. I'll drive."

The Mustang had barely rolled to a stop when Catherine jumped out and, heedless of the cars whizzing by, ran around and slid behind the wheel. Now she saw the blood on Father Garibaldi's arm. "You need a doctor!"

"I'm all right. Let's keep going."

Catherine eased the Mustang out into the flow again as she squinted through the windshield, the wipers going *whump whump.* "Here," she said, pulling a handkerchief out of the pocket of her sweater. "Keep pressure on the wound."

There was a gas station up ahead. "I have to call Danno," she said as she pulled in and parked by the phone booth.

But when she got back into the car a minute later, starting the engine and pulling back onto the highway, she said, "A man answered. He identified himself as a detective. He said Danno had been taken to a hospital. When I asked if he was going to be all right, the detective asked me who I was. So I hung up." She pounded the steering wheel. "I don't like this. I really do not like this!"

"What now?"

She looked at Father Garibaldi. "First we need to get that arm taken care of."

"I'll live. Let's just put some space between us and the guys who were shooting at us, okay?"

They stayed with the traffic until they came to the Highway 154-San Marcos Road turnoff. Catherine pulled off at the last minute, causing more angry honking. She looked in the rearview mirror; two other cars had turned off with her.

Father Garibaldi said, "May I ask you something? Back there, when we were cornered in that alley and that patrol car came by, why didn't you signal to the policemen for help?"

She eased up on the accelerator. One of the cars behind her pulled into the next lane, zipped past and disappeared into the rainy night. The other car, however, slowed with her. Her grip tightened on the wheel. "I might have if the gunmen hadn't taken off."

"But still—"

"I can't go to the police."

"Why not?"

"I just can't." She looked at him. "I'm wanted in thirty-two states."

"What!"

"For tearing those little tags off pillows."

He stared at her. Then he smiled. And then Catherine, despite herself, also smiled, and she released a short, stress-relieving laugh.

They were heading up into the mountains now; the highway narrowed, grew winding. They started to pass roadside signs: Chumash Painted Caves State Historical Park; Rancho San Marcos; Stagecoach Road. Through the rain Catherine glimpsed pine trees and rocky canyons. The traffic was lighter, making it easier to tell if they were being tailed. She checked the rearview mirror again. The car that had stayed behind her now turned off onto a small residential road, leaving blackness behind.

"Keep your eye out for a gas station or coffee shop," Catherine said. "I need to call and find out where they've taken Danno." She looked at Garibaldi. "What are you doing here, Father? In Santa Barbara, I mean. And why were you at Daniel's apartment house?"

"I was looking for you."

"Me! Why?"

"There was a big commotion at the Isis Hotel yesterday morning. The place was crawling with government people looking for you. Mr. Mylonas, the manager, was very upset. They seemed to think you had done something wrong and he staunchly defended you, telling them that you had gone home on a family emergency. They were hinting that you had stolen something."

She peered through the windshield. "I think I see a light. It's a motel! And it looks like the vacancy sign is on."

Garibaldi kept his eyes on her as he said, "Mr. Mylonas told me that a package had come for you. He was worried because it had come registered and insured, and his clerk had signed for it before they knew you weren't there to pick it up. Mr. Mylonas didn't know what to do. He didn't want to send it back because he didn't trust the postal clerks in Sharm el Sheikh. A registered package usually means something valuable. He said he would never forgive himself if it was stolen. I asked him where you live and when he said California, I told him that I was flying back to the States, going home by way of Los Angeles, and that I would be glad to deliver the package. But I went to your place in Santa Monica and you weren't there."

Catherine slowed the car and pulled off the highway. "How did you know I'd be here?"

"I didn't. I was taking the package to the return address on the label. Dr. Daniel Stevenson on Pedregosa Street, Santa Barbara."

"The package is from Danno?" She pulled the car under the porte cochere in front of the motel office. "Wait here."

When she came back a few minutes later, she said, "I took a room." She started the engine and drove around to the side, where a few cars were parked in front of dark cabins. "Number fifteen . . . it's at the end. I'm going to park around back, among those trees. If anyone drives by they won't see the car."

They hurried inside and as Father Garibaldi closed the drapes and locked the door, checking to make sure no one had seen them, Catherine turned on the lights, turned up the thermostat, and then went straight to the phone. "I'm going to find out what hospital Danno was taken to."

But when Father Garibaldi pulled the handkerchief away from his arm and rolled up his shirtsleeve, she put the phone down. "That definitely needs to be taken care of."

"And me fresh out of Band-Aids," he said, grimacing as he exposed a long, ugly gash.

Catherine thought for a moment. Then she took the bloody handkerchief, wrapped it around her own hand, and said, "Lock the door behind me."

When she came back a few minutes later, Father Garibaldi was in the bathroom, running water in the sink. "I got us some food," she shouted to him. "At least I think it's food." She gave the apple a dubious look. "I have a feeling that vending machine hasn't been restocked since Watergate. How's the arm?" she called out.

He emerged from the bathroom, shirtless and clasping a towel to his wound. When Catherine turned to him, she experienced two swift reactions: first she stared, then she coughed and looked away. When did priests start having bodies like that?

"This hurts like hell," he said, peeling away the towel, "but it isn't deep. Just a graze."

Catherine turned back around, trying not to look at the sculpted pecs and biceps, the dark chest hair glistening with either water or perspiration. "Are you sure it's only a graze? No bullet?"

"I think the bullet took out someone's porch light."

"Sit down," she said, and she proceeded to open the small first aid kit she had brought back from the office.

"How did you get that?"

"I told the manager that I lost the key to my luggage and cut my hand trying to pry it open with a knife. He looked at me like I was one fork shy of a place setting." Catherine tried to apply antibiotic ointment to the wound, but her hands were shaking too badly.

"Hey," Garibaldi said. "It's okay. We're safe here."

"I've never been shot at before! And I'm worried about Danno!"

He took the ointment from her and said, "I can do this. You go find where your friend was taken."

Catherine went through the phone book, opened it to the listing for hospitals. She found the right one on the fourth call. "Yes, Daniel Stevenson," she said, anxiously clutching the phone, "I just want to know—What? Oh, uh. I'm his sister. Yes, thanks, I'll hold." She covered the mouthpiece and whispered, "I found him!" While she waited, she looked at Garibaldi, wondering when the last time was that she had seen a man's bare back look so—

She tore her eyes away, forced them to focus elsewhere.

Her eyebrows shot up. "'What on earth are *those?*"

Father Garibaldi looked where she was pointing—at his black satchel, to which were strapped two thirty-inch rattan sticks, shiny with lacquer. "Pangamot canes."

"Panga-*what?*"

"Pangamot. It's a Philippine martial art."

She stared at him. "You're into martial arts?" She looked at the canes. "Do you actually *fight* with them?"

"Sometimes."

She met his gaze. "Don't you find that—"

"Find it what?"

She brought her attention back to the phone. "Yes, I'm still here. Daniel Stevenson, yes. How is—" She listened. "Oh, I see. Yes, thank you. I'll try again later."

She hung up. "He's in surgery. They won't know anything for a few hours." She sat there for moment, staring at the cradled phone while rain pelted the windows and the lights flickered. "Why do people need to kill each other?" she said. "So help me, if Danno is seriously hurt, someone is going to pay." She went into the bathroom and closed the door.

When she came out a few minutes later, she saw that Father Garibaldi had put on a fresh shirt—black and short-sleeved like the other, neatly tucked into his blue jeans. But she noticed that he had left the Roman collar off.

"Are you okay?" he asked.

"No," she said.

"Maybe this will help," he said, holding out the package from Mr. Mylonas.

Although the return address was Daniel's apartment on Pedregosa Street, the postmark, Catherine noticed, was Cozumel, Mexico. She carefully picked open the brown paper, revealing a cardboard box. There was a letter on top; she read it through tears: *"Hey Cath, Surprise! What you are holding came from the tomb, no kidding. The tomb was empty when I found it because it had been plundered centuries ago, but artifacts have cropped up over the years from an unknown source. I found this particular treasure in a little shop in Cozumel, and I knew right away that it was from 'my' tomb because in one of the murals a woman whom I presume to be the queen is placing corn on an altar to what appears to be an earth goddess, one of the more peaceful deities in the Mayan pantheon'. Anyway, in the mural she is wearing the enclosed. And when I saw it in the shop I was struck by how exactly the color of the jade matches your eyes. Merry Christmas and Happy New Millennium, Cath. Tour devoted Danno."*

She opened the small box and found a jade pendant nestled in a bed of cotton wool. Lifting it out, she saw that it was a miniature jaguar suspended on a leather thong. She put it over her head, lifting up her hair and then settling the amulet between her breasts.

She gazed down at it for a moment, her eyes misting. Then she suddenly stood, retrieved Daniel's laptop case, set it on the table by the window, and started to open it.

"What are you doing?"

"Daniel said that he knew who was after us, that he had written it in his journal. His journal is in this computer."

As she lifted the lid of the case, she drew in a sharp breath.

"What is it?"

"It's me," she said. "A picture of me, in Danno's laptop case!"

Garibaldi reached into the case and brought out a small black device that resembled a pager.

"That's Danno's tone-dialer," Catherine said. "A necessary tool in our line of work. Most places we go still have rotary-dial phones. Impossible to call your answering machine and retrieve messages." Catherine found the on-off switch on the computer, booted it up. "I don't believe it!" she cried.

"What is it?" Garibaldi said. Then he saw the screen:

Please Enter User Password

"I don't know Daniel's password," she said.

"Make a guess."

She tried a few based on what she knew of Daniel's interests, typing in *Spock, Klingon, Asimov,* but with no success.

"There are some pretty common ones," Garibaldi said. "Try thunderbolt." It didn't work. "How about phoenix?"

Catherine vacated the chair. "You try some."

Father Garibaldi took her place and began rapidly typing, entering word after word, each time getting the response: Invalid Password. Please Try Again.

"Where did he go to school?"

"Berkeley."

He typed in "Stanford." No luck.

"Try Immaculata," Catherine said.

"This could take forever," Garibaldi murmured.

Suddenly a brilliant light filled the room. Father Garibaldi shot to his feet and pulled Catherine back against the wall. When the light swept past, Garibaldi moved the curtain an inch and looked out. A white van pulled into the space outside room sixteen. It said Oaks Campgrounds on the side.

He let the curtain fall. "False alarm." He looked at Catherine, her face inches from his, and saw the fear in her eyes. "You okay?"

"All things considered," she said in a shaky voice, "I'd rather be in Philadelphia."

"I'd settle for Duluth."

They returned to the computer, Catherine at the keyboard this time. Garibaldi regarded her photograph inside the laptop case. "Try your own name," he said.

When it didn't work, she typed "Alexander."

Invalid Password. Please Try Again.

"Now what?" she said, glaring at the message on the screen. "We could do this forever and not come up with the password."

"Let me try something." With the laptop still plugged in, he lifted it from its black leather carrying case and set it down on the table. Then he felt around the edges for release catches and lifted up the keyboard to reveal the computer's inner workings. "Sometimes," he murmured, "you can override the password if you just . . ." As he studied the layout of the hard drive, cards, and other electronic components, Catherine said, "Don't you need your glasses?"

He gave her a startled look. "What made you think I wear glasses?"

"The indented lines over your ears."

His hand automatically went up. "They still show? I mean, it's been months since I had the operation. Radial keratotomy," he added. "I got tired of dealing with glasses." He gave her a long, thoughtful look. "That was pretty observant of you."

She shrugged. "Ninety percent of archaeology is being observant."

"And the other ten percent?"

"Imagination. The ability to construct an entire civilization from a tiny fragment of pottery."

He returned his attention to the computer and focused on the green motherboard with its transistors and circuits. "Ah, Delilah," he murmured after a moment, "what a dimpled dragon you can be."

Now it was Catherine's turn to look surprised.

He reddened slightly. "Victor Mature to Hedy Lamarr in *Samson and Delilah.'*"

"Great," Catherine muttered. "I'm on the run with Roger Ebert."

"Here it is!" he said, after a brief inspection of the motherboard. "I need a piece of metal. Do you have any bobby pins?"

She ran her fingers through her long hair. "Sorry, no pins."

"How about a paper clip?"

Catherine searched through the pockets and compartments of the laptop carrying case, coming up with a spare battery, a dogeared copy of *Hawksbill Station* by Robert Silverberg, an empty gum packet, a Bic pen, scraps of paper and—"Success!"

As he unfolded the paper clip, Father Garibaldi pointed to a spot on the motherboard and said, "See where it says J-A237? That's a jumper. If I can manage to cause a short . . ." Catherine watched as he adjusted the paper clip so that its two points spanned the minute prongs which were about a centimeter apart, and then touched down on them and bridged the jumper.

The message on the screen changed.

"What did you do?" Catherine said as he closed and secured the keyboard, pulled up the other chair and sat down in front of the computer.

"I reset the master password," he said.

The screen now read: Your Setup Information Has Changed. Press F2 to enter SETUP, F3 for license information.

"Will this get us into the system?" Catherine asked.

"Let's see," he said as he pressed F2.

The screen now read at the top: SphinxBios SETUP

As Garibaldi clicked on SECURITY from the menu, he murmured to himself, "To make sure we've disabled all the passwords." Now the screen said:

User Password Is Disabled Set User Password: [Press ENTER]
Password on Boot: [Disabled]
Diskette Access: [User]
Fix Disk Boot Sector: [Normal]
Virus Check Reminder: [Disabled]

"Okay, save values and . . . exit!" He pressed Enter, the computer completed its boot, and the c-prompt appeared in the upper left-hand corner of the screen.

"Uh oh," Catherine said. "I'm afraid Daniel never updated his software. I don't know how to operate DOS."

"It's been a while since I've worked with text commands," Garibaldi said.

Next to c:\> he typed SCI and hit Enter.

BAD COMMAND

Catherine said, "Daniel wouldn't have used Scimitar. He detested Dianuba Technologies and wouldn't touch their software."

"Okay, then let's try this." Garibaldi typed WIN and the Windows desktop appeared.

And all of Daniel's files.

"There you are," he said, getting out of the way so Catherine could have the keyboard.

She scanned the icons. "Now I just have to find which file is Danno's journal." When she came upon *Captains Log,* she said, "This has got to be it!"

She double-clicked and:

Personal Journal of Daniel Stevenson

"Bull's-eye," Garibaldi said. "Okay, so what are we looking for?" She began scrolling through the journal entries. "The night we left the Sinai there was a big commotion going on at the camp. Danno said he saw a familiar face in the crowd, an American."

Garibaldi looked at her. "7 was in that crowd."

"I think this is it." They read the entry: *"A guy with a crazy scar on his face and spooky white hair. I know I've seen him somewhere before. But where? Of course, there it is right before my eyes! I've looked at that hideous mug nearly every day for the past two years. He works for—"*

"My God," Catherine whispered.

"What is it?"

She shifted the computer around so that he could read the monitor. Garibaldi's dark eyebrows arched. "Miles Havers? *The computer mogul!"*

MIDNIGHT, AND THE computers were cooking.

Teddy Yamaguchi knew that people thought he didn't have a life. They were wrong. Computers were his life, and there was nowhere else on the face of the earth he would rather be at that moment than surrounded by a state-of-the-art communications center. For a twenty-eight-year-old who just barely managed to graduate from college, Teddy made an incredible salary in Havers's employ; he lived rent free in a cottage on the vast Havers estate, and the fact that he was on call twenty-four hours didn't bother him because as long as he did his job for Miles Havers, Teddy was free to make use of the equipment all he wanted during his time oft.

Sometimes his assignments for Havers were a challenge, but tonight's job, at this midnight hour, was simple: "Find Catherine Alexander."

Piece of cake.

Positioning himself at the Balarezo-986 210MHz 10-gig HDD computer with a 128,000 bps modem, Teddy watched for signals from Catherine Alexander's credit card accounts, bank accounts, telephone calling cards, gasoline cards, Social Security—even her library card— anything that might show up somewhere in a computer system.

He had to laugh. It was like his favorite computer game, *Pulse:* find the girl, the treasure, and the golden idol and make it back through the maze before Gordon got you. No one had yet beat Teddy's record time getting through Pulse, and no one could match him for finding and bringing in Catherine Alexander.

Grabbing a fistful of snack food from the bowl at hand—a mix of Cocoa Puffs and jelly beans sprinkled with brown sugar and powdered instant coffee—Teddy felt himself zip into high gear as he entered the digital interstate.

Sometimes he couldn't believe his luck.

Back in 1995, when he was a Stanford undergrad, he had been arrested and charged with conspiring to distribute millions of dollars' worth of illegally copied commercial software over the Internet— stolen from Miles Havers's company, Dianuba Technologies. Touted as the largest single instance of software piracy uncovered up to that time, the case was thrown out by a federal judge who decided that the student hadn't committed a crime; the copyright act that covered software did not specifically criminalize Teddy's alleged conduct because he apparently had not benefited financially from the venture. But because government officials felt they had to charge him with something, they had then tried to indict him on conspiracy to commit wire fraud. When that didn't work either, Miles Havers himself had unexpectedly stepped in, startling everyone by publicly forgiving the young man, saying, "We've all sown wild oats."

The software that Teddy had given away on the Internet had been the newest game designed by Havers's company, which Teddy had stolen and then illegally copied just before it was due to be released on the market. Because it was a hot new game rumored to have the clout to knock all competition out of the arena, an estimated two million users copied the stolen software, cheating Havers out of millions of dollars of profit. His act of forgiving Teddy Yamaguchi had been condemned by other software manufacturers, but applauded by the public.

Havers didn't suffer losses for long.

When the second version of the game came out six months later, this time selling in software stores and hitting bigger than even Myst or Doom, analysts estimated that Havers had not only recouped his previous losses but had ended up making *more* profit than if the original version of the game had been released through legitimate channels.

Teddy had thought the whole thing a gas because the joke was on the Justice Department. No one knew it, but Miles Havers had planned it all from the beginning, personally recruiting Teddy Yamaguchi to steal from his own company!

Teddy had been suspicious at first, when Havers had approached him with the outrageous deal. But Teddy, superhacker that he was, had quickly grasped the situation. Miles Havers could have just put out a beta version with a built-in expiration date on the Internet and let users get a taste of it, the way other companies did, "teasing" games on the Net, hoping to hook new players—create the addiction, the philosophy went, and you'll never go broke. But Havers, keen observer of human nature, had taken the strategy a step further, reasoning that *stolen* software, like forbidden fruit, was always sweeter. He even boasted that he liked to think of this method of marketing, commonly known as shareware, as "crack- ware" since it was just as addictive as crack cocaine and ten times more profitable.

When Havers had invited Teddy to come to Santa Fe and work for him, the young Asian American hadn't even had to think about it. And in the four years since, Teddy had been part of Havers's whiz team that had increased company profits from $800 million to $7 billion annually.

No, not a bad life at all, especially considering the stock options that came with his monthly paycheck. Five years from now he was going to take his handful of millions, open a bait shop on Maui, and keep himself in state-of-the-art computer hardware for the rest of his life.

Teddy glanced over at his boss, who was sitting at the other end of the room in an exotic atrium of rare and fragile plants around a rock pool and waterfall, a scene so perfect that it looked as if everything had been clicked into place with a mouse. Teddy's end of the room, where computers, monitors, printers, and fax machines took up most of the space, didn't have any plants, but it did have a giant window that gave out onto a spectacular view of the Sangre de Cristo Mountains and a snow-dusted desert of sage and mesquite.

Teddy sometimes forgot that the vista was a computer-generated illusion, since Miles Havers's private communications center was housed in a concrete bunker one thousand feet from the main residence, and fifty feet underground.

Smart man, Teddy thought as he munched another fistful of sugar-caffeine rocket fuel. Miles's personal motto was "The computer is power. And power over the computer is absolute power."

As he turned away from his boss, only distantly wondering what was going on—Teddy didn't care what Havers wanted Catherine Alexander for, all he cared about was the chase, being pitted for once against the wit of a real human being instead of a string of code—he addressed his computer screen. Riding the wave of a coffee-cocoa-sugar rush, he started pulling up a history of Dr. Alexander: courses she had taught, conferences she had attended, papers she had presented, organizations she was affiliated with. Somewhere in all of this was the golden key that would find her and bring her back through the maze before the game clock ran out.

SITTING AMONG THE ferns and vines he so cherished, listening again to the conversation taped in Daniel Stevenson's apartment,

Miles Havers made sure he was out of Teddy Yamaguchi's hearing Teddy often wore a T-shirt that read: *Information, Like Water, Seeks Its Own Level,* and Miles knew that, like most hackers, Teddy held to the absurd notion that information *wanted* to be free. Havers knew what drove the young man: it was the thrill of the hunt, the challenge of getting in without getting caught—that was always the hacker goal, the information retrieved being purely secondary. But Miles knew that Teddy also held to another hacker creed: that you could do whatever you wanted *as long as no one got hurt.*

And since he knew this about Yamaguchi, that the kid liked to think of himself as a knight of the I-way bound to certain rules and ethics, Miles was careful not to let Teddy know about Security Consultants, Inc., and that their instructions were to get the scrolls at any cost— even the cost of human life.

As Miles listened now to the taped conversation between Catherine Alexander and Daniel Stevenson, he paid particular attention to Stevenson's mention of his journal, and also of setting up a cyberspace lab. Havers then referred to his handwritten notes of his conversation with Titus. *"She ran with a blue nylon gym bag and a black case."*

A black case.

Miles tapped his fingers on the armrest of the stone bench.

A black case like the kind a laptop computer is carried in? he wondered.

Maybe the journal wasn't a book, maybe it was in a computer.

The computer Catherine Alexander had with her.

As he was about to reach for his portable phone, Miles was startled by the sound of Teddy's voice, suddenly echoing from the far end of the room: "I've got a name, Mr. Havers! Lives in Malibu, runs the Freers Institute. Dr. Julius Voss."

"I HAVE TO call Julius!"

"Whoa, hey, wait a minute," Father Garibaldi said. "I'm not getting this. How could your friend Daniel possibly connect the guy with the scar to *Miles Havers?*"

"I don't know," Catherine said. "But Danno wouldn't have just made it up." She looked at the laptop screen and reread from Daniel's journal: *"Of course, there it is, right before my eyes."*

And then it came to her, the old yellowed newspaper clipping taped to Danno's refrigerator—an item about Havers's purchase of the Copernicus Diaries from the Russians back in 1997. Catherine had seen that old clipping every time she had gone to Daniel's place, and she pictured it again now: a UPI news photo of Miles Havers, attractive and rich, standing with a smiling Russian, a small knot of men in the background, the caption reading: "Computer mogul Miles Havers purchases rare fifteenth-century diaries." Next to it, another clipping, headlined: "Miles Havers Announces Releasing Copernicus Diaries for Public Display." There had been a major public outcry when Havers had bought the diaries before the world even knew they existed—they had come to light after the breakup of the Soviet Union, when many treasures thought to be lost during World War II had come to light. Danno had been one of the loudest voices opposing Havers's private acquisition of the diaries, which had resulted in embarrassing Havers into donating them to the University of Warsaw. The clippings were taped to Danno's fridge as a reminder of one of the few victories in his life.

In both photographs there was a man in the background; he had short white hair and a scar on his face. A Havers flunky.

Catherine rose from the table. "I have to warn Julius. He might be in danger." She sat on one of the beds and picked up the phone. "But I won't tell him where I am or what I suspect about Havers," she said as she dialed the phone. "The less he knows, the safer he'll be."

But Julius wasn't there, instead she got his answering machine. Catherine thought for a moment. Disguising her voice, she said, "Dr. Voss, this is Mrs. Meritites. You removed my gallbladder last year. I just wanted to let you know that I continue to enjoy excellent health and in fact I have never felt better. You needn't return this call as I am going out of town for a much-needed vacation, away from phones and interruptions. I'll give you a call when I am back from my holiday. I hope—" She stopped, drew in a breath, then said, "I hope all is well with you."

When she hung up she felt Father Garibaldi's eyes on her. "That wasn't your voice," he said. "How will he know it's you?"

"He'll know."

"You didn't warn him."

"I did," she said. "You just couldn't tell."

"Mrs. Meritites?"

"An Egyptian queen who died of gallbladder disease about four thousand years ago. Julius did a postmortem on her mummy. There was some flack about it at the time, internal rivalry at the institute that involved archaeological espionage. Julius found out later that his phone had been tapped and his notes secretly photocopied. The report was published by another man before his own report came out. I'm counting on Julius remembering that to alert him that his phone might be tapped."

"Are you going to tell me what it is Miles Havers is after? You said something about scrolls."

She got to her feet, began to pace. "You don't want to get involved, Father, believe me."

"Dr. Alexander, I'm a funny kind of guy. I tend to take it personally when a couple of escapees from *Pulp Fiction* shoot at me. The way I see it, I'm already involved."

She stopped and looked at him. Two electric-blue eyes framed by black lashes and black eyebrows shot across the room and went right through her. She nearly jumped out of her skin. For an instant, with the storm raging outside, causing the lamps to flicker, the moment was cast in a surreal light. Catherine flashed on the memory of how the sight of Michael Garibaldi had affected her a few moments ago, when he had come out of the bathroom not wearing a shirt. He was a priest, but she felt herself responding to him on a level involving chemistry. This was something new, and she didn't like it.

Picking up the nylon bag, she brought it to the table, moved the laptop to the side, and undid the zipper. A moment later, Father Garibaldi was staring in disbelief at six neat piles of ancient papyrus.

Catherine quickly explained about the dynamiting and the first fragment, the discovery of the tunnel and the basket, and finally, about smuggling the papyri out of Egypt. "The Bedouin woman you intervened for. That was Danno. Your heroics almost exposed our deception."

His eyes were riveted to the papyri. "What's in these books?"

She fished the single sheet of legal-sized notepaper from the gym bag. "This is all I've translated so far."

97

As Garibaldi read it, the lights flickering again and thunder rumbling in the distance, Catherine saw the digital clock on the nightstand between the beds click over to midnight.

Father Garibaldi frowned. "This woman, Perpetua, invokes the name of Jesus!" He looked at her. "What year were these books written?"

"The Greek is second century."

"Second century? Are you sure?"

"The story itself might be older, possibly first century. Sabina, who's dictating to Perpetua, refers to someone named the Righteous One, who I think might be Jesus."

"How can you determine when the story takes place?"

"I'm hoping something in the scrolls will date them, such as the name of a reigning emperor or a governor. But I have to hurry." Father Garibaldi reached out to touch the first book, his fingertips caressing the fragile paper. "Hurry? Why?"

"Because of the photographs Danno was holding. If Havers gets them then he has everything he needs to find the seventh scroll."

"Whoa! Hey, back up. *Seventh* scroll?"

"These six are incomplete. Another book follows."

"Do you have any idea where it might be?"

"Perpetua tells Aemelia to take it to King Tymbos. Ever heard of him?"

When Father Garibaldi said, "King who?" Catherine snatched up her purse and said, "I'm going to the hospital and wait for Danno to come out of surgery."

"I don't think that's a good idea. Unless you plan on going in disguise."

"Give me your clothes," she said. "I'll go as Barry Fitzgerald."

"Singing Tooralooraloora?"

She threw her purse down. "Dammit, I can't just do nothing!"

"Wait until morning," he said. "They probably won't be able to tell you anything about his condition until then anyway."

"All right," she said, reaching into the gym bag for her yellow legal pad and pen. "But there's no way I'm going to be able to sleep. I want to see what's written in these scrolls." And then, she decided, when Father Garibaldi was asleep, she would slip out and drive back to the hospital. . . .

"PERPETUA," STEVENSON WAS saying on the tape. "Sabina . . . Aemelia . . . King What's His Name . . ."

Havers stopped the tape. *Who were these people?*

He looked at the photographs he had received from Titus, spread out on his black granite desk. The papyri resembled the Dead Sea Scrolls, only in better condition. Their value? It depended. Were they early Christian? A lost gospel, perhaps? Hungerford had boasted to Zeke that the fragment they had found after the dynamiting had the name Jesus in it.

Leaning over the desk, Havers scrutinized one of the clearer pictures. He couldn't speak or read Greek, but certain words seemed to crop up more often than others—Ae|xe\i,a, Saliva, nepireTua. Calling up what he knew of the Greek alphabet, he took a stab at a rough transliteration: Aemelia, Sabina, Perpetua.

Personal names. Women's names. Which meant that, unlike many of the scrolls found in the Qumran caves, these were not inventories of temple treasure, or books from the Old Testament, or rules of conduct for a secret society. Hungerford had told Zeke that Catherine Alexander had described the Jesus fragment as a letter of some sort.

One thing he knew, he didn't have much time. If Catherine Alexander was the idealist he suspected she was, he could already guess her plan: to translate the scrolls and release their contents to the world, possibly even turn the papyri over to a museum or university for *public* viewing.

The thought made him shudder.

Like the Copernicus Diaries, which had not been looked upon in decades, or the Solstice Kachina that was handled only by a select group of priests, it was the fact that these papyri had been seen by only two people in two thousand years that made them desirable to Miles.

So he had to get them before Catherine Alexander made them public.

But how to find her? Titus had men watching the hospital where Stevenson had been taken, but Miles doubted she would be careless enough to go there. And although Teddy Yamaguchi had set up electronic flags, Miles didn't think she would be foolish enough to use a credit card. So how—

Just then the private door chime sounded, he looked at the monitor of the security camera, and saw his wife.

Erica came in wearing a peach silk peignoir over a white lace nightgown, her tanned face slightly puffy from sleep, her ash blond hair, Havers noticed, disheveled in a sexy way. "I woke up and you weren't there," she said.

He drew her into his arms. "I'm sorry, darling, I didn't mean to disturb you."

Miles did business around the world at all hours. Still, Erica liked to be sure he was all right. "I wasn't sleeping well anyway," she said.

"The insomnia? Are you sure you don't want to see Dr. Sanford about it?"

"No. I think it's just having the children here for the holidays. And Coyote Man."

Havers frowned. The old shaman. "Do you want me to ask him to leave?"

"Oh no! I want him here! He's going to take me to a sacred site tomorrow, on Cloud Mesa."

"I didn't know there was anything there."

"There isn't, at least not to the naked eye. But Coyote Man says that if you know how to look, you can see the invisible spirit roads that the gods and ancestors travel along. You know, like the Aboriginal songlines in Australia."

"Spirit roads," Miles said with a smile. "It sounds romantic." He kissed her. "I'll be in in a little while."

As soon as she was gone, he returned to his desk, where he silently regarded the photographs Titus's men had picked up in Stevenson's apartment. As he sifted through the stack, he noticed that not all the papyri were in a good state of preservation. In fact, some had gaps in the writing where the papyrus must have disintegrated; in one place, an entire sentence was missing. He tapped his finger on the polished granite. What had Stevenson said when he found the P245 papyrus in the British Museum? *That Catherine might want to find copies of the scrolls to help her with the translating.*

How had Stevenson put it? "Let your electronic fingers do the walking and never leave the safety of your home."

Unexpectedly, Erica's voice echoed in his mind: "invisible spirit roads. . . ."

"WE'LL *BOTH* GET to work," Father Garibaldi said, and he pulled out a chair and settled himself in front of the computer. "While you're translating, I'll get us logged on to the Internet. I am assuming that, because this computer has a modem, your friend was online."

"Danno did a lot of his work through the Internet."

As Father Garibaldi double-clicked on the icon for *Internet Utilities,* Catherine said, "You don't have to do this. I know how to do research on the Web."

"We can accomplish twice as much if we divide the work. My Greek's rusty, but I'm fluent on the computer." He double-clicked on TCP Manager, and when the Trumpet Winsock screen came up, he murmured, "Let's hope your friend wrote a login script. And let's pray the modem works."

As he clicked on Dialer in the menu, Catherine held her breath and hoped that the modem hadn't been damaged when the laptop was tossed into the wet grass.

But they heard the reassuring sound of the modem dialing. In the next instant, "Welcome to OmegaNets Santa Barbara, CA POP**" appeared on the screen. But immediately below it was the word login followed by a colon and the blinking cursor.

"Danno didn't write a login script," Catherine said.

"Which means we need a password again. This isn't something we can override with a paper clip. Any ideas this time?"

Catherine thought for a moment—Daniel was always writing notes to himself, he even forgot his own phone number on occasion. Where would he write down his user name and password? On a hunch, she reached out and gently peeled her photograph away from the inside of the laptop case. Flipping it over, she read: *Cath, Graduation Day, June 15, 1979.* Underneath, in a different color ink, Daniel had written: *dstevens, Klaatu.*

Garibaldi typed them in; Catherine kept her eyes fixed on the screen. And then:
PPP
Script completed

PPP ENABLED

IP is 670.65.324.000

"We're in," Father Garibaldi said, and he double-clicked on the icon for NetScape. "Fasten your seatbelts, we're getting on the highway!"

"INVISIBLE ROADS," ERICA had said.

Miles quickly sat down, booted up his computer, went straight to Internet Access, and logged on.

DAY FIVE

C atherine awoke with a start.

Trying to remember where she was, she lay still and listened for sounds of her camp waking up, for the call of the muezzin from a distant minaret. Instead she heard something she couldn't at first identify. And then she recognized it.

Rain.

In the Sinai?

She sat up, and it all came back. She didn't remember falling asleep in the chair where she had been examining the papyrus, but she saw that, at some point, Father Garibaldi must have carried her to the bed, removed her sandals, and covered her with a blanket. She looked at the next bed. It was made but rumpled, as if he too had slept on top of the covers. She looked over at the table under the window, exposed to a milky morning; Daniel's computer was propped open. Then she remembered: Father Garibaldi had said he was going to log on to the Internet.

She saw the closed bathroom door and heard the shower running. Swinging her feet to the floor, she cradled her head—Danno, in the hospital—she had fallen asleep; she hadn't gone to see him. Then she picked up the phone.

No dial tone.

Cursing softly, Catherine rose and padded to the luggage. The first thing she checked were the scrolls. They were still there, safely between the covers of the paleobotany text. They didn't appear to have been disturbed. She glanced again toward the bathroom. Michael Garibaldi could have taken them while she was asleep. But he hadn't. *Could* she trust him?

She regarded his black satchel. Hearing the water running in the bathroom, she quickly opened the bag and glanced inside, noting at once the priest's stole, a bottle of oil, a silver pyx for carrying the Eucharist to the sick, and some books: a small Bible, the Liturgy of the Hours, and the latest Tony Hillerman.

"I really am a priest."

She spun around. He emerged from the bathroom wearing black drawstring pants and a black T-shirt. "I'm sorry," she said. "I had to be sure."

"I don't blame you."

She eyed his T-shirt and its cryptic message in silver letters—*Dong Meyong Pangamot*—and then she glanced at the varnished rattan canes, which were propped against the wall. "Dong meyong. . . . It doesn't exactly sound warm and fuzzy. Is it like karate?"

"In that it's a martial art, yes. Why?"

"I just find it odd that a priest—" She stopped herself. "What happened on the Internet?" she said. "Were you able to get back online?" Shortly after they had logged on the night before, the storm had knocked out the mountain phone lines, ending Father Garibaldi's foray onto the Web.

"No luck. We'll have to try again." He watched her for a moment, then he said, "How are you feeling?"

"Like I'm having an out of body experience."

"The shower's available and the water's good and hot."

"First I'm going to try the phone again. I have to know how Danno is."

TO GIVE CATHERINE some privacy in their room, Father Garibaldi struck out into the chilly morning. And as he joined other travelers at the motel office, where free donuts and coffee were being offered, he paused to observe the gray sky hanging low over the surrounding mountains, and to sort his troubled thoughts.

The dream had returned.

It was exactly the same as it had been years ago, nothing had changed. It was the same scene, the same players, the same heart-wrenching drama he couldn't seem to escape from. Except that . . .

This time the dream was slightly different. This time, as well as the old man and the boy, there was—

He turned and looked back in the direction of their motel room, and he pictured Dr. Alexander as he had found her peering into his black bag, a knot of worry between her brows.

In the dream there had been someone new, standing just at the edge of his vision. He realized now that it had been a woman. Who was she? And why had she entered his dream now?

He pictured Catherine again, frowning at the pangamot sticks. Was it she? But if so, why was she in *that* dream?

Father Garibaldi was startled out of his thoughts by a sudden clanging sound as a motel guest bought a paper from the news rack outside the office. Pushing the dream from his thoughts, Michael dug into his pockets for change.

CATHERINE WAS COMBING out her long auburn hair, still damp from the shower, when Father Garibaldi came in from the outside, saying, "The gas pumps are now open, and the rain has let up." He had also brought coffee and donuts, and a newspaper. She noticed that, while she had been in the bathroom, he had changed into jeans and black clerical shirt with the Roman collar.

She also noticed something guarded about his manner.

"Any luck with the phone?" he asked.

"Totally dead. We'll have to go to the hospital."

"Dr. Alexander," he began.

"If they ask me for ID I'm sunk, but," she eyed Michael's black shirt and white collar, "I'll bet they'd let a priest in to see Danno!"

"Dr. Alexander," he said again.

She froze. Her eyes went to the newspaper in his hand.

"I'm sorry," he said as he handed it to her. "It's in the B section, bottom of page three."

She found the item: *"Local archaeologist Dr. Daniel Stevenson, who was attacked last night in his Santa Barbara apartment, died early this morning of stab wounds. Police have not released details, but they suspect foul play. Witnesses say a woman was seen fleeing from the scene. . . ."*

Catherine's knees gave way. She sank to the bed and closed her eyes. "I knew it," she whispered. "Somehow, I already knew—" She covered her face with her hands. "Oh God. Danno."

"I am so sorry," Father Garibaldi said.

Catherine began to cry, coughing out harsh sobs into her hands. The bed moved and she felt Father Garibaldi's warmth beside her. Putting his arm around her, he didn't say anything, just let her cry.

She curled her arm around his neck, pressing her face into his shoulder as she wept. It wasn't happening. It wasn't real.

Danno! "Those bastards!"

"Dr. Alexander, you have to call the police."

She drew back, angrily dashed the tears from her cheeks. "Why?" she cried. "What do I tell them? That Miles Havers had him killed? Do you think for a minute they'd believe me? Danno's dead, Father! Are the police going to bring him back?" She stood up, went to the door, flung it open to the gray day, and gulped in the air as if she were drowning.

"I can't believe this is happening. Oh God, what do I do now?"

"Would you like me to pray with you?"

She turned around. "Pray! For what? To whom? Prayer won't bring Danno back!"

Suddenly she was remembering Daniel's words from thirteen years ago, when he had come upon her the night of her mother's funeral, as she had sat in the darkness with a bottle of sleeping pills. "That's not the answer," Daniel had said.

"I stopped praying long ago, Father," she said, suddenly growing quiet as she stared at the newspaper on the bed, with its small, barely noticeable item on page three of the B section, an insignificant mention of the passing of Daniel Stevenson, thirty-six years old and her best friend.

He never got a chance to tell me his news about the Maya murals.

Catherine started collecting her things. "I have to get going. I have work to do."

"You're right," Garibaldi said.

"You're not coming with me."

"Yes, I am."

"Why?" she shouted. "And why are you still with me? Why don't you leave?"

He touched the bandage on his arm. "I have a personal stake in this, remember?"

She tipped her chin, a challenge. "Isn't your parish going to wonder where you are?"

"I still have a few vacation days left. They aren't expecting me yet."

"And when they do?"

"I'll deal with that then."

"Do what you want," she said, angrily throwing toiletries into the gym bag. "I know what I have to do."

Five minutes later they were in the car and facing the highway. "Which way, Dr. Alexander?"

Fighting back the tears, Catherine looked ahead into the dismal day, and then back over her shoulder at the highway that led southward to Santa Barbara and, ultimately, back to Malibu and Julius—to safety and security. "The men who murdered Danno," she said in a grim tone, "are not going to get away with it. When Miles Havers decided to take me on, he made a mistake, because now he's going to get more than he bargained for."

"So, which way?"

"I need to run tests on the scrolls, and some textile fibers I found on them. And there's software—" Her voice broke. "I need to download. There's only one place that might be safe enough to do it. North," she said, keeping her voice hard-edged, determined. "We'll use the foundation's research lab in San Jose."

"North it is."

As Father Garibaldi guided the Mustang out of the lot, Catherine reached into her gym bag and brought the paleobotany book into her lap. Carefully lifting the cover, she unfolded the first brittle page.

Keeping Danno in the front of her thoughts, she began to read. . . .

There were strange omens the night I was born.
My mother later told me that a fortune-teller came to our

house with an urgent message concerning the destiny of the child about to enter the world under this roof. I was not to learn the significance of this prophecy until many years later.

Forgive me, dear Perpetua, I get ahead of myself. First, greetings to Aemelia, my sister in The Way. Let me embrace you with the kiss of peace, and the news that my mother was also a deacon, as I was also intended to be, before destiny intervened and altered the course of my life forever.

I was born in Antioch in Syria. My father owned a shipping line and so we were wealthy. All who knew my mother envied her. But what no one knew was that she was secretly unhappy, for theirs had been an arranged marriage, and it was only after they married that she discovered my father was incapable of love.

I was their only child.

When I was ten years old, we took a long journey far from our home upon the advice of my father's physicians who, unable to cure him of a crippling back ailment, suggested he try the famous healing waters of the Sea of Salt. And it was there, in the wilderness of Judea, that we heard a man preaching.

He spoke in his native tongue, but there was a man to translate, who changed the words into Greek so that the foreigners in the audience could understand. Although that day on the Sea of Salt took place many summers ago, I recall clearly the desert teacher's face, the sound of his voice, and how the people listened, and asked him questions and called him "rabbi." My father walked away from the gathering, I remember, to return to the baths and the doctors there. But my mother remained, and I with her, to listen to the teacher.

When we returned to Antioch, my father declared that the healing salts of the sea had cured his back. It never troubled him again.

In my sixteenth year, my mother and I went out into the city to visit the astrologer, as was my mother's weekly habit. But when we came to our usual route, the main road that led through the Epiphania District into the heart of the town, my mother said, "We will go a new way today." Presently we came upon a crowd in a marketplace we had never visited before, where camels and pigs were sold, and slaves and donkeys.

Those were uncertain times, dear Perpetua, a time of spiritual unrest when people were seeking answers. The city was a stewpot of different beliefs, each quarter with its own temples, each street corner its shrine, each intersection its statue of a god, even the emperor in Rome, we were told, was now to be worshipped as a living god.

There was a man addressing a small crowd. My mother's habit had always been to hurry past such gatherings, but on that day she stopped and listened. The man spoke of forgiveness and how forgiveness opened the door to the way of light.

That was the day my mother changed forever.

She was never after that able to say why she had chosen to go that route or to stop and listen to the preacher, but we went straightway home afterward and at once she forgave my father for the cold and distant and unloving man he was. It was as if the preacher's words had dissolved the seed of bitterness that had been lodged in my mother's heart for so many years. A new light shone around her after that, and she became happy and young again.

The man in the marketplace had said many things which we did not understand. He said, "Vengeance belongs to God," and the crowd said, "Whichgod?" He replied, "There is but one God."

He said, "Forgiveness is ours, " and the crowd said, "Why should we forgive?"

"So that you can overcome death. We of The Way never die."

He said, "Nothing happens by chance. Everything is part of a greater design. What will be will be. But out of forgiveness flows peace. And with peace comes the light and eternal life."

And I realized that this was true, for I saw how it had changed my mother.

We went back every day to the marketplace, and then we invited the preacher into our home. We gathered together our servants and slaves, our friends and neighbors, and we *listened to him speak. We asked questions about the things that troubled our hearts—for those were perilous times in the empire—and he said, "The Righteous One said, Seek and ye shall find. Knock and it shall be opened to you."*

But the greatest message from the Righteous One was this: he overcame death.

As the teacher stayed in our house and taught us the wisdom of the man he called the Righteous One, and as he healed the sick and the lame as he had been taught by his Master, I came to realize that the Righteous One was the man we had heard in the Judean Desert.

We asked the teacher, "When will the end of the world come? Will it be today? Tomorrow? In our lifetimes?" because the empire was rife with war; there were outbreaks of pestilence on the borders; colonies were rising up against their overlords; the people in the cities were discontent, and they were afraid, locking their doors at night, trusting no one. Our teacher replied, "You will recognize the end by the signs. To each of you, I promise, will these signs be revealed."

My mother said to me, "This is the true faith, Sabina. And now we must spread the message as far and wide as we can."

The meetings were held in our house. Perpetua tells me that this is no longer the practice, because of persecution. But in those days we were not persecuted. We were able to meet freely, and the gatherings were always in the home of one person, who oversaw the weekly reading of the Message, and who prepared and distributed the love feast. People came from all over the city, eager for the message, and our membership grew until we had to hold our meetings in the garden. My mother conferred deaconship upon other members, so that they could hold meetings in their homes. Thus did the Community grow and flourish.

We weir happy in our new faith and ignorant of the tragedy that was to come and that was to set me on the quest that would take me to the ends of the earth.

And where destiny led me can only be marveled at, for in my eight decades of life I came to know kings and peasants, statesmen and thieves; I learned the art of healing, I brought babies into the world and sat with the dying; I traveled to the farthest ends of the empire and I witnessed many strange and wondrous things. And in all the towns and cities and villages, among all the wise men and sage women, the fools and the wicked, the learned and the unlettered, the hopeful and the despairing, I learned many secrets and the answers to many mysteries. But foremost among those answers were these, Perpetua:

First: to me was revealed the hour when the Righteous One will return.

Second: I know the day, the hour, the minute of the End of Things.

And thirdly: I know this now, that we are not alone. In the universe there is Another, which is greater and higher, and which is known by many names—the Good, the One, the World-Soul, the divine Artificer, Creator, Nature, Cosmos, Logos, Supreme reason, the Eternal ones, God.

You wonder how can I be certain of these things? I have proof, dear Perpetua. And when I reveal to you this proof, you too shall have unshakable faith.

And I bring you something else: a Gift. And this I will give to you, for it is a Gift to all of humankind from the Supreme.

IT HAD BEEN such a strange message that at first Julius had thought it was a prank. But then he had realized that the caller used the name Meritites—the name of the mummy he had examined last year. After playing the tape a few more times, it had dawned on him that the caller was Catherine, disguising her voice.

Calling to tell him that she was safe and going into hiding and didn't want anyone to know where, not even him.

But why the disguise? Why Meritites and the phony voice? And why the insistence that she was all right?

He wished he hadn't gone to the institute after their argument, that he had stayed with her. When he had come home to an empty house and the note—"I have to go away for a few days"—he had dialed Daniel Stevenson's number, hoping she might have gone there. But there had been no answer.

So Julius had come here, to her condo on Fifth Street in Santa Monica. Using his key to let himself in, he had half hoped, half expected to find her here, poring over the scrolls, her long auburn hair spilling over her shoulders the way it did whenever she was absorbed in a project, because she sometimes forgot to comb her hair back into a clip.

But she wasn't there. The coffeepot was cold, her bed had not been slept in, and a pile of mail and newspapers, brought in by a neighbor, waited on the dining room table.

In the bedroom he saw a photograph of Catherine and him on the beach in Honolulu. They had attended a conference together, they had made love for the first time there, at the Halekulani Hotel. Julius could still hear the whispering surf beyond their lanai, see the moonlight spilling across the bed, feel Catherine's soft skin and inhale her mixed scent of coconut suntan oil and freshly washed hair. That was the first thing that had attracted him to her, that mane of auburn hair, which she often wore loose, sexy and inviting.

"Catherine," he whispered, "wherever you are, please call me. Come home. We'll work this out together."

"LONG REDDISH HAIR," the witness said to the sketch artist in the police station. "No, not that red, more like chestnut. Yes, like that." Although the incident had happened quickly—the woman bursting out of Dr. Stevenson's apartment, not watching where she was going—the neighbor had gotten a good look at her; the likeness, she told the artist now, was nearly exact.

"Do you have any idea who she was?" the Santa Barbara detective asked.

The woman shook her head. "Dr. Stevenson was rarely home."

"What about the guys chasing her?"

"I didn't get a good look at them."

"She met up with a man outside," the detective said, raising his voice a little because the squad room on this December morning one week before Christmas was pure bedlam. With robberies, carjackings, burglaries, and drunk driving—all up during the holidays—keeping everybody hopping and manpower stretched thin, he didn't have the luxury to spend the time on this case that he'd like; he still hadn't even got the evidence over to the lab. "The guy she drove off with. Did you get a good look at him?"

"Sorry, officer."

On the other side of the squad room, a short plump woman in a blouse, jeans, and sandals, with a macrame tote slung over her shoulder, was calling out friendly greetings to officers as she threaded her way through the chaos toward the detective and the witness. She rarely had to flash her press badge; after six years working the crime beat for the *Santa Barbara Sun,* she was a familiar fixture around the station.

She had come this morning to see if there was a story behind this archaeologist's murder. But so far all she'd been able to find out was that Stevenson had been on the fringe, a Chariots-of-the-Gods type who believed there were pyramids on Mars. A kook.

But significant enough, she noticed, to warrant getting murdered in a curious way: apparently it was the work of punks and yet it seemed that the only thing taken were some photographs.

After getting a look at the artist's sketch, she followed the detective through the squad room where ringing phones, clattering typewriters, humming faxes, and absolutely everyone talking at once created a deafening pandemonium. Faintly heard beneath the din was a radio station playing "Santa Claus Is Coming to Town."

"Any leads on who killed him?"

"I can't comment on that just now," the detective said, and he kept going until he disappeared into the captain's office.

She stood there for a moment, wondering if the cop's uncharacteristic brusqueness was due to holiday stress or if it was because of the case, when she happened to glance at his desk and spot a pile of paper envelopes, the kind that come from an evidence collection kit. They were labeled *Stevenson 12.17.99; Det. Shapiro,* and under them there appeared to be the edge of what looked like an eight-by-ten black-and-white glossy photograph between plastic sheet protectors.

Keeping an eye on the captain's office and another eye on the chaotic squad room, she turned her back on the desk, stretched out a finger, and drew the photograph out from under the evidence envelopes. Then, with the coast continuing to remain clear, she turned around and looked down.

Then she looked again.

What was *this?*

It looked like papyrus. With ancient writing on it.

She frowned. She had seen something like this before. But where?

Checking to make sure the detectives were preoccupied and that no one was watching her, she eyed the photograph a little more closely. Although at first glance the papyrus appeared to be a single sheet, careful scrutiny revealed a tear in the lower half so that it looked as if two pieces had been found separately, pieced together, and photographed.

What was this document?

Even more intriguing: *where* was it?

She thought of the sketch of the woman who had run from the scene. Who was she, and how was she connected to this papyrus? The picture was going to get buried in the Metro section, that was certain; run for maybe a week with a number to call, and then disappear.

She stared at the photograph again. Had Stevenson actually found something?

Making sure no one was watching, she turned the photograph over and discerned a penciled note on the back, not in the detective's handwriting: *"Jesus fragment, found 12/14/99, Sharm el Sheikh."*

Jesus fragment!

She didn't waste any more time. Making sure she wasn't being observed, she quickly reached into her tote bag and brought out the palm-sized, hand-held digital video camera she carried with her everywhere. Equipped with a flashcard containing 250 megabytes of memory, it took superior pictures that, when downloaded into a computer and then printed out, were hard to tell from the originals.

Keeping the camera steady, she scanned the photograph, then she dropped the camera back into her bag and was walking out of the station house before anyone knew what she had done.

"TOUCH ME . . . ," THE woman's voice softly purred. "Embrace me . . . kiss me . . . whisper to me . . . tell me your secrets . . . I'm here for you . . . as far away as . . ." The image of a man's hand glided onto the screen. ". . . your finger." And then a man's voice, loud and authoritative: "Dianuba 2000. It's all you'll need."

The lights came on and the people gathered in Miles Havers's office congratulated one another on another brilliant ad campaign.

"It's going to be a thousand times bigger than when Windows 95 was released," said one visitor.

"It's brilliant!" said another. "I mean, how many hits do you estimate Yahoo gets a day? A million? With this new software it will be two hundred million—*five billion* hits! There's no limit!"

Miles himself was silent. The software was his brainchild, he knew its potential. He had based it on a very simple concept: basically, take an unmoderated newsgroup where posts are automatically forwarded around the world without review and expand it a millionfold. Dianuba 2000 was going to connect every single one of the one hundred million persons currently on the Internet and connect them in a way that was light-years beyond anyone's dreams. And Miles's company had kept the project under such tight security that the competition had only a suspicion of what the new software was capable of—total, instantaneous global connection.

At the click of a button.

"What about the antitrust suit?" one of the visitors asked—a major stockholder who had been invited to the screening of the new ad. Others in the room echoed his concern about the nongovernmental interest groups and online services that were charging Dianuba Technologies with monopolistic practices, claiming that the new software would put all competition out of business. They wanted the government to force Dianuba Technologies to sell the global Internet connection separately from Dianuba 2000, which was due to be released in fourteen days, at one minute past midnight on January first.

But Miles wasn't worried about the antitrust suit. "I have an angel," he said with a cryptic smile, "a shining, black guardian angel."

He went to the window and looked out, his suite on the third floor overlooking the campus of twenty buildings and 12,900 employees that made up Dianuba's "science park." From here, across lawns so perfect they looked like AstroTurf, he could see the main employee parking lot. It was full today, of course—a Saturday. But it was always full on Sundays as well. That was how Miles gauged the success of a company: if there were workers' cars in the lot on a Sunday or holiday, it meant the company was healthy and growing. A dead lot meant a dead company.

But *his* company would never be dead. Not with tiger-power driving it.

When his eyes focused in more closely and he saw his own reflection in the window, he flashed himself a smile. But then suddenly he was seeing another image, a familiar image that had been haunting him for thirty years. *Slanting, almond-shaped eyes . . .*

No, he wouldn't think about it. He *had* to believe it had been a tiger, because the alternative—those eyes, almost human—was insupportable.

He turned sharply away from the window and went to the computer terminal on his desk, punched a key, and the latest NASDAQ listing appeared. The price of Dianuba stock had closed the day before up $2. Miles held 79,000,000 shares, which meant he was $158 million richer.

And soon, most likely within the next twenty-four hours, he was going to be richer by six scrolls as well.

Teddy Yamaguchi had hacked into the Internet access provider Daniel Stevenson had used. Armed with the IP address, all they were waiting for now was for Catherine Alexander to log on, and as soon as the connection with OmegaNet went through, they would trace it right back to her.

"I WANT TO get back onto the Internet as soon as we can," Catherine said as she pulled the car into the parking lot of the foundation's research lab, taking a space away from the overhead lights. "We're bound to find something that will help us date the scrolls and find the seventh."

After she killed the engine, she and Father Garibaldi regarded the low-profile building nestled among grassy berms softly illuminated against the night. Despite the late hour, there were still some cars in the lot, and lights glowed from a few windows.

"How do we get in?" Michael said.

"Security's pretty tight. Several museums use the foundation's labs for analysis of art objects. The *Mona Lisa* spent some time here, back in the seventies."

"Someone's coming out!"

They sank down in their seats and peered through the windshield as a foundation employee, carrying a briefcase, came through the front entrance and headed toward a Lexus.

"Wouldn't it be something," Father Garibaldi said quietly, "if the preacher Sabina mentions turned out to be St. Paul? Antioch was the first city where he preached. That's where Christians were first called Christians."

Catherine didn't say anything. She knew that Father Garibaldi was thinking in terms of the men who had helped construct the early Church; she hadn't told him about her own personal hope that the scrolls might shed light on the *women*. She glanced at him as they sat in the darkness. He was still wearing the Roman collar, symbol of the masculine power behind the Church. She wondered how he would react to the concept of Christian priestesses.

What would he think if he knew I was searching for proof that men have no right to be Pope?

"What I think would be amazing," she said as they watched the Lexus drive off, "is if the scrolls offer proof that a man named Jesus really existed."

Garibaldi looked at her. "You don't believe Jesus existed?"

"I'm a scientist, Father. I deal in facts and hard evidence. As far as I'm concerned, the Bible is a collection of myths."

She massaged her neck. They had been on the road for nearly ten hours, taking turns driving, stopping only for gas and drive-through burgers. Catherine had read as much of the first scroll as she could: *"I know the hour when the Righteous One will return. . . ."* Catherine glanced at Garibaldi again and wondered what his thoughts were on the coming millennium. Did he believe the end was near, that the Second Coming was at hand?

The Second Coming. . . . *Had* Sabina been given that secret knowledge?

"I think the coast is clear," Michael said. "What's the plan?"

Catherine tapped her fingers on the dashboard. Then, reaching for the blue gym bag, she slung it over her shoulder and said, "Grab the laptop, will you?"

"You mean we're just going to walk in?"

"Why not? I have clearance. And I've brought assistants in with me before."

He stared at her. "I'm your assistant?"

"Lose the collar, though," she said, and she was out of the car and hurrying toward the building.

The guard at the security desk was unfamiliar to her; the last time she had worked here was over a year ago. As he slowly stood up, she quickly scanned his name tag, and offered a smile. "Hi, Gordon. The place looks quiet tonight."

"May I see your identification, please?"

"Sure." As she fished around in her purse, she glanced at his left hand, saw the gold band. "How's your lovely wife these days? I'll bet the holidays are keeping her busy."

He studied the ID card, then he typed something into his computer console. "My wife is fine, thank you," he murmured. Handing the ID back, he held out a clipboard. "Sign here, Doctor." He looked at Garibaldi. "Both of you, please."

When they stepped out of the elevator onto the third floor, Catherine looked up and down the deserted hall, then said quietly, "I need to download the Logos program. But I also need to run a test in the chem lab."

Garibaldi said, "Point the way and I'll do the downloading while you're in the lab."

They went down the hall, looking into offices where computers sat dark and silent. They were hoping for one that was already running, to avoid triggering alarms. "It isn't a secure program," Catherine said. "At least it wasn't when I used it a year ago."

"What does it do?"

"It's an indispensable tool for dating and translating ancient Greek writings. It started out as a catalog for the papyrus collection at Duke University. Then it was expanded to include other collections. You scan a word and it finds matches that have already been dated. It can save weeks of work."

They came to the last office and saw the glow from a monitor.

"Someone's using it," Garibaldi said. "They might be right back."

"I don't think so," Catherine said as she looked over the neat desk top. "There's no coffee or tea, no soda, no food. The chair is pushed under the desk. And look, they've already torn off today's calendar page. This person is long gone."

"Dr. Alexander, if you ever leave the archaeology business, you could open a detective agency."

She sat down and, as she searched the files for Logos, she said, "Jesus' ministry is generally believed to have lasted three years, until his crucifixion in 32 or 33 C.E. So if Sabina was ten when she heard him preach near the Dead Sea, that would place her birth around 20 c.E. And if she lived into her eighties, as the scrolls indicate, then she met Perpetua around the year one hundred. Which is why determining the date of the scrolls is so important. Come on, Logos, where are you!"

"Is this program that vital?"

"For me it is. My mother was the best paleographer there ever was. She spent years cataloging brushstrokes, densities of ink, the formation of letters. Just like you would be able to tell eighteenth- century handwriting from contemporary—just look at the Declaration of Independence—my mother could look at an ancient document and put a date to it. But I don't have her skill, I need all the help—Here it is!"

As Catherine vacated the chair so that Michael could take her place, she said, "It's too big for a floppy, you'll have to download directly onto the laptop hard disk."

"Could be a problem," Michael said as he inspected the computer. "No, wait, we might be in luck. It has an infrared port. Keep your fingers crossed. . . ."

They watched the laptop screen.

Then:

CONNECTION ESTABLISHED PROCEED

Catherine started to leave.

"Wait a minute," Michael said. "Is this program on a network server?"

"Yes, why?"

"Then we can't download this file."

"Why not?"

"It won't be complete. We need to capture the uninstalled program." He typed \pub\applications\logos.

On the laptop screen: g:\ Michael typed: copy *.* c:\

"How long will it take to download?"

"Unfortunately infrared is slower than a direct connection, but we don't have the proper cable for a direct connection. Maybe ten minutes."

"Make it seven." And she was gone.

MILES HAVERS TURNED away from the lights of Dianuba's campus as he listened to the phone ring at the other end. A familiar voice picked up. "Titus," he said, "I'm faxing you a list of places Alexander might visit."

"It's coming over my machine now."

"My hunch is the first place she'll head to is north, to the foundation. It's just outside San Jose."

"San Jose? Hey, my friend, give me something difficult! As it happens, I just sent two of my best consultants to that area. I can divert them to pick up your lady. But just to be sure, I'll send agents to the other locations as well."

Miles hung up and thought for a moment. Deciding that it wouldn't hurt to have a backup, he picked up the phone and dialed again. "Senator, hello!" he said after a moment. "Yes, Erica and I are looking forward to seeing you and Francie at our New Year's Eve party. Senator, I was wondering if I could ask a favor. I need to get in touch with the director of a scientific research facility near San Jose and I believe she's a friend of yours. . . ."

CATHERINE TURNED ON the lights in the chem lab and scanned the counters for a workstation. Staying alert for the sound of footsteps, she collected a box of fresh slides from the top of a refrigerator where someone had taped a note: "!!Danger: Nitrocellulose!! Do *NOT* remove from fridge!!"

Catherine first placed a few textile fibers she had harvested from the papyrus onto a slide and then she treated them with hydrochloric acid. She held her breath as she watched for a reaction. If the color remained unchanged, it was one proof that the fibers had been dyed a true Roman purple.

The color didn't change.

But the definitive test was yet to come. Keeping her eye on the threads under the microscope, and listening for sounds out in the hall, she applied a drop of hydrosulfite of ammonia onto the slide. She held her breath again. If the threads turned bright yellow, it meant they had been dyed with an extract from the murex shellfish, a method of dyeing used in the early centuries of the Roman empire, later abandoned. Yellow threads would mean the scrolls had been wrapped in cloth dating in the age of the Caesars, placing Sabina's scrolls closer to the time of Jesus.

Downloading Complete. . . . Father Garibaldi would have liked to run "Install" and make sure the program was going to work, but there was no time. He and Catherine had been there for twelve minutes already, and he didn't like the way the security guard in the lobby had looked them both over. "Time to go," he murmured as he shut down the computer and left the office.

But when he turned the corner at the end of the hall, he overheard the guard from downstairs talking on a cellular phone: "Yeah, she's up here, workin' with her assistant. The name? Let's see . . . yeah, the assistant's name is Daniel Stevenson. Huh? Stevenson is what! Yes sir! I'll detain them both until you get here."

Garibaldi found the lab, hurried inside. "The fibers turned yellow!" Catherine said excitedly. "That means they're old!"

"And that is exactly what we won't grow to be if we don't get out of here, fast!"

"What—"

"We've been found out. Orders are to detain us."

Taking the emergency stairway, they ran down to the first floor, made sure the corridor was clear, then made a dash for the exit door.

It was locked.

They tried another. Also locked.

Michael said, "We could try setting off the fire alarm. It would unlock these doors but it might also have the guards running to all the exits and grabbing us before we can get away."

"How about if we start a fire in one of the upstairs offices?"

"I don't know if we could get away from the scene fast enough. What we need is something on a timer. Something that doesn't go off until we're at the opposite end of the building."

"Nitrocellulose!" Catherine said. "Flash paper! There's some in the lab refrigerator."

As they hurried back, slipping quietly onto the third floor after making sure the coast was clear, she explained, "It's just ordinary paper treated with nitrate to make it highly flammable. Danno introduced me to it in college when he was involved in sabotaging the administration's efforts to raise student fees. In case the cops paid them a surprise visit, they could destroy the evidence literally in a flash."

"Sounds dangerous."

"It is."

MILES PICKED UP the phone on the first ring. It was Titus. "I have my San Jose team on the line. They've just turned off the highway. They say they have the building in sight."

"THIS IS HIGHLY volatile," Catherine said as she carefully placed the flashpaper into the wastebasket. Then she positioned the infrared lamp over it and switched it on. "The heat will cause it to ignite."

"How long will it take?"

"I have no idea."

"I love precise science," Michael said as they ran for the door.

Hurrying down the hall, they heard a guard coming. They ducked into a small utility room and hid among mops and brooms as they waited for him to pass. "Just how big an explosion is that flashpaper going to create?" Garibaldi whispered.

"I have no idea."

"Enough to blow up the building?"

"Possibly."

"I see," Garibaldi said. "Then I suggest we vacate the premises as quickly as possible."

Just as they reached the farthest exit from the chem lab, they heard a muffled explosion. An instant later, fire alarms went off. And the exit doors sprang open.

As Michael and Catherine flew out into the night, a car came squealing up, headlights blinding them, and a voice shouting, "Hold it right there! Don't move!"

THE FIRST SCROLL

MY MOTHER KNEW *the art of midwifery, a skill she had learned from her mother and which she was teaching to me in that summer of my sixteenth year.*

One night, we were summoned to help a young wife in a difficult childbirth. She had been laboring for a day and a night, and after my mother delivered the baby, the woman sank into a deep, exhausted sleep. The infant did not thrive; it died while the young wife slept.

My mother wrapped the infant in a cloth and took it to the temple of Juno, where unwanted infants are left exposed on the steps to die. There she left the dead child and took one that had only recently been left. She brought the living baby back and placed it at the young mother's breast. When she awoke, she was overjoyed to see her child.

Before my mother had become a follower of The Way, she never would have committed such an act of mercy.

In my seventeenth year I married. My young husband was also of a wealthy family and although the marriage was arranged, I knew I should grow to love him. Four months later, I became pregnant.

It was in the winter of the great riots.

Perhaps you have heard of that terrible time, Perpetua, when pestilence spread through Antioch and many people died. The populace made sacrifice night and day in the temples, but their cries of mourning never ceased. And then they noticed that the disease had not reached the wealthy districts of the city. In their grief and outrage, the people sought a scapegoat. Because we of The Way were a new faith, they blamed us.

The mob came during the night, with torches and clubs. Prayers did not save us. My parents were slaughtered; my young husband fought bravely before he, too, was killed. Members of The Way who had sought safety in our house were also killed, as were our servants and slaves. I alone survived, although I lost the baby.

My physical wounds eventually healed but my heart did not. I thought I would die of grief And my soul cried out one question, to which I received no answer.

And then I heard rumors that the Righteous One was preaching his message in a distant land. Because I had heard the story of his execution many times, how he had died and come back to life again, I knew that he would have the answer to the one question that burdened my heart.

He was in the East, I was told. And so to the East I would go. And thus began the journey that was eventually to reveal to me the Seven Truths that ans)ver all questions, dispel all fears, and bring certain riches into the lives of those who know them. The first I have already shared with you: that we are not alone, that there is a Source of Life in the universe. The second Truth—which endows us with power—was made known to me in the ancient city of Ur Magna, on the banks of the Euphrates River.

I was eighteen years old, and it was the fourth year of the reign of Emperor—

DAY SIX

DECEMBER 19, 1999

C atherine awoke to find that the world had vanished.

As she unfolded herself from the backseat of the Mustang, where she had slept all night under a borrowed blanket, she gazed out at the ghostly realm beyond the windows. A dense fog shrouded everything in a white silence; she could only just make out phantom-like shapes in the mist: the colossal redwoods.

Sitting all the way up and rubbing her stiff neck, she saw that the front seat was empty. She hadn't heard Father Garibaldi leave the car.

Now she saw that others were stirring as well, the various travelers who, like Catherine and Michael, had pulled into the refuge of a mountain rest area for the night. After speeding away from the foundation's grounds the night before, they had headed west toward the ocean, up into forested mountains in hopes of finding a motel with a vacancy. Finally, they had had to stop. Michael had been able to borrow a couple of blankets from a family in a Winnebago; he had then taken the cramped front seat, allowing Catherine the dubious luxury of the back.

Last night . . . Another close call. If it hadn't been for a second lab explosion, bursting out the third-floor windows and showering the parking lot with glass, creating the confusion she and Father Garibaldi needed to make a dash to their car and subsequent escape—

She shook her head. It was too scary to think about.

As she got out of the car, stretching and inhaling the bracing salt air, she saw through the mist people trudging to and from them bunker-like restrooms, or sitting at picnic tables. The Winnebago was warming up its engine, so Catherine returned the blankets to them, with a sincere thank you. She and Father Michael would have frozen without them.

Michael.

She looked around for him, decided he must be in the restroom.

Catherine had wakened during the night to hear him moaning in his sleep. She had given him a gentle shake and the nightmare had subsided. And then she had watched him for a while, studying his face in the ghostly glow of the rest area lights, recalling the way he had held her yesterday morning while she had wept on his shoulder until she thought her heart would shatter.

Although his dream seemed to have subsided, a shadow of its effect could still be seen on his attractive features as he slept, an inner conflict that had left its imprint. He was a man of peace not at peace, she thought. A man who followed Jesus but carried martial arts weapons.

The showers in the restroom were coin-operated and cold water only. But Catherine fed as many quarters as she could into the timer, relishing the icy water on her body. She dried off with paper towels and changed into her only fresh set of clothes.

When she returned to the parking area, the mist was completely burned off, with a bright sun shedding light on towering redwoods and families packing up to leave the rest stop.

She saw Michael at their car, wearing jeans and a Loyola University sweatshirt. He was checking the air in their tires while talking to a man in a cheap, rumpled suit. Their voices were low, and they were laughing about something.

When Catherine drew near, she heard the stranger say, "If you're thinkin' of heading south, don't bother. The coast highway is jammed. Every yuppie New Ager in the country is descending upon Big Sur as if they think that's where the Martians are gonna land! I'm from

Redwood City. But I do business all up and down the coast. Hoping to get home for Christmas." He flashed a grin at Catherine. "So, you folks on vacation?"

She offered him a weak smile and said quietly to Michael, "May I have a word with you, please?"

They walked away from the car, with Catherine keeping her eye on the stranger. "What were you and he talking about?"

Michael shrugged. "Nothing." He scanned her face. "How are you doing? Holding up?"

"I'm okay," she said slowly, as she watched the stranger wash the windshield of his dusty white Pontiac and lob the paper towel into the waste receptacle as if it were a basketball. She looked at Michael. "How's your arm?"

He flexed it a little. "Still attached."

"Father Garibaldi, that man is not what he seems."

"What do you mean?"

"I don't like the way he's watching us without watching us."

"You think he's a cop?"

She shook her head. "He isn't police. Look at the way he's stalling. As if he's waiting for everyone else to clear out so he can pick us up. A real cop would just flash his badge and take us into custody, witnesses or no."

"Are you sure this isn't just paranoia?"

"He said he was from around here, but his car has rental plates. And I saw the time on his watch. It's three hours ahead."

Father Garibaldi's eyebrows arched. "Eastern time?"

"Whatever, he isn't local."

"I hear you," Michael said. He scanned the rest area. There were only two cars left; everyone else had moved on. "I suggest we get going while there are still witnesses around."

But as they headed back to the car, the stranger's partner appeared from the restrooms.

"Uh oh," Michael said, "he's got company."

"Let's split them up, confuse them. You make a run for the car and I'll dodge back into the ladies' room. There's an exit on the other side. Drive around and pick me up."

As Michael got into the car, Catherine ran for the bathroom, joining a woman with two children. The stranger's partner ran after her, stopping when she disappeared inside.

By the time Catherine got to the other exit of the bathroom, Michael had the Mustang rolling. The other car was also rolling, with the partner jumping in.

Michael approached, Catherine readied herself to grab the passenger door. But instead of slowing down, he sped up.

"Hey!" She fell back against the concrete block wall and watched in disbelief as, with the Pontiac in pursuit, Michael took off down the highway, with everything with him—her purse, the laptop, and the scrolls.

The desk was deceptive.

Ten feet wide by eight feet deep, the Plexiglas surface was illuminated from underneath by the push of a button, which caused an electronic map to appear, showing the current location of every one of Titus's "advisers" around the world. The touch of another button enlarged the map of a small African country where employees of Security Consultants, Inc. were in the process of "putting out a fire." Another tap on the smooth desk top and a tiny Asian nation mushroomed to show hot spots of insurrection, drug trafficking, illegal arms movement, each flagged with a tiny red light indicating the presence of a Security Consultants agent.

Titus drew most of his recruits from the military, but many were also ex-CIA and ex-FBI operatives who liked the work but wanted better pay. Titus was generous, and his agents did clean, swift jobs without asking questions.

The map Titus was inspecting at the moment, as he sat in his twentieth-floor office with his back to the rainy Seattle day, resembled a planetary landscape, with state borders glowing orange, cities pinpointed in blue, highways in green, and points of interest, such as missile sites and top secret government installations, in sunshine yellow—a neon panorama floating in the black liquid crystal space beneath the translucent desk top: California.

And the red light inland from the coast, just south of San Francisco, indicated the presence of a top team.

They had missed picking up the Alexander woman at the research lab, so Titus had had to launch a wide search for the blue Mustang she had gotten away in. Who was the guy she was running with? Titus had run a trace on the license plate and found the car rental agency it had come from. But although he had accessed their customer files with no difficulty and had found a record of the Mustang having been rented at Los Angeles International Airport, the client's name and credit card number had been mysteriously erased. As if someone had known ahead of time that people would be looking for him.

Titus checked his watch. His agents should be reporting in at any time. He surveyed the map again, then reached over to brush a speck of dust from the polished desk top, which had absolutely nothing on it except for a small figurine.

Of a tiger.

Catherine decided not to stick around. The guys in the Pontiac might come back.

The only problem was, if she left the rest area, then Father Garibaldi wouldn't be able to find her. So she decided to follow the footpath alongside the highway, which provided adequate coverage from passing motorists while she could still watch the traffic. And as she trekked along, she thought back over what had happened—in particular how, when she had come out of the showers, Garibaldi and the stranger had been speaking in a friendly way.

As if they already knew each other?

Catherine picked up her pace, following the trail as she made sure that she couldn't be seen from the highway, but that she herself had a clear view of it. Cars zipped by, campers and RVs, and occasionally a truck. But no blue Mustang.

The way Michael and the stranger had been laughing. And then had suddenly talked louder when she came out.

A setup? The whole thing staged, to enable him to get away with the scrolls while making it look as if he was running from attackers?

But he had had earlier opportunities to take off with the scrolls.

Maybe he needed a buyer first.

"Dammit!" Catherine whispered as she increased her pace along the wooded track.

Back at the rest area she had seen a sign pointing to a ranger station in this direction. She would wait for Father Garibaldi there. If he didn't see her at the rest area or along the highway he was sure to look for her there.

If he was coming back.

Of course he was. Why wouldn't he? He couldn't have been in cahoots with those two guys.

There was another reason why he might not come back. They might have caught up with him. . . .

The hours passed and her anxiety grew. When she suddenly shivered, Catherine realized that the sun was no longer overhead, but slipping behind the giant trees. To her right was the redwood forest, deep and mysterious. To her left, the highway, and on the other side, more redwood forest. Up ahead, the highway seemed to disappear into a wooded horizon. Shadows were starting to stretch, and fog was rolling in from the ocean. It also seemed to Catherine that the traffic was thinning.

Where was Father Garibaldi?

When her teeth began to chatter, she realized it was more from fear than cold. What if they caught him? Would they kill him, too? Like Danno—No. She wouldn't allow herself to even consider it.

Then what was taking him so long?

The day was growing darker, and the track along the highway was becoming harder to follow. A few cars were whizzing by now with headlights on. And Catherine was starting to get cold. Her sweater was in the blue Mustang, with Father Michael.

How long *was* this damn highway?

Were there wild animals in these woods?

Catherine felt her fear shoot up another notch. The sign back at the rest area—it *had* said the ranger station was in this direction, hadn't it?

If you don't find it, then what?

Stick out your thumb.

But Catherine quickly discarded the hitchhiking idea. With the fog and darkness descending, she couldn't make out the cars behind the headlights. The two in the white Pontiac might be searching the highway for her right now

There it was! The ranger station!

As Catherine ran down the road, her legs feeling leaden after so many miles of plodding through brush and grass, she looked for the blue Mustang, hoping Michael had stopped here first to look for her.

But as she drew near to the small log building, she realized there was no blue car. Neither was there an official ranger vehicle. No vehicle of any sort.

The station was closed.

"Hey!" she said, pounding on the door. Someone *had* to be in there! She peered through the window. The place was dark and deserted.

She chewed her lip as she looked around. The woods were dark now, and menacing. When she heard a rustling to her right, she gasped. Two golden eyes peered at her through the growth and then vanished.

Catherine circled the cabin, fighting down her rising panic. Pretty soon it was going to be night, with no stars or moon, no street lights, just plenty of darkness and thick fog and a freezing cold. On top of that, she realized she hadn't eaten since the night before.

She tried the door. It was locked. She rattled the windows. No way to get in. And then, off to the side, in an area with picnic benches—a pay phone!

To her relief, it was in working order and there was even an intact telephone directory.

She quickly thumbed through the book, found a towing outfit that specialized in mountain and off-track service. So what if she didn't have a car? The driver could hardly refuse her a ride into town.

And then what?

We'll deal with that then.

But when Catherine dug into her pockets, she found them empty. She had used all her coins back at the rest area.

As she searched her surroundings, she tried not to panic. The fog was dense. And the temperature was dropping. And she hadn't heard a car pass by in a long time.

Go back to the rest area.

But—which way? She could now barely see a few feet in front of her.

And then she heard a car motor in the distance. After a moment she realized it was drawing closer. And then, through the fog, she saw headlights.

Michael!

"Hey!" she shouted, waving her arms. "I'm over here!"

But it was a white car and it seemed to be traveling too fast.

Catherine turned and started to run.

The white car followed, chasing her along the fire road that led from the ranger station into the forest. Catherine veered off the road and plunged into the woods.

"Hey! Catherine, wait! It's me!"

She stopped and turned. It was Michael.

She flew into his arms, and stayed there, holding on to him, for a very long moment.

"You don't know how worried I've been!" he said as he drew back, his hands still on her arms. "I've been searching for you for over an hour!"

"Why did you leave me!"

"I figured if they're after the scrolls, they'd follow me and you'd have a chance to get away."

"What took you so long coming back?"

"When I finally managed to shake those guys, I left the Mustang on a residential street and walked to the nearest rental agency. I've had the laptop on, hoping you would find a pay phone and call."

"The laptop! I tried to make a call—I didn't think of calling the laptop," she said breathlessly, ". . . a towing service, but I used all my coins on that shower!"

They climbed into the car, where hot air from the heater enveloped Catherine. "It was a good idea to get rid of the Mustang," she said, relishing the blessed heat. "Now there's no way they can find us."

"Guess again." Michael handed her a newspaper, and when Catherine unfolded it she cried out.

She was looking at her own face.

On the front page of the Sunday paper.

HER FACE WAS so beautiful Julius almost hated to cut it.

He had to remind himself that his knife wasn't going to disfigure her any more than nature already had, because this ancient queen's beauty was no longer perceived on her real skin-and-bone face but on the funerary mask that had covered it. Whenever he performed an autopsy on a mummy, he liked to have the mask, or a statue, or some representation of the specimen nearby, to remind himself that he was working on what had once been a living person, who deserved the same care and respect as any recently deceased man or woman.

Julius held life sacred, and he approached the body of another with reverence; it was a temple of God, not to be abused or desecrated. And always, when about to incise the brittle, desiccated flesh, he silently recited the Hebrew prayer *Barukh Dayan ha-Emet*—Blessed are You, the True Judge.

However, on this quiet Sunday morning at the institute, which Julius nearly had all to himself—except for a Seventh-Day Adventist lab technician who, like Julius, had celebrated the Sabbath the day before—he was having an uncharacteristically difficult time concentrating on his work. It had been two days since Catherine had left, and in that time, except for the cryptic "Mrs. Meritites" message on his answering machine, he had not heard from her.

He was worried sick.

"Here you go, Dr. Voss," the technician said brightly as she deposited a thick Sunday paper on a stool. "I'm off for the rest of the day. Christmas shopping!"

"Thanks, Tracy," he said, noticing that she had also left a fresh cup of coffee and a Danish with the paper, as she always did. "Please let security know I'm still here," he called after her. "Last week they locked me in!"

As Tracy's footsteps faded down the hall, Julius turned away from the mummy and, peeling off his rubber gloves, picked up the coffee and pastry and the newspaper, and went into his office, where the open window admitted salty' ocean air and the first kiss of dampness that meant fog was rolling in.

Oh Catherine, where are you?

Maybe he should try Daniel Stevenson again, and see if he had heard from her. Or perhaps he should contact the foundation that was funding her dig in the Sinai—

The cup suddenly slipped from his hand, splashing hot coffee on his pants; the Danish thudded to the floor.

JESUS SCROLLS FOUND? the headline screamed. Below it, a photograph of a papyrus with ancient Greek writing. And next to that—

Julius was thunderstruck.

"Have you seen this woman?" it said beneath Catherine's picture.

As he quickly scanned the article—Daniel Stevenson, murdered; a woman seen running from his apartment—Julius sat down just as his legs gave way. He rapidly devoured every word of the story.

Witnesses said the woman drove off with a man. What man? Daniel's murderer? Had he kidnapped Catherine? Was her life now in danger?

Was she already dead ?

My God, Catherine. How did I let this happen ? Why didn't I stay with you ? Why did I have to be so damned self-righteous?

Santa Barbara, the story said.

But that was two nights ago. She could be anywhere by now.

Drove off with an unidentified man. . . .

Julius shot to his feet. There was only one thing to do. Go to the police. Tell them who she was and what he knew. Help them find her.

Five minutes later, he was pulling out of the institute's parking lot. He didn't see a car pull away from the curb behind him.

AS THEY DROVE slowly along the fog-bound highway, Catherine stared at the front page of the newspaper, with the police artist sketch, the photograph of the Jesus fragment, and the headline: DOES ANCIENT DOCUMENT GIVE DATE OF SECOND COMING? "It says the police are looking for me in connection with Danno's murder. And look at this sketch! It's almost like a photograph of me."

"Is that one of the scrolls?"

"It's the photograph I took when I pieced the fragment together with the first page of the first scroll—Perpetua's letter. I didn't keep the fragment. I left it behind in my tent. I thought Havers had gotten all the photographs, but apparently he didn't. It says the police found some photographs in Danno's apartment. But I took over a hundred, which means that although Havers may have gotten some, he didn't get all of them." Catherine read the caption under her picture: *Have you seen this woman? Anyone with information as to her identity or whereabouts please call Det. Shapiro at the Santa Barbara Police Department: 1-805-897-2300.* "It will only be a matter of time before one of my friends or colleagues sees this," Catherine said, thinking of Julius.

"And the byline isn't a San Jose writer. It says Associated Press, which means it was picked up on the wires. That story, along with those two pictures, is probably running in other newspapers around the country. Maybe even," he added, glancing at her, "around the world."

Catherine suddenly remembered Hans Schuller at the Institut Radiologique in Zurich. She had planned to call him and see if he had been able to carbon date the specimen she had sent to him from the Sinai. But now she couldn't. If he saw this news story, he might not want to assist her. He might even tell the authorities.

Catherine angrily wadded the newspaper and flung it down. "As soon as we find a place to stop, I'm going to call the police. I didn't kill Danno. But I know who did!"

"Be careful," Michael said. "If whoever you call has Caller ID, they'll know where the call is coming from."

"My alarm clock isn't working," she said, throwing up her hands. "That's it. I'm at home, fast asleep in my nice safe bed, having this awful nightmare, and my cheap Sony knock-off that I got with a free coupon isn't working!"

"There's a vacancy," Michael said, pointing to a motel up ahead, on a small street that led to the beach.

"Thank God," Catherine said. She had been worrying they were going to have to spend the night in the car again.

It was the See-Side Inn, twenty miles south of San Francisco, and Michael checked them in while Catherine stayed hidden in the car.

Once inside, they quickly opened bags from Sav-Mart, where they had stopped for clothes and supplies, paying for the purchases with Michael's traveler's checks. As Catherine unpacked a bag of oatmeal cookies and juice, she stopped and looked at Michael. "What's all that?"

He set some tools on the table, and plugged in what she guessed was a soldering gun. Then he opened the laptop and took out Daniel's tone dialer.

"This is in case we get separated again," he said as he sat at the table and proceeded to unscrew the back of the dialer. "I don't want to risk another incident like this morning."

Catherine watched in fascination as he carefully melted the solder on the circuitry board and removed a tiny metal cylinder. "This is the crystal," he said. "It's what gives the dialer the tone. And this," he said, holding up a tiny, square component he had purchased at the Sav-Mart electronics counter, "is a crystal that will give us a different tone."

He worked slowly and carefully, like a jeweler, soldering the new crystal in place. After replacing the back of the dialer and installing the batteries, he punched the buttons to test it. "Hear that?" he said. "This is the tone that makes a telephone think money has been deposited. In hacker lingo it's a 'red box.' Unlimited free calls anywhere in the world." He handed it to Catherine.

"Is it legal?"

"Of course not. Keep it on you at all times. If we ever get separated again, you can reach me through the laptop modem."

She gave him a long, thoughtful look. "Garibaldi, who are you *really*?"

He smiled as he put the tools away. "If I tell you, then I'll have to kill you." He looked up at her. "Seriously, I *am* Father Michael Garibaldi. Want to see me make you go from zero to guilty in sixty seconds?"

"I'm going to wake up any minute, I just know it." She drew up a chair and sat next to him. "Let's test the Logos software."

While she removed the hand-held scanner that came with the laptop, uncoiled the cable, and plugged it into the computer, Michael booted up and located Logos.

They waited. Then:

SCSI Device Not Loaded

"What does that mean?" Catherine said.

"It means the scanner isn't working."

"Isn't working! Why not?"

"Well, you may have just hit upon one of the major metaphysical questions in the field of computer hardware."

"In other words, you don't know."

"I'm sorry, it looks like you're going to have to do the translating the old-fashioned way."

"All that work for fipthing. And nearly getting killed!" She brought herself up short. "All right. And in the meantime, let's get online," she said.

"I'VE GOT MY men searching the area," Titus said to Havers over the videophone. "But it's a large area. And she could be laying low."

"Maybe we can't catch her physically," Miles said, thinking of invisible highways, "but there is another way. If Dr. Alexander wants to translate those scrolls quickly, she is going to have to get online help.

Mr. Yamaguchi has already located the server and IP address she'll be using. As soon as she logs on we'll have the phone number. A trace takes two minutes."

"I'm standing by," Titus said.

"LET'S HOPE DANIEL paid his Internet bill," Father Michael said as he booted up the laptop.

Catherine was sitting on one of the twin beds, carefully unfolding the second papyrus scroll. She had reached the end of the first one, now completely translated and stored in the box her new jeans and blouse had come in. But the folds of the second scroll were proving to be less resilient than the first, and in places appeared to be in danger of tearing.

"That was the fourth year in the reign of Emperor—"

Who? Catherine wanted to shout. Emperor who? But the broken-off fragment was lost.

With an impatient sigh, she gave up and stood behind Michael as he typed on the keyboard. He was making a sound; she thought he was groaning, and then she realized he was humming. "What's that?" she asked.

"Catching the spare change of angels as they fly over."

She gave him a surprised look. "You're a Laurie Anderson fan?"

His ears reddened. "Want to hear me sing *Walking & Falling?*"

"I'll pass." She watched the screen:

TCP Manager
Internal SLIP driver COM1
Baud Rate = 54600 Compression IP Buffers = 32

Michael pulled down Dialer from the menu and clicked on "Login."

User Name appeared. He typed: *dstevens* Then, Password:

But as he started to type *klaat*—Catherine suddenly grabbed his wrist and said, "Wait! Shut down!"

"Why?"

"Shut down! Hurry!"

He quickly pulled down Dialer and clicked on "Bye."

The words NO CARRIER appeared on the screen.

"What was that all about?"

"If Havers might think of tapping Julius's computer, don't you think he would monitor Danno's Internet account? It would be child's play to Havers to hack into OmegaNet and wait there like a spider for us to log on."

"And as soon as we do, he puts a trace on it—right back to here! Damn, why didn't I think of that?"

"What now?"

He picked up the phone book, flipped to the Yellow Pages listing for Internet access providers. "Here's one. They guarantee instant access."

"MR. YAMAGUCHI," HAVERS said, as he slipped into his tuxedo jacket. "Mrs. Havers and I are going out for the evening. There is a good chance Dr. Alexander will sign on with a new access provider."

"No problem, Mr. Havers. All she has to do is use her credit card."

"THE MINUTE WE'RE in," Michael said as he watched the computer screen, "we'll have to move fast. If Havers is monitoring your credit card, he should know soon which provider you've accessed." In order to sign on to an Internet account, a credit card was required. They had tried Michael's, only to discover that he had gone over his limit; LinkNet had refused it. So they had to use Catherine's. "But he won't be able to trace your location until he hacks into the provider's system. That's why I picked an Orange County server. It will throw him off."

Catherine returned to the papyrus, and as she gingerly drew the stiff leaves apart, watching in alarm as the brittle edges broke, even disintegrated in places, she wondered what had happened to her dig. Was it still going or had the authorities closed it down? What about the dynamiting? Was Hungerford's project proceeding or were there archaeologists there now, excavating out the well, exposing the skeleton?

"Still no access," Michael announced, and Catherine heard him dial the provider's number again.

"What if it doesn't work?"

"We'll figure something out. Although I have to admit, I haven't been faced with a challenge like this since the time Sister Mary Agnes got herself locked in the sports equipment room and I had to pick the combination lock to get her out. With Father Murphy standing there offering me ten bucks to leave it till morning!"

Deciding to work on the papyrus later, Catherine collected one of the Sav-Mart bags and disappeared into the bathroom. She emerged a moment later with a towel around her shoulders, and her hair hanging down straight and wet. She held out a pair of scissors. "We'd better get this over with."

Michael rose from the computer, frowning at the scissors. "Are you sure you want to go through with this?"

She looked over at the newspaper with her likeness on the front page. "I have no choice. Will you do it? I'm afraid that if I try it myself it will come out a mess."

"I've never cut hair without the aid of a soup bowl before," he said, taking the scissors.

She saw how stiffly he moved his arm. "How's the wound?"

"It hurts, but it looks like I'll still be able to play the tuba."

As he was taller, Catherine had to look up at him. He was wearing a plaid shirt from Sav-Mart and, like herself, stiff new jeans. She noticed, for the first time, a trace of aftershave or men's cologne. Catherine was momentarily unbalanced. Although the Roman collar had unsettled her, a constant reminder that he was a priest, in street clothes he was simply another male, a sexy male, requiring her constantly to remind herself that he was a priest. The collar, at least, had taken care of that.

"How short do you want it?" he said as she sat in the chair. "Short, but not as short as yours."

"Yeah." He laughed. "People tell me crew cuts are out. But I wear my hair this way for a very practical reason."

"What's that?"

He seemed to hesitate. "Pangamot," he said. He didn't elaborate, nor did Catherine prompt him to.

As he positioned himself behind her, surveying the thick curtain of auburn hair, he said again, "You're sure about this."

"I've been meaning to get a trim."

"Is that all you want? A trim?"

"Make it eight inches."

He lifted a lock of hair and sliced the scissors into it, and Catherine heard, out in the parking lot, beyond the closed drapes and locked door, a car go by with its radio on. The station was playing "Joy to the World."

"It's hard to believe," she said as she tried to ignore the auburn tresses falling one by one into the wastebasket, "that Christmas is only five days away. Julius wanted me to take a leave from the dig and come home to celebrate the holiday with him. If I had, I wouldn't have been there when Hungerford dynamited. And none of this would be happening. And Danno would be alive." She touched the jade panther around her neck. "I never got around to buying him a Christmas present this year," she whispered.

"You said Julius is your fiancé." *Snip snip.* Another hank of hair gone. "When are you getting married?"

"We aren't officially engaged. And as far as getting married . . . God, I wish I could call him. Just to talk to him."

"With luck, and a little persistence," Michael said as he moved around the chair, carefully and gently cutting away, "we'll find all the answers you need on the Internet and you'll be home with your family and friends before you know it."

Family and friends. How strange that sounded. No family, Catherine thought. Not even a distant cousin. Friends? She hadn't really thought about it, but now that she did, she couldn't come up with the names of people she really thought of as friends. There were colleagues, of course, and acquaintances by the number, but someone she could call friend? Julius was one, Danno had been the other.

Have I really kept myself that isolated all these years?

She felt Michael standing close behind her, handling her hair. "I have no family," he had told her the night before. What about friends? Did priests have friends, real friends?

"You were in Israel," Catherine said now, becoming more and more aware of his nearness, his fingers brushing her neck. She had never realized before what an intimate act hair cutting could be. "Why did you leave before Christmas?"

"Have you ever been in Jerusalem during a religious holiday? It took me five hours just to get halfway down the Via Dolorosa!"

"So you headed for the wide open spaces of the Sinai."

He hesitated. The scissors stopped. She felt him behind her, breathing softly.

"Yeah," he said finally, resuming snipping. "The wide open spaces. And what were you looking for in the Sinai? The manager at the Isis said something about the Exodus route."

"I'm looking for Miriam."

"The prophetess."

"You know about that?"

"Well, I am a priest. I know about Miriam. 'Hath the Lord spoken only by Moses? Hath he not also spoken by us?'"

"Numbers," Catherine said in amazement. "Chapter twelve. I believe that Miriam was a co-leader with Moses, but my theory isn't very popular among Bible scholars."

"Of course not. How are we going to keep women in their place if we let it out that maybe they had clout in Bible times?"

And suddenly the moment was imbued with such a feeling of deep intimacy that Catherine felt briefly giddy. Father Garibaldi was aware of it, too, she knew; she sensed it in the way he took pains to touch only her hair, the way his fingers would snap away if they accidentally brushed her skin. She realized that he mustn't have much physical contact with a woman, and certainly not in a way so personal as cutting her hair.

When Catherine looked into the wastebasket, she was startled to see how much he had cut away. But she had told him to make it very short, as different from her newspaper picture as possible.

"How's that?" he said at last, standing back.

Catherine patted her hair. It felt even all around, but shockingly short. Her neck was completely exposed, making her feel strangely naked. She had had long hair all her life; this new cut made her feel suddenly vulnerable. "Bangs," she said.

His eyebrows rose. "Bangs! Are you sure?"

Catherine had surprised herself. The idea of bangs had only just popped into her mind. "Yes. Please."

But when Michael positioned himself in front of her, combing her hair forward over his hand to protect her eyes from the shears, she drew in a breath and held it. His legs were touching hers, and the waistband of his jeans was inches from her face. She realized in that moment why she had asked for bangs.

He worked quickly; she sensed his reluctance, his discomfort. She closed her eyes, felt the back of his hand on her eyelids. Snip snip. He paused, combed more hair forward, unhooking some strands from behind her ear. His touch felt like a lover's caress. Catherine was appalled to realize that her cheeks were burning. "All done," he finally said, stepping away, sounding relieved. Catherine went to examine his handiwork in the mirror over the dresser. "I look like Buster Brown," she said.

"I'd say more like Louise Brooks."

"Now for the next step." She reached for the Sav-Mart bag, but Michael got to it first, bringing out the box of Dazzl-Em Ultra-Blonde. "It says here you're supposed to do an allergy test forty-eight hours in advance."

"No time for that."

He gave her a serious look. "Are you sure about this?"

"I need to change my appearance as drastically as possible. And anyway, now's my chance to see if blondes really do have more fun. But this is something I can do on my own."

He nodded, headed for the door. "In that case, I'm going to go see if I can find an out-of-town newspaper."

She went into the bathroom and stood at the sink. She was surprised to see that her cheeks were still inflamed. As she unfolded the plastic gloves and slipped them on, she recalled the feel of Michael's fingertips grazing her neck. As she removed the cap of the developer bottle and poured in the coloring gel, she thought of him standing close to her, towering over her, the sharp scissors snipping close to her skin. She shook the bottle to mix the solution, and then proceeded to squeeze it into her hair, and she thought about Michael, how he was starting to affect her. Ammonia filled the air and stung her eyes, but the memory of his aftershave was stronger. In the mirror, behind her, she could see the rattan sticks he carried with him everywhere.

Who was he, really? What about his past, his background? Who was his family, why did he become a priest?

Finally, the blonding gel all used up, she swept her short hair up into a frothy cap. The instructions said to let the dye set for forty-five minutes.

So she sat down at the computer and dialed the provider. When User appeared on the screen, she typed in "phantom," the password she and Michael had decided upon.

An instant later: Incorrect Login. Service had not yet been activated. She dialed again and entered the password.

Incorrect Login

Surely they should have access by now. Was there something wrong?

She typed again, heard the modem dialing and the phone at the other end ringing . . . she held her breath as she stared at the screen. A moment later she heard a new sound, like a rusty hinge opening—the computer "handshake." The account had been activated.

Quickly clicking on NetScape, and then again on NetSearch, she briefly considered the search engines offered, deciding on Lycos at Carnegie-Mellon University. She clicked on *Search Large Data Base.*

Click. And the Search Form appeared, with the cursor blinking at Keyword. She thought: Which first?

As she started to type in Sabina, she hesitated. Her glance went again to Michael's lacquered canes. What had he said it was called?

Chewing her lip for a moment, Catherine backspaced to erase Sabina and typed in: *pangamot.* She hit Enter.

Lycos came up with twenty-nine hits. She chose an article recently published in *Soldier of Fortune magazine: "To the pangamot warrior, self-defense is passive. The pangamot combatant is aggressive, trained in lethality. There are no rules. And the winner receives as a prize, not a trophy, but his life."*

A hypertext link sent her to the Filipino Martial Arts Web page, which displayed graphics of men in fighting positions, brandishing the same lethal rattan sticks as Michael's. The object, it appeared, was to kill.

She heard the front door open and close, felt Michael come in and stand behind her. "You could have asked me," he said when he saw the screen. "I would have told you whatever you wanted to know."

She didn't look at him. "You said pangamot was for self-defense."

"I never said that."

"It's a combat art. You're into violence."

"I'm not into it. I control it."

She looked up. "You mean you control your opponent's violence?"

He shook his head. "My own."

She suddenly felt cold, and vaguely repulsed. But she had to know.
. . . "Why *do* you wear your hair so short? Tell me."

"Because one of the moves in pangamot is grabbing your opponent's hair and flipping him—"

She turned away. "I shouldn't have asked."

"Tell me why it upsets you so much."

"Because I hate violence, in any form, and—" *Her father kneeling
submissively with the others.*

"And?"

Because you're a priest, she wanted to say. Because it disturbs me
that a priest would practice so violent a sport.

He regarded her for a moment. Then, unstrapping the cane sticks
from his black satchel, he held them out to her. "Here, take them."

"No."

"They're just two pieces of rattan, varnished and polished. Maybe
if you handled them it would help defuse your fear of them."

Catherine stared at them, held in momentary thrall by the long,
hard sticks. "It's not the canes I'm afraid of," she said. She looked up,
met his eyes.

"I'm sorry," she said. " I don't want to talk about it anymore. I
shouldn't have brought it up." She walked to the bathroom. "I have to
rinse this stuff out of my hair."

"Okay," he said after a moment, laying the sticks down. "I'll start a
search on the computer. What shall I try for first?"

Where to begin? Catherine's mind swirled with keywords: *dia- konos,*
The Way, Antioch, the Righteous One. What was the most vital thing
she needed to determine about the scrolls?

Their age, she thought. We need to know when they were written. "Sabina said everyone was upset about news of the Roman legions
being slaughtered. If the Roman general was Quintilius Varus, then
we have our dates."

But then Catherine's eye caught one of the newspapers they had
collected during the drive up the coast. A headline leaped off the page:
DOES ANCIENT PAPYRUS PREDICT END OF WORLD? And she thought: The
seventh scroll. We have to find that first. "Tymbos," she said. "Look
for King Tymbos."

And Michael typed *Tymbos* and clicked on Start Search. . . .

"SHE'S ON THE NET!"

"Thank you, Mr. Yamaguchi," Miles Havers said, and as he hung up the carphone, he pressed a button that moved a panel beneath the limousine's VCR, exposing a small computer. Entering a few commands on the keyboard, instantly linking him to Teddy Yamaguchi back at the house, Havers dialed another number, reaching Titus in Seattle. Although alone in the limousine—Erica was riding in the one behind, with her daughter and grandchildren—Miles spoke softly into the phone. "Catherine Alexander has used her credit card to sign on with an access provider. LinkNet in Orange County. I have started a trace on her." He paused when he saw the lights of the pueblo ahead, and the crowds gathered beneath the stars. Coyote Man had called a special powwow for prayers and dancing to coax Solstice Kachina back to his people. "My wife and I are attending a function," Miles said, "so Mr. Yamaguchi will inform you as soon as he has located Dr. Alexander. Titus," he added, before hanging up. "I trust your men have their instructions. They are to pick up the laptop computer and collection of papyrus books and see that Dr. Alexander is taken care of."

As the limousine inched its way through the crowd, Miles typed a command on the computer keyboard and that morning's front page appeared. The Jesus Fragment and its English translation. He gazed at the last line on the page: "Take it to King—"

"King who?" he whispered, leaning toward the monitor. "Take it to King *who?*"

"SORRY, NO TYMBOS," Michael called out. "King or otherwise. Are you sure we're spelling it correctly?"

Catherine emerged from the bathroom combing her short, damp, and nearly platinum hair. Michael stared at her. "You look different."

"That's the idea," she said as she frowned at the computer screen.

Michael couldn't take his eyes from her. Now that the long hair was gone, Catherine's neck was exposed. Unlike her tanned face and arms, it was milk-white, and slender, looking almost like fragile porcelain. The newly cut hair—not a professional job but choppy— looked as if it had been shorn as some sort of punishment, and the

145

drugstore dye job made Catherine look like a little girl who had gotten into her mother's things.

Back at the research lab, she had been tough and decisive; if she had been afraid, it hadn't shown. But now she looked so . . . *vulnerable.* And Michael was rocked by a sudden, intense desire to protect her.

Catherine turned away from the computer and went to the box that held the first scroll, brought it out. At the top of the second leaf she pointed out to Michael: TYMBOE.

"You're right," he said, "no doubt about it. Could it be an anagram maybe? The early Christians had a real passion for that. You know, like *ichthus.*"

"It's possible," Catherine said. The anagram of *ichthus,* made up of the first letters of the phrase, *Iesous Christos Theon Uios Soter*— Jesus Christ, Son of God, Savior—resulted in the Latin word for fish, thereby creating one of the early symbols of the Christian faith. Had Perpetua resorted to a similar secret code?

Noting the hour on the computer screen, Michael said, "I figure we've got time for one more search and then we'd better log off. Make it a good one, professor."

As he sat with his hands poised over the keyboard, waiting to type in the word, Catherine mentally ran through her list. Aemelia, Perpetua, Sabina, The Way, the Righteous One. Without the women's last names, it was going to be difficult if not nearly impossible to find them. And The Way, the Righteous One, were too broad; Lycos would offer thousands of choices of phrases that contained any of those words.

Returning to the bed where the second scroll had been partially laid out, she read the first line: *I joined the caravan of a man who was an alchemist delving into the occult mysteries of life and death. . . .*

I joined the caravan of a man who was an alchemist delving into the occult mysteries of life and death.

He had studied the great sorcerers and wizards of Persia, and was driven by a quest, searching for the ancient formula to eternal life. He told me that, long ago, the world was inhabited by giants. It was called the Golden Age and people lived extremely long lives. He showed me evidence of this, in the writings of Plato and Socrates, and in the scripture of the Jews, where it is recorded that men named Adam and

Seth and Methuselah each lived for nearly a thousand years.

He was by faith a Stoic, but he also believed in the Eternal Ones from whom, he said, mankind once knew the secret for longevity. But that secret, he said, was lost long ago. Yet it could be found again, if one but looked.

And so, in order to travel in safety to the East, in search of the Righteous One, I joined the caravan of Cornelius Severus. . . .

http ://home. mcom. com/home/internet-search. html
SEARCH ENGINES
InfoSeek Search
InfoSeek is a comprehensive and accurate WWW search engine. You can type your search in plain English or just enter key words and phrases. You can also use special query operators:
Enter: Cornelius Severus
RUN QUERY   *CLEAR QUERY TEXT*
http://www2. infoseek. com/Titles?qt= Cornetius+Severus
InfoSeek Search Results:
You searched for: *Cornelius Severus*
There were no WWW pages that matched your query.

As Miles walked with his family toward the center of the pueblo, where the ceremonies had already begun, he held a small cellular phone to his ear.

"I've got her IP address," he heard Teddy say. "In two minutes I'll have the phone number she's accessing from."

Miles assisted Erica, who was dressed in a white evening gown, around the temporary bleachers toward the area roped off for special guests. The bleachers were packed with Native American families, sympathizers, tourists, and the media. The buzz was that Coyote Man was going to play a magic flute that would draw Solstice Kachina from out of the earth. It promised to be a good show.

"Tracing now," Teddy said over the phone.

Havers held his breath.

MICHAEL LOOKED AT Catherine. "Want to try for one more search?"

She regarded the cursor blinking on the screen. "No," she said. "Log off."

File Exit
Dialer Bye
PPP DISABLED
NO CARRIER

THE AIR FILLED with the aroma of Indian fry bread and the sounds of the drums, all eyes were fixed on Coyote Man as he played his sacred flute. Miles quietly excused himself and left. No use hanging around for something that wasn't going to happen.

As he reached his limousine, standing out among the cars, pickups, and four-wheel-drives, the chauffeur opened the passenger door and Miles slipped in. First he called Teddy, to be given good news and bad news. The good: that the faxes Miles had been anxiously awaiting had begun to arrive from Cairo—the start of the translation of the scrolls. The bad: that Catherine Alexander had logged off the Internet before Teddy could trace her.

"Very well, Mr. Yamaguchi," Miles said. "It is time to set the trap. Please begin the program."

He telephoned Titus in Seattle. "Her laptop contains data that might possibly be incriminating to me. I have no doubt, Titus, that others are going to join the search for Dr. Alexander. And I cannot stress enough how essential it is that we find her first."

As he hung up, a transmission was coming over the limousine's fax machine. It was from Cairo. The English translation of the first of the scroll photographs.

THE LIGHTS WERE on unusually early in the papal apartments overlooking St. Peter's Square.

And as he waited to be admitted to see His Holiness, Cardinal Lefevre paced anxiously, his thoughts in turmoil.

God's Dogs. Yes, that was it. That's what we were called. A play on the name of our order, Dominicans, named for our founder, St. Dominic, but mutilated—*Domini Cane*—so that it meant the dogs of God.

Why did they hate us so? Pierre Lefevre asked himself as he paced outside the Pope's study in the Apostolic Palace overlooking St. Peter's Square, where the Vatican civil guard was starting to have difficulty containing the swelling crowds. We were only trying to protect the faith from heretics and devil worshippers. We were reviled when we should have been applauded.

And now we are needed again. Will we be God's Dogs once more?

"Your Eminence?" A young priest interrupted his thoughts. "His Holiness will see you now."

Once they were alone, the Holy Father came straight to the point. "The Egyptian ambassador to the United States has requested an urgent meeting at the White House. I have been told that it concerns the papyrus that was found in the Sinai. Which can mean only one thing—that the Egyptian government wants the papyrus restored to them."

"It would seem so, Your Holiness."

"For what purpose, do you suppose?"

"To put on display."

His Holiness regarded Lefevre, an old friend from seminary days. "You think this is so? They would do this?"

"If the scrolls are Christian, and if they predate any gospel record in existence, and if they can be authenticated beyond a doubt as a genuine *eye-witness* account of Our Lord's ministry. . . ." He held out his hands, indicating the obvious.

His Holiness nodded. The scrolls would attract crowds, bringing money back into Egypt. Yes, they would put them on display. "Do you think we have anything to fear from what is written in the scrolls?"

"If they are connected to a document which we already have, then there is a great deal to fear."

His Holiness knew which document Lefevre referred to. "I am sending someone to Washington," he said finally. "I have already informed the American government of our desire to attend that meeting. We need to let our concern be made known."

"I can leave at once," Lefevre said.

But His Holiness said, "This is going to require someone special." He already had the person in mind, someone who would be successful in persuading the President of the United States of the diplomatic urgency of the situation.

"Father Garibaldi," Catherine wrote on a sheet she tore from her yellow legal pad. *"I'm sorry to do this to you, but I have no choice."*

She paused and looked at his sleeping form on one of the twin beds. Her own bed had not been slept in, despite the midnight hour.

And her bag was packed and waiting by the door. She resumed writing:

"I can't expose you to any more danger. I'll be spending the rest of my life mourning for Danno, I don't think I could survive if I were to be the cause of your death, too.

"I hope you'll forgive my taking some of your money. Look for the spare change of angels as they fly over."

She signed the note, picked up her bag, and slipped out into the foggy night.

THE SECOND SCROLL

HE WAS KNOWN *by many names: Healer, Savior, Heavenly Shepherd, Only Begotten Son. And when he was slain, they called him the Sacrificial Lamb. When I asked among his followers and was told that he had been born of a virgin and had come from Jerusalem, that he had been crucified, buried, and then resurrected, I knew that I had found the Righteous One.*

The caravan of Cornelius Severus had come to a great caravansary on the bank of the Euphrates River, on the plains surrounding the ancient city of Ur Magna. It had taken us many weeks to arrive there, and I was anxious to speak with the Righteous One. But when I went to the temple, I was told by the priests that it was not so simple to speak with him; I must first be purified and enter into the secret initiation.

This I did gladly, for I was the last member of the Fabianus family, and I had to ask the Righteous One the question that burdened my heart.

The neophyte period lasted forty days, in which we fasted and meditated, and learned the teachings of the Savior. When the day of our initiation arrived, we took immersion baths and dressed in white robes. And then we were led into secret rooms beneath the temple which symbolized the underworld, for we were to undergo a ritual death. The High Priest led us in mystic prayer, which continued without cessation for many hours, accompanied by the rhythmic sounding of bells and a constant stoking of the incense fires. He intoned: "Trust ye in your risen Lord, for the pain which He hath endured, our salvation hath procured." And in this atmosphere of mystical fervor, we began to experience charismatic phenomena.

Some of the neophytes fell to the floor in ecstatic trances, others began to speak in tongues, while yet others saw the spirits of the dead. Of these charismatic gifts, the one that I received was the gift of prophecy, for as the spell of the mystic prayer came over me, I experienced a wondrous revelation.

When the initiation was over, we were brought out from beneath the temple and into the light, where families and friends were there to receive us and to rejoice with us in our new "birth."

This was when I learned that the savior I sought—the Righteous One—was not the one who dwelled in this temple! For this "messiah," as they called him, was Tammuz, a very ancient savior, who dwelled long ago in the Great Temple at Jerusalem, and who had also been slain and resurrected.

I was told I had sought out the wrong god. But there was another savior worshipped in Ur Magna, also born to a virgin, and when a star appeared in the heavens to herald his birth, a delegation of magi and astronomers went to adore the new child, taking gifts. He was the Redeemer, and he lived Wo thousand years ago. But after speaking with his followers, I learned that this savior's name was Josa. He was not the Righteous One.

While I was disappointed that I had not, after all, found the Righteous One, I was elated all the same with the new insight that I had received beneath the temple—the gift of prophecy. And with this new sight, I saw clearly what I had not seen before. It is this, dear Aemelia and Perpetua: that we are divine.

As I would some day come to learn, indeed receive proof, that there is a Source of Life in the universe, so it was revealed to me that we spring from that Source. We are made of it. You and I are made of god-stuff. As the child resembles the parent, we are divine.

Remember this, Perpetua and Aemelia and all my sisters in The Way, for it is part of what I will eventually come to understand as the Seven Truths—which are a formula for attaining a life of happiness and richness, a life in which there is no fear but only understanding, and knowing who we are, where we are going.

THE PROPHETESS

The third Truth, which empowers us even further, was revealed to me in faraway India.

DAY SEVEN

MONDAY
DECEMBER 20, 1999

"Dr. Alexander? *Dr. Alexander?*"

Catherine didn't hear him over the running water. She had turned the shower up as hard as it would go and as hot as she could tolerate it and so she didn't hear Father Michael pounding on the bathroom door.

But in the next instant she felt a sudden draft. And his voice, coming through the steam, startled her. "Dr. Alexander, we have to get out of here, *now!*"

Then she heard the door slam shut and the draft was gone.

A few minutes later and barely dry, Catherine came out in jeans and a T-shirt, hastily pulling on her socks. She was surprised to see Michael packing her things and putting them by the door with his own bags. "What is it?" she said, hopping over to her shoes.

And then she stopped and stared.

Gone were the jeans and short-sleeved clerical shirt. Father Michael Garibaldi was now wearing a long black, ankle-length cassock that buttoned from the collar all the way down to the hem, with a rosary of jet beads hanging from the black grosgrain sash around his trim waist. A flashback exploded in her head: the night of her mother's death, Father

155

McKinney arriving at the hospital dressed in a cassock. She had never seen him in one before, and she had accused him of choosing it as a weapon in his power play, expecting the clerical garb to influence her mother.

The things she had accused him of that night, and the Church, and God . . .

"Why arc you dressed like *that?*"

"There's no mention in the papers about the guy you ran with," he said, locking the laptop case, setting it by the door, "so I don't think Havers or the police know about me. I figure that by dressing like this I'm buying us some time. People will see the priest and pay no attention to the woman with him."

"Why are we leaving?"

He tossed the newspaper to her. "You've been ID'd."

Catherine couldn't believe it. There was her face on the front page again, except that this time it wasn't a police artist's sketch but a recent photograph. The caption identified her as Catherine Alexander, Ph.D., of Santa Monica, California. *Wanted in connection with Wo murders, burglary, international theft and smuggling, industrial sabotage.* Catherine quickly scanned the article. *"Dr. Alexander is believed to have been involved in a break-in and burglary at a science research laboratory in Silicon Valley where bombs placed in wastebaskets caused considerable damage. . . ."*

The story was a long one. Absolutely everyone, it seemed, was being questioned: the director of the foundation, Mr. Mylonas at the Isis Hotel, Samir, U.S. customs agents. Catherine searched for Julius's name. It wasn't there.

"We can't hang around here," Garibaldi said. "Someone might remember seeing you last night, before you changed your hairstyle."

She watched him tuck the pangamot sticks under his arm. "Father Garibaldi, I started to leave you last night."

"I know. I wasn't asleep." He looked at her. "What made you come back?"

"The fog was murder on my hair."

Their eyes connected for one skipped heartbeat and then they heard a siren in the distance, and when they realized it was drawing closer, they grabbed their things, jumped into the car, and Michael floored it out of the parking lot.

"DR. VOSS, ARE you aware that smuggling artifacts into this country is a crime? And are you aware that this is what Dr. Alexander is suspected of doing? Where is she now? What is her connection with the murder of Daniel Stevenson?"

Julius rose from his desk and massaged his temples. He couldn't get the imaginary interrogation out of his mind. It had come to him the day before, as he had pulled up to the police station with the intention of telling them about Catherine. In the end he hadn't gotten out of his car. "You say this woman's name is Catherine Alexander," the police would say. "And you know for a fact that she smuggled scrolls into this country?"

It would have been blowing the whistle on her.

So far, up until last night anyway, the authorities had not known Catherine's identity, what her connection to Daniel was, or that she was in possession of stolen artifacts. And Julius, changing his mind and pulling out of the police parking lot, had decided they weren't going to learn any of that from him. Besides, as of last night, Catherine had still had a chance to clear herself.

But that was last night. The foggy morning had delivered a rude awakening in the form of the *Los Angeles Times,* with Catherine's real face on the front page, and her identity.

Julius thanked God she was still alive. Seeing her on the front page had upset him, but the relief to discover that she seemed to be okay was overwhelming. The article didn't mention anything about the man she had supposedly left Daniel's apartment with; so it didn't appear she had been kidnapped after all.

He picked up the paper and read the article again. It said the police found nineteen photographs. But Catherine had told him she had photographed every scroll page, over a hundred. Had whoever killed Daniel taken the rest?

He threw the paper onto his cluttered desk and thrust his hands into his pockets. He felt so helpless. He wanted to do something for her. But what?

And then he thought: *find the seventh scroll.*

How? Surely Catherine was also searching for the seventh scroll, and so was the person who had killed Stevenson. And God only knew how many others were involved in this insane treasure hunt, all of whom appeared to possess the "map"—whether it was scrolls or photo-graphs of the scrolls, which possibly contained clues.

As he paced his office, he tried to think back to that rainy after-noon at his house, when Catherine had shown up unexpectedly from Egypt and laid a most astonishing bounty of papyrus on his coffee table. What had she said? "Perpetua tells Aemelia to take the final scroll to a king should she fear persecution." But King who? What had that name been?

Julius rubbed his forehead, his temples, and his neck to get the circulation going, hoping it would dislodge the blocked memory. He closed his eyes and pictured the bundles of papyrus. Catherine had opened one out. He remembered bending over it, scrutinizing the ancient Greek writing that, although barely discernible in some places, had been remarkably clear in others. A name had jumped out at him.

Whose name? It wasn't the king; someone else.

Picking up the newspaper, he read the translation again, noting the names: *Aemelia, Perpetua, Sabina.* It would be a simple matter to scan indexes to papyrus archives and see if any contained a fragment bearing one of these names. But such a process, even on a computer, would be lengthy and time-consuming. And Catherine, he feared, didn't have much time.

If only he could recall the name he had read on the papyrus!

He went to the door of his office and started to open it. But he stopped. He had no idea where he was going. He certainly couldn't work. And by now other staff members would be arriving, carrying their morning papers. Everyone knew that Julius and Catherine were an item, there would be talk, questions, or worse, polite awkward silence.

He shouldn't have come in today. He should be out in the world, doing something for Catherine.

But, dammit, what?

In all his life he had never felt so helpless.

He went to the window and looked out. Although it was eight o'clock in the morning, the Christmas lights festooned across Wil-shire Boulevard were already on. They weren't supposed to light up until dark, but apparently the overcast morning was sunless enough to fool the light sensors. Tepid red and green lights nestled in tired tinsel—the decorations were much more fabulous at night.

Fabianus.

Julius drew in a sharp breath.

That was the name! Fabianus!

Turning away from the window, he crossed to the wall of shelves crammed with books and journals. Who was Fabianus? he wondered as he scanned titles, looking for a place to start. Sabina's father? A man she married? Possibly the king to whom the seventh scroll was given?

He went to his desk and booted up his computer, mentally running down the list of search engines: Lycos, InfoSeek, OmniSearch. . . .

"Mrs. Meritites. . . ."

He stopped.

That was why Catherine had used the mummy's name in her cryptic phone message! To remind him of the petty jealousy last year, the intramural rivalry the queen's discovery had sparked—one ex-colleague had even had Julius's phone tapped!

He frowned. Why would Catherine think someone would tap his phone and computer? In irritation he shut the machine down. If he couldn't use his computer, how was he going to search for the seventh scroll?

He looked at the newspaper again, lying on his desk. Local and federal law-enforcement agencies were contacting anyone who had any connection to Dr. Alexander. He knew that it was only a matter of time before they found out about him. How to avoid them until he had at least thought everything through?

Quickly grabbing his tweed jacket, the newspaper, and his battered leather briefcase, Julius left his office, hurried through the maze of corridors and laboratories that made up the institute, then he delivered himself into the gloomy morning filled with salty ocean dampness and the threat of rain, and thinking, I'll go up to the cabin. Too late he saw the TV vans, the news crews, cameras, and the police car pulling up to the curb.

MILES HAVERS FELT his ears pop as his private jet began its descent. He consulted his watch. The flight had taken just over six hours.

It hadn't been necessary for him to come. Miles could have sent his attorney to handle the transaction. But the scrolls meant too much to him to trust anyone but himself to close the deal.

If the police possessed nineteen of the photographs, one of which had been printed in the newspapers, Miles reasoned that all he had to do was find copies of the other eighteen.

So far, he had located only three: one in the Duke University archive, the second at the British Museum—both of which were small fragments in poor condition, with neither shedding any new light on the life of Sabina Fabiana. But the third papyrus, in the personal collection of a Mr. Aki Matsumoto, wealthy Japanese businessman, had been written up in *Archaeology* magazine, along with a photo of the excellently preserved sixth-century parchment, said to be a copy of a second-century papyrus. The name Fabiana could be clearly read.

Miles intended to possess that document.

The yellow light on the intercom beside his seat flashed several times, the pilot's signal that they were on the approach to Hilo Airport. Miles looked down at the aquamarine ocean below, the islands strung out like scattered emeralds. It had been a difficult decision, to personally make this trip, leaving Erica at home to deal with the house full of guests and to oversee preparations for their New Year's Eve bash in ten days—a star-studded gala that was promising to be Oscar night, the Inaugural Ball, and the Cannes Film Festival all rolled into one. But Miles was possessed. He knew what a deep satisfaction it would bring, if he could greet his guests knowing that, far below the house in his private museum, the rare and relatively "virgin" Sabina scrolls were housed.

The jet landed and taxied to the far side of the airport, where private planes shared service hangars with small freight airlines and flying schools. The steward, who had seen to Havers's needs during the six-hour flight, opened the cabin door and admitted a sultry Hawaiian breeze. He came back a moment later to inform his employer that the contact had arrived.

Miles looked out the window and saw a sleek black Mercedes limousine parked out on the tarmac, its smoked-glass windows rolled up.

The unseen passenger in the rear seat, Miles knew, was Mr. Matsumoto, a small soft-spoken man with pale skin and mournful eyes. Matsumoto, on the other hand, did not know the identity of the man he was doing business with. In delicate negotiations of this sort, Miles always preserved his anonymity; all written and telephone contact with Matsumoto had been conducted through Miles's attorney. And he had purposely not come in the corporate jet, with the Dianuba logo on the side, but his own smaller Hawker Siddeley HS-12T executive jet, plain white with no identifying marks.

Miles handed an envelope to the steward, who already had his instructions, although he didn't know that the envelope contained photographs of Aki Matsumoto's fourteen-year-old daughter in bed with a popular kung-fu movie star. The steward then left the plane, approached the limousine, and, while Miles watched unseen from the jet, handed the envelope through the chauffeur's window.

Havers had offered Mr. Matsumoto a generous sum of money for the Fabiana parchment, but had been turned down. So Miles had changed to another kind of currency, one that he suspected Matsumoto might find more persuasive. He saw the chauffeur take the envelope; a moment later another envelope was handed in exchange to the steward, who immediately brought it aboard the aircraft.

Remaining seated in the plush comfort of his dove gray leather chair, Miles opened the stiff cardboard slip cover and inspected the parchment, along with the certificate of authentication that it had been accurately dated to 568 C.E. Then he handed the steward a second sealed envelope, which contained the negatives to the photographs in the first envelope.

While the transaction was being wordlessly concluded at the limousine, Miles scrutinized the document for key words that he had learned to recognize—*Aemelia, Perpetua, Sabina, Cornelius Severus.* There were none that he could identify, nor any other words that appeared to be proper names. The word *Fabiana,* however, was clear and distinct at the bottom, where the document appeared to end in midsentence. Handling the sheet with care, he placed it in the onboard computer's scanner, and immediately faxed the image to Cairo, with the added post scriptum that a clearer photographic image would follow as soon as he returned to New Mexico.

The limousine drove away and the steward came back on board. Since the jet was still refueling, Miles decided to step outside and stretch his legs. He lifted his face to the tropical sunshine, feeling good about his transaction and about the chase for the scrolls in general.

Dr. Catherine Alexander had been identified in the newspapers. Now that she was a prisoner of her own face, there was little she could do without risking being spotted. She wasn't free to roam the world as he was, picking up fragments here, documents there. She couldn't even go into a library to use an encyclopedia!

The odds were definitely on the side of the tiger.

"THE URGENCY IN this matter, Mr. President," the Egyptian ambassador was saying, "is compounded by the fact that we have reason to believe that certain private parties are after the scrolls. We cannot allow the papyrus to fall into their hands."

The President glanced at his aide, the only other person in the Oval Office besides the two visitors. "Mr. Dawud," he said to the ambassador, "on what does your government base its suspicions that there *are* scrolls?"

Dawud, a small energetic man who spoke quickly with staccato gestures, said, "First of all, papyrus was found. And then Dr. Alexander found a basket in a nearby well. She emptied the basket and refilled it with rocks, leaving it for us to find after she left. We have examined the basket and found flakes of papyrus, as well as reddish-brown fibers which match fibers found on the skeleton in the well." He started to sit, but then remained standing, a man whose thoughts were flying ahead of his words. "Mr. President, if Dr. Alexander did not steal scrolls from us, then why did she leave Egypt so abruptly? Why is she in hiding? Why did she visit a research facility and then set off explosions in order to create a diversion when she left?"

The President turned to his adviser. "Do we know yet what Dr. Alexander was after at the facility?"

"They've determined that she downloaded a software program, sir."

"What kind of a program?"

"It's called Logos. A tool for translating ancient Greek."

"Mr. President," Dawud said, "I am sure that I need not remind you of the terrible state of Egyptian economy due to the loss of the tourist industry. And I know that I do not have to impress upon you what these scrolls could mean to our economy should we be able to display them. As it is, the loans your government is making to ours are barely enough. . . ." He let his voice trail off dramatically, to make his point.

The fourth person in the room had said little so far. Tall and aristocratic in a tailored suit, white hair impeccably kept in place with gold clips, she spoke in an arch tone, her words those of someone used to being in authority. "Mr. President, with all due respect to Mr Dawud, need I remind you that if the scrolls are indeed Christian then they rightfully belong to the Church?"

The President had locked horns with her before, on issues involving abortion, contraception, sex education, and gay rights, all of which she staunchly opposed. Her voice alone was strong, but it was the voice behind her that the President was listening to now, because Dr. Zorah Kane, professor of medicine at Harvard University, wasn't here tonight as an independent agent speaking for herself but as the appointed representative of a greater power: the Vatican. His Holiness himself had selected her to oversee this matter on behalf of the Church. "I assume, Mr. President, that I can report to His Holiness that we can expect the full cooperation of your government?"

"Mr. President," Dawud interjected. "The scrolls were found on Egyptian soil—"

As Dr. Kane began to retort, the President offered words of diplomatic assurance to both visitors, adding, "Federal agencies have already been brought in, so we should have results very soon." At the same time he mentally cursed Catherine Alexander, whom he had never met, for putting him in this spot.

TITUS THRUST HIS hands into his pockets as he studied the map glowing beneath his desk top. Lights and numbers sparkled and winked, just like the Seattle skyline behind him, twinkling against the night sky. He focused on the bright light labeled "San Francisco."

"My guess is she headed there," he said to the other man in the room. "Big city. Lots of people. Lots of places to hide."

His assistant, a man who had been with Titus from the beginning, when Security Consultants, Inc. had been operated out of Titus's one-room apartment, picked up the tiger figurine on the desk and, examining it, said, "We've searched as far south as San Simeon and as far east as Fresno. There's no vacancies the length of the coast. People are huggin' the ocean like it was life's blood. Must be thinkin' that's where the apocalypse is going to happen."

"Or *not* happen," Titus murmured. "She's in this area somewhere. But where . . . ?"

"What's her biggest need?" the other man asked.

Titus absently scratched a scar on his chin, a memento from his days with the CIA. "Her biggest need? The client says she needs Internet access. And she needs it anonymously."

"Anonymous Internet access?" The other man grinned.

CATHERINE HAD BEEN worried that they would stand out in the crowd and be easily spotted. But the late-night denizens of the At Dot Com Cafe showed no interest in the Catholic priest in a long black cassock and his platinum blond companion with the blue gym bag slung over her shoulder. In fact, Catherine noticed as she looked around the noisy cybercafe on Sutter Street in San Francisco, she and Father Garibaldi looked depressingly normal among the nerds, Netheads, Webaholics, chat freaks, hacker wannabes, and newbies who sat glassy-eyed at monitors, fingers flying over keyboards.

The cafe boasted fifty-six computers with direct Internet access, and the tables were fitted with Internet connections for customers' laptops. The walls were made to look like giant circuit boards, and signs warned that patrons making too frequent use of the words *cyber* and *techno* would be thrown into the street. The air was filled with the smell of coffee and chocolate; above the din of clattering keyboards, conversations were shouted from table to table, consisting mostly of talk about the new Dianuba 2000 software, due to be released one minute after midnight on New Year's Eve.

Michael leaned close to Catherine and murmured, "I think we'll be able to accomplish a lot here."

She agreed. "Our top priority is dating the scrolls. Sabina mentions visiting the temple at Ur Magna. We know the temple there was destroyed by an earthquake far back in history, but I don't recall the date. If Ur Magna was destroyed before Jesus lived, then the Righteous One couldn't possibly be him. And I'm sure that once that was known, then everyone would back off and leave us alone, Havers included."

Michael took her arm, protectively. "Let's see if we can locate a couple of available computers next to each other. Stay close to me."

THE MEN IN the white Pontiac waited on the tarmac as the private jet taxied to a stop. Four men disembarked. Two got into the Pontiac, the others into a rental car parked alongside. The leader of the new arrivals had brought with him a list of all the cybercafes in the San Francisco area.

"Let's go," he said.

THEY HAD TO wait for a computer, so they took a booth in the coffee bar, where Catherine picked up a newspaper lying on a chair. She skimmed it, then quietly read to Father Michael: "U.S. Customs Service said today that Dr. Catherine Alexander entered the country through JFK airport four days ago, on December 16. Customs officials have no idea how the manuscripts made their way from the Sinai to the United States, and wish to question Dr. Alexander in this matter. Although Dr. Catherine Alexander has not yet been formally charged with any offense, authorities in both Egypt and the United States believe that two murders—one of American construction engineer J. J. Hungerford, and the other of archaeologist Dr. Daniel Stevenson—are connected to the smuggled scrolls and to the disappearance of Dr. Alexander, who is believed to be hiding somewhere in Southern California."

"The paper still describes you with long red hair," Michael said, "which means those guys back at the rest stop weren't cops."

"Havers's men."

"Or someone else's. I think the manhunt is growing and that your chances of surviving out in public are getting thin fast. I am really getting worried for your safety."

She looked at him. "Are you?"

He couldn't put it into words, his growing feeling of protectiveness of her. When four guys took the next table, Michael slipped closer to Catherine, stretched his arm along the back of the booth. As he scanned the cafe crowd, he watched Catherine as she, too, kept a sharp lookout. He noticed how she tipped her chin now and then, an unconscious gesture of challenge or defiance. He could picture her singled-handedly taking on an army, fists flying to the very end. He also noticed, from this angle, that her hair was uneven behind her ear, where he hadn't trimmed it properly. The sight of it made him ache; he wanted to brush it back, make it less obvious.

Suddenly he was remembering his dream from the night before, the same one from his past, and yet not the same. A new player had entered the scene—a woman—and this time not just on the periphery but in the center of the action. He still couldn't see her face, but she seemed to be trying to tell him something.

"Yes," he said finally.

Catherine brought her gaze back to him. "Yes what?"

"I am worried about you."

And for an instant, the cafe and the crowd vanished; the vinyl booth was the universe in which Michael and Catherine saw only each other.

Then he drew back and shifted his posture. "It's getting increasingly dangerous for you, Dr. Alexander," he said, using words to create distance.

"So you think I should quit, turn myself in, is that it? You saw the news today." They had stopped for lunch in Daly City at a diner with a TV set suspended over the counter. There had been an update from the Sinai where the Egyptian government was excavating Catherine's well. They had exposed the skeleton, which they had determined to be female, and had discovered that her hands and wrists had been bound. "They said it looked as if she had been buried alive. She was martyred for those scrolls."

"So that's why you're risking your own life, because of a possible Christian martyr?"

"Father Garibaldi," Catherine said; then, quickly glancing around, lowered her voice. "My mother was more than a professor of theology. She dared to challenge accepted Bible translation. She had the courage to point out that in Genesis, the tradition that Eve was created as a helper to Adam was the result of male bias. The Hebrew word doesn't mean 'helper,' it means 'strong equal.' And in Deuteronomy," she continued passionately, "verse thirty-two, it says 'You were unmindful of the rock that begat you, you forgot the god who fathered you.' But the Hebrew term that was translated as 'fathered' actually means 'writhing in labor.' I would bet the rent, Father, that the men who translated the Bible didn't like the image of God writhing in labor like a woman. So they altered it. And Paul's use of the title *diakonos*—"

Michael held up his hand. "Whoa, I'm on your side, remember?"

"You can't be. When it comes to Catholic dogma we have to be on opposite sides of the fence."

"I don't think the Church treats women shabbily. Catholics are the ones who venerate the Blessed Mother, don't forget."

"The veneration of Mary and the treatment of human women are two very different things, Father Garibaldi. When I learned that I couldn't receive all seven Sacraments because I was a girl, I ran home crying, only to have my mother explain that Holy Orders was one of the Sacraments and that girls can't become priests."

"Well, that's—"

"Father Garibaldi, I was a passionately devout little Catholic girl, and I wanted more than anything to help serve at the altar. But only boys were permitted. And some of those boys, I tell you, were obnoxious little twerps who secretly drank the sacramental wine and made fun of the priests behind their backs. I wouldn't have done that, and yet I wasn't worthy to serve as an altar girl! And in 1965, when I was two years old, my mother applied to teach at Yale and was turned down because they didn't want a woman on staff!"

"I didn't make the rules," he said quietly.

"There were only women at the foot of the cross, women took the body down and gave it a decent burial, women held vigil at the tomb while the apostles were away in hiding, afraid for their lives, and when Jesus reappeared the first person he revealed himself to was a woman. *When did the men take over?*"

"You're preaching to the choir. I've never been opposed to the ordination of women as priests."

The waiter came by then with two coffees and a bowl of pretzels. Catherine waited while Michael paid with cash, asking the waiter to let them know as soon as a computer was free. Then she continued: "In 1973 my mother came out with a small scholarly book titled *Mary Magdalene, The First Apostle.*"

Michael nodded. "It was on the seminary's forbidden index."

"So you never read it."

"No, I read it." He smiled. "I still had a lot to learn about obedience in those days."

"The reason that book caused such an uproar," Catherine said, "is because my mother's previous works had all focused on women in women's roles, even a paper proposing that Mary Magdalene had been Jesus' *wife* didn't cause a stir, because my mother was dealing with the

Magdalene in a *traditional female role.* However, with the *Apostle* book, she had overstepped the bounds. She had dared to place Mary in a *man's* job, and that was not to be tolerated."

Catherine paused. Then she said, "Father Garibaldi, nowhere in the New Testament does it say that Mary Magdalene was a prostitute. That particular tradition can be traced back to the early centuries, when many factions were still fighting for power over the Church. By declaring Mary to have been a prostitute, the Church stripped her of dignity and power, and robbed her of her true status, which was as the *first* apostle."

A sudden eruption of cheers in the next room startled them. They heard excited chatter about hacking into AlphaWorld. Catherine turned her back on the commotion, her eyes shining with passion. "The Greek word *apostle,* Father Garibaldi, means one who has witnessed and has been sent to preach the Word. Mary Magdalene fulfilled these criteria in that she witnessed both the empty tomb *and* the risen Christ and then proclaimed the news to others. But later, *Peter* lay claim to be Jesus' successor as head of the new Church by virtue of the fact that *he* had been the first to witness the resurrection! Am I right?"

Michael nodded.

"So for two thousand years men have succeeded Peter as supreme Pontiff, basing their papal authority on his. An authority that was in fact stolen! Now tell me, Father Garibaldi, what if scrolls were found that could prove Mary Magdalene was Jesus' successor—Sabina's scrolls maybe, that *predate* the gospels. Can you imagine the impact on the Church? It would be like going to someone's house, knocking on their door, and saying, 'May I see the deed to your house?' You look at it and then you produce a deed with an older date and you say, 'I'm sorry, this house is really mine. You have to move out.'"

He thoughtfully stirred his coffee. "So that's why you've been fighting to hold on to the scrolls," he said. "You're on a mission to finish your mother's work."

An image flashed in her mind: the news photo of her father, kneeling with the others. It had been on the front pages around the world.

"My mother was silenced," Catherine said bitterly, pushing the image away. "But I am going to take a stand, I am not going to be silenced. Yes, I have broken the law. I did steal artifacts from Egypt and smuggle them into this country. But sometimes you have to break the law in order to do the right thing. If Sabina has an important message for us, then the world deserves to hear it."

She felt for the jade amulet around her neck, her connection to Daniel, and as soon as her fingers curled around it, she could feel Danno in the jade, sense his strength there, his terrier pugnacity, urging her to go on. "It said miscreant, Cathy," Danno had said to her long ago, after the day Sister Immaculata had humiliated her in front of the class, calling her a filthy little girl. Catherine had asked Danno about the sign Sister had hung about her neck as she stood on the stool. "It said miscreant." Although neither of the ten-year-olds had known what it meant.

"And there's one more reason why I won't give up," Catherine said as she pulled her Visa card out of her wallet. "They killed Danno."

"GOT HER!" TEDDY shouted. "She just used her credit card again!"

"To sign up with an access provider?" Havers said.

"In a roundabout way," he said with a grin. "Dr. Alexander is in a cybercafe in San Francisco. It's called the At Dot Com. She just paid for five hours' online and two pastrami sandwiches."

The Third Scroll

HIS FOLLOWERS ARE *baptized, his mother was a virgin, and in his lifetime he performed miracles, healed the sick, made the lame to walk, and cast out devils. On the night before he died, he celebrated a last supper with his twelve disciples, and in memory of this his followers, who call him Son of Man and Messiah, partake of a sacramental meal in which they eat bread marked with a cross. And when I heard that his triumph over death and his ascension to heaven are celebrated at the spring equinox, I knew that I had found the Righteous One at last.*

I was eager to ask him the question that burdened my heart.

We had come to Persia following Cornelius Severus's thirst to discover the secrets of alchemy, astrology, and living forever. And so when Severus met with magi, I went to the temple of the Savior whom I thought was the Righteous One.

But when I sought to enter into the mysteries, as I had done in Ur Magna, I was told that this religion is forbidden to women. And it was in this way that I learned I had not found the Righteous One at all, for the savior the Persians worshipped turned out to be Mithra, who is also worshipped back in Antioch and in Rome, where every year- on the twenty-fifth of December the faithful celebrate his birth.

In Persia I met also the followers of Zoroaster, a prophet who had been born to a virgin mother, and who lived hundreds of years ago, yet whose life and works were so similar to those of the Righteous One that I wondered if Zoroaster had been reincarnated in Judea.

According to his many followers, the birth of the prophet Zoroaster marked the beginning of the final three thousand years that the world would exist; he is to be followed by three saviors, they said, each arriving at a thousand-year interval. At the appearance of the last, which the followers calculate will be two thousand years from now, Judgment Day will occur, those who fought against evil will be offered the drink of immortality, and a new creation will be established.

This is what the Persians preach: "Then will come the general resurrection when the righteous shall enter into heaven and the wicked shall be purified by molten metal. From that day forward, all will enjoy happiness and sing the praises of the Eternal One."

But Zoroaster turned out not to be the Righteous One, whom I still sought. And so when Cornelius Severus told us that he was traveling on to the Indus Valley, I again joined his caravan. For, while in Persia, I had heard of a Savior in India, called Redeemer, and born of a virgin, crucified, and resurrected. The stories of his birth were familiar to me, that when he was born on the twenty-fifth of December, wise men brought him gifts of gold, frankincense, and myrrh. And so I knew for certain that to India was where the Righteous One had gone.

And there in the Indus Valley, dear Perpetua, dear Aemelia, I was to receive yet another revelation—the third of the Seven Truths.

DAY EIGHT

Tuesday
December 21, 1999

When Julius emerged from the rear entrance of the institute, he didn't go straight to his car in its reserved space, but instead walked across the lot and out to the street where a car was parked at the curb. He knocked on the window, startling the driver.

"I'm going to grab a bite to eat at Johnny's in Culver City," he said when the man rolled the window down. "Do you know where that is? Just go straight down Pico and turn right at Sepulveda. After that I'm going to do some Christmas shopping at Santa Monica Place. And then I'm going to pay a visit to my rabbi at the synagogue over on San Vicente. I'll try to drive slowly so you don't lose me."

Julius had no idea who the man was or who he worked for—the police or a private party, or maybe he was a reporter—but he had been following Julius for two days. And it so annoyed Julius to have his privacy invaded this way, that he had decided to let this goofball, whoever he was, know that he was very much aware of him.

When they arrived at the synagogue in the late afternoon, Julius waved to the guy, wondering when he took the time to eat or visit a rest room, and went inside.

Rabbi Goldman had been at the synagogue for as long as the oldest

173

member could recall; what his age was, no one knew. He greeted Julius with a bright smile and sharp, lively eyes. "Such a pleasure it is to see you, Julius!" he said as they shook hands.

"Thank you for seeing me on such short notice, Rabbi Goldman."

"What can I do for you?"

"I was wondering, Rabbi," Julius said as he looked around the cluttered, musty interior of the rabbi's residence, the home of a true book lover and scholar, "if I might use your computer for about an hour?"

THE CROWD SCREAMED as the bull raced toward the half-naked girl, and then they cheered when she deftly grabbed the animal by the horns, leaped onto its back, and did a somersault, landing on her feet behind the bull in an exact re-creation, the management of the Atlantis Hotel boasted, of the ancient Minoan sport of bull-leaping as it was practiced on the island of Crete over three thousand years ago.

Right in the middle of the hotel lobby.

But bull-dancing wasn't the strangest feature of Las Vegas's newest and tackiest resort hotel, Father Garibaldi thought as he threaded his way through the crowds toward Reception. As weird and outlandish as some of the Atlantis features were, none beat the fact that the twenty-story hotel, set on an island in the center of a sixty-acre lake, didn't have a single elevator.

The motif of the resort, which faced the Beau Rivage across Las Vegas Boulevard, was, according to one critic, "Mars Meets Minos," one of the main attractions being the Minotaur's Maze beneath the colossal hotel, while above were ancient frescos and columns, statues and pillars, but super-futuristic architecture as well, including, zigzagging across the open space of the world's largest atrium, the anti-gravity "spaceships" that ferried guests to and from the hotel's four thousand rooms. Although the ships did indeed give the impression of flying completely without support, the illusion, according to hotel guidebooks, was created by lights, lasers, and trompe l'oeil architecture hiding the very solid rails upon which the Martian ships "flew."

The Atlantis was such a popular attraction that it was always booked to capacity, always teeming with gawking tourists. "We'll be safe there," Michael had assured Catherine when they had left San Francisco. "No one will find us in those crowds."

But even so, as Michael reached the desk to speak to the concierge, and he noticed how people stared at him, he realized that he stood out after all. Priests in long black cassocks were not a common sight in a casino.

Still, he considered his attire good camouflage, and this hotel a wise choice for a place to hide. Nonetheless, he was on the alert, his senses more heightened than ever. If anyone got to Catherine, it was going to have to be through him, and they had better be prepared, Michael vowed, for a fight.

And would you kill to protect her? a voice whispered at the back of his mind.

Let's hope it never comes to that.

But would you ?

A memory, unbidden, flashed in his mind: the feel of Catherine in his arms when she had wept against his shoulder upon the news of Daniel's death.

Michael forced his attention to the busy street beyond the restaurant's large window. Las Vegas, he thought, a town like no other. Always a crazy, over-the-top place, this month it seemed that even Vegas was weird for Vegas. He had felt it as soon as he and Catherine had driven into town and seen the heavy traffic, the crowds on the sidewalks. There was urgency in the air in these final days of 1999, a frantic pulse that signaled fear, uncertainty, desperate hope. The end of the world was coming—maybe. Or maybe God was coming. Maybe it was spaceships, or maybe just another New Year's hangover. People had come to Vegas, Father Garibaldi suspected, to enjoy a last hurrah in this modern Sodom, to gamble away the mortgage in the hope of grabbing the jackpot before tomorrow didn't come, or perhaps to do something wild, have a fling with a Vegas showgirl, commit sins that otherwise wouldn't be committed, because the world was going to end. Or maybe it wasn't.

"There you are, Father," the concierge said as she handed Michael his temporary Internet account card. "Your user name and password, which only you know. You may log on any time you wish."

One of the newest services offered by the bigger hotels was Internet access through the hotel's own system, the guests being charged a small fee for online time. Business travelers used the service for conferencing and creating virtual offices; for vacationers, the kids were left safely in rooms to cruise the Net while parents went downstairs to gamble.

As Michael headed back across the lobby, passing through the sunlight spilling like a golden waterfall through the tall glass doors, he stopped to buy a newspaper at a kiosk that was supposed to be either a Martian fountain or a Minoan sarcophagus. And as he looked around at the crowd, he heard his question again: *What would you do to protect her?*

And he replied with passion: *I will do whatever is necessary.*

"IT'S CALLED THE Methuselah Syndrome," the guest on the local Santa Fe talk show was saying. "The desire to live forever, or the delusion that one is going to live forever."

"So tell me, Doctor," the host said with a smile, "do you believe these scrolls might contain an ancient magic spell that will enable people to live forever? It certainly is what a lot of people are hoping."

The guest cleared his throat, assumed an air of importance. "Unfortunately, John, we do not know what is in the scrolls, or if the scrolls even exist—or, for that matter, if Catherine Alexander herself still exists! But all this hysteria about living forever has come from one phrase, or rather just two words, that appear in the fragment that has been published in newspapers. *Zoe aionios,*" he said, "which means 'eternal life.'"

"But does it mean eternal life here on earth or in heaven after we die?"

Miles Havers silenced the TV set and went to pour himself a chilled Perrier at the wet bar in his gray and burgundy office. The Second Coming and Living Forever! How the public had latched onto those two phrases in the fragment: *parousia* and *zoe aionios.* What would people do, he wondered, if they knew that the author of the scrolls had in fact traveled in the company of an alchemist searching for the ancient secret of longevity?

They would kill to get hold of it.

As he went to the window to look out at the festivities taking place on the green lawns that abutted his private golf course, he marveled at all the "crackpottery," as his father would call it, going on around the world. The news these days was about nothing but the approaching millennium. The New Jerusalem had been sighted by a watch group in Montana; it was moving toward Earth through space, they said, and would arrive on New Year's Day. Other groups were declaring that astronomers were keeping secret the discovery of a black hole over the North Pole, because it was the gateway to Heaven. Still others claimed to have actually seen the megaliths at Stonehenge move on their own.

In readiness, no doubt, Miles thought wryly, for the return of their Venusian creators!

He sipped the sparkling water and watched the hundreds of children squeal with delight on the carnival rides or line up to see Santa Claus, or shyly approach the generous barbecue buffet before greedily helping themselves. It was Erica's annual Christmas party for disadvantaged children, rounded up from the Indian mission, hospitals, orphanages, even homeless children, all transported to the Havers estate for a once-a-year taste of largesse before being taken back to their miserable existences.

He saw Coyote Man, off to the side.

"We went to Cloud Mesa!" Erica had said breathlessly the night before. "Coyote Man explained that centuries ago the Star People arrived there, flying out of the sky on solar-seed pods. He said that on auspicious nights, if you turn your eyes to the sky, you'll see flying triangles and cosmic bells and tongues of fire!"

Cosmic bells! Tongues of fire! Miles did not like the crafty old shaman. He didn't like the way Coyote Man looked at him sometimes—into him. It was almost as if he could see the tiger.

Goldstein, ten years ago, calling in the middle of the night, saying in a haunted voice: "Hey, Miles. It was a tiger, wasn't it?"

Goldstein had committed suicide shortly after that. *Six went in, and six came out. But only three survived. . . .*

Where were the backbones anymore? Miles wondered. Aki Matsumoto—his obituary had been in the morning's paper. Sepuku, they called it. Ritual suicide over some family dishonor that he wouldn't divulge.

And for what? The sixth-century parchment Miles had obtained from Matsumoto had turned out to be worthless. The translation that came from Cairo had been accompanied by the message that the Fabiana mentioned here was in no way connected to Sabina Fabiana. So the thirteen-hour trip to Hawaii and back had been for nothing.

Time was being wasted!

And that fiasco at the cybercafe! Titus's men rushing in to nab the two pimple-faced nerds who had stupidly picked up Alexander's abandoned credit card and tried to go for a free ride on it!

The intercom buzzed. "It's up and running, Mr. Havers."

"Thank you, Mr. Yamaguchi." All right, the trap was now operational.

The trap he had carefully laid in the Internet, bait for a certain unsuspecting archaeologist to bite on so that he could reel her in.

IT WAS IN the Indus Valley that I received the third of the Immutable Truths. . . .

Catherine paused in her work to look over at Michael at the computer.

They had been able to get a business suite at the Atlantis, which meant two bedrooms with private baths branching off a central living room equipped with two desks, a fax machine, two modem jacks, two separate phone lines, and even a supply of staples, paper clips, rubber bands, and steno pads.

They had ended up not using the services of the At Dot Com Cafe. When Catherine had noticed some suspicious-looking men outside, their conservative suits and haircuts making them stand out in the colorful crowd, she had purposely left her credit card near the cash register, hoping someone would spot it and decide to have a free ride on her Visa account. She liked to imagine the looks on the faces of Havers's men when they moved in, thinking they had caught her.

Watching Michael now, his handsome face set in concentration, she thought about the night before last, when she had tried to leave him. She had written a note and gone out into the fog with the intention of going on alone. What had made her turn back? At the time, she had told herself it was because of the scrolls. She had walked three blocks in the cold and mist and had realized that, for the sake of the scrolls, she was better off staying with Michael.

But was that really the reason?

That first night, in the motel outside Santa Barbara, Michael coming out of the bathroom with no shirt on and Catherine feeling a jolt go through her.

He's a priest, she reminded herself now, something she was having to do with increasing frequency. A priest like Father McKinney, only better packaged.

But it wasn't just that—Catherine knew there was more to Michael Garibaldi than a sexy body. Ever since they had been separated at the rest stop and Michael had found her in the fog at the ranger station, he had stayed close to her, attentive and watchful. When they were in a crowd, he always placed himself between her and anyone who could be a threat; she felt his hand on her arm at all times, sensed his alertness, his readiness to defend her. It was a new experience for Catherine, to be with a man who was so protective of her.

"We're on!" Michael said suddenly. As she joined him at the computer, bringing two chilled glasses of 7-Up with her, Michael went to Net Directory, clicked on it, and clicked again on Lycos.

When Search Form came up, he typed in Ur Magna, and they both held their breath. "Four sources found!" he announced.

"The dig," Catherine said, pointing to the fourth entry in the list. "Click on that."

And a full-color image came up of an archaeological dig in a tawny desert. "The ruins of Ur Magna," Michael read, "currently undergoing reconstruction by a team composed of—"

"There!" Catherine said. "Ur Magna was destroyed by a massive earthquake in—"

"One hundred a.d.!" Michael finished. "Which means Sabina was there in the first century."

"Which increases the odds that Sabina's Righteous One is Jesus!"

"What next?" Michael said, hands poised over the keyboard. "There's nothing we can't find now, especially with this faster software. Sorry," he quickly added. "Guess I didn't have to mention that." The computer system of the Atlantis used Dianuba Technologies software, including the swift new Scimitar.

"It's all right. I would get a certain satisfaction out of beating Miles Havers by using his own software! See if you can find the URL for the Papyrology Page."

As he typed, Michael turned to her briefly to send her a smile, and Catherine felt the jolt again. Only a few times in her life had she experienced such a high—the adrenaline rush brought on by danger and the thrill of discovery. She and Michael might be sitting at a harmless computer, but she had a sense that they were running through cyberspace, a pair of daring adventurers defying death, going for the prize. And he felt it, too. Catherine realized that she was somehow sensing what he was feeling; she saw the excitement in his eyes, and the way he smiled—this man who only a week ago had been a total stranger—sent secret messages that said: *We're in this together, it's Us against Them.*

Catherine suddenly had to get up, walk around the room and work the restless energy out of her. She glanced at the TV, which was on but muted. There was her face on the screen again. She turned up the sound.

An anchorwoman was saying, "A spokesman for the FBI said today that they expect to arrest Dr. Catherine Alexander at any time now."

Michael rose from the desk. "Isn't there anything else going on in the world?" he said in irritation. "This is becoming a circus!"

"In related news," the anchor continued, "the Egyptian government is demanding that the Santa Barbara police department turn over the rest of the photographs to them. But the police are saying that the photographs are evidence in a murder investigation and cannot be released. Egyptian authorities are taking their protest directly to the White House."

The news was followed by an in-studio interview with a man who was introduced as a spiritual specialist. "Dr. Cochran," the anchorman said, "why is there such a growing spiritual movement in this country?"

"Because the Boomers are aging, Steve. We're starting to bury our parents. It forces us to face our own mortality and to ask, What comes after?"

"Then why isn't there a bigger return to the traditional church?"

"Well, Steve, I'm a former Catholic but now I'm a New Ager, like a lot of my friends. And I speak for all of us, I think, when I say that we rejected the faiths of our parents because they don't suit today's needs. Frankly, Steve, a lot of us think Catholicism is just too old."

Michael shook his head and murmured, "A faith lost in the dust of centuries. Don't you think it's ironic, to reject a faith because it's old?"

"All he did was exchange rosaries and saints for crystals and angels," Catherine said. She changed the function from TV to radio, tuning across several music stations until she came to a call-in talk show. "We have with us tonight Dr. Raymond Pearson," the host announced, "founder of the Historical Jesus Society. What can you tell us about this papyrus fragment, Dr. Pearson?"

Michael went back to his desk, picked up his 7-Up and scowled at the TV/radio console. "Well, Edie," Dr. Pearson replied, "for one thing, paleographic examination places the writing around the first or second century of the Common Era. We know it was written by a woman, and that she is most likely addressing early Christians—the word *diakonos* would indicate that. And, of course, there's the word *Jesus* in it. If these scrolls were indeed written by members of the very earliest Christian church, then they might tell us what Christianity was all about when it started."

"Dr. Pearson, some Church spokesmen say these scrolls might be blasphemous or heretical."

Pearson chuckled. "Rather than feeling threatened by these scrolls, Edie, today's established churches should embrace what the scrolls can tell us about the beginnings of our faith, free of the myths and mysticism and fables that have attached themselves to Christianity^ over the centuries. The final result could be liberating."

"Are you saying, Dr. Pearson, that the New Testament doesn't tell us what the original Christian Church was like?"

As Catherine stood and listened, she sensed Michael behind her.

"Probably not," Dr. Pearson said. "The gospel known as Mark was written around the year 65, Matthew and Luke are generally believed to have been written twenty years later, John around the year 95. You see, despite intensive search, no original manuscripts of the four gospels have ever been found. They've been lost through time."

"Then how can we even trust the New Testament?"

"Because we do have early *copies*. For example, in 1925 a small fragment of papyrus was found in the Egyptian wilderness and sold to archaeologists in Cairo. Analysis revealed that it was a Greek text containing the gospel of John, but written a hundred years after the crucifixion. In fact, it's the oldest fragment of the New Testament we have. The first bits we have from Luke and Matthew are no earlier than the year 200—that's one hundred and seventy years after Jesus' execution. Finally, a scrap of Mark from the year 225."

"So what you're saying, Dr. Pearson, is that Mark was written around the year 65, and yet it isn't until the year 225 that we get our first copy?"

"Precisely. Makes you wonder what kind of changes the gospel underwent in all that time."

"Okay!" the host said. "The phone lines are open, you know the number, ask Dr. Pearson a question. Texas, you're on the air."

"Listen, Dr. Whoever You Are, you are going to burn in hell for what you've just said—"

"Thank you, Texas. Nebraska, you're on next."

"Dr. Pearson, are you saying that the New Testament isn't the revealed word of God?"

"Oh no, I believe that it is. But we don't know what those *original* revealed words were."

Catherine felt Michael shift behind her, sensed his alertness.

"We know there was a power struggle after Jesus died," Pearson said. "This is clearly documented in Acts. And in the first hundred years there were many different Christian sects all over the Roman Empire, each with different beliefs, rules, and so forth, and everyone arguing over which was the True Faith. There were many gospels and letters being circulated; some groups clung to Peter's teachings, others to Paul's. Remember, Peter insisted that new converts be circumcised, Paul disagreed. These disputes continued for another two hundred years, with splinter groups breaking away and setting up their own churches, each saying that theirs was the True Faith, but each with different rituals and prayers and visions of who Jesus was and what He said. In the fourth century, the most powerful 'camp' won out and put together what they called the New Testament, choosing only four gospels from the many that people were reading at the time, declaring all others to be heretical. However, if the scrolls that Dr. Catherine Alexander allegedly smuggled out of Egypt are in fact an eyewitness account of the Lord's mission here on earth, then we will get our first real look at Christianity's origins and intentions, before all the splintering and fighting. And which might also reveal to us a Church vastly different from the one we recognize today."

"Thank you, Dr. Pearson. Los Angeles, you're on the air. What is your question?"

"First of all, you're full of *<bleep>*, Professor. I think Dr. Alexander is the Antichrist, sent to earth to sway good Christians from the True Path in these final days before the Apocalypse. And if you—"

Catherine gasped. "The Antichrist! He's calling me the Antichrist?"

"Thank you, Los Angeles. Reno, you're on the air."

"Jesus is coming, we know that, and He is going to establish His Thousand-Year reign on earth. My question is, if these scrolls that woman is running with tell us the day and the time, why don't the authorities do something about it and get those scrolls from her so we can prepare?"

"I'm sure the authorities are doing their best to find her. Thank you, Reno. San Francisco, you're on."

"This message is for Catherine Alexander. You are going to burn in Hell, you *<bleep>*."

"Well, folks!" the host said. "Sounds like the public is making its opinion known! St. Louis, you're on."

"Tell that bitch—"

Michael strode across the room and switched the radio into silence. He looked at Catherine. "Are you all right?"

She glared at the dark console. "Why are they saying those things about me? Why is everyone against me?"

"I guess because you've been silent. They're taking your silence as an admission of guilt. People need to hear your side of it. Look," Michael said, "I don't like the way things are going. With all this millennium madness that seems to be robbing people of reason, something serious could happen to you if you were spotted and recognized. Fanatics might kidnap you, or worse. And I'm afraid that even if you were to turn yourself in now the police might not be able to guarantee you protection. Too many crazy people are convinced that either you are evil or the scrolls are."

"Then I have to let people know the truth! I have to tell them my side of it!"

"Great, but how? You can't make any phone calls. They'll be traced."

"I'll use the Internet. I'll post somewhere, and ask them to pass along a message."

He nodded thoughtfully. "It might work, if you post to a site where the most people will read it so you'll have a chance at least of one person passing your message along."

She sat down at the computer and tried to think. "I can't post to WELL or ECHO," she said with a frown, "because they require a subscription. UniCom would be the best, nearly everyone's on that, but they also make you sign up first. Same with the Dianuba Network."

"Well, you can't post to a Usenet group because they'll be able to track you through the header. Which is too bad, because by cross-posting you could reach a lot of people."

"How about IRC? There are some very popular channels on Internet Relay Chat."

"Havers has probably anticipated that you would think of that and already has someone watching for you on the popular channels. As soon as you start your message, he picks up the address of the host server and traces you right back here."

"He can't watch all of them," she said. "There are thousands of IRC channels!"

"True, but most of them usually only have three or four people online at a time. Dropping in on one of those chats doesn't even give you good odds on getting your message believed, let alone passed on."

There had to be a way, Catherine thought as she regarded Danno's laptop case, with its peeling Dianuba Technologies and Microsoft Bob stickers. Opening the case, she brought out the dog-eared copy of *Hawksbill Station* by Robert Silverberg. "This was Danno's favorite book," she murmured. "It's a story about a group of men, isolated from their world and their time, misfits. . . ."

She quickly started typing.

Michael pulled up a chair and sat next to her. "What are you doing?"

"I worked with Danno for a summer down in Mexico. He was looking for a Mayan temple. Every morning and every evening, without fail, Danno spent an hour on the Internet, and I believe it was on Internet Relay Chat." She clicked on the IRC Manager icon. "And I think the channel was called Hawksbill."

"What are you going to say if you find the channel?"

"I'm going to tell them who I am, that I'm innocent, and then I'm going to ask them to spread the message as far and wide as they can." She typed *pasadma.ca.us.uyidernet.org.* Then she hit: Enter.

"How big a group is this?"

She clicked on the icon CONNECT. "Two years ago it had ten members." She kept her eyes on the monitor. *Tour Host is pasadena. ca.us.undernet.org. Server created on 7/23/96 at 16:43 PST. 2,000 users, 1500 invisible on 127 servers.* "I know it's small," she said, "but if I post anonymously to a BBS that a hundred people read, that's the end of it. A hundred people know I'm innocent with no guarantees they'll spread the word. But with this group I think I can count on member loyalty."

On the screen she read:

MOTD: Fake user @host is not allowed on this server. Persistent
    abusers of this rule will have their host banned from this server.
Bots are allowed on this server only with server op approval.
    Absolutely NO clone bots allowed.
End of/MOTD command

"Pray that it's still there, Father," Catherine said as she typed: */list -min 4.*

On the right hand side of the split screen, names and numbers began to appear:

#altair 4
#boychat 7
#dogs 5
#doomsday 9
#england 12
#friendly 32
#german 6

"There it is!" Michael said. "Hawksbill!"

"There are only four people in it. I hope they remember Danno." She highlighted *#hawksbill* and double-clicked. On the screen, You Have Joined Hawksbill appeared, and in a side window the "handles"—nicknames—of everyone currently in the room were listed: BENHUR, DOGbert, spaCeman. The fourth, Jean-Luc, had the @ sign before his or her name, indicating that he or she was the channel operator. "They're still here," Catherine said in amazement.

"Do you know these people?" Michael said.

"No." But Catherine experienced a sudden sense of deja vu: three summers ago, sweltering in the Yucatan rainforest with Danno, she had peered over his shoulder as he had logged on to his morning chat with old friends he had never met. She recalled now these same curious names.

As soon as she joined, an icon in the lower left corner of the screen started flashing and emitting a beeping sound. It read:

IRC private hawksbillbot.

"Uh oh," Michael said. "They're telling you you can't log on, you're a stranger. They'll kick you out if you stay."

Catherine typed */leave* and hit Enter. She then went back to Server/Connection to see what nickname Daniel had entered. It said Klaatu. "I don't understand," she said. "This has to be it."

"Try again then."

She logged back in, ignored the flashing icon, and scrolled down to where the conversation was already in progress.

[spaceman] I'm telling you its a conspiracy. His atlantis theory and
*   everything. Someone wanted him to shutup*
<SERVER> RarebiV.johnjay@mach1.wlu.ca has joined this channel
[Jean-Luc] Yo, Rarebit you rabbit. Long time no see:-))
[Rarebit] Did you read about it? Hawksbill is finished
*   [BENHUR] Conspiracy my aunt mildred's garter!*

"Do you know anything about these people?" Michael asked as the conversation went on in non-location cyberspace.

"Danno didn't even know if they were male or female. That's the rule at Hawksbill Station. They're exiles, they don't talk about their previous lives."

"If they didn't know each other's real identities, then they won't know that the Daniel Stevenson they might have heard about in the news was one of their group."

"Danno created this channel. He was the founder. He and another friend, this Jean-Luc person I think. Look at what they're saying. They're talking about Danno's death."

And then:

> [Jean-Luc] Klaatu: sorry, this is a private channel. You have to leave.

"Not the password problem again," Michael groaned. "We don't have a lot of time, Doctor. If Havers is monitoring the IRC, or if the FBI is . . ."

As she tried to think, she stared at the dog-eared book, Hawksbill Station. Then she picked it up, turned to the first page, and read opening lines, "Barrett was the uncrowned king of Hawksbill Station. No one disputed that. He had been there the longest; he had suffered the most; he had the deepest inner resources of strength."

As she quickly clicked on Server/Connection, deleting Klaatu and entering a new nickname, she said, "Danno probably belonged to more than one channel and used a different handle for each one. I think I've found the one he used here."

She clicked on #hawksbill again and typed, "Greetings, fellow exiles. "

> <Barrett> Greetings, fellow exiles.
> [spaceman] What the heck?!!!
> [BENHUR] Barrett is dead, man :-(
> [Jean-Luc] Leave this channel

Catherine typed: I am Barrett.

> [Jean-Luc] You cant be
> *Rarebit is filled with consternation
> *DOGbert is fainting at the sight of a ghost
> [spaCeman] Throw the impostor out!
> [SERVER] You were warned.
> <Barrett> Wait please I need you
> *DOGbert picks himself up off the floor
> [Jean-Luc] What gives your dead >:-1
> [DOGbert] This isnt funny man, were greeving
> [DOGbert] *grieving*
> <Barrett> I need your help. Dr. Catherine Alexander did not murder me. She is innocent. She was my best friend.

[spaCeman] Your causing grief. We loooost Barrett you magot
<Barrett> Catherine Alexander was my friend. She needs your
*   help badly*
[Jean-Luc] PROVE YOURSELF!!!!!!!!!!!!

"They don't believe you," Michael said, looking at his watch. They had been in IRC for fifteen minutes. "You're going to have to convince them that you really are Daniel's friend and not an impostor. And you're going to have to do it quickly."

She thought for a moment, then she rapidly typed: *"I'm the Cat!"* Danno's signature line.

She hit Enter and waited.

When there was no response, she typed, */me is begging you to listen*, which translated on the other screens as *Barrett is begging you to listen.*

[spaCeman] Whose Catherine alexander?
[DOGbert] Why should we help her
[BENHUR] deth to impostors
[Jean-Luc] Are you Janet?

Catherine stared at the screen.
Michael frowned. "Who's Janet?"
"I have no idea."
"Did Daniel have a girlfriend?"
"He would have told me."

[Jean-Luc] Repeat: Are you Janet?

"They're waiting for an answer."

She bit her lip. Daniel had never mentioned a Janet. "This is my only chance to get their help. I have to win their trust now or forget it. But what if it's a test and I answer yes and it was supposed to be no?"

Michael's gaze fell upon the snapshot of Catherine taped to the inside of the laptop case. "I don't think it's a test," he said after a moment. "I think Daniel must have talked about you, but called you Janet instead of your real name."

"Why?"

He picked up the science fiction book and flipped through it. "Here it is," he said, showing her the page. "Janet was Barrett's lover."

"Lover!"

"I think Daniel was in love with you."

Catherine stared at Michael for a moment, then she quickly typed:

<Barrett> Jean-Luc, yes. Janet.

They watched the screen. Nothing happened for another moment, then it began scrolling quickly.

[Jean-Luc] Barrett: we missed you.

[BENHUR] Is it really you???? < :-)

[DOGbert] The Station isnt the same since you left us. Who killed you. man? Why dont the police get him?

[BENHUR] BRB

[SERVER] BENHUR has left this channel

[Jean-Luc] Barrett: Why were you killed?

[spaCeman] Were mad as hell. What can we do?

<Barrett> Because of what I possessed.

[SERVER] Sugar!~kharvey@scgrad.demon.co.uk has joined this channel.

[DOGbert] Who killed you?

[SERVER] TrilogY!^tombak@ix-or1-22.ix.vetcom has joined this channel

[sugar] BENHUR found me in a MUD Said to join you guys. Whats this about Barret's back?

<Barrett> Jean-Luc: a Bad Guy killed me.

[SERVER] Maynard!~rismith@alice.brad.ac. us has joined this channel

*Trilogy is making faces and saying noway man. Barrets dead!!!!!!

[spaCeman] Just shut up and listen

[Maynard] Hi guys! Anybody get laid lately?

[SERVER] Zipcode!zelinksi@ouray.cudenver.edu has joined this channel

[sugar] Mayn-Man! Welcome back!!!!!

[DOGbert] No sex talk on this channel

[Maynard] Sorry ;-p

[Jean-Luc] Maynard, Barrett is here

[SERVER] Benhur!~George@Sebaka-I.DialUp.PolarisTel.Net has joined this channel.

[Maynard] No way man.

[sugar] way

[Jean-Luc] Barrett: You still there?

[Maynard] I read about it in the paper. He was murdered by a chick that ran from the scene.

[SERVER] Zipcode has left this channel

<Barrett> Catherine Alexander did not kill me. She is innocent. She needs your help, the Bad Guy is after her and wants to kill her too. She was my best friend and now she needs the help of my friends.

[SERVER] Carlos!mmongo@dianuba.com has joined this channel

[TrilogY] Yo, Carlos.

[Carlos] Whats the hap? Benhur pulled me out of alphaworld

[Jean-Luc] Its Barrett

[sugar] Exiles stick together. Barrett, tell us what to do.

[Carlos] Barrett was good, he kicked ass.

<Barrett> Contact Dr. Julius Voss jlvoss@freers.org. Tell him Catherine Alexander is safe and unharmed. Pass the word to everyone on the Net that Dr. Alexander is INNOCENT and that she is being unfairly persecuted. Tell the police that she does NOT know who killed me, that my murderer is after her too and she needs protection.

[TrilogY] Is she the chick with the scrolls?

Catherine thought for a moment. Then she typed:

Help Dr Alexander find Tymbos. Is it a place, a person, or an anagram? I will join you again to see if you have found him/her/it. But I will join under another name because Bad Guy is watching for me. DO NOT TELL ANYONE ELSE ABOUT TYMBOS.

"IS THAT WISE?" Michael said. "If they spread the word Havers might pick it up."

"I'm counting on their loyalty to Danno. I'll log on in a couple of days to see if they've found Tymbos. As I recall, Danno said one of these people was an astrophysicist. Maybe he or she can break the code!"

[sugar] Barrett: what is tymbos?
[TrilogY] Ditto
<Barrett> A person. Or maybe an anagram.
[Jean-Luc) anagram: like what?
<Barrett> Are any of you Christians?

There was a brief silence, then:

[Carlos] John 3:16

"For God so loved the world," Michael recited softly, "that he gave his only begotten son, that whosoever believeth in him should not perish, but have everlasting life."

Catherine typed: *ichthus*

[Carlos] Iesous Christos, theou uios soter
[sugar] Barrett: is tymbos a sentence in Greek or latin?
<Barrett> I don't know, greek I think, help me Tymbos is where the seventh scrol might be.
<Barrett> scroll
[sugar] Barrett/Janet: Does Dr. Alexander have scrolls?
[Jean-Luc] Do they predict the end of the world like everyone says.
[Carlos] the Second Coming?
<Barrett> Dr. Alexander is borrowing something that belongs to all of humankind. When she is done with it, she will give it to the world as a gift. She is one of us. She is running for her life on the Internet. The persecution must stop. And my killer must be found before he kills again. Please disperse this message in the name of a friend we will all miss

Catherine watched the monitor. Her words remained the last ones at the bottom of the screen. "They aren't saying anything," she said.

"They're probably messaging each other privately, trying to decide if you're legit."

They continued to stare at the screen. No new words appeared; the dialogue didn't scroll upward.

"I don't like this," Michael said. "Better log off."

"Wait," Catherine said. "I'm sure we can trust them."

"And I'm not so sure."

Catherine waited another minute. When nothing more appeared on the screen, she typed a final message:

<Barrett> I can't join this channel again because I might get caught. But I will contact all of you in a couple of days. Watch IRC. I will create a channel. *please believe in me* Keep the vigil. . . .

She then typed */leave,* and clicked on the Disconnect Server icon.

File Exit
Dialer Bye
NO CARRIER

THE FOURTH SCROLL

THIS TIME I *was more cautious in my hope, for twice now I had thought I had found the Righteous One, only to be disappointed.*

Cornelius Severus was a man of great dignity and influence; he carried with him a letter from the Emperor that opened doors otherwise locked. And as I had by now been with his company for nearly two years, and in that time had put my midwifery skills to good use—delivering his wife of their third son—Severus invited me to join him in the company of rajahs and queens. I told these noble men and women that I was seeking a wise man whom we of The Way called Redeemer. I told them of his virgin birth, and how he had healed the sick, worked miracles, and preached in parables.

They said, "Yes, he was here!" And I was disappointed to know that I had missed him. But when they said, "He was here twelve hundred years ago," I asked his name, and they said it was Krishna, whose followers are legion. Krishna's earthly mother was a virgin who had been impregnated by a god, they told me, and his birth was announced by a star and attended by wise men and angels and shepherds, who came to honor him. The people who follow Krishna sing a hymn to his mother: "In thy delivery, O favored among all women, all nations shall have cause to exult." He survived a slaughter of innocents when an evil ruler ordered all firstborn to be put to death. And then Krishna was baptized in the River Ganges and he entered into a life of curing lepers, raising the dead, and preaching that the poor are the chosen of God, and that goodness redeems a man from sin.

And what of his death? I asked.

And they said, "Our Lord and Savior Krishna died young and alone, and ascended bodily up to heaven. He was born so that he would suffer and die for the sins of the human race." And in their temple sculptures they depict Krishna suspended upon a cross, his feet pierced.

"But do not mourn," they hastily added, "for the Lord rose again after three days dwelling in the land of the dead. He cast off his shroud and walked among the living again!"

In Persia I had learned that Mithra also rose after spending three days in the underworld, and it is well known that the gods Prometheus and Mars also, upon their executions, sojourned three days among the dead and rose again to walk among the living. And so did my own Lord, the Righteous One.

And I wondered which of these gods was the true one.

A letter arrived from my lawyer in Antioch, the man who had handled my parents' estate and who now handled my finances. I had received a large inheritance from my mother and father, and this man sent me regular reports on the management of my money. He had joined the Community when my mother was deacon, and so he also regularly sent news of the progress of The Way.

In this letter he had included another, written by a woman who had known the Righteous One personally. She had been among the first of his followers and her name was Maria. It was the habit of the Community to copy letters written by those who had known the Righteous One, and disperse these copies among members of The Way in other cities and communities. By this method did the word spread. In Maria's letter, she wrote: "Greetings to the Community in Antioch, from your sister, the kiss of peace. Please receive into your bosom thy faithful servant, Andreas, who carries this letter to you.

"Bless the words of the Righteous One when he said: I am the First and the Last, the honored One and the scorned One. And I am with you forever.

"Remember to keep the words of Solomon, who said that the death of the righteous is only an illusion, they will have everlasting

life if they believe. The power of God saves all who have faith. The upright man finds life through faith. Death is an illusion. Freedom from death is through peace. And peace comes from forgiveness."

I made copies of the epistle and gave them to my friends in India.

As I began to despair of ever finding the Righteous One, I started alive and preaching his message. But the stories now were conflicting, for they continued to report him being farther east. And I wondered, can there be a farther East than India ?

In his hunger for knowledge, Cornelius Severus visited a small community of people who are merchants from far-off China. They invited us into their homes arid they shared their tea and the stories of their gods. In the home of one family I saw a shrine to the god Yu, who, these people told me, was born of a virgin mother back in the mists of time. Her name was Shing-Mon and she was impregnated by the god known as the Father of Mercies. Yu's birth, they said, was heralded by a new star in the sky.

Another group of Chinese merchants were eager to speak of the holy man they followed, sharing the story of his life which, like Tam- muz and Mithra and Krishna—and as I was to learn later, like Prometheus, Zeus, Hercules, Plato—began with his birth to a virgin mother. Like Krishna, his birth was attended by wise men and angels. He traveled the land with twelve disciples and preached that we should respect others as we would want them to respect us. This holy man's name was Confucius and his followers in China are many.

In every Chinese home that I entered, I asked the same question: Was the Righteous One in China? But they did not know of him.

Dear Perpetua, in my zeal to find the Righteous One so that I could ask him my one question, I journeyed as one blind! I looked but I did not see! I have told you that it was there in the Indus Valley that I received the third of the Seven Immutable Truths. This is so. Yet I did not know it at the time! It was there before me, and yet I was blind to it. Only years later were my eyes opened and I saw the Truth that was revealed to me in India.

But I will share it with you now, for it is a truth the world is in urgent need of knowing.

It is this: that there is no death.

As the Righteous One taught us, as the preacher in Antioch told us, there is no death. How can I know this, you ask ? It is for this reason: You know that there is the Source, and that we were created out of the Source. The Source is divine, therefore we are divine. And being divine, we are eternal.

Therefore: We all return to the Source. And so we do not die.

I have told you that I have proof of this. And I do. But I shall divulge that when the time comes. For now, keep these three Truths close to your heart: that we are not alone; that we are divine; that we are eternal.

For a fourth Truth follows, and it is one which you can make use of, dear Perpetua, dear Aemelia, as an instrument with which to guide and empower your lives.

DAY NINE

"**N**ot again!" Michael shouted, and he pounded his fist on the desk.

Catherine, who was deeply absorbed in Sabina's story, looked up. "What's wrong?"

"Everyone and his grandmother must be trying to get in," he said, gesturing impatiently at the computer monitor.

She rose stiffly from her desk. She had been bent over the scrolls for hours; her neck and shoulders throbbed. When she saw the sky beyond the window turning orange, she was surprised. Where had the time flown? As she sat next to Michael she saw the Sorry, Cannot Connect To Host message on the screen. Then she saw the address he had been trying to access: *http://christusrex/archivio/vaticano.html*

"The Vatican Library?" she said.

"There are thousands of manuscripts and documents in there, many of them not even translated or cataloged. I thought it would be a good place to fish for a wild card. But no luck. It's a busy line."

He leaned back in the chair and stretched his arms over his head. When Catherine saw how the fabric of his black clerical shirt strained over toned, hard muscles, she looked away and centered her gaze on the molten sunbeams streaming through the window, casting the last light of the day onto the rich teal carpet. She forced herself to think of Julius, to remind herself how much she loved him, to concentrate on him.

What was he doing at that moment? How was he feeling, what was he thinking? "Going along with this insane plan is not supporting you, Catherine." It was one of the last things he had said to her, that rainy afternoon in Malibu, five days ago. Did he still feel that way, that helping her would only, as he put it, destroy her?

She wondered if the Hawksbill members had gotten through to him. If they had, perhaps her message helped him to understand why she was doing this, and why she couldn't stop.

If only she could log on and find out if her plea to Daniel's friends last night had worked. But she and Michael dared not access newsgroups or IRC channels for fear someone might be able to trace her IP address back to this hotel. The Web was safe because it was anonymous. At least, they hoped it was. With thousands of sites around the world, it wasn't possible for Havers to be watching all of them.

She went to her desk, stood over the new text she was translating: *You ask me about my personal life in these years, dear Perpetua. Of that there is little to say. . . .*

"If only," Catherine murmured.

Michael looked up. "If only what?"

"I wish Sabina would give us details, describe what she sees! I have a good imagination, but it's letting me down. I want to see what Sabina sees—the people, the cities. . . ."

Michael quickly returned to the monitor, avoiding her gaze. "I'm afraid I can't help. Never did have much of an imagination."

She rubbed her neck. "I feel like a caged animal."

"How can you say that?" Michael said, as he tapped the computer screen. "In the last few days we've traveled thousands of miles on these invisible highways. I visited Duke University a little while ago, zipped from there to Beijing, toddled back to the Oriental Institute in Chicago, and now that the Vatican is busy, I think I'll roam the academic halls of the University of Stuttgart. Care to come along?"

He was already typing, but the address, Catherine noticed, did not contain *uni.stutt.edu.* "What are you looking for?" she asked.

"When I accessed a page in San Francisco I saw mention of a

directory for private antiquities collections. It wasn't a hypertext link, though, so I've been trying to find it through another route."

Catherine glanced at the notepad beside the computer and saw Epistle of Maria/Mary" to his list of searches. And she wondered: What if Maria—the Greek version of the name Mary—turned out to be Mary Magdalene? Although Mary had been a common name back then, Sabina said that *her* Mary had known the Righteous One. Was there a copy of that epistle in existence? According to Sabina, the Community in Antioch had made copies, and Sabina herself had made some. Could there be a Mary Magdalene letter somewhere in the world today?

"Here it is!" Michael said. "The list of private collections."

She leaned close and frowned. *"Fred's Page?"*

Michael clicked on the highlighted hypertext link and suddenly they were looking at a Web page that, for some mysterious reason, displayed the photograph of a homely little dog named Noodles. Michael scrolled down to the text, which consisted of the dog's statistics—age, weight, date of birth, first hairball—until he came to: Dog's Owner. Michael clicked on it, and up popped *Fred's Home Page.*

"He collects collections!" Catherine said, marveling at the photograph of a goofy-looking guy hugging an inflated *Jurassic Park* velociraptor.

Michael scrolled down the list. When he came to Historical, he clicked on it. Ancient, *click.* Artifacts, *click.* Writing, *click.*

When a new list materialized, Catherine quickly read it. "I've never heard of some of these! They must be *small* collections."

As Michael scrolled down, saying, "Let's take a look," Catherine said, "Wait, stop there." She was familiar with many of the collections on the list, knew their papyri. But when Langford Collection cropped up, she frowned. She had never heard of it.

Michael palmed the trackball so that the cursor was pointing to LANGFORD. As he was about to click, Catherine said, "Wait a minute. Before we log on, do a cross check on Lycos."

"Why?"

"I don't know. I've got a strange feeling about this."

A minute later they were reading:

You Searched For: Langford There were 0 hits.

"SHUT DOWN." CATHERINE said.

"Why?"

"Something's wrong."

"Don't you even want to see what's in the Langford Collection?"

She stared at the blue letters. And the bad feeling grew. "Log off," she said, putting her hand on his arm. "Please."

After the screen went dark, they sat in the stillness, listening to the gentle whisper of warm air from the air conditioning vents as the hotel's central heating maintained a perfect 72-degree climate within the cold embrace of the surrounding desert. Catherine eyed the remnants of their lunch brought up from room service earlier. It had been hours since they had last eaten, but she wasn't hungry.

When she heard Michael sigh, she said, "Why don't you go for a walk? You've been at this computer all day. You're free to leave, I'm the one who has to stay here."

"I don't know," he said with a soft laugh. "Vegas is a dangerous place for me."

"Why?"

"I have a weakness for gambling. It's something I've never quite been able to overcome. When I was young I'd bet on anything—the horses, sports, even what color dress Mrs. Nussbaum was going to wear at the bakery!" He looked down at Catherine's hand, still on his arm.

She jerked it back, as if she had been burned. As they looked at each other for another moment, Catherine continued to feel the smooth skin, the hard muscle of his forearm beneath her fingertips.

"Catherine," he said quickly. "There is something I have to tell you."

But before he could say anything more, they felt their chairs suddenly start to shake. And then they realized that the whole room was also starting to shake.

"What the—?" Michael said, jumping up.

"It's an earthquake!"

They ran to the window and looked out. At first all they could see were the brilliant lights of Las Vegas splashed against the dusky sky. Other buildings didn't seem to be shaking, nothing seemed to be falling down. As the trembling increased, accompanied by a low menacing rumble, they realized what it was: Atlantis was sinking.

Again.

Upon one of the islands surrounding the hotel in its sixty-acre lake had been constructed someone's vision of the lost civilization of Atlantis, complete with temples, pillars, gigantic statues of gods. And twice a day, regular as clockwork, Atlantis sank—island, temples, gods, and all. During the day, the spectacle wasn't as dramatic as it was at night, when the temples were lit with torches, and flames erupted from what appeared to be newly formed volcanic fissures. There were even sound effects—stone crashing down, people screaming.

As Catherine watched the apocalyptic event, her mind filtered out the onlookers crowding around the lake to watch and cheer on the disaster, but focused instead on the island itself. Although intellectually she knew that it was an illusion, like a Disneyland ride, with hidden mechanisms and wheels and pulleys and a computer choreographing the whole stunning cataclysm, the realism of the show suddenly filled her with fear—as if the show were a preview of what was going to happen on the night of December 31, eight days from now. Her pulse began to race and her breath caught, as flames leapt to the darkening sky, and pillars that looked as if made of solid granite swayed and cracked and toppled, making tremendous crashing sounds. Waves of water rose up, like tsunamis, engulfing the island. An enormous statue of a goddess, dominating the highest point of the island, swayed and spun dizzily until it, too, crashed into the water, rolled like a log, and then sank.

Finally it was gone, completely wiped out, Atlantis, an entire civilization swallowed up with not a trace of island or life left on the smooth still waters of the lake.

Catherine and Michael remained silent for a moment, then Catherine said, "How can they make an amusement out of violence? Did you hear those spectators on the sidewalks down there? They were watching an act of utter destruction, accompanied by a very realistic soundtrack of people screaming and dying, and those spectators down there were laughing!"

"It's only a show. It isn't real."

"So if it's an illusion it's all right? And how many illusions must we watch before we become completely indifferent to violence?" She turned away. "I'm going to take a bath. I need to get this stiffness out of my neck and shoulders."

He regarded her for a moment, as if debating saying something, then he said, "I think I'll check out the health club facilities this hotel has to offer. With six swimming pools I should be able to get in a few laps."

When he disappeared into his bedroom, closing the door, Catherine remained at the window to watch the submerged island slowly reappear from the lake's depths, being set up to be destroyed again at another time. She tried to explore her feelings and identify the new fear that was starting to coil around her heart; it wasn't just her fear of Havers or the fear that she wouldn't find the seventh scroll in time. Something frightening was developing, dark and unknown and unwelcome. Of all the threats that were dogging her, this terrified her the most. It had to do with Michael.

She closed her eyes and conjured up his image; she could see him perfectly, every detail of him, down to the tiny black mole behind his right ear, the neatly clipped hairline at the back of his neck, the scattering of gray over each temple. Then she tried to conjure up Julius, the black liquid eyes, the romantic Semitic features. But he didn't come in as sharply as Michael did. She tried to recall the scent of Julius's aftershave, but she couldn't quite, remembering only that it had once struck her as a melancholy fragrance. Father Michael wore Old Spice—traditional, masculine, the original "man's" scent. She had now spent a compressed five days and five nights with him, over a hundred hours in his constant company. Did that translate into five weeks in a normal relationship, or maybe even five months? She was astonished at how deeply his physical appearance was imprinted on her mind. But she still knew little about him, where he had come from, why he had entered the priesthood.

Christmas was two days away. Weren't priests required to celebrate Mass on Christmas?

She heard him come out of the bedroom and a moment later saw his reflection in the window as he stood in the center of the room. He was carrying his black satchel. And he had something in his other hand, but she couldn't see what. Even though he was now wearing the black clerical shirt and Roman collar all the time, it was getting harder and harder for her to see him as a priest.

"Father Michael," she said, keeping her back to him, "do you think the Hawksbill members passed my message on to Julius?"

"Do you want to log on and see?"

She turned and faced him. "No, I don't want to log back in to Hawksbill yet. If Havers found out about it and is waiting for me there, then it will have to be my last log-in and you and I will have to move on. I'm going to give them a few days, see if they've come up with anything on Tymbos."

"Who knows?" Michael said with a smile. "Maybe Jean-Luc is the chief archivist for the Library of Congress."

Catherine smiled back, and their eyes met across the room. And they both fell silent.

As he started to go through the door, Catherine said, "Father Michael. Christmas is in two days. Do you want to go home?"

And she was startled to see his expression darken suddenly; she saw the muscles in his neck tense up, and she remembered how he had started to tell her something, just before the "earthquake" had struck.

He shook his head without saying anything, then he turned abruptly and was out the door. As it shut behind him, Catherine glimpsed what he carried in his other hand.

The Philippine fighting sticks.

MILES'S PAGER WENT off.

He discreetly checked the message on the display: it was an Internet address. The signal that someone had logged on to his newly constructed Web page. "Pardon me, Senator," he said, and rose from the table where one of Erica's lavish dinner parties was in progress.

Downstairs at the computer consoles, Teddy said, "Sorry, Mr. Havers. I was just about to call you. I'm afraid you came down here for nothing."

Miles looked at the screen where his Website "hits" were recorded. The pager at his belt was programmed to alert him the minute anyone logged on to the Langford Collection page. "It wasn't her?"

"Some surfer in Oslo."

Havers moved to the next workstation. "Nothing here either?"

"Not yet." They had accessed Stanford's Netnews Filtering Service, which scanned the thirteen thousand newsgroups and their several million messages for the names of those who logged on. There was a slim chance that Catherine Alexander might try to seek help from fellow archaeologists.

Eventually, she was going to venture out onto the Net and she was going to trip.

I met Satvinder in a haul of fish. . . .

Catherine frowned. Then she reread the sentence she had just written: *I met Satvinder in a haul of fish.* It didn't make sense.

She picked up the magnifying glass, moved the lamp closer to the papyrus, and tried to make out that last word.

A^pa. Definitely "agra."

Opening out *Strong's New Testament Greek,* she looked up the word, "#0061-GSN: *agra*—a haul (catch) offish. KJV: draught."

She returned to the papyrus, brought the lamp even closer so that she felt the heat from the bulb begin to toast her hair, slowly moved the magnifying glass up and down between the page and her eyes, and squinted hard over the word.

Then she saw it, the tiny *o* sandwiched in between the ^ and the *r.*

"*Agora!*" she cried. "Catherine Alexander, you idiot! Sabina met Satvinder in the *marketplace,* not in a haul of fish!" Danno's scanner would have caught it, if the damn thing had worked.

She put her pen down and looked at the time. It had been a while since they had watched the sinking of Atlantis; why hadn't Michael come back from the health club yet?

Getting up from her desk she paced the room, trying to place a name to what was bothering her. It wasn't just the snail's pace at which the translation was going, it was something else. . . .

She looked over at the computer, dark and silent. Suddenly needing to do something, she sat down, booted up, dialed the hotel's Internet access, and entered the temporary user name and password. As she was about to log on to the Web, she stopped, thought for a moment, then, on a hunch, clicked on NewsReader.

Request Latest Group List From Server?

She clicked on *Yes.*

DOWNLOADING . . .

Catherine knew she could safely log on to these because she wasn't joining them, simply reading them from her hard disk. When the list of groups appeared, she began to scroll, stopping at *alt. bible.prophecy.*

She clicked on it, found a discussion about End Times, and clicked again.

Organization: University of Cambridge, England
Lines: 26
Message-ID: <4pvrpd~50q@favor.csx. cam.ac. uk
NNTP-Posting-Host: usen. chu. cam. a-uk
Subject: Re End Times

»>Apocrypha supports Bible prophecy of the last days.
»> Steve

»Steve, you're full of it. Apocrypha isn't God's word.
» Give proof. Ray
Sorry I took so long to reply. Been gathering your proof. Ref: P245 British Museum, P14 Broderick Archive, Duke University et at. The Millennium is upon us, pal, according to documentation outside Canon.

Catherine went back over the papyri cited but realized she was already familiar with them—nothing there to shed light on Sabina's scrolls. She logged off and returned to the main list, searched again until she came to *alt.archaeology.* Clicking on it, she scanned the articles. She suddenly stopped and stared.

1999 11/30 Daniel Stevenson "Atlantis"

She clicked on it.

Xref: news.omeganet.com sci.archaeology
On 25 Nov 1999 18:44:37 + 0100, stan@moonbeam.vamp.co.aus writes:
>Atlanteans - Mayans

>*Stevenson: You posted this rubbish a couple of months ago*
>*and you were told then it is rubbish. Why are you now*
>*putting us all to the expense of downloading it again?*
>*Stevenson: You are a waste of bandwidth.*

Catherine felt her anger flair. Danno, being attacked as usual. That was how he had always been, always the underdog, always fighting for someone's rights or for an unpopular cause. *Danno sitting at his desk, tears rolling down his cheeks in empathy with the tears of shame on her own face as she stood on a stool in front of Sister Immaculata's fifth-grade class, watching the kids point and giggle.*

Catherine had a sudden urge to enter the newsgroup and flame this jerk in Australia. But she couldn't. The instant she logged on, her e-address would show and anyone reading her posting at the time, or even later, would be able to trace her back to this hotel.

She shut down and when the screen went dark she gazed for a moment at her photograph taped to the inside of his laptop case. Why had he put it there? "I think Daniel was in love with you," Michael had said.

Michael . . .

The thing that was bothering her seemed to have something to do with Michael. It had been nagging at the edge of her mind ever since he had left to check out the hotel's pool facilities.

Feeling her restlessness grow, she turned on the TV, hoping for the comfort of a human voice. Instead, the late-night news was introduced with a lead-in that nearly screamed: "Stolen scrolls are declared the work of the Antichrist."

She changed the station. Ted Koppel was interviewing a well-known physicist who was saying, "This is the beginning of the End of Things, Ted. Synchronicity is real. How many of us are noticing more and more coincidences? It's an indication that things are coming together—all the threads, the realms, the currents of the universe are starting to touch, and when they touch the result is coincidence. With more and more of them happening, it means that the coming together is escalating, the planes and currents and invisible spheres are touching more frequently, until finally every single point in the universe will touch and the cosmos will implode on itself, returning to the primordial Dark. I've calculated it out mathematically. The final event will occur at the stroke of midnight, December 31, 1999."

Catherine clicked the TV into silence and began to pace again.

When she saw on the coffee table the Liturgy of the Hours, its dark green leather binding stamped in gold with the *chi-rho*—the capital P with the x over its stem, standing for the first two letters of *Christos*— she thought of how many times in the past five days she had seen Father Michael reading from its pages, his lips some times moving, a whisper escaping now and then. She was curious: Was it in English or Latin? Were they prayers or just sayings, words of comfort, hymns perhaps? Catherine had never read the Liturgy; the missal had been the book of her Catholic youth.

She picked it up and opened it, and saw that it was indeed arranged according to hours and days. She turned it to December 22, the Evening Prayer, and she read:

God is light: if we live and move in light, there is love
    between us.
Without love the world cannot be at peace: rid our world of
    hatred and fear.
Help husbands and wives to find comfort in sorrow and
    strength in trials; grant them enduring love.
Lord, keep all the dead in your care: those we have loved and
    those no one remembers.

Catherine closed her eyes. *Keep all the dead . . . those we have loved . . .* And for an instant she felt a whisper of peace.

But then a conversation from long ago suddenly came back: Catherine in the eleventh grade asking Stanley Furmanski how he pictured the afterlife.

"I imagine it's just like the beforelife," he had said.

"You mean before we were born?"

"Do you remember any of it?"

"Of course not."

"There you go."

And she thought: Is that it? A nonstate? Is that where my mother went? *Is that where Danno is?*

She closed the book and put it down. *Keep all the dead. . . .* It was a nice prayer, but it was a Catholic prayer, and she couldn't separate it from the institution that had written it.

She thought of Michael again. And then it came to her, what was bothering her. "Six pools in this place," he had said, "I should be able to get in a few laps."

But he had taken the pangamot sticks with him.

Going back to the computer, she booted up, clicked on Lycos, quickly typed in pangamot, and jumped on the hypertext link that sent her straight to the Web page of the Filipino Martial Arts. She hadn't accessed it since the night Michael cut her hair, and when the home page came up now, with its symbol of crossed sword and cane, she wondered if somewhere in here she would find an explanation for Michael Garibaldi.

Having only briefly read the introduction before, she now jumped on links until she reached the *Frequently Asked Questions,* and she began to search among them, for answers. . . .

THE LAP POOL was on the fifteenth floor, adjacent to the health club, and when Catherine didn't find Michael there, and was told by the attendant that no one registered to her room had signed in, her suspicions were confirmed.

Checking the weight-lifting rooms, the circuit machines, the indoor running track, and then stopping in at the juice bar and pro shop, inquiring at the masseuse station and even the boxing workout area, Catherine finally headed down a hall where schedules of dance, yoga, and aerobics classes were posted. Two of the rooms had late-evening groups in progress, but the rest, Catherine discovered as she walked to the end of the corridor, were dark and empty.

When she reached the fire exit, she was about to turn around and leave when she thought she heard something.

Glancing into the room at the end, she didn't see him at first, the lights were out and he was a shadow in black drawstring pants and T-shirt. He seemed to be dancing. Catherine stayed back, out of sight, and watched.

"A common misconception," the FMA Web page had explained, *"is that Filipino martial arts are stick fighting only. But FMA are made*

up also of empty-hand skills such as kicking, punching, trapping, and grappling."

Michael stood with feet apart and knees bent as he moved in slow motion, his right hand rising up and then gliding down with fluid grace, up again and down, in a way that made Catherine think of a woman elegantly sewing, but very slowly, every muscle and sinew under control, his balance perfect, body in total harmony.

"To compare with other martial arts: tai chi is circular, internal, and soft, whereas pangamot is linear, external, and hard."

Michael stood with one foot forward in a stance that made Catherine think of tai chi, but when some of his movements ended crisply, as if coming up against a glass wall, Catherine surmised that these must be the killing moves.

"In the Philippines, contestants do not pull punches in tournaments. It is not unusual for someone to get severely injured, or even killed."

He was reflected in the mirrored walls, with mirrors casting back reflections from other mirrors so that a hundred Michaels could be seen from all angles, affording Catherine many views of him, all of them, to her surprise, different. In one view he seemed almost to be smiling, and in another she thought she glimpsed his sense of humor. But another mirror cast back the face of an angry man, and in another he appeared troubled, as his body moved slowly in the shadow dance of lethal fighting.

Catherine couldn't take her eyes from his breathtaking body, and she found herself imagining him making love, using that same exquisitely controlled power: *linear, external, hard.*

"The 12 Angles of Attack are as follows. . . ."

How did an agent for peace reconcile with training himself in an art meant for one purpose only? How could he justify being a priest and a martial arts combatant?

"The rattan sticks, or canes, are sometimes referred to as Sticks of Death. . .

Although Catherine hated what she saw, she found herself drawn to it all the same, and suddenly she wanted to join him, stand behind him, press her body to his, lay her arms along his and move with him, to feel that violent, controlled energy flow from his body into hers.

And the thought that she might actually do it, spontaneously join him in a dance that repelled her, act upon an impulse that went against everything she believed in, frightened her. Michael had tapped into a part of her that she had not known existed. A part that was beyond her control. . . .

Finally he came to a halt, clasping his hands beneath his chin and giving a small bow to his invisible opponent. Pausing for a moment, standing completely still, he then picked up the rattan sticks and twirled them for a moment like batons, as if he were preparing to lead a parade. But then he struck a combat stance, one foot in front of the other, legs apart, knees bent, and he began slowly to sweep the sticks in a complex routine, first the right stick behind his neck, the other brandished in front of him like a sword, and then the first gliding out, with the other rising up and back, crossing over its mate to trace a lethal X in the air—like intricate clockwork moving on hidden cogs and wheels, slowly at first and then gaining momentum, going faster and faster, fury and power building until Catherine could hear the sticks scissoring the air, slicing it into bloodless ribbons.

Michael advanced with the canes, attacking his unseen adversary, releasing his breath in short, harsh gasps as he dealt swift and powerful blows. He sprang to the side, blocked an imaginary strike, dropped to a knee and swept the sticks through his enemy's legs. Up on his feet again, bouncing on the balls of his feet like a boxer, striking this way, that, gaining force, charging the atmosphere with fury so that Catherine held her breath, felt her body go rigid with excitement and anticipation.

She thought: He keeps himself trained in a combat art, he is keeping himself fit in order to kill. Why? Who is he preparing to kill? What did the martial art bring to him that Catholicism could not? *If prayer doesn't work, then maybe the pangamot sticks will.*

Catherine backed away from the door, from the scene that at one time would have disgusted her but which now—

An image formed unexpectedly in her mind—a memory, from long ago. Catherine had been very young at the time when she had gone searching for her parents. She had come upon the open door to their bedroom, and had seen them inside. Her mother, standing in the center of the room, and her father kneeling, his arms around

Nina's legs, his face buried in her abdomen, Nina with her hands on his head as if in benediction. They were fully clothed, there was no sex going on. But in their pose, in the gentle, tolerant, and understanding look on her mother's face, Catherine had seen something that transcended sex and romance and creature-love. It was total, surrendered Love. The sort that she suspected few people found, and then experienced only once.

As she looked again at Michael, the image in her mind changed, it became Catherine standing in the room and Michael with his arms around her, his face pressed into her abdomen, her hands resting on his head.

And the *feeling* it delivered to her was an emotional punch so strong that it caught her off guard and made her nearly cry out.

She turned away from the sight of Michael, away from the memory, and fled down the hall, her running footsteps silenced by the hallway carpet.

INSIDE THE DARKENED dance studio, Michael came to a standstill, pangamot sticks at rest. He was breathing heavily, sweat bathed his body. He saw his myriad reflections in the mirrors, saw the tension in his neck and jaw.

For the first time after a workout, he didn't feel restored.

His dream. The woman now taking center stage so that he could see her more clearly. Dressed in white, her sandals covered with the dust of ancient roads, standing at the entrance to a temple, her arms outstretched to him, hands open, as if to embrace him. She seemed to want to lead him inside. There was a smile on her face.

The memory of it made him shudder; the fighting sticks slipped from his hands and clattered on the hardwood floor.

The woman in the dream was Catherine.

"If only I could see," she had said earlier. "I want to see what Sabina sees." And he had replied, "I can't help you."

But the thing was, he *could* help her, because he was seeing what Sabina had seen. His dreams were filled with visions of temples and highways, camel caravans and people gathered peacefully around campfires, talking softly beneath the stars. But he couldn't tell Catherine about it, for then he would have to tell her the rest . . . that he wanted to go into those outstretched arms, let her lead him into the temple, and that he couldn't because where he was going, no one else could follow.

Michael picked up the pangamot sticks, drew in a deep breath, and began again.

On the third floor of the FBI Headquarters building at Tenth Street and Pennsylvania Avenue in Washington, D.C., special agents were working overtime in the sci-crime lab.

Latent Fingerprint Section chief Wally Walters was trying to identify prints that had been lifted off a blue Mustang found abandoned near Castle Rock State Park in northern California. They had been matched to prints taken earlier from the exit door of a research lab outside San Jose, and now he was developing them on the computer's image enhancer by means of converting the print into a digital image for clearer comparison. The final step was then to send the prints to Fingerprint Identification Division, the largest operating unit within the FBI, employing over two thousand people and housing a file containing over two hundred million fingerprints.

"It's a bitch of a case, Wally," his assistant said, as he came in with a brown bag of sandwiches. "So far, Catherine Alexander hasn't committed any crime that we know of for certain. It's all rumor and speculation. You want pastrami or cheese? Maybe there are stolen scrolls, maybe not. Maybe she's the one who ran from Stevenson's apartment, maybe not. Maybe she caused an explosion in the research lab—I think this is the coffee with cream and sugar. We need something solid to bring her in on."

Wally unwrapped his sandwich. "The guy she was with in the research lab downloaded software onto a computer. Chances are, she uses the Internet as well."

"Hey, maybe we can pick her up on a legality. Title 18, maybe," the assistant said, referring to the section in the U.S. Code that prohibited the transmission in interstate or foreign commerce any communication containing a threat to kidnap or to injure someone. "Theoretically, if Alexander slips up and makes threatening comments to anyone over the Net, we can pick her up and she could get up to five years in prison."

"If she loses her cool," Wally said, suddenly sitting up, alert. The

chief had been with Latent since before it was separated from Ident Division to become part of the sci-crime lab, and just when he thought he'd seen everything and the job started to get boring, something juicy would crop up to renew his faith in America's criminals.

Like now. The computer had found a match.

"Well, well," he said as he read the name of the person to whom the prints belonged. "Now *this* is interesting. . . ."

THE CRY PIERCED her subconscious.

Waking with a start, Catherine stared at the dark ceiling, wondering for a moment where she was. Then she looked at the clock on the nightstand. It was just past midnight. She had only been asleep for a few minutes.

She listened to the silence. What had woken her?

Another cry, anguished.

She sat up. It had sounded like Michael.

Catherine had been in bed when he had finally returned from the health club an hour ago. She had heard him go quietly into his room and close the door.

"Why don't you leave me alone!"

Jumping out of bed and running across the suite, her white nightgown flitting ghostlike through beams of moonlight, she paused to listen at Michael's door. He seemed to be breathing heavily, groaning, as if he were ill.

"Father Garibaldi?" Catherine called out. "Are you all right?"

She pressed her ear to the door. She thought she heard a sob.

"Father?" she said. She knocked. "Michael?"

Opening the door a crack, she peered in. Moonlight streamed through the window, illuminating the twisted sheets, the blanket heaped on the floor. And Michael, in the grip of a nightmare, his skin glowing with sweat. When she saw how his head rolled from side to side on the pillow, and the torment on his face, she stepped into the room. "Michael?"

His eyes were shut tight; his teeth clenched, making the veins in his neck stand out. Because he was shirtless, she saw the muscles of his chest and arms flex and strain as he wrestled with an unseen demon.

Catherine went to the bed and stood over him. She put her hand on his shoulder, gave him a gentle shake. "Michael, you're dreaming. Wake up."

"No," he murmured. "Don't do this. . . ."

She sat on the edge of the bed. "Wake up," she said sharply. "You're having a nightmare. Michael—"

"Oh God!"

Suddenly his eyes snapped open.

"You were dreaming," Catherine said. "You're all right. It was just a dream."

He drew in a deep breath and released it with a shudder. Then he pushed himself up to a sitting position, blinked a few times, trying to focus on her face. Suddenly he pulled her into his arms and buried his face in her neck. Catherine automatically drew him to her and held him as she felt his body shake with stifled sobs.

He clung to her for a long moment, not speaking, breathing softly into her neck. Then he drew back.

Catherine saw the dampness on his cheeks, wiped it away. "Are you all right?" she said.

"You brought me back from a very dark place," he whispered.

The look in his eyes held her for a moment; she saw fear in them, and a naked vulnerability that shocked her. "Do you want to talk about it?"

He nodded.

Catherine returned to her room to put on her robe, and as she tied the sash tightly, she reached for the jaguar pendant, curled her fingers around it. A vision flashed in her mind: the gold cross Michael always wore, lying against his bare chest—

In the sitting room, she turned on lights, and when Michael came out, she saw that he had gotten fully dressed. He had put on a plaid shirt and jeans; he had even, she noticed, put socks and shoes on.

He looked at her, their eyes met, and the air in the room seemed to shift, even the light, Catherine thought, subtly changed. She felt his arms around her again, her own hands pressed into the firm muscles of his bare back, his hand on her hair, his lips pressed to her ear.

"I'm sorry I woke you," he said.

"I wasn't sleeping. Do you want to tell me about the dream?"

He went to the minibar and took out a cold Evian. "It was pretty bad. I'm glad you woke me up."

"Do you often have nightmares?"

He drank long and deep, nearly emptying the entire bottle before taking a breath. Then he went to the window and parted the drapes to admit cold, platinum moonlight. Catherine gazed at his silent, broad-shouldered silhouette against the desert stars.

When he didn't reply, she said, "I went looking for you earlier. I saw you in one of the dance studios. I watched you," she said. "Pangamot isn't for self-defense. It's for killing. Why do you do it?"

"I do it for a lot of reasons," he said softly.

"Have you ever . . . killed anyone?"

"With pangamot? No." He left the window and took a seat in the chair opposite the sofa, to face her. His eyes were filled with restless shadows as he stared darkly at the bottle in his hands.

"Can you control your power?" she said. "If I were to strike you—"

He snapped his head up. "Oh God, Catherine, I would never hurt you. You've got to believe that. Please don't ever be afraid of me."

She held out her hands in a gesture of helplessness. "Maybe if I understood why you do it. Before, when I thought it was like karate, when I thought it was self-defense, I could accept it. I told myself you did it for mental discipline, or to keep fit. But now I'm confused."

"You want to know how I can be a priest and be involved in a combat skill?"

"Yes," she said. *And I want to understand why my body is aroused by something that my mind and heart tell me is wrong. Michael,* she wanted to cry, *I don't like what I've discovered about you. But worse than that, I don't like what I've discovered about myself.*

He seemed to consider his next words before saying, "I grew up in a house where hitting was the main form of communication. My dad would hit first, ask questions later. Drunk or sober, it didn't matter. It made me into a real tough kid, the local bully with a chip on his shoulder. One night, some friends and I got drunk and decided to trash the neighborhood church. The priest didn't call the cops. Instead he sent for Father Pulaski, a big Polack from a parish across town. He took me behind the church and beat the shit out of me. Then he enrolled me in a karate class at the YMCA. That was the start of my career in martial arts. And that was when I discovered—"

"Discovered what?"

He regarded her with a clear gaze. "That there is something inside me that I need to keep under constant control. I can't describe it, but it terrifies me."

"Is that what the nightmare is about?"

"When I was sixteen, Catherine, there was a store in our neighborhood, one of those old-fashioned mom-and-pop types. The owner was an old guy, I don't recall his name. He was from Europe, had a thick accent. His wife had died a few years before, and he was running the place on his own. A nice old guy, always giving candy to the kids.

"I was in there one night, it was late, I was the only customer. He was getting ready to close. He always called me Mikey, so he said, 'Make your selection, Mikey, I don't want to miss the late news.' And that was when the punk kid came in. Older than me, but skinny, and strung out on something. He went up to the cash register and pulled a gun, demanding the money. He didn't know I was there. The old guy stood behind the counter saying something like, 'You don't want to do this, sonny. It'll ruin the rest of your life.' The old man saw me come down the aisle. I stopped. The punk didn't see me. The old man was watching me. The scene kind of froze. For a minute it seemed like there was no sound, as if the world had stopped for an instant. The old man's eyes were fixed on me, pleading with me to do something. But I didn't. I just stood there. And then the punk shot him. Three times in the chest. The kid vaulted over the counter, grabbed the cash, and ran.

"And that, Catherine," Michael said, "is what visits me in my dreams. I'm in that store again, and I'm just standing there as that punk takes an innocent life."

"It wasn't your fault. You were only sixteen—"

"I had thirty pounds on that punk easily, and I didn't do anything."

"He had a gun."

"And I had the advantage of surprise." Michael stood up. "Anyway, it was after that that I went wild, and thought it would be cool to spray graffiti inside a church."

"How did you end up being a priest?"

"It was Father Pulaski who set me on that path."

Michael went into his bedroom and returned a moment later

with a watch Catherine had seen him take out and wind every so often. It was an antique watch, on a chain, the kind she imagined prosperous Victorian businessmen wore festooned across their prosperous stomachs.

"He gave me this the day he died," Michael said, handing it to her. "It was given to him by his mentor, who I believe received it from *his* mentor. It's very old, you can barely make out the inscription. . . ."

Catherine took the watch, cradled it in her palm.

Michael stayed on his feet, pacing. "Father Pulaski was a big, boisterous Pole who always spoke in decibels. When I told him I was thinking of entering the priesthood, he said, 'You've been called to the service of the Lord, lad!' I said, 'What do I do now?' And he shouted, 'Why, you answer, boy, you answer!'"

Michael stopped at the window, put his fingers to the glass. "Father Pulaski was opposed to the New Mass, he kept the Latin Mass until the day he died, even though he had been ordered to switch to the secular. I remember when the Bishop came to talk to him. Father Pulaski shouted, 'All right, so the mass has to be said in English now! You could at least have kept some of the Latin! You could have at least kept the Kyrie!' None of us had the heart to remind him that the Kyrie was the only *Greek* in the Mass!" Michael looked at Catherine. "Father Pulaski took up a collection and sent me to school, where I discovered I had a talent for math and computers. When I finally got my degree in computer science in 1984, I was twenty-seven and I'd already been an ordained priest for six years."

Catherine gently placed the antique watch on the coffee table. "Why are you still with me, Michael?" she said. "Why haven't you gone back to your safe parish?"

"Why are *you* still here? Why aren't you back at your safe dig, or in a safe university somewhere?"

Catherine looked at her hands, studying her palms as if reading her own fortune. Then she said, "I've told you about my mother, her work. She was a sweet, gentle woman, and deeply religious. The last thing she wanted to do was attack anyone's faith. If anything, she hoped to illuminate faith. But the Church saw her as a threat. And because she taught at a Catholic college, the Church had the power to censure her. At first she resisted; finally they sent a man all the way from Rome, to talk to her. The man from the Vatican was a Dominican, he worked in the office of the Inquisition."

"It's no longer called that, not since 1965."

"I know. They've given it a clean name—the Congregation for the Doctrine of the Faith. But it was called the Inquisition for six hundred years, and just because it's been called something else for the last thirty-four doesn't make it something else. I know what the Congregation does, Father Garibaldi. Their purpose is to investigate anything that might threaten the Church, and I know that these investigations are always done in total secrecy."

She nodded, lowering her voice. "Oh yes, I know all about the Congregation, how the tribunal is set up, with a judge who is called the Assessor and an aid called the Commissar, how they investigate anyone who might threaten Church unity. They tried to work through our parish priest, Father McKinney. He would come over to the house and tell my mother to stop the attacks on the Church, but she always got into spirited debates with him, telling him that the Church had an obligation to evolve with the needs of its members. I suppose when the Vatican representative finally came out, Father McKinney took it as a sign of his own personal failure to control this heretical woman. He felt that my mother had humiliated him."

"What happened?"

"The Inquisition wrote a recommendation to the Pope that my mother be stripped of her post at the college and declared no longer qualified to teach Roman Catholic doctrine. She was even told that she was no longer a Catholic theologian, and she was forbidden to write or publish anything more. And she complied. However," Catherine said, "for Father McKinney it wasn't enough. I'll never forget that Sunday. . . . I was ten years old. During his sermon, Father McKinney spoke of heresy and he was looking directly at my mother. It was a terrible moment, the whole congregation silent, staring at us. My mother, holding her head high, got up and walked out, right in the middle of Mass, and she never went back.

"After that," Catherine said, "it was just my father and me every Sunday. I felt people staring at us, and in school the other kids called my mother names and said we were all going to burn in hell." Catherine closed her eyes to a sudden, unbidden image: *the fifth-*

grade class giggling and whispering while she stood on the stool as
punishment, her face burning with shame as the wetness began to
trickle down her legs.

"What people didn't know," Catherine continued, "was that my
mother held her own private service every Sunday morning. She
continued to believe, but she refused to take the Sacraments. And so
she was excommunicated."

"Is that why you left the Church?"

"No, it happened later, when my father died." Catherine
unfolded herself from the sofa and joined Michael at the window. She
squinted at the powerful beam of light shooting up from the tip of the
Luxor pyramid, like a highway to another galaxy. "He went to Africa
on a peace mission," she said quietly, "taking medicines and Bibles.
There was a coup—one tribe rising up against another. My father and
his party were caught in the middle. They were executed as spies. My
father, a priest, and three nuns. It was in the news—they kept showing
photographs of the bodies—"

"I remember. I didn't know that was your father."

"He was brought back and given a big Catholic funeral and he was
buried in a Catholic cemetery. My mother died a few months later—
pneumonia, the doctors said, but I knew that it was of a broken heart.
My parents loved each other deeply, they were devoted to one another,
and without my father, my mother found no reason for living."

She looked at Michael. "The night my mother died, she told me she
wished to be buried at my father's side, so that they could spend eternity
together. But the only way that could be accomplished was if my mother
were to confess and receive absolution. She agreed to it, after years of
having separated herself from the Church she had so loved—"

Catherine drew in a deep breath, released it slowly, aware of
Michael's eyes on her. "Mother asked me to send for a priest. I telephoned the church, and the man who came was Father McKinney.
And there was, I don't know, something in his eyes when he entered
that hospital room, a kind of triumph, as he approached my mother's bed. It was as if he had come to their final moment of reckoning,
the moment of power play, and only one was going to come out the
victor. All my mother wanted was to die in peace and join my father.
But Father McKinney . . .

"I left the room. I shouldn't have, but I did. I thought my mother would want the privacy. I don't really know what happened. A short while later Father McKinney came out, red-faced with anger, and he stormed off without a word to me. I went back into the room and my mother was crying. I knew she hadn't received absolution or the Last Sacrament. I knew she wasn't going to die a redeemed Catholic. I did what I could for her. I even tried to find another priest, but it was too late."

She heard Michael murmur something. She didn't hear it distinctly, but it sounded like, *"Ora pro nobis."* Pray for us.

"My mother was not buried next to my father, or even in consecrated ground, but in a public cemetery. She had wanted to spend eternity with the man she loved."

Catherine turned to him. "Father Garibaldi, did the earthly Church, and a mere man with the title of Father, have the power to condemn my mother to a lonely eternity, or perhaps even to none at all?"

"I can't answer that," he said, "without knowing what happened between your mother and Father McKinney. But if your mother confessed directly to God," he added gently, "then she was forgiven."

Catherine pictured her mother against the antiseptic hospital pillow, breathing her last breath, comforting her daughter instead of being comforted by her. "Don't grieve," Nina had whispered. "I go to join your father."

But did she?

"Where did my mother go after she died? Where is her soul now, if she had a soul?"

"We don't *have* souls, we *are* souls. It's the body we have—temporarily."

"And what happens when we die?"

"When we die we are rewarded with the loving presence of God."

"What about people who die unconfessed? What about hell?"

"As a priest I am required to preach the punishments of hell. But in my heart I can't believe that our Heavenly Father created us so that He could cast us into eternal torment."

"And Purgatory?"

"I believe in Purgatory, and that we stay there until someone prays for our release."

"Then it helps if those on earth pray for the souls of the departed?"

"Yes."

"Will you pray for my mother?"

"Yes. But you can pray, too."

She turned away from him, away from the view of the sinful, seductive city. "It wouldn't work, coming from me."

"Why not?"

"Because I don't believe."

"So you want me to believe for you?"

She regarded him again. "I *want* to believe. I wish I *could* believe, as my mother did."

"Catherine, everyone is born homesick for heaven. The trick is finding the way back."

How? she wanted to know. *How?*

"So now I understand," Michael said, walking away from the window. "Father McKinney is the reason you didn't like me when we first met."

She watched as he drank down the last of the Evian and set the empty bottle on top of the minibar. "Father McKinney wasn't completely the reason," she said. "I am uncomfortable around people of deep faith."

"Is that why you won't marry Julius?"

Her eyebrows arched. "What makes you think that?"

"I don't know. Maybe it was something you said. Or didn't say."

"Julius is a religious man, and he abides by the rules and laws of his faith. I couldn't live with someone like that. He would be a constant reminder of what I am lacking."

He regarded her for a moment, then said, "Do you hate Catholicism that much?"

"I love Catholicism. It's a beautiful religion. Although I no longer believe in God, I miss the incense, the saints, the compassionate Virgin, the comfort and solace. And that is what I am so angry about. All that was taken away from me."

"You can get it back."

"No I can't." She looked into Michael's smile and recalled how, at Our Lady of Grace School, the kids would always be surprised to see a pretty nun or a good-looking priest, how they'd think, What a waste.

How many girls, she wondered, in Father Michael's parish, harbored secret crushes on him? "Michael, is Catholicism the true faith?"

"I believe it is."

"If you had been there with my mother, at her bedside, what would you have done?"

"I would have asked her if she was sorry for her sins, and then I would have absolved her. Father McKinney's personal dispute with your mother, and the issue of what she wrote about, had no place in the confessional."

"And is she with my father now? Are they together?"

"I don't know the answer to that, but I can assure you that prayer will help."

She nodded. Then she cleared her throat and said, "Anyway, now you know why pangamot upsets me. It's because of the senseless and violent way my father died." She faced him. "I am repelled by violence of any kind. And it confuses me that you . . ."

"I understand," he said. But Catherine heard a hardness in his voice, and she saw how he looked at his watch, as if searching for the hour of his fate on its face. He was suddenly agitated, and it surprised her.

"I'm going out for some air," he said abruptly.

She blinked. "I'll go with you."

He strode to the door. "I'd rather go alone. Don't wait up." And then he was gone.

Catherine stared at the door, wondering what had just happened. Then she quickly got dressed and went after him.

A night porter vacuuming the hall said the man who had come out of her room had taken the elevator up to the roof. There was a garden up there, he said, fountains and pagan temples. Catherine was in the elevator before he could finish describing it.

Few guests were in the rooftop paradise, where the desert wind blew so chill and sharp that as she walked among tropical ferns and palms, Catherine almost expected to see snow. She found Michael standing at the edge, his face set toward the black desert that spread ominously beyond the border of the dazzlingly lit town. She went to stand next to him, relishing the feel of the cold wind cutting through her short hair.

After a moment Michael said without looking at her, "Do you know how it has made me feel to know that something I do repels you? That pangamot frightens you? That *I* frighten you?"

He turned to face her and she saw the anguish in his eyes, as if he were living a waking nightmare. "Catherine, you asked me why I stay with you, why I don't go back to my safe parish. I'm going to tell you something I have never told anyone, not even Father Pulaski." He spoke quickly, as if afraid of losing his courage. "I thought for a long time that the incident in the store was God's way of calling me to His service. That He had placed me there in that moment so that my path would change and turn toward Him. That was why I became a priest. But . . . I've started having doubts. Not about my faith, but about my vocation."

He waited, as if to see what her reaction might be. He continued: "For years I didn't have the nightmare, but then it started coming back, and now I am being forced to relive that night over and over. Even during the day, the face of the old man haunts me. I've become obsessed with it, trying to figure it out."

"And have you?"

"I think it's my own conscience, coming back to haunt me after all these years."

"But why? Michael, you don't know that you could have saved him."

The wind picked up, frigid and cruel. Catherine wrapped her arms around herself, even though she wore a jacket. But Michael, wearing only a shirt, seemed unaware of the freezing wind. "It's not about that! Catherine, the day that I was ordained, do you know what I felt? Not joy or religious exaltation. I felt *relief.* I felt that I had finally been forgiven for not acting that night. But, my God! That's no reason to enter the priesthood! A man becomes a priest because he wants to serve God, not because it's a place to hide from his guilt! I tried to tell myself that serving God was a way of making up for my failure that night, but that isn't it. I took Holy Orders as a way to obtain my own salvation. I became a priest for selfish motives. I'm a fraud!"

"Michael—"

"Catherine, I told you I was in Israel on vacation. That's not true. I was there on a personal pilgrimage, I went to examine my conscience to see if I was fit to stay in the priesthood. And then I ended up in the Sinai, and became involved in newly discovered scrolls that might shed light on God's message. And that is why I've stayed with you, to see if the scrolls contain the answers."

"What answers, Michael? Whether you should stay in the priesthood?"

He didn't respond.

"If that isn't it," she cried, the wind carrying her voice out over the desert, "then what? Tell me!"

"I can't. Not yet. Maybe never."

"Michael, please let me help you."

He suddenly took her by the shoulders, startling her. "You really want to help me, don't you? You hate priests and yet you want to help one." He looked up at the sky, probed the stars, brought his gaze back to her. "Do you know what a paradox you are, Catherine? You say you abhor violence and yet you fight when all the odds are stacked against you. There are guys out there who are ready to kill you, but you're not going to give in, are you? We're the same, you and I, Catherine. We're wrestling old demons, only we're fighting in different arenas." He dropped his hands away from her arms, attempted a smile. "In pangamot, you would make a formidable opponent."

"It's easy to fight," she said. "The hard part is—"

"Is what?"

"I loved my father, Michael. I worshipped him." *Filthy little girl, said Sister Immaculata, pulling Catherine down from the stool. Your father has been sent for. Maybe he can knock some respect into you.* "It was my mother's break with the Church that started his missions around the world. It was obvious to everyone that my father felt driven to make up for her supposed sin. When he was killed, I said terrible things to my mother. I blamed her for his death. God help me, Michael, I didn't mean any of it. And then a few months later she died and I never got around to telling her I was sorry!"

Catherine started to cry, and when she said, "Oh dammit," Michael pulled her into his arms to shield her from the harsh desert wind. He held her while she fought the tears, fought for control, he held her to him and murmured, "Let our prayer come into your presence, Lord, as we humbly ask for mercy: and as in your love you counted your handmaid, Nina Alexander, among your people in this world, so bring her now to the abode of peace and light, and number her among your saints. Eternal rest unto her, O Lord, let perpetual light shine upon her. May she rest in peace. We make our prayer through our Lord. Through Christ our Lord. Amen."

"Amen," Catherine whispered. She remained in Michael's sheltering embrace. But when she felt his hand start to trace the curve of her back, and her own sudden shock of desire, she drew away, needing to let the freezing wind blow between them. "We'd better go downstairs," she said, turning away to wipe the tears from her face, to hide her embarrassment that he had seen her cry. And so he wouldn't seen her inflamed cheeks. Her desire for him was growing; she was appalled at her spiraling loss of self-control. "We have a lot of work facing us tomorrow," she added.

"Catherine," he said. "About tomorrow . . ."

She turned around. "What about tomorrow?"

"I'm afraid we're going to have to leave the hotel."

"What do you mean?"

"I thought you were asleep when I got back from the health club so I decided to wait until morning to tell you." He paused. "I visited the steam room after my workout, and when I came out I found my locker standing open. My wallet was gone."

"Gone! You mean stolen?"

"I reported it to the management, but they don't hold much hope of recovering it. Catherine, aside from the twenty dollars you have, we are flat broke."

"YOU NEED TO get down here, Mr. Havers," Teddy said. "Something *weird* is going on!"

As Miles hung up the phone and started to get out of bed, Erica stirred beneath the sunrise-hued satin sheets. "Darling . . . ?"

"I just have to see to something, dear. Go back to sleep." Slipping into his maroon dressing gown of hand-stitched raw silk and tightening the sash around his narrow waist, he watched Erica drift back off to sleep.

As he entered the subterranean communications center, where Teddy Yamaguchi sat alone among millions of dollars' worth of electronic equipment, Miles glanced over at the special fax machine to see if any more translations had come from Cairo. The tray was empty.

He also hadn't received any good news from the three technicians at Dianuba he had assigned to run independent searches for anything remotely connected to the Sabina scrolls. "What is it?" he said. "Did Voss receive more e-mail?"

Teddy had had no trouble hacking into the Freers Institute system and hijacking Julius Voss's mail. Although he had encountered an encryption program protecting their e-mail, it was Keep- Out, a security' software program designed by Dianuba Technologies. Teddy could get in, but he couldn't stop the computers at the other end from issuing a warning to users at Freers that their system had been broken into and their files were being scanned. It didn't matter. With Voss, Teddy didn't care about being subtle. He knew that, in this game, everyone knew that everyone was watching everyone else!

The first message had appeared last night, a cryptic note from someone in England, saying simply, "Catherine is alive, she's okay." Teddy and Miles had been puzzling over it, wondering if Dr. Alexander had left the country, when another message had come over for Voss, this time from someone in Denver, saying the same thing. The third message had followed a few minutes later, from Seattle, a repetition of the first two, but with the added, "and she didn't kill Daniel Stevenson." When a fourth had come through, saying, "She still has the scrolls and she is going to give them to mankind as a gift when she is done with them," Teddy had immediately put a trace on the senders, but had ultimately found no connection between them and Dr. Alexander.

Since then, a trickle of curious messages throughout the day, but nothing of significance. Until now.

"No, not Voss's e-mail," Teddy said. "Something really strange. Watch this." He was in his usual posture for working at a computer, tilted back in his chair, the keyboard in his lap, arms tucked into his sides, fingers jackhammering like ten little pistons. Teddy never once glanced down at the keyboard, his eyes were fused to the screen as if a network of neurons and dendrites created an invisible bridge from the monitor to his brain and down to his fingers, the rest of his body being purely extraneous.

When he said, "I dropped in on a channel called Felines," Havers knew that he was referring to an Internet Relay Channel—otherwise known as "real time chat." Teddy liked to relax by cruising the chat channels, dropping in and out to see what was jumping in cyberland, fueling himself with geek food, tonight being, Havers noticed, Skittles and Ding Dongs washed down with Snapple. "They were talking about the Los Angeles Lakers," Teddy explained, "when all of a sudden— Well, see for yourself."

Havers watched the monitor. After the usual MOTD, Ping and Pong, and "refresher," the ongoing dialogue came up.

> [catbox] Whachoo all planning for New Years 8-j
> [CelsiuS] Mike, the difference is two.
> <SERVER> Franciel~fjames@kendaco.telebyte.com has joined this channel

"What are we looking for?" Havers said. As far as he could see, it was just the usual inanity; Internet chats had replaced the pickup bar, with the dialogue just as vacuous.

"Wait," Teddy said.

> [Mike] Hi, francie!
> [catbox] Welcome francie. Where you from?
> [Francie] Dr. Catherine Alexander is running for her life. She is innocent. She is being pursued by Bad Guys. Pass the word.
> <SERVER> FRANCIE has left this channel.

"What!" Havers said.

"That's how it's been going. People hopping in and out, saying that Dr. Alexander is innocent."

Miles pulled up a stool and positioned himself in front of the next monitor. Logging on to the IRC' using his old hacker nickname, Avenger, he started joining channels, jumping in and out as if he were cruising.

> <SERVER> Welcome to #Planets
> [figgy2] Hi Avenger! Here's a coke.
> *figgy2 hands Avenger a coke
> <SERVER> Moondoggylphil@actcom.co.il has joined this channel

[bOzO] figgy2, answer my questions.
[MoonDoggy] Someone is trying to kill Catherine Alexander. She has the scrolls and is protecting them for all of us.
<SERVER> MoonDoggy has left this channel.

"It would seem," Havers said. "That our clever doctor is bar-hopping. And she seems to be jumping around the IRC at random. If we could manage somehow to get ahead of her, be in a channel before she logs on, catch her host address—"

<SERVER> Forty-One plus. Be cool. For my services /msg Foxy [cream] Christmas shopping! Aaarrrrgh!!!!!!

[ToTo] A size six, I think. No. maybe an eight. Gollee, you there girl?
<SERVER> Maynard!~rismith@alice.brad.ac.us has joined this channel.
[cream] Hi, Maynard. You ef or em?
[Gollee] ToTo: had to let the cat in. What were we talking about?
[Maynard] Tell everyone you know that Dr. Catherine Alexander did NOT murder Daniel Stevenson. She is I.N.N.O.C.E.N.T. And the COPS will *not* get her.
<SERVER> Maynard has left this channel.

"This isn't Dr. Alexander, Mr. Havers," Teddy said, having abandoned his relaxed posture and now sitting upright before two screens, monitoring both at the same time. "All those host addresses. These are all different people!" Teddy's eyes were bright, like two fiery opals, as he watched the screens in fascination. "And they're all over the map!" he said as he jumped in and out of channels as quickly as Catherine Alexander's champions did.

"Who are they?" Havers said as he joined #Geology just in time to see:

[Carlos] Tell the cops to leave Dr. Alexander alone.
<SERVER> Carlos has left this channel.

Teddy shrugged, a quick, sugar-fueled gesture. He looked as if he were wired directly into the computers. He typed *#Zippers*, hit Enter, and was greeted with *Hi, Mouse*, his IRC handle. And in the next instant:

<SERVER> Carlos!mmongo@dianuba.com has joined this channel.

"Carlos!" Teddy barked. Carlos had just jumped out of the *last* channel. Teddy left #Zippers and joined #German.

[LadyGray] Ola, mouse. Sorry. Wie geht's. I'm in spain. where are
     you?
[corVette] That's five countries we have now, man\
<SERVEFt> Figgy2!ashame@ppp26. cac.psu.edu has joined this
     channel
[Troy] Hallo Figgy2. Halo maus
[Troy] mouse
[figgy2] Tell everyone in Deutschland that Catherine Alexander
     did not kill Daniel Stevenson, she did not steal any scrolls
     from anybody, she wants to be left alone, and she has secret
     knowledge of the New Millennium. Pass it on.
<SERVER> figgy2 has left this channel.

Teddy let out a yelp. "This is unbelievable! The wires are frying! The Alexander chick is getting everyone on her side!"

Havers didn't say anything as he swiftly and wordlessly dropped into channels and then left. Like Teddy, he was noticing the pattern, an ocean swell building into an enormous wave as people in other channels, hearing the message, picked it up, dropped out of the channel, and joined another, passing the message along.

#Cars:
[LadyGray] There is someone in trouble. Katharine Alejander. Tell
     people to help.
<SERVER> LadyGray has left this channel.
#SameLove:
<SERVER> Corvette!~Johnson@ix-ch/2-04. ix.netcom.com has
     joined this channel [wicker] Have to spend downtime with the
     fam):-(

[MisterT] Hi corvette! Do you own one
[CorVette] Catherine Alexander . . .

Havers stood abruptly, thrusting his hands into the pockets of his maroon dressing gown. Except for the hum of recirculated air coming through the vents, and the steady trickle of the waterfall at the "grotto" end of the bunker, the only sound in the room was the rapid-fire c*lack*, *clack* as Teddy's hands flew over two keyboards. His eyes reflected the glows of twin screens where information changed as swiftly as camera shutters. All those chat rooms around the world, existing only in microcircuitry and ISDN lines—names without people, words without voice, rooms without walls—

And in just nine days, one minute past midnight on New Year's Eve, all these chats and channels and bar-hoppers were going to be instantaneously and globally linked by Miles's new software, Dianuba 2000.

The power of it.

#jazz:
[chuck] I dont know. N'Orleans, maybe. Et vous?
<SERVER> Corvette!~Johnson@ix-ch/2-04.ix.netcom.com has
*   joined this channel [FATS] Yo, Vette!*
[chuck] bonjour
[CorVette] Tell everyone that Catherine Alexander . . .
#Forty+
[midWICH] I cant decided between Stonehenge or Peru. Where
*   are you from anyway:)*
<SERVER> Fatsl~babyface@aol.com has joined this channel
*   [DeltaCom] Why Peru?*
[DeltaCom] Riverside. And you??:))
[DeltaCom] Welcome, Fats.
*   [FATS] Listen up. Help the lady who is running with the scrolls. . . .*

"Where did it start?" Miles asked. Twenty-four hours ago Catherine Alexander had been called the Antichrist. Now she was a hero.

Teddy shook his head. "No way of finding out. It could have been anywhere, an IRC channel, a newsgroup, even a MUD. It's growing, too! Look, three names just joined this room, and I saw them in other rooms. Everyone's picking up and moving, dropping in and out of channels so fast I can't keep up. The whole Net is alive! They don't even know who Catherine Alexander is, but they're all taking up her cause and running with it. Man, this chick oimrthe IRC!"

Havers knew that Catherine Alexander wasn't just on the IRC— newsgroups would be buzzing about her now, every Web chat would be filled with the sight of her name; e-mail, zipping back and forth across the globe, from Iceland to New Zealand, Johannesburg to Germany, all talking about this woman no one even knew. Even her photograph, Havers had no doubt, was being transmitted around the world in bytes by the millions.

I will give the scrolls to humankind as a gift, she had had the audacity to declare publicly. *And so the cybermasses,* Miles thought, *never ones to have a life in the first place, had taken up a cause they knew absolutely nothing about. Run, Cathy, Run might be their rallying cry, even though they wouldn't know "Cathy" if she spat in their faces.*

As he watched Teddy surf the IRC like a maniac on a tsunami, Miles smiled and nodded to himself. *Very well, Dr. Alexander,* he thought. *Ton give me no choice.* Time for the tiger to move in for the kill.

This was going to be fun.

The Fourth Scroll

I MET SATVINDER *in the marketplace of a city where cows roam the streets unmolested for they are considered sacred.*

Satvinder was a physician, but because she was a woman, she was restricted to tending only female patients. We met at the astrologers' stall, and when it was revealed that we were born under the same sign, we became friends. For the rest of the time I spent in India, I spent it with Satvinder, who taught me her ways, as I taught her mine.

Satvinder was a follower of a man who was begotten by the Lord of Hosts and born of a virgin named Maya. He preached a life of poverty and chastity, kindness and humility. His followers expect him to come again to earth, that his return will signal the End of Things; he will judge the righteous and punish the wicked and create a new earth. His name is Buddha, and he lived jive hundred years ago.

You ask about my personal life in these years, dear Perpetua. Of that there is little to say except that I continued to remain alone. There was a man in Cornelius Severus's retinue, a scholar like Severus, and a knight. He asked me to marry him, and I declined, for I was done with marriage and the hope of a family. There was room in my heart for only one thing: the question which I must ask the Righteous One.

I learned much during my sojourn in India, but my greatest revelations were yet to come. I told you that we are eternal and that we return to the Source and there is no death. But, in life, we are as sailors lost upon a stormy sea. We need to find our way home.

I have found that way, Perpetua. And its simplicity will aston-ish you. For the next three Truths form the threefold path that will become the guiding star, to help you navigate your way Home, back to the Source and to eternal life.

I heard from travelers of a god named Logos—the Word Made Flesh—whose followers say he spoke the Word and the universe was created. And so when Cornelius Severus announced his departure from India, once again I joined his party, for they were bound for Alexandria, the home of Logos, whom I hoped to be the Righteous One at last.

DAY TEN

Catherine was getting worried. She had searched all over the Atlantis for Michael, but he was nowhere to be found.

She had awoken at sunrise to find him gone, and the last twenty dollars missing from her purse. Suspecting that he was down at the casino trying to replace the money stolen from his locker the night before, she had decided to search for him.

Although she was wearing enormous sunglasses, and the police did not yet know about her new short blond hair, Catherine was still wary of being spotted. "These fanatics might kidnap you, or worse," Michael had said. But that had been the other night, w hen the whole world had seemed to be against her. Now, public opinion appeared to have executed an about-face. As she passed the news kiosk in the lobby, she saw a newspaper headline: LEAVE ME ALONE! It w'as accompanied by her photograph. She knew that the story would be about how' the Internet was exploding with talk of Catherine Alexander.

Her plea to the cyberworld had produced incredible results. On the radio this morning she had heard Detective Shapiro in Santa Barbara quoted as saying, "We haven't accused her. We only want to question her. Witnesses say she was being chased by men with guns, so we doubt she killed Daniel Stevenson."

Still, Catherine wasn't going to relax her guard. As she brow'sed the kiosk, w'ondering where Michael had gone to, she kept a watch on the crowd; but everyone's attention, it seemed, was commanded by the attractions going on in the hotel's football-field-sized lobby.

As she was about to turn away, her eye was caught by a display of audio cassettes, in particular *Chant3,* religious chants recorded at a monastery in Spain. On an impulse, she purchased the tape, charging it to their room, and slipped it into her blue gym bag. And as she turned away from the kiosk, she finally saw him, walking toward one of the spaceship elevators. He wasn't wearing the cassock or Roman collar, so he looked like a tourist.

She ran across the lobby, breathlessly catching up with him at the foot of a three-story statue of the goddess Athena that was really a video arcade. "Michael, I've been looking everywhere for you!"

He hoisted up the laptop case. "We needed new batteries." He also had his black satchel with him, she noticed, and the pangamot sticks. He looked around and said more quietly, "Good news. We don't have to leave after all. I managed to get some money, enough to take care of us for a while." When she gave him a questioning look, he said, "Don't worry, I didn't use the twenty dollars. I stood in the doorway of the casino and almost went in. But I didn't."

"But how—?"

"I'll explain later," he said. "We'd better get back up to the room, before someone notices you."

He put his hand on her arm, and Catherine felt a jolt go through her, making her think of their rooftop embrace the night before. She had slept restlessly after that, her dreams filled with disturbing visions of Michael, shirtless in the moonlight, battling an unseen adversary with the pangamot sticks.

She had also dreamed of him kissing her.

"I've thought of a new Web site to log on to—"

Suddenly, two men were blocking their path. One of them showed a government ID card, as he said, "Dr. Alexander, will you come with us please?"

"Pardon us," Michael said. "You're blocking our path."

"This is official business—"

"Yeah? And who are *you* supposed to be?" Michael said impatiently. "The poor man's Jack Lord?"

"Just come with us, please, Dr. Alexander," the government agent said, ignoring him.

"I suggest you leave the lady alone."

"Please stay out of this, sir." The man took hold of Catherine's arm, and Michael went into action before anybody saw it coming. His right fist went up, the other shot out, and the man was flying off his feet with a surprised look on his face.

"Run, Catherine!" Michael shouted. *"Go!"*

She vaulted into the crowd, pushing people out of the way, and when she looked back she saw Michael grab the second man by the hair and flip him over like a rag doll. His partner, recovering quickly, was already up and charging at Michael in a blur of karate moves. Catherine had started to turn back when she saw the first man, staggering to his feet, wipe blood from his nose and start to come after her.

She turned and ran, zigzagging blindly through the crowd, dodging in and out of groups of people, nearly colliding with a luggage rack rolling by. As she sped past the elevator launchpads, where a towering mirrored wall reflected the colossal lobby, she saw the government agent running through the crowd, searching for her.

Up ahead she saw the underground attraction, Minotaur's Maze, with a rope across the cavernous entrance and a sign that read, CAUTION: CLOSED FOR SERVICING—DO NOT ENTER.

She quickly climbed over the rope and delivered herself into the blackness, with one backward glance to see her pursuer heading her way. There was no sign of Michael.

The maze was intended to be a re-creation of the labyrinth on Crete where the bull-headed man-monster had dwelled, feeding on the victims who became lost in its pitch-black tunnels. The ride was taken on boats, cruising dark canals.

Catherine hurried along the narrow walkway bordering the main canal, her shoulder grazing walls that had been made to look as if they were rough-hewn rock. The air was dank.

She paused to look back and listen. The light from the entrance didn't reach very far inside; she was now in total darkness. Fumbling inside the gym bag, she felt for her pocket pen-light, found it, and flipped it on, casting a pencil-thin wand of light down onto the narrow ledge. She was inches from the murky water.

Thinking that she could find an emergency exit, or doorways to equipment and control rooms, she ventured forward, into the abyss.

She had no idea what the ride was all about, but she imagined that it delivered thrills and a sense of danger. From the Minotaur, she wondered? Would there be recordings of heavy breathing, beastly moans, perhaps shadows on the walls, showing the monster coming closer, lunging—

She ran into something that clattered loudly. She cried out. Training the frail beam of light over the wall, she found herself face to face with a human skeleton hanging from iron manacles.

She inched forward, passing torches in wall sconces that clearly were supposed to flicker with atmospheric light but which were now dead. She turned corners, trying to get her bearings, only to end up in blind alleys or encounter trompe l'oeil doorways that looked real but weren't, and corridors that seemed to go on forever but which she walked right into. A crazy maze, like something out of a Road Runner cartoon, except that it wasn't funny.

She tried not to panic. It was only an amusement park ride, she told herself, right under a busy hotel lobby. But she couldn't hear a sound, and the only light was from her feeble pen-light, a beam that she noticed was starting to go dim. Was it possible to get lost in this maze? What if the ride was closed for days or weeks, with no workmen going in or out? What if they had constructed it so realistically that it truly was a Minotaur's maze, intended to trap hapless victims?

She stopped and strained her ears to listen. But all she heard was her own ragged breath and thumping heart.

She came to a junction where red-painted columns framed frescoes of graceful bull-jumpers and bare-breasted snake goddesses. Had she seen one just like it before, or was this the same one?

Am I going in circles?

She tried to remember which way she had turned last time. It had been to the right; this time she went left, feeling her way along the wall, trying not to fall into the canal. The delicate papyrus scrolls in her gym bag—it wouldn't take much water to ruin them beyond all recognition.

She stopped and listened again. This time she thought she heard something. Following it, she presently came to an intersection that seemed to have a source of light. Flicking off her pen-light, she realized that she could see.

Following the light source, wondering where it was leading, she came to the cave-like exit, and she realized in dismay that she was back at the entrance. With the government agent standing just inches away, his back to her as he scanned the crowd.

She slowly retreated, careful not to catch the attention of a passerby, who might stop and look at her, making the agent turn around to see what they were gawking at. And as she did, she saw a sign she had not seen before: *Warning! This Is a True Maze. Do Not Enter on Foot or When Ride Is Not in Operation.*

Catherine's mouth ran dry. Surely the sign was there to enhance the thrill of the ride. If the maze were truly dangerous, they would have a gate across it, wouldn't they?

She glanced back over her shoulder at the black void. The penlight wasn't going to last much longer, certainly not if she was going to waste time going in circles.

She looked at the agent again. He showed no signs of moving.

Where was Michael?

Catherine backed away into the protection of the darkness, but was still able to keep an eye on the agent. When she saw him turn and survey the entrance to the maze, her heart skipped a beat. And when he approached the rope, squinting into the tunnel, she backed up a few more feet. He was going to come in!

She tried to think, tried to recall what she knew about the legend of the Minotaur's Maze. It had been designed so that no one could find their way out, and clearly this ride had been designed with the same illusion. But a Greek hero named Theseus had slain the monster. . . .

Quickly digging into her gym bag, Catherine felt for the cassette she had bought earlier. She fumbled with the cellophane wrap, nearly dropping it, then she snapped the case open and, keeping her eye on the agent who was stepping over the rope, plucked at the ribbon of tape until she had a generous loop. She stretched it until it broke, then she quickly tied it around a torch sconce, making certain it was secure, and began to make her way backward along the narrow walkway, slowly unraveling the *Chant3* audio tape as she went.

Now she knew she wouldn't go in circles. And she was already sufficiently familiar with the tunnels that she didn't use the pen-light, saving it only for emergencies. She was able to go swiftly, having an edge over the agent, who possessed neither light nor familiarity with the maze. But she went cautiously, unspooling the tape, being careful not to snap it, trying to keep track of her turns, whether left or right, so that when she hit a dead end and had to backtrack, she made a mental mark that she must turn the other way. And once, when she felt ahead on the wall and her fingers encountered the ribbon of tape, she realized that she had gone in a circle around one small section of the labyrinth and hadn't even been aware of it.

In the darkness, and in her fear, she lost all sense of direction. She discovered that it was possible to make turns and yet have the odd sensation of going in a straight line. She paused occasionally to listen for her pursuer. She heard something fall into the water. Then she heard something slip or scrape, followed by a sharp intake of breath and a softly spoken curse.

He was still in the maze, still coming after her. Like the Minotaur.

Finally she saw a faint light at the end. And she saw new frescoes here, no more bull-leapers, but strangely clad people with curious skylines behind them, and what looked like spaceships flying through the air.

Before making a bid for freedom, she went back into the darkness, memorizing the way, and broke the tape, letting it fall into the water, in case the agent had picked up on it and was using it to find her. Then she retraced her steps until she saw light.

Catherine pursued the light almost giddy with relief. She had found the exit to the maze! And as soon as she was free, she was going to run as fast as her legs would go.

But when she emerged, she discovered to her horror that she was on one of the islands that surrounded the hotel, which was itself on an island. And then she realized which island it was.

The one that periodically sank.

Suddenly frantic—the agent could be out any minute—she looked across the water toward the shore and, beyond, the sidewalk teeming with pedestrians. Across the way stood the fabulous Beau Rivage resort, gleaming in the morning sunshine. How to reach the shore without getting the scrolls wet?

As she was trying to figure out a way to get off the island without going back into the maze, she experienced a quick spell of vertigo. And then the ground began to rumble.

Atlantis was about to sink!

She looked back into the mouth of the maze, and when she saw the agent climbing his way up from the darkness, she dashed away from the cave and headed up the slope toward a cluster of white marble temples. Catherine had witnessed their destruction four times already, and each time they reappeared as good as new. But she knew what was about to happen. The island was about to be swallowed up by the sea.

The rumbling grew until the ground started to shake, nearly throwing her off her feet. Small statues toppled; delicate fountains folded up and disappeared. At this proximity, while the ground shook and felt like a genuine earthquake, Catherine could see the hinges and springs that enabled the pillars and porticoes to "collapse." The sound effects were deafening. When she heard the screams pouring from hidden speakers, she thought for a moment that she wasn't alone on the island.

And she wasn't. The agent had seen her and was now running after her.

The main temple stood on a knoll, at the top of an elegant marble stairway lined with beautiful urns and statuary, cypress trees and fountains. As Catherine scrambled up the stairs, she looked back. He was getting closer.

Water around the island was starting to churn. Catherine hugged the blue gym bag, trying to protect the scrolls. She could see the spectators gathering at the fence to watch the spectacle, shouting and cheering, cameras clicking away.

And then the island started to sink.

Amid the groaning and creaking, the volcanic special effects began, steam and smoke, lava geysers and fireworks. Catherine coughed as she plunged steadily upward through the inferno, blinded by the smoke. She felt the heat from the lava—she had no idea what it was made of, but it looked and felt hot.

The island started to shake sideways; it was breaking apart.

Catherine lost her footing, fell onto the marble. The agent was right behind her. He grabbed for her ankle. She kicked back at him, missing his face but catching his shoulder.

She heard cheers from the crowd. Could they see her? Why didn't the hotel management stop the program?

Maybe they can't.

As the island continued to break up, the water began rising rapidly. The lower half of "Atlantis," where the labyrinth exited, was now completely submerged. Only the temple, on high ground, remained.

Catherine scrambled upward, her shoes and jeans wet, holding the gym bag as high as she could from the splashing water. A statue toppled and rolled over the agent. He looked surprised as it bounced off him.

Then she heard a terrible cracking sound. Looking up, she saw in horror the gigantic statue of a goddess start to sway. Catherine tried to remember which way it fell. It was the same each time, she knew, *but which way?*

The statue began to spin crazily on its pedestal, giving the impression that a ton of marble was about to come crashing down. But Catherine glimpsed the mechanism underneath, and the statue's hollow core.

She fell again; the gym bag slipped out of her hands. The agent reached out and clamped his hand around Catherine's ankle. She tried to wrench free. The rising water was lapping at the edge of the stairway, nearly touching the gym bag. The crowd on shore was roaring with delight. And the statue was now swaying this way and that as it prepared to come down in a spectacular fall.

Grabbing the gym bag, Catherine swung it high in the air and brought it down on her pursuer's head.

He didn't let go of her foot.

The water was churning upward. Catherine continued to climb to the altar, with the agent hanging on to her foot, climbing with her.

The statue swayed menacingly. Now, off toward the hotel, Catherine saw boats zipping across the water in her direction—hotel security.

She couldn't let them catch her.

She kicked at the agent. And then she looked up at the statue. He looked up, too, and for an instant his grip relaxed. Catherine yanked free and clambered up to the temple sanctuary, all that remained above the turbulent water.

She looked back at the agent, who continued advancing. Then she ran to the edge of the sanctuary, where four pillars and the swaying statue still stood.

Catherine looked across the water and saw Michael climbing the fence, running down to the grassy edge of the water. He waved at her to jump. But it was too far and she couldn't plunge in with the scrolls.

The statue. She remembered! It fell *away* from the island, into the lake. And stayed afloat for just a minute before sinking.

She was going to have to be fast.

The agent leapt toward her, and his fingers curled around the handle of the gym bag. His eyes met hers in a look of triumph.

And then the statue started to fall. Catherine screamed, startling the agent, giving her the moment she needed to catch him off guard. She delivered one hard, swift kick, knocking the breath out of him, and then she spun around and jumped off the marble platform, seemed to hang for a long moment suspended in midair, and then she landed on the statue's pedestal, just barely keeping the gym bag dry.

The goddess now lay stretched out on the water, but was sinking fast. Catherine ran the length of the colossal body, slipping and sliding as the statue rolled like a log. She reached the head just as the government agent also managed to leap from the sanctuary as it was swallowed up by the water; he grabbed onto the pedestal, hoisted himself up, and scrambled after Catherine.

She was only a few feet from shore, but the crown of the goddess was now submerged and Catherine was up to her knees in the water, and rapidly going down.

"Catherine!" Michael shouted, his arms outstretched. "Throw me the bag! Hurry!"

She swung it high in the air and felt her heart stand still as she watched the blue bag and its priceless contents carve an arc against the blue sky and land—right in Michael's hands.

The crowd roared.

"Come on!" he shouted, hooking the bag over his shoulder and holding his arms out. "Jump!"

She looked back; the agent was slogging his way along the submerged statue. The water was now up to their waists. And the hotel security boats were drawing in, causing the water to churn and the sunken statue to roll sickeningly.

"Stay where you are!" came a voice through a bullhorn. "We will pick you up!"

The lake was heaving with waves. She looked helplessly at Michael. There was no way she could jump.

And then suddenly, a tremendous roar filled the air; the statue lurched beneath her feet. She held her arms out to steady herself as the statue started to come back up.

They had stopped the sinking and were reversing it!

The crowd on shore went wild. But Catherine saw policemen pushing their way through toward Michael.

"Hurry!" he shouted, arms outstretched. "Jump!"

The statue came up, up. The agent reached out behind her, his fingers grazing her blouse. A security guard tossed a rope to her.

And then Catherine jumped, pushing herself off the now surfaced crown of the goddess, and landing right in Michael's arms.

She heard the crowd erupt in frenzied cheering as she fell against him and he held her tightly. Then he said, "Let's get out of here!"

They raced through the crowd, dodging the police, and made it to the hotel's entrance, where they seized a taxi, jumped in, and went squealing off.

JULIUS COULDN'T BELIEVE his eyes. He had found it. Stumbled upon it, actually, while looking for something else. Right there on the page, the very thing everyone was searching for.

The end of the story. The fate of Sabina Fabiana.

He had borrowed the antique volume from Rabbi Goldman: a gigantic tome published a hundred years ago, at that time probably the most comprehensive catalog of ancient documents, scrolls, codexes, manuscripts, and letters housed in private collections, some of which Julius knew would be too small or esoteric to warrant a listing on the World Wide Web. And as he had gone through it, hoping to come across a listing of ancient papyri, he had stumbled upon a curious medieval manuscript written in Latin and labeled *Thomas of Monmouth, attributed. XIIth C.* And there, leaping off the page, the name Sabina Fabianus.

He felt sure Catherine didn't know of the existence of this parchment; there was no way she could locate it through the Internet and he doubted she was risking exposure by doing any search through actual library books.

He gazed at the document in awe. His Latin was shaky but sufficient to let him know that this was the instrument through which he could finally help Catherine.

But instead of being relieved, he found himself unexpectedly troubled, suddenly wondering if he should even tell her about the parchment at all. It was a contest between his conscience, he realized, and his love for her. He had always held himself to a strict code of ethics, and he didn't want to betray that code. But he didn't want to betray Catherine either.

The phone rang, and he heard the caller say to his machine, "Dr. Voss, this is Camilla Williams from *Eye Witness News.* We were wondering if we could schedule you for a live interview on our show—"

Julius went into the kitchen and hit the "stop" button, silencing her. He briefly considered unplugging it, but there was always the slim chance that Catherine might call.

As he was about to return to the living room and the now worrisome document, he caught his reflection in the shiny door of the microwave oven. He had suspected he must be looking tired lately, but he wasn't prepared for the smudged eyes and drawn cheeks. Was it any wonder? He had barely slept or eaten in the past twenty-four hours, traveling like a madman from computer to computer—from Rabbi Goldman's to the downtown L.A. library to the archaeology' department at UCLA back to Rabbi Goldman—torturing his brain for a way to help Catherine. He had been unsuccessful in finding Fabianus anywhere on the Internet or the Web, or anything connected to Sabina and the scrolls.

It was when he had finally blurted the whole thing to Rabbi Goldman that the wise and patient old scholar had brought out a dusty book with brittle pages, placed it in Julius's hands, and said with a smile, "It might not be as fast as a computer, but its drive never crashes."

Julius went to the sliding glass doors that opened onto a weathered sundeck, and stepped out into the bracing ocean air. There was no sun on the deck now, just comfortably warped redwood furniture, pots of red and pink geraniums, and a starfish he and Catherine had found one night in a tide pool.

It had been the second time they had made love, on the beach under the stars—just before they had been startled by a surprise invasion of grunion hunters with sacks and flashlights. The memory made him smile. And then it made him want to cry. Catherine . . .

He had finally had to tell the police what he knew. Yes, Dr. Alexander is in possession of papyrus documents. No, I don't know exactly how she brought them into the United States. No, I don't know precisely where she found them. He had told semitruths, trying not to lie but trying to save Catherine at the same time. He felt as if he were being torn apart. Where did a man's conscience end, he wondered, and his love for a woman begin? Did one have to exclude the other? In this case, he thought grimly, it did.

His eyes were drawn to the horizon, far out across the nacreous Pacific to where the clouds hung low and slivers of sunlight kissed the water. Beyond that horizon, on the other side of the great curving earth, lay Hawaii, and the Halekulani Hotel, where he and Catherine had made love for the first time. If only there were some way to turn back the clock, reverse the days and the seasons, go back to a more innocent age and begin again, knowing what lay ahead and this time avoiding it.

When he heard the phone ring again inside the house, he listened, hoping it might be Catherine. But a man's voice came over the answering machine, another tabloid reporter, offering to pay Julius for his story.

Even though he hoped she would call, he knew she could not. When all those e-mail messages had come in from strangers around the world, assuring him that Catherine was all right, his computer had sounded a warning that the system's encryption program had been overridden and that his mail was being scanned. Catherine had been right.

Furious with himself and his helplessness, Julius went back through the house, stripped off the sweats he had worn for a day and a night, and got himself under the hottest shower he could tolerate. But the water didn't help. When he emerged, he was still torn. If he told Catherine about the Thomas of Monmouth document, then he would be assisting her in something he believed was wrong. If he *didn't* tell her, then her search could go on for weeks, maybe even months, increasing the danger to herself.

As he dressed, he thought about the phone conversation he had had that morning with his mother—she had called very upset, having heard about Catherine in the news. She had said: "You carry a heavy burden, Julius. Don't carry it all alone. Put yourself in God's hands. Ask Him to guide you."

And suddenly Julius was thinking of the comforting ambience of the synagogue, the Ark containing the scrolls of the Torah, the single lamp burning, to symbolize that the light of the Torah would never be extinguished, and over the Ark, the inscription in Hebrew: *Know before Whom you stand.*

He thought, I'll go to the synagogue and pray.

But when his father's voice, from long ago, joined his mother's, saying, "Baal Shem-Tov told us, 'He can be found wherever one lets Him in,'" Julius bypassed his car keys and instead opened a special drawer in his bedroom dresser to bring out the *tallit* and *tefillin*—prayer shawl and *phylacteries*. Although Julius regularly recited the shaharit, the morning prayer, he realized now that he had fallen into a routine of mindless repetition while getting ready for work.

This morning he would take the time for proper, conscientious prayer.

Taking up the first *tefillin,* he placed the *bayit*—the black leather cube containing passages from the Torah—on his left arm, encircling the upper arm with the black leather strap and then winding it seven times around the lower arm down to the hand, wrapping it diagonally across the hand, between thumb and index fingers as he pronounced the blessing: *"Barukh, vetzivanu le-ha-ni-ah Tefillin*—Blessed are You, He who has commanded us to wear *tefillin."*

Taking up the second *tefillin,* he placed the *bayit* on his forehead, drawing the black leather circlet down onto his head with the knot at the back, the two bands brought forward over the right and left side of his chest, as he recited: *"Barukh, vetzivanu al mitzvat Tefillin, Barukh Shem kevod malkhuto le-olam va-ed*—Blessed are You, He who has commanded us concerning the Mitzvah of tefillin, Blessed be His glorious Kingdom for ever and ever."

Returning to his hand, he unwrapped part of the strap, encircled the middle finger and then the fourth finger, wrapping the rest between his thumb and index finger, reciting:

> *"And I will betroth you unto Me forever;*
> *Tes, I will betroth you unto Me in righteousness and in justice,*
>   *and in loving kindness and in compassion.*
> *And I will betroth you unto Me in faithfulness;*
> *And you shall know the Lord."*

Before he picked up the *tallit*—the blue and white shawl fringed at the four corners—he looked at the clock on his night table. It was not yet noon; officially, then, still morning. Holding the silk garment between his outstretched hands, he offered a blessing: *"Barukh attah, vetzianu le-hit'atef ba-tzitzit*—Blessed are you, He Who has commanded us to wrap ourselves in *tzitzit?*

Drawing the *tallit* momentarily over his head and body, and then down upon his shoulders, Julius picked up the Siddur, the prayerbook, went to the sliding glass doors that led to the sundeck, and opened them, admitting the ocean breeze.

In a clear, resonant voice, he recited: *"Sh'ma Tisrael: Edonai Elohenu Adonai Ehad! Barukh Shem Kevod Malkhuto le-olam va-edl* Hear O Israel: The Lord Our God, the Lord is One! Blessed be His glorious Kingdom for ever and ever!"

Then he opened the Siddur and began to chant: *"Barukh attah Adonai Elohenu Melekh ha-Olam*—Blessed are You, Lord our God, Ruler of the Universe," his voice ringing out over the sand where sea gulls and sandpipers foraged among dried seaweed and kelp.

He began to sway in time with the chant: *"Hamotzi lehem min ha-aretz*—You are He Who causes bread to come forth from the earth"; his voice grew in strength, he felt his spirit lift. He felt the sacred vowels and consonants fill his mouth and pour from his lips: *" Osseh maaseh bereshit*—You are He Who performs the act of the creation."

And then he delivered himself into the Amida, the Silent Devotion, ending with the Sim Shalom, "Establish Peace."

When he finally lifted his gaze from the prayerbook, he saw that the sun had won the battle with the clouds; blue sky and sunshine now blessed Malibu. Julius felt strangely refreshed, as if he had eaten well and slept deeply. His mind was clear; there was no more confusion or indecision.

He went into the living room and gazed down at the reproduction of the illuminated manuscript in Rabbi Goldman's antique catalog, and Julius saw his path clearly. He knew what he had to do.

Going into the kitchen, he dialed the number of *Eye Witness News* and asked for Camilla Williams. And as he waited to be connected to the famous anchorwoman, his eyes strayed again to the living room, to the remarkable book that contained an account of the last days of Sabina Fabianus—how and where she died, and the fact that she had died before her complete story could be told.

"She left behind six scrolls on alchemy and sorcery," the document clearly stated. "Of the seventh, told in legend, there is no knowledge, *for it was never written.'"

"DR. ALEXANDER?" MORE firmly: "Dr. Catherine Alexander?"

The elderly lady in the window seat nudged Catherine and said, "I believe he's talking to you, dear." Catherine looked up and saw the official badge inches from her face.

"Dr. Alexander? Airport police."

Catherine felt the eyes of the rest of the passengers on her. "I beg your pardon?" she said.

As soon as the jet had taxied to the terminal, the flight attendants had asked everyone to remain seated. And then they had opened the door, admitting two plainclothes policemen while two in uniform remained by the exit.

"Will you come with us, please?" said the man with the badge.

"You've made a mistake. My name isn't Alexander."

"Then may we see some form of identification, please?"

She offered a helpless shrug. "My car was stolen in Vegas. My purse and all my luggage were in it."

He moved behind her, to clear the aisle, while his partner took a few steps back. "Will you come with us, please?"

"But you have the wrong person."

"Then I'm sure we can clear this up in a few minutes."

Los Angeles International Airport was a madhouse, with cranky holiday travelers made even crankier due to heightened security. The four airport police officers escorted Catherine through the crowded terminal, one walking on either side of her, the two uniforms right behind, upstairs to private offices where phones were ringing and harried airline agents were trying to cope with delayed flights, an overloaded computer system, and a new terrorist alert.

"Where are you taking me?" Catherine asked when she saw that they appeared to be looking for a vacant office. "I mean, this isn't standard procedure, is it?"

When they didn't reply, she said, "I know this airport. Your head-quarters are in that direction, at the 96th Street airport entrance."

Her two escorts exchanged a look. Finally the one on her left said, "We have a slight problem with overcrowding at the moment." He was also the one who had shown his badge on the plane. So far his partner was mute.

"Am I under arrest?"

"No, ma'am, we just want to ask you a few questions."

It briefly crossed Catherine's mind that they weren't who they said they were. But as she sized them up—a tall African American and a shorter, slighter blond guy—she saw "cop" all over them. Even though they wore suits instead of uniforms, the haircuts, the way they walked, the poker faces gave them away. Plus the fact that people rushing past them in the halls seemed to know them.

Finally they came to an office with kangaroo posters on the walls, an Anzac hat hanging on a hook, a stuffed koala with a Christmas bow around its neck. There was only one person occupying the office, and after the blond cop held a brief exchange with her, she said, "Sure! Make yourself at home. I was just about to go for lunch anyway."

She picked up a sweater and purse, shot the guys a flirtatious wave, and then she was gone.

The blond cop closed the door, blocking out the noise from the corridor, and locked it while his partner said, "Have a seat, Dr. Alexander. This shouldn't take long."

Catherine quickly scanned the office, noting the computer, and that it was on. "I told you. I am not Dr. Alexander. Will you please tell me what this is all about?"

When they politely explained that it would take only a few minutes to clear up a matter of her identification, Catherine realized that they were stalling for time. They were waiting for someone.

She sat down and folded her arms, tried to appear calm while she did some fast thinking. She had had only a minute to prepare after seeing the policemen hurrying through the boarding lounge toward her arrival gate, quickly surmising that they were coming to pick her up.

"You say your luggage was stolen?" the African-American cop asked now.

"That's right."

"Then you filed a report with the police."

"Well, uh, I didn't have time. I had to catch a plane."

"Is someone meeting you? Someone who can vouch for you?"

"Look, I know my rights. If I'm under arrest, then I want a lawyer present. *And* I get to make a phone call."

"You can make your call in a few minutes, Dr. Alexander."

"Stop calling me that!"

He looked down at her legs. "Where did you leave your wet clothes?"

Her heart skipped a beat. Catherine had quickly changed clothes back at McCarran Airport, cramming her wet jeans into a trash receptacle. "I don't know what you're talking about."

"How did you pay for the ticket if your purse was stolen?"

"I already had my ticket . . . in my pocket." She tried to stay calm. She put her hand on her chest, to feel for Danno's jaguar.

When Michael had given her money to buy a ticket, peeling bills from a large roll, he had explained: "Hartmann's Antique and Rare Gifts in the hotel lobby. The sign said they were open twenty-four hours, so I figured they catered to desperate gamblers who were out of money and looking to hock valuables." He had sold Father Pulaski's watch.

So now, when she laid her hand on her chest, seeking the comfort of Danno's jaguar amulet, it wasn't there. Because when she had gone searching for Michael, she too had noticed the twenty-four-hour sign on Hartmann's Antiques and Rare Gifts. Mr. Hartmann hadn't given her nearly what she thought the Mayan pendant was worth, but she knew that Danno would understand. He always understood. . . .

Catherine standing on the stool while Sister teaches the fifth-grade class. Tears of sympathy streaming down Danno's cheeks as

Catherine starts to feel something trickle down her legs. The kids giggling and then laughing until they're hysterical while Catherine Alexander, whose mother everyone knows is going to burn in hell, stands there peeing her pants. But then the laughter dies and they're silent and embarrassed for her. And the silence is worse than the laughter because Catherine knows they sense her utter shame.

She kept her eye on her two guards. The blond one anxiously paced, frequently checking his watch, while the tall black guy, Catherine noticed, who was chewing a lot of gum, unwrapped a fresh stick and folded it into a mouth already crammed with gum.

HAVERS WAS ON his private golf course when the call came. He excused himself to take it on a cellular phone, out of the hearing of his companions. It was Titus. "Alexander was almost picked up in Las Vegas."

"Vegas! By whom?"

"CIA."

"How did they manage to track her there?"

"I don't know. My guess is, they have a source that we don't have. But don't worry, we haven't lost her. Dr. Alexander boarded a plane at McCarran Airport and landed a short while ago in L.A. The FBI is sending an agent to pick her up. But my guy will get there sooner."

"And the man she was with?"

"The ticket clerk at McCarran said Alexander boarded the plane alone. The LAX cops said she was sitting next to an old lady, and no one on the plane fit the guy's description. The agents in Vegas said they weren't sure if he was with her or just a bystander coming to a lady's rescue."

"Who are you sending?"

"Rosenthal. He's good and he's nearby."

THE PHONE ON the desk rang. The blond cop answered it. He listened for a minute, then said, "Give him this number," and hung up.

"Okay, Lionel," he said to his partner. "The feds have some-one on the way. When he gets here, he'll call first on that line before coming up," and he gestured to the phone on the desk. "His name's Rosenthal. We're to turn the woman over to him." He went to the door. "I have to get over to United. There's a riot or something at the ticket counter."

After he was gone, Catherine said to the cop named Lionel, "I'm telling you, I'm not who you think I am."

"You can sort all that out when the government man gets here. We were just told to escort you off the aircraft and hold you until they came for you."

She glanced at the newspaper on the desk, and the headline that, for once, wasn't about her. "So, Lionel," she said, "what do you think about O.J. getting murdered?"

No response.

"Who do you think did it?"

Still no reply.

She tried to think. All she needed was to be alone in the office for one minute. "Do you suppose I could have a glass of water?"

He went to the door, looked out, caught someone in passing, and a moment later a Dixie cup filled with water was delivered.

"Thanks," Catherine said. She took a sip, then pressed her finger-tips to her forehead. "I have a raging headache. Do you suppose you could scratch me up an aspirin somewhere?"

"Maybe there's some in the desk."

"Never mind." He clearly wasn't going to leave.

When she saw him unwrap another fresh stick of gum and push it into his mouth, she said, "You know what I could really go for right now? I'm desperate for a cigarette. Maybe there's some in this desk—"

"I don't know whose office this is," he said abruptly, standing up. "We shouldn't be nosing around. There's a machine down the hall. Don't touch anything." He locked the door behind himself.

Catherine had seen the cigarette machine; it wasn't far, he w'ould only be gone a few seconds. She hurried to the desk, but when she picked up the phone she saw that there was no number written on it.

"Dammit!"

She tugged at her lower lip, trying to flog her memory. There was a way to find out the number of a phone—what was it?

Then it came to her. Picking up the receiver, she quickly dialed 1-800-MY-ANIIS. A moment later a computer-voice at the other end said, "Your ANI is 213-555-4204."

She got back to her seat just as Lionel returned. She noticed the pack was open and he smelled of cigarette smoke. "Thanks," she said, taking one. But as he lit it for her, she said, "I have to go to the bathroom."

"Dr. Alexander—" he began.

"I know my rights. You can't deny me the use of a bathroom. And anyway, you have the wrong person. I want you to know that I have some very important friends. I'm going to see to it that you're demoted to baggage handler—"

"Okay, okay," he said. "Empty your pockets first."

"Why?"

"Just a precaution."

She turned the pockets of her jeans inside out. "See? No metal file, no bomb."

"Okay, let's make it quick." After he escorted her down the hall to the ladies' room, he stopped and took her cigarette. "Just in case you were thinking of starting a tire in the wastebasket."

"You watch too many cop shows, Lionel."

Inside, she quickly looked around and saw with relief that there was a pay phone. Then she reached under her blouse and pulled Danno's tone-dialer from her bra, where she had placed it just before the cops had boarded the airplane. Lifting the receiver of the pay phone, she dialed 1-0-ATT followed by the number on Danno's modem. A recorded voice said, "Please deposit one dollar." Praying that Michael's illegal modification worked, and that he had the laptop turned on, Catherine pressed the preprogrammed button on the dialer, then fixed the dialer to the mouthpiece. She heard the five-pulse signal go over the line, ending with the computer voice saying, "You have a credit of twenty-five cents," and the line at the other end began to ring.

Michael answered on the second ring. He had been waiting for her call.

"They're holding me at the airport," Catherine said quickly, watching the door. "I'm upstairs in the Bradley terminal, in one of the Qantas offices. An agent is coming for me. His name is Rosenthal. They're expecting him to call first on the phone where I'm being held." She gave Michael the number of the phone in the Qantas office and hung up.

SEVERAL CARS ARRIVED at once, driving out into a secure area. "Wait here," Rosenthal said. He gestured to the men in the other cars to disperse according to a prearranged plan.

Two of the men positioned themselves at the security entrance, to stall the federal agents when they got there.

Rosenthal made the call from the baggage area.

THE DESK PHONE rang. Lionel picked it up. "Franklin here. Yeah, we're holding her. What's your name? Rosenthal? Okay, we're expecting you. Come on up. We're in the office at the end."

He looked at Catherine. "Whatever it is you did that you say you didn't do, it must be something to have so many people after you."

Catherine smiled and resisted the impulse to wipe her perspiring palms on her jeans.

Rosenthal. It *had* to be Michael.

They heard a sharp knock at the door, and when Lionel opened it, Catherine's eyes widened as she saw the tall man in a black coat, black leather gloves, and a wide-brimmed hat. He did not look like a federal agent.

"Busy, huh?" he said to Lionel. "I'll take her off your hands."

"I'll need the paperwork first—"

"Wait!" Catherine said. "Lionel, don't fall for this. He's no government man."

"Sorry, Dr. Alexander—"

"Dammit, I am not Dr. Alexander and you can't let this man take me!" She suddenly bounded out of her chair and ran for the door.

Rosenthal ran after her, grabbed her, while Lionel drew out his gun.

"Let go of me!" she screamed.

"It's okay," the agent said to Lionel, pulling Catherine's arm up behind her back. "That won't be necessary. I've got help waiting out in the hall. This is one dangerous woman. Wanted in thirty-two states."

"Get her out of here."

As they hurried down the hall, Catherine whispered, "Where did you get the clothes?"

"I borrowed them." And as they passed the open door of a Lufthansa office, Michael quickly removed the coat, hat, and gloves and tossed them inside. "I don't think they were even missed."

As they approached the elevator, the doors were opening and two men in dark suits stepped out. When Catherine spotted the wired earpieces, she said, "Michael—"

"I see them." He took her arm and steered her toward the escalator, joining a group of flight attendants and ground personnel in jumpsuits. Pushing their way through, Catherine and Michael delivered themselves into the crowd and disappeared.

"DO YOU HAVE the scrolls?" Catherine asked five minutes later as they were speeding away down Imperial Highway toward the ocean.

"The lady who was sitting next to you needed help getting her things down from the overhead bin. While I was at it, I retrieved your stuff as well."

"It's a good thing you thought of us buying tickets separately and not sitting on the plane together." She looked him over. He was back in civvies again. On the plane, he had changed clothes in the restroom, so that when the cops came on board they had seen a Catholic priest sitting in the tail section.

"I hope I didn't hurt you," he said.

She released a short laugh. "You've been trying to twist my arm ever since we met!"

"So what happened back there?"

After Catherine recounted her ordeal in the office, Michael said, "When asking for water and aspirin didn't work, what made you think asking for cigarettes would?"

"I saw a nicotine patch on his neck, and the way he was stuffing sticks of gum into his mouth, I knew he was a man desperately trying to quit smoking. I was counting on him not being able to pass up an opportunity to cadge a cigarette for himself."

Michael smiled. "Sherlock Holmes strikes again."

She returned the smile. "You're not so bad yourself." Adding: "For a priest."

To her surprise, Michael slowed the car, pulled out of traffic, and parked on the grassy edge of the beach. He killed the engine, turned to her and said, "You don't know how worried I was. Catherine, if they hurt you in any way—"

"They didn't," she said, caught up in his sudden passion. Then she smiled, tried to make light of it—her emotions spiraling out of control. "At least you didn't burst in with two guns blasting."

He took her by the shoulders. "I told you last night that I can control my power, that I would never hurt you. But you have to know, Catherine, that if anyone so much as touches you, by God, they'd better be insured. Catherine—"

She held her breath, mesmerized.

"Catherine, I have a confession to make."

THE FOURTH SCROLL

I FOUND THE *Righteous One in Alexandria.*

The Stoics say that God is everything you see and every movement you make, the totality of all things seen and unseen—God is the soul. But I have seen the Creator. With my eyes, Perpetua, I have seen the Source of Life.

The Stoics also say that everything is predetermined, except for our will. And this is true. God dictates how we move, but not where. If we are thrown into a raging river, that we swim is a given. But in which direction is left to us.

We have been thrown into a raging river, dear Perpetua, dear Aemelia, and we are swimming. But which direction should we choose? And how do we choose?

I learned this answer in Alexandria, a city of scientists and inventors, intellectual enlightenment and religious freedom. But Alexandria is also a city of many gods and their followers. Here, for example, I encountered the thriving cult of Hercules, he of the Seven Labors. Hercules was born to a virgin, as you know, the only begotten son of his father, and when he died he went to the underworld and then ascended to heaven. Like the Righteous One, Hercules is known to his many followers as Savior, the Good Shepherd, Prince of Peace.

Many goddesses are worshipped in Alexandria: the mother of Hercules, who was taken up to heaven by her divine son to become Queen of Heaven; and the mother of Bacchus, who is called Son of

God, as she too ascended bodily to heaven to be crowned Queen of the Universe. But the greatest Queen of Heaven is Isis, the Savior Goddess, whose mysteries first revealed to me the Threefold Path to eternal life—the instrument which I spoke of to empower you and to guide you on your way Home.

But first I met with members of The Way, whose community was flourishing in that populous coastal city. They greeted me with the kiss of peace and I gave them a copy of Maria's epistle, which had not yet reached that shore. I asked the deacon where I might find the Righteous One, as I had heard he was here. But she said the Righteous One dwells in Alexandria in the hearts of his followers, not in the flesh. She asked me why I thought he might be here, and I told her about travelers in India who had spoken of a savior who is called Logos, which is another name for the Righteous One.

She said the travelers had been speaking of the false god Hermes, who had a great following in Alexandria.

I wondered how a god could be false, and so I went to the temple of Hermes, which faces the sea, and I spoke with the priests there. And when they told me that Hermes, a very ancient savior-god, was the Word Made Flesh, the Redeemer through whom we achieve eternal life, I asked if I could be initiated into his mysteries. They welcomed me.

As neophytes we were taught the hymns and prayers to Our Lord and Savior, we fasted and were immersed in ritual baths. And then, as with Tammuz in Ur Magna, we were led into the Holy of Holies for personal communion with the Savior.

Here is why, dear Perpetua, I had thought I would find the Righteous One in Egypt: because Hermes was born of a virgin mother named Maia, and he was laid in a manger while three wise kings came to pay homage.

During the temple initiation, we fasted for three days. There was not the loud chanting of Tammuz, but a studied quiet that led us to delve deep into unplumbed regions of our spirit. And after a while, the neophytes began to experience mystical phenomena. A young woman cried out, "Oh God!" and the god in the chamber replied, "That is you."

And that was when we saw—was it Him ? Or was it Her? For the

Cosmic Soul revealed itself to us in different guises. Some of the initiates saw a man with a crown upon his head, shafts of golden light shooting from his eyes. To others, the Creation Principle appeared as a woman in blue robes with stars beneath her feet. And what did I see? O blessed day—my eyes beheld the bearded preacher I saw long ago beside the Sea of Salt.

Perpetua, I saw the Righteous One.

And to me he granted this revelation: That we are born believing.

We are born with spiritual clarity, Perpetua. He said: There is no anger in a baby, no jealousy or resentment or envy or hatred. The newly born soul is pure. But then we experience the soul-tarnishers: hunger, disappointment, loss, pain, fear, injustice. And our bright new souls grow dim.

And suddenly I understood what Satvinder had taught me about Buddha, when he said: "Perfection is inherent in all people. Seek the help of the enlightened to be shown the way to your own nature. When one is enlightened, one will attain perfect wisdom."

I had asked Satvinder: "What is perfect wisdom?" And Satvinder had replied: "When you realize your original nature."

I had not understood these words at the time, but in the holy sanctuary of Hermes I suddenly did. Our original nature, Perpetua, is the birth-soul.

I was still in my mystical state, and so I asked the Righteous One: Why do savior gods die young, violent deaths?

And he said: So that they will be noticed, and remembered.

I heard a voice whisper in my mind: They came, and they will come again, to remind us of the lost birth-soul that is still within us, and that we can regain it by undergoing death and rebirth. When a believer has made his way through death and resurrection, he rediscovers that new-soul he was born with, pure and understanding, and he sees with crystal clarity. And this is what the newborn sees: the Gift of Faith.

I did not comprehend at the time, for it took me many years to understand what the Righteous One whispered in my vision at the Temple of Hermes. What I came eventually to realize was that faith is a gift from the Creator—a gift to the newborn. And I will show you, Perpetua, how you and Aemelia can receive this Gift.

And so it came to me the true meaning of The Way—for it is not the way forward, Perpetua, but the way back to the beginning. As we shed the earthly accretions of anger and fear and envy, we peel away layers until we expose the birth-soul within us. We regain the Sight we were born with but lost.

And then we believe.

You ask me how do we achieve this? By understanding the fourth of the seven great Truths, which I myself did not fully grasp until I underwent death and rebirth through the Savior Goddess, Isis.

The fourth Truth, Perpetua, is the first step that will take us back. . . .

DAY ELEVEN

"Millennium madness meets Internet mania!"

Miles looked up from his work to watch the news that had just come on.

The way the female news anchor was smiling, the story w'as obviously a humorous one. "Dr. Catherine Alexander, who remains at large and is being sought by various police agencies, was nearly caught today by the FBI. Except that she turned out not to be the fugitive archaeologist at all but a Seattle housewife! The FBI w'as led a merry chase early this morning when they received word that Dr. Alexander had gone online through what is known as the Internet Relay Chat."

The male co-anchor joined in, also laughing. "For those of you who haven't yet joined the computer age, this is what alerted the FBI to the suspect's location. What you are seeing on your screen right now is how the computer screen appeared to agents monitoring the Internet."

<@CaAlex> The scrolls predict the end of the world. They also say when Jesus is coming back. And if the cops don't leave me alone I WILL BURN THEM

The computer image faded and was replaced by a w'oodsy setting. The voice-over explained: "Federal agents traced the Internet Relay Chat channel to this rustic home on Bainbridge Island w here computer buff and local tavern owner Barbara Young claimed she w'as 'just having fun.' The FBI agents," the anchorwoman said when she came back on, "were not amused. Elsewhere in the news . . ."

Miles turned off the TV and looked at his watch. Titus was over-due reporting in.

He had so far been unable to catch Catherine Alexander; neither, it seemed, had anyone else. The fiasco on the sinking Atlantis island had made the front pages, of course, and the police at LAX had had some explaining to do. But it was of no consolation to Miles.

Maybe it was time for the tiger to change his strategy. . . .

"There ain't no tigers in Vietnam, man!"

It was First Sergeant Perez who said it. But he didn't say it within the Colonel's hearing. Perez might be reckless but he wasn't suicidal.

Summer of 1968, and it had rained without stopping for days, during which time the men had huddled inside a foul-smelling field tent, wondering what fresh hell they had been dropped into. Food rations had run out Wo days before so that now, as they finally trekked single file through the steaming jungle, they were beyond hungry.

Private Miles Havers, twenty years old, had never known hunger like this. Back at the base, where food was plentiful, he had fanta-sized about sex. Now that food was scarce, he fantasized about eating. Starvation, he realized, honed a man's priorities.

But there was something worse than hunger. Two terrible realiza-tions were beginning to dawn upon the members of the small combat unit. First, that they had become so far separated from their squad that they were probably hopelessly lost—it had been a long time since they had passed a village or a rice paddy; were they even still in the Republic of Vietnam? The second, bigger fear, was that their leader, the Colonel, had gone around the bend.

"Listen up, gentlemen!" the Colonel called out at the head of his dispirited, ragtag group, five stressed-out "lurps"—soldiers on Long Range Patrol deep into enemy territory. "Charlie's in the neighbor-hood. Charlie's got his eye on us."

He didn't need to remind them. His men were so aware of the ubiquitous Viet Cong that their nerve endings quivered as if they had been flayed alive; even the sunlight on their faces seemed to scrape like sandpaper. The sound they were all listening for was the metallic snap of a round being chambered into an AK-47, because that was the signal that bullets were about to fly at the hellfire rate of 350 rounds per minute, turning the jungle into a meat grinder.

Even more terrifying was the threat of pungi stakes—green bamboo stalks sharpened to deadly points and placed in camouflaged pits along jungle trails. It had elevated walking to a whole new challenge.

Hacking his way through the dense undergrowth, the Colonel called out cheerfully, "Just remember what the great Sun Tzu said, gentlemen. That which does not kill you makes you irritable as hell!"

The Colonel had changed. Miles thought maybe it had happened when the Major and Second Looey had been airlifted out—or what was left of the Major and the Second Lieutenant. The Colonel had stood there looking down at the blood on his pants—the Major's blood and maybe even a few chunks of the Major himself—the Colonel had stood there smiling and saying, "Well I'll be."

That was why Miles couldn't stop thinking about the radio. The Colonel had told them it had got sucked into the mtid back there when the downpour had caught them unprepared. But if that was so, then why had the Colonel been holding the handset?

Don't say it.

Because the Colonel must have purposely destroyed the radio.

But why, for God's sake?

So he could go on this insane tiger hunt.

"Tigers hunt alone, gentlemen," the Colonel said as he removed a damp cigar butt from the pocket of his green and brown camouflage fatigues. "Typically traveling tip to twelve miles in search of its dinner, the tiger relies more on sight than sense of smell, and when the quarry is sighted, it crouches undercover and waits for the right moment to attack."

He stuck the cigar into his mouth and spoke between clenched teeth while his starving, weary men plodded behind. "The stalk is very impressive, gentlemen. Assuming a semicrouching posture with head high, the tiger moves slowly and with extreme caution, carefully placing each foot on the ground, pausing frequently. When it strikes, it is in a few bounds. A tiger attacks from the side or the rear, and it never—keep this in mind, gentlemen—a tiger never springs high into the air nor does it launch itself from a distance. When it seizes its prey, the tiger's hind feet do not leave the ground."

The unit came to a small stream, trudged across it, eyes and ears sharp for the enemy.

The Colonel kept up his lecture: "The prey is seized by the neck and jerked off its feet. The tiger then drags its dinner to dense cover and commences to feed on it over a period of days. The tiger always begins," the Colonel said with a grin, "on the arse. And he doesn't stop until there's only skin and bones left. The tiger we are searching for, gentlemen, is a man-eater. She killed a villager while protecting her cubs. Once she ate the villager, she decided she preferred the taste of human flesh to that of the usual deer and wild pig. She has since stalked and eaten thirteen people. The locals call her Soul-Stealer, because she has stolen fourteen souls."

Perez came up behind Miles and muttered, "The Colonel's lost a few shingles from his roof, if you ask me."

Goldstein produced a pack of Camels and passed it around, but everyone was too jittery to light up. There was something wrong with the Colonel's eyes. There was a scary dark spark in the center of each pupil, and when he looked back at his men with those eyes, Miles felt his bowels fill with ice. Suddenly the Colonel was more frightening than Charlie and the whole North Vietnamese Army.

Miles couldn't stop thinking about the compasses. It was weird how he and the others had all managed to lose their compasses. Only the Colonel had one, taking a reading on it now and then without sharing it with the others.

Where the hell was he leading them?

"Keep your eyes and ears peeled, gentlemen, " he said. "A VC patrol has been reported in this area."

"Patrol my ass, " said Jackson, the only black soldier in the unit. "I heard it was a brigade, man. A North Vietnamese Army brigade loaded to the teeth with Soviet armor and artillery. I mean, what the hell are we doing out here?"

"Hunting tiger, son, " the Colonel quipped with a grin.

Perez said quietly, "The Colonel is loopier than a jumping bean. Section Eight. Oh Jesus, I'm hungry."

For the hundredth time, Miles checked the magazine in his Colt .45 automatic and then bolstered it. The other weapon, slung over his left shoulder, seemed to gain a pound with each step he took. It was an autoloading Ithaca model 37 shotgun, and because it spread the shot horizontally, it did a lot of quick, efficient killing. And it scared the crap out of Miles Havers.

Charlie's in the neighborhood. Charlie's got his eye on us.

"Hey Sarge," whispered Corporal Smart, who was eighteen but could pass for Uvelve. "What if we do find a tiger?"

And again the Colonel overheard, even though he was yards up ahead. "There's a tiger out here all right, son. Heard about her back at the Ponderosa," he added, referring to the Trench villa that had been turned into a bar at military headquarters in Saigon. "Big one, too, they said. Our man-eater for sure."

"Sir, don't you think—"

"Panthera tigris," the Colonel merrily sang out. "Largest of the cat family. Lives anywhere he goddamn pleases. Ton'll find him in snow and bamboo, rain forest and desert." He chuckled. "Tigers own the world. "

"May I ask sir," Perez said, "why we are going after this tiger?"

The Colonel suddenly stopped in the track, turned, and planted a frankly astonished look on his raggedy combat unit. "I should think, First Sergeant Perez," he said, "that that was rather obvious." Then he turned and resumed marching.

"Now," Corporal Smart murmured, his teeth chattering. "I. Am. Really. Scared."

Miles was scared, too, for the first time since landing in this nonsensical nightmare. He hadn't had any opinions about the war one way or the other; by the time he had wondered if he should burn his draft card and run to Canada, he was doing push-ups at Ford Ord. But now he had only one ambition: to get out alive, back to the U.S. and Erica.

"Sir, " Perez said, "do I have permission to deploy the men to search for food?"

"Not necessary, son. Tou'll be feasting before the night is out."

They stared at each other with large eyes set in gaunt, dirty faces. Feasting on what? they all wanted to ask.

"But here's an appetizer to put you on," the Colonel said, and he stopped and harvested dark green leaves from a tall plant sprinkled with unusual red flowers. He doled the leaves out like Holy Communion, admonishing: "Chew well, it's the juice you want."

"Hey, Sarge?" whispered Corporal Smart, pimples standing out on his boyish chin. "We supposed to live on grass?"

Perez frowned in thought. He looked at the frightened faces around him. And he knew what they were thinking: it was happening more and more, GIs turning on their officers. "Fragging," it was called, rolling fragmentation grenades into officers' tents, blowing the bastards sky high.

"Let's just stay cool," Perez said.

The leaves turned out to be not so bad, tasting sort of like spinach, with a sharp edge that reminded the men of caffeine. With their stomachs protesting so loudly for food, they began to chew the leaves the way the Colonel was, chomping and swallowing as if they were eating Caesar salad with croutons. And suddenly they were more ravenous than ever, eating down the leaves and stripping more from the bush, cramming their mouths with imagined delicacies.

And soon the jungle was humming with brand-new hues. It was if they had landed in Oz and everything was carved from emeralds. The damp ground seemed to sigh lovingly beneath their boots, as if they trekked across a woman's breast. The air solidified, turned into silk. It tasted like the Fourth of July. Miles felt his ears become extra-sensitive; he swore he could hear the fog rolling into the Golden Gate, on the other side of the world.

"Uh oh," Jackson said at one point, but didn't elaborate.

Miles squinted through the thick ropy jungle vines and saw in the distance a bright red pagoda rising out of the mist, its curved eaves gleaming with gold.

He blinked.

The pagoda vanished. It was only a dead tree.

"Tigers hunt at night," the Colonel said as the sun began to retreat from the jungle. They heard bird calls that sounded like little girls laughing, and once, when they stopped to pick more leaves and

eat them, Miles swore he could hear the petals of a night-blooming flower opening up. "A tiger's forelimbs and shoulders," the Colonel said, "are heavily muscled, and the paws are equipped with long, sharp, retractile claws. The skull is foreshortened to increase the shearing leverage of the powerful jaws. The tiger is one strong mother."

Goldstein started to hum the tune to "Ruby, Don't Take Tour Love to Town." He had a beatific smile on his face.

Corporal Smart said, "Oh wow."

Perez was holding his hand up before his face, sniffing his wrist.

Miles paused to regard a big shiny popcorn machine standing among the ferns. It was the old-fashioned kind, on a cart with big wheels and a top made to look like a circus tent. He smacked his lips in anticipation of a salty, buttered snack.

But then the popper winked out of existence and became just a mundane pile of rocks again.

"There she is!" the Colonel said in a hushed voice, stopping so abruptly that Smart bumped into him. "What you gentlemen are looking at," he whispered as he parted elephant-ear leaves to peer into a clearing, "is your Indochinese tiger, which is darker than your Indian, and lighter than your South Chinese tigers. Hunted to near extinction in the last century. Isn't she a beauty?"

They peered through the foliage. "I don't see a tiger."Goldstein said.

Neither did Miles. Just a dark clearing with grass that looked like pearls. The newly born moonlight was playing games with the laws of nature: shapes were shifting and changing, stretching and springing back. But something was moving through the brush. They could hear it, feet softly padding over rot and decay.

"Jesus," Corporal Smart said. "There she is."

And there she was indeed, just entering the clearing, a sleek beauty gliding on streamlined haunches, her fur like snow in the moon's glow, slashed with dramatic black stripes and softly blushed along the back in sunset colors. She was so beautiful that the men were momentarily breathless.

Why doesn't she scent us? Miles wondered.

She swung her head and looked right at them with slanting, almond-shaped eyes. She licked her lips with a surprisingly delicate pink tongue. She froze, as if sensing danger.

269

The Colonel stood up, fearless, faced the six hundred pounds of sheer cat, and fired a single clean shot into her breast. She went down with a startled gasp.

The Colonel rushed into the clearing, whipped out his knife, exposed a white underbelly, and executed a swift, neat slice from her throat down to her loins.

The tiger screamed, her outrage flying up to the stars. Then the Colonel dropped to his knees and plunged his hands inside and began scooping out riches—kidneys, intestines, ruby red liver—all smothered in hot blood-sauce. "Eat hearty, gentlemen!" he cried.

The starving men didn't hesitate.

Perez was the first to dive into the gaping belly, emerging with arms red to the elbows, his fists clutching something yellow and glistening. "Sweetbreads," he said triumphantly, and proceeded to devour it.

As Miles went to join the feast, he glanced at the tigress's face. Her eyes were open, and for an instant she looked almost human. And then he felt his hunger bellow for him to get moving, and he joined the feeding frenzy.

The men lobbed offal at one another, and painted red stripes on themselves, laughing like kids in a sprinkler on a hot summer day. They gorged on tiger-spirit, telling themselves that they were consuming Soul-Stealer's soul, and maybe even the souls of the people she had eaten. They filled their mouths with morsels warm and sticky and tasting of salt and iron. Miles stripped off his shirt and slapped a handful of congealing blood on his white skin, absorbing tiger-power through his fatigued and bewildered flesh.

He could have sworn that the tigress's heart was still beating as he hacked it in tnvo and tossed a portion to Jackson. And as he gnawed on tough cardiac muscle, he pushed a nagging thought from his mind, an ugly thought that kept whispering: She was still alive when the Colonel slit her open.

And then the thought was gone, because they were no longer thinking men but limbic creatures boiled down to their rankest components of survival lust. They didn't hear the approach of the chopper, and later none of them would even remember how they had gotten out of that clearing. Perez, Smart, Goldstein, and Jackson would all later declare that their first memory was waking up in a military hospital in

Saigon. But Miles would remember briefly coming to on board the HH-53 rescue helicopter, and hearing someone say, "Jesus, what did these guys do? They're covered in blood but they aren't wounded."

"Look at their mouths, they ate something."

"But what? There was nothing there. "

"I saw something. . . ."

THE PHONE RANG, jarring Miles from his thoughts. It was Titus, calling at last. "Sorry, my friend," he said. "Apparently the agent who claimed her at the airport is an accomplice. Catherine Alexander's really gone to ground this time. We don't know where she is."

"Time to flush her out," Miles said.

"I've got an open line to the CIA," Titus said. "As soon as they know something, we'll know something." Miles knew his friend could make this promise, because Titus had been with the Central Intelligence Agency for seventeen years, before retiring and starting his own "security" company. He still had friends in the agency, which he had joined when he had been discharged from the army back in 1970.

Like Miles, Titus Perez—now a CEO but formerly a first sergeant—had the tiger-power. *Six went in and six came out, but only three survived. . . .*

"I'VE BEEN THINKING," Michael said as they walked down the quiet residential street in Washington, D.C., the sharp wind in their faces.

"What about?" Catherine's voice was muffled by the big woolen scarf that concealed nearly all of her lace. They had finally been driven to leave Mrs. O'Toole's Bed & Breakfast to search for a computer. It had been three days since Catherine had contacted the Hawksbill group, asking them to look for Tymbos. She needed to know if they had found anything.

"What Sabina said about returning to the birth-soul." Michael brought his hands up, blew into them. "Jesus said something similar. He said that unless we become as little children we cannot enter the kingdom of heaven. I wonder. . .

"What?"

"If it was Jesus she heard in the temple at Alexandria."

When Catherine looked at Michael, she noticed how the cold air gave him a ruddy look, a man created for the outdoors, not for church cloisters. "I have a confession to make," he had said yesterday after their escape from Los Angeles International Airport. But before he could say another word, a police car had pulled up behind them and for one frozen, heart-stopping instant, they thought they had been caught. "You can't park here," the cop had said, letting them go with just a warning, but the fear had been enough to make them drive on in silence, until they got to John Wayne Airport and a flight to Washington, D.C. After the plane lifted off and Catherine was able to relax a little, she asked him what he had been about to say. And he had said, "It was nothing. Just that I had been worried that I wouldn't be able to get you out of LAX before the feds claimed you." But he had avoided looking at her as he said it, and Catherine hadn't pressed it.

They had arrived in D.C. last night to find the temperature a chilling twenty degrees and dropping. Before heading into the city, they had separated at the airport, Catherine going in search of a gift shop that might offer winter wear, Michael to find a Traveler's Aid to see about accommodations for the night. Catherine had met him thirty minutes later with two shopping bags stuffed with down jackets, mufflers, gloves, and knitted caps, and Michael with the news that he had found a bed and breakfast for them to stay at.

At the street corner now, as they waited for the light, he searched her face. "Are you all right?"

She knew what he meant. It had been eleven days since Hungerford's blasting had delivered up the Jesus fragment—eleven days of running, hiding, grabbing sleep here and there. "Does it show? Do I look awful?" she said, trying to smile.

He returned the smile, but she saw something flicker in his eyes just before he turned away. Catherine thought: He wants to tell me I look beautiful.

She drew in a sharp breath, startled by her thoughts.

And then suddenly Michael was looking across Wisconsin Avenue. "Do my eyes deceive me?" he said.

Catherine looked across the street. And then she saw what he was staring at.

A computer store, all lit up for Christmas, crowded with shoppers, and a big friendly sign on the window that read:

DIANUBA 2000
Come In And Try Out The Newest Internet Software!
FREE!!

"Stay close to me, Catherine," Michael said as they made their way through the chaotic store looking for the demonstration computers.

They saw evidence of Havers's power everywhere. His software dominated the market; people standing in line at the cash registers were holding armfuls of computer games and PC software created by Dianuba Technologies; women were buying up the interactive CD-ROM romance game "Butterfly3." And people were two-deep at the counter, putting in their orders for Dianuba 2000, due to be released at 12:01 January 1, if the Justice Department didn't intervene.

Catherine and Michael found the demonstration computers, where people were happily cruising the Web, struggling with MUDs, discovering the joys of real-time chat in virtual worlds. While they waited for an available computer, Catherine cautiously scanned the holiday crowd. She paused on two women at a terminal, both laughing about something one of them was demonstrating to the other. As she watched them, Catherine realized they were mother and daughter, and that the daughter, in her twenties, was introducing her mother to the world of computers. Seeing the way the older woman's face lit up as she mastered the mouse, rewarding herself with colorful graphics and jazzy music, Catherine thought that it wasn't much different from the way a mother introduces a child to new experiences—except that now it was the daughter's turn to amaze and delight her mother.

Mother, why didn't you live long enough to let me teach you something?

She looked away and saw Michael watching her. His glance went to the mother and daughter, and then back to Catherine, and she saw in his eyes, in that instant, that he knew exactly what she had been thinking. And then she realized that she knew what he was thinking.

When did we start reading each other's thoughts?

Finally a computer was free. Someone else was about to step up to it, but Catherine was quicker.

While Michael stood lookout, she worked swiftly. It was Scimitar software, faster than what Danno had in his laptop, so that she was in IRC with the click of the mouse.

With relief she saw #Hawksbill listed, which meant they were online and not out Christmas shopping. The question was, were they monitoring the IRC for her return? She was tempted to join the channel but knew she didn't dare. If Havers had somehow found out about Hawksbill, he could be there now, chatting them up with a name taken from the novel. And watching for her to log in.

So she typed: */join #janet.* Hit Enter, and #janet 1 appeared in the right hand window. All she could do now was wait, and stare at the blank screen with her name at the top—*@Janet*—all by itself, waiting for someone from #Hawksbill to notice and log on.

She looked over at Michael, who had managed to divert a salesman. But she saw another one glance over at her, and start to move her way.

She turned back to the blank screen. "Come on," she whispered. "Notice me. Notice Janet."

"Excuse me?" someone said behind her.

Catherine looked into a smiling face. "You don't seem to be doing anything there," he said, "and I'd like to test the software, if you don't mind."

Catherine threw herself into a massive coughing fit. He moved away, found another available terminal.

With a quick glance at the salesperson who was definitely making his way through the crowd toward her, Catherine stared at the blank screen. "Come on," she said a little louder. "See me. Ix>g on."

And then the salesman was there. "So!" he said. "What can I tell you about Dianuba 2000? Are you already familiar with the Internet?"

He looked at the screen. "Oh, you won't find much action in IRC today. It's Christmas Eve, everyone's out shopping!" he said jovially. "And don't forget, a lot of those channels are in Europe, where it's evening already and they're busy opening their presents." He reached over, started to type on the keyboard. "What would you like me to show you? Hey, UNIX a problem? Let me show you how, using this amazing new software, with just one finger you can Telnet your way into Multi-User Dimensions and—"

Catherine flew into another coughing fit, harder this time, catching Michael's attention. "Excuse me," he said, pushing his way through and tapping the salesman on the arm. "I was wondering if you could answer some questions about the latest OS-2?"

Catherine turned her head, coughing ferociously into her muffler.

"Yes," the salesman said with a slight look of disgust. "Of course, sir, come this way."

When they were gone, Catherine desperately wanted to remove the woolen hat and scarf, but she couldn't risk exposing her face. Instead she concentrated on the blank screen, where her name continued to sit by itself, *@Janet,* waiting for someone to join.

She looked at her watch. How long had she been standing here? She sensed other customers milling around behind her, waiting for a turn at the free ride on the Internet. The blank screen was bound to make someone impatient, or suspicious—

<SERVER> Jean-Luc!^mason@ouray.cudenver.edu has joined
    this channel
<SERVER> Sugar!~kharvey@scgrad.demon.co.uk has joined
    this channel

Catherine nearly cried out with relief. They had noticed her!

<Janet> Hi everybody!!!!

<SERVER> Maynard!~rismith@alice.brad.ac.us has joined this
    channel
[Jean-Luc] Janet, we've been waiting for you.
[sugar] Hi! :)))
<Janet> Thank you for finding me.
<SERVER> Benhur!~George@Sebaka-1 .DialUp.Polaris. Telnet has
    joined this channel

Catherine w'as about to type, *Did you find tymbos,* when a customer came and stood behind her. A coughing fit sent him on his way.

[Jean-Luc] Janet, we've seen your picture in the newspapers. Your very beautiful, we hope they don't catch you

<SERVER> Carlos!mmongo@dianuba.com has joined this channel

[BENHUR] Janet: merry Christmas

[sugar] What does it say in the scrolls???? Is the world going to end on new years eve? Should I accept a date with Frankie or just stay home and die? Hehehehehehehe <SERVER> Trilogy!^tombak@ix-or1-22.ix.vetcom has joined this channel

[DOGbert] I don't want to die.

<Janet> The scrolls say that because we are from God we are divine and being divine we are eternal, there is no death

[Carlos] :))

[Jean-Luc] Janet, you can't come here anymore. The FBI is monitoring the IRC channels.

[spaCeman] But not us not Hawksbill

[BENHUR] Not yet

[Carlos] We think

[sugar] Janet: did you read about the woman in Seattle saying she was u?

[spaCeman] And the FBI went to check her out:))))))

<Janet> yes. was that you?

[TrilogY] We thought it would take the feds and everybody off your trail):-p

[Jean-Luc] We're crying wolf, were setting up other channels so that if Dr. Alexander really does set up a channel they won't move so fast. Theylll think its another joke ;-)

Glancing around to make sure no one could see, Catherine quickly typed, "Did you find Tymbos?"

[Jean-Luc] No Tymbos.

[TrilogY] sorry

[sugar] we tried. :(

[BENHUR] Looked all over

Catherine stared at the screen, acutely disappointed. Then she typed:

<Janet> Everybody: better go now. It isn't safe
[DOGbert] good luck
*DOGbert gives Janet a hug *TrilogY dittos
<SERVER> Dogbert has left this channel
<SERVER> Trilogy has left this channel
[sugar] take care :-)
*sugar kisses Janet {{{{hugsDH}}}}
<SERVER> Sugar has left this channel
[Jean-Luc] Will yu ever come back to us?

Catherine stared at the screen, reading the words and gestures of people she had never met nor probably ever would. She didn't know if sugar was a woman or spaCeman a man, if they w ere in their twenties or seventies, if they were all in the United States even.

<Janet> Jean-Luc: probably not *Janet embraces all of you
<Janet> Thank you for helping me
[Maynard] We did it for Barrett, too. He created this channel. He made us.
[BENHUR] We're with you in spirit.
<SERVER> Maynard has left this channel
<SERVER> Benhur has left this channel
<Carlos> Janet: God go with you and keep you

Catherine looked at the righthand screen. There were only two names left: *@Janet and Jean-Luc*

[Jean-Luc] Janet <Janet> Yes?
[Jean-Luc] Who wrote the scrolls?
<Janet> A woman named Sabina. A prophetess [Jean-Luc] No <Janet> No what?

A long moment passed before the reply scrolled up:

[Jean-Luc] YOU are the prophetess. . . .

/leave
DISCONNECT SERVER
NO CARRIER

THE HEADLINE READ: *Woman Touches Photo of Scroll—Is Cured of Cancer!*

The fact that it was not on the front page of the *New York Times* or Italy's *Oggi*, but an American tabloid called the *National Enquirer*, did not diminish its impact, as far as Cardinal Lefevre was concerned. It merely pointed out the pervasiveness of the insanity. The Vatican was being deluged with phone calls and telegrams from everywhere attesting to the healing powers of the so-called Jesus Fragment.

As he approached a door with a bronze seal that read *Archivio Secreto Vaticano*, he nodded to the priest on duty at a desk, typing away at a computer. Changes had been made. There were now computers down here. The Vatican had joined the Internet back in 1995. Cardinal Lefevre remembered that astonishing moment, four years ago, when twenty thousand manuscript pages were suddenly let loose into cyberspace, offering people around the world stunning images of medieval miniatures and illuminated documents, accessed with the mere click of a mouse.

He entered one of the main storage rooms, which was only a small part of the thirty miles of shelves containing archive material. He knew that people misunderstood the name of this library, "secret" not meaning in this case hidden or classified, and certainly not forbidden, but simply "private," owned by the Church. The Secret Archive was in fact open to scholars and students.

However, on this chilly afternoon on the eve of Christ's birthday, Cardinal Lefevre's steps took him through the open section of the library and into the back, truly a secret area, where massive storage vaults protected thousands of undocumented and uncataloged manuscripts.

He had just received by special courier an envelope filled with photographs. On the back, each had been numbered in pencil, dated 12/15/99 and initialed C.A.—Catherine Alexander. There were additional notes in ink: the date Dec. 17, 1999, a case number, and a police detective's initials.

These weren't all the photographs, of course; only a handful could be obtained as he had to share with the United States government and the Egyptians as well. But they were enough to satisfy His Eminence that what Catherine Alexander had found in the Sinai was something that could not be ignored. Especially not by the man who had helped draft a document, published by the Congregation for the Doctrine of the Faith, which specifically addressed the functions and obligations of the theologian—a title embracing archaeologists as well. In that document, Cardinal Lefevre had made it very clear that theologians who dissented from the established teachings of the Church were committing a sin, in keeping with the 1990 updated version of the catechism, which states: "The task of giving an authentic interpretation of the Word of God has been entrusted to the living teaching office *of the Church alone.*" This extended to ancient documents that so far only might be Christian.

There had been the expected outcry from biblical scholars and historians when the new catechism came out. Dr. Alexander herself had sent off a strongly worded letter protesting the elevation of dissent to an actual sin. But what would these people have? His Eminence wondered. If God's Word was allowed to be freely interpreted by anyone who chose, then chaos would ensue and the Church would collapse. Lines had to be drawn, parameters set, and structure established. It was in fact the daily battle of Cardinal Lefevre's office in the Congregation to see to it that the foundation of Mother Church was not eroded by dissenting theologians.

In particular, he thought darkly as he unlocked an inner vault with a special key, angry young women who stole valuable Church property—if these scrolls were indeed Christian documents—with the intention of translating and, worse, interpreting them for the rest of the world, according to her own twisted bias!

Cardinal Lefevre knew Catherine Alexander. It was he who had sent a Vatican representative to California twenty-seven years ago to order Dr. Nina Alexander to cease her heretical teachings.

Like mother, like daughter, he thought as he brought out a strongbox.

He paused. But O my dear God . . .

Dr. Alexander had no idea the scope of this issue, of that Lefevre was certain. She thought the Church feared women, and that the scrolls would place power in their hands. But what was at stake here was something far bigger. It went beyond Church politics, beyond the power of popes and priests. What Cardinal Lefevre dreaded most was that the scrolls contained something that would shatter the faith of millions.

It had nothing to do with Mary Magdalene. It had to do with the heart of Christianity—Jesus himself. . . .

His hand shook as he regarded one of the scroll photographs and read the ancient Greek: *"When the Savior was a child, he was lost for three days, and his parents frantically searched for him until they found him in the Temple, teaching the priests. Then did Isis rejoice at finding her blessed son Horus. . . . "*

Lefevre trembled with fear. *How will so many saviors affect the worship of the True Savior ?*

He set his fears aside and focused on what had brought him down here, to the deeper regions of the Secret Archives: the word at the top of the first photograph. *Tymbos,* it said. The name of the king the deaconess was to take the scrolls to, should she be persecuted for their sake.

He lifted out the papyrus fragment, found in 1932 in ruins in North Africa, preserved for nearly two thousand years in the Algerian sands. Written in the Greek of the Roman Empire, it appeared to be a letter: "Now that you have been told the precise hour of the Righteous One's return, and the day of the End of Things, your heart can be at peace. For the gift of living forever is yours, as the Righteous One promised. We will never die."

Paleography and radiocarbon dating had placed this fragment around a.d. 100-150. And since Righteous One was one of the Messiah's titles in the Bible, the Vatican had preserved this fragment, on the suspicion that it might be part of a lost gospel.

Was this from the Sabina scrolls? Lefevre wondered now, as he felt a cold finger of fear trace down his spine. Had the author of this letter read the Sabina scrolls and made a copy? Or was the author perhaps the deaconess Aemelia herself, or maybe even Perpetua? This fragment had been found near the ancient city of Timgad. *Tymbos?* the Cardinal wondered. Was there enough of a similarity between the names to make that leap?

There were rumors on the Internet that Dr. Alexander did not have all of the Sabina scrolls, that she was searching for a seventh. *Was Timgad in fact where the seventh scroll was buried ? And was it still there today, in the drifting sands of North Africa, waiting to be found . . . ?*

"ISN'T MODERN TECHNOLOGY grand?" Titus said when his assistant brought in the report. Twenty-four hours ago he had obtained a photograph of Alexander with her new look, and a police sketch of the man who had claimed her at LAX. These had gone out on the wires to every airport, train station, bus depot, newspaper, TV station, and post office, and results were starting to come in.

He picked up the phone that was a direct line to Miles Havers. "We're getting some sightings, my friend," he said with a smile. "Couples matching these descriptions have been spotted in several places. I'm getting my men on it now. We should be able to weed out the false alarms with no problem. And you know what I've heard, my friend? That the man she left Vegas with is a priest. Do you know what this does for us? Tonight is Christmas Eve. If you were a priest, Miles, where would you go on Christmas Eve?"

"I WON'T BE long," Michael said. "The church is just three blocks away and around the corner." He waited for Catherine's response.

Bent over the papyrus, her hands in rubber gloves purchased from the local drugstore, she was painstakingly folding back the first leaf of scroll number five. "Four scrolls down and two to go," she said. "And we're no closer to finding the seventh than when w'e started." Catherine straightened and turned to him. "I know you want me to go with you, but I can't."

He walked up to her, reached out as if to touch her face, but stopped himself. He was remembering a moment from earlier, when they were in the computer store waiting for an available terminal. They had both been watching a mother and daughter together, and when Michael had turned to Catherine, when his eyes met hers, it had occurred to him that he suddenly knew what she was thinking. It made him remember the only other time in his life when he had connected with someone in that way—w'hen he w'as young and his father would come home drunk, and Michael wanted to have it out with him for terrorizing the family. His mother would settle wise eyes on her son and send a message of love and patience, and unspoken words that said: "Let him be, Michael, you don't understand. Maybe someday, when you're older."

Michael never got a chance to reach that age of understanding, because his mother had died of cancer before her forty-fifth birthday, and his father had wasted away in the alcoholic ward of a county hospital.

But he would never forget how his mother's eyes could speak and only he could read the message. He had forgotten w'hat that w'as like, until today when his eyes had met Catherine's and he had known what she was thinking.

"Isaiah," he said now, quietly, almost touching Catherine's face. "Sixty-six, twelve. 'And I shall extend peace to her, like a river.'" She w'as held briefly in his gaze. And then she turned away. "Catherine," he began. And then he said, "Hey."

She saw that he was staring at the TV set. "Isn't that Miles Havers?"

"It is!" she said, quickly turning the volume up.

Havers w'as making a live press announcement from his Santa Fe home. "I don't know' howr word got out that Dr. Alexander and I are in these negotiations for the purchase of the scrolls," he w'as saying in his trademark charming tone, his smile lighting up the screen. "But I can assure you, I had no intention of any of this getting out."

"What!" Catherine said.

"Mr. Havers," a reporter said, "are you saying that there are in fact scrolls? You can confirm this?"

"Yes, I can. And the reason I want to buy the scrolls from Dr. Alexander is because I am afraid she is going to destroy them. These scrolls belong to humankind, not just to one person. I thought that my offer of fifty' million dollars would persuade her to share the scrolls with the world. So far Dr. Alexander has refused my offer."

"I don't believe this!" Michael said.

Catherine changed channels. On another news program: "Billionaire Miles Havers, chairman of Dianuba Technologies, disclosed today that he is currently involved in private negotiations with Dr. Catherine Alexander to arrange for the purchase of ancient scrolls for the sum of fifty' million dollars—"

"I don't get it," Michael said. "Why is he doing this? What does he gain?"

Catherine shook her head, nonplussed. She clicked the remote and got a Baltimore station: ". . . this admission came after an anonymous tip to the *New York Times* from someone who claims to be close to Miles Havers. The unidentified source said that the scrolls in question did come from the Sinai Peninsula, that they are definitely Christian in origin, that they were smuggled illegally into this country, and that the seller of the scrolls is the one who found them, Catherine Alexander, still at large."

"It has to be Havers himself doing this," Michael said. "If the tipster had been anyone else, Havers would be denying everything. So he's made this whole thing up."

"But why, Michael? What does he get out of this?"

"Maybe he thinks he can force your hand, make you come forward and deny it all."

When the news program segued into a commercial, Catherine turned off the TV. "Well it won't work. I'm staying hidden and silent, and I'm going to keep translating the scrolls." She looked at Michael. "You'd better get to church. Midnight Mass is in an hour."

"Are you sure I can't persuade you to come with me?"

"The fifth scroll is in worse condition than the others," she said. "I have to start work on it."

But he didn't leave. And when she felt his eyes on her, she turned to him and said, "Michael, I can't go with you."

"Why not?"

"Because the night my mother died, I cursed the Church, and I also cursed God. I can't go back."

"Of course you can. You can always go back."

Suddenly she was remembering what he said two nights ago, at the Atlantis: "Everyone is born homesick for heaven. The trick is finding the way back."

How? she had wanted to ask.

But now she was remembering what Sabina had written: *"And so it came to me the true meaning of The Way—for it is not the way forward, but the way back to the beginning."*

Did Sabina find the way back?

Catherine shook her head. "I wouldn't know the way, Michael."

"Then let me show you the way."

And she looked at his outstretched hand.

THE NIGHT WAS bitterly cold, with a wind that cut like knives. But a crowd was streaming through the open doors of the church, while cars continued to pull up in front, congesting the narrow street.

So many believers, Catherine thought as she looked up at the Gothic spires supporting the dark, starless, and moonless sky. She heard the organ inside, playing "O Holy Night," the light pouring through the open doorway looked like liquid gold. Catherine watched the people delivering themselves into the light, some somber, others cheerfully waving to friends; there were elderly moving slowly on canes, and children who ran to ogle the magnificent, brightly lit Nativity' scene on the lawn.

As she and Michael drew close to the church, Catherine felt her heart begin to thump. Despite the frigid temperature, she started to perspire; she suddenly needed to throw off her coat, to expose herself to the cleansing night air.

Finally, at the foot of the steps, she stopped.

Michael looked at her. "What is it?"

"I can't."

"There's nothing to be afraid of."

"Michael, I *can't.'*"

When he saw how pale she was, he led her around to the side of the church, into the private garden where a ghostly birdbath stood among frost-blanketed shrubs. Catherine sank onto a stone bench and pulled off her scarf, lifting her face to the cold wind and inhaling deeply.

"Why did you come with me?" Michael asked, searching her face. When she didn't respond, he said, "You did it for me, didn't you?"

"I'm worried."

"About what?"

"That you're going to leave the priesthood."

"Why does it worry you?"

"Because it won't solve anything, Michael. If you leave, you'll only add more guilt to what's already troubling you."

"So you thought that if I could bring a soul back to the fold, I would decide to stay? Catherine, you can't go to church for *my* sake. You have to go for your own."

"Do you still have faith, Michael?"

He gave her a confused look. "What do you mean?"

"All those savior gods Sabina found—"

"They aren't new. They're in the history books—Hermes, Tammuz, Mars. They don't weaken my faith in Jesus, if that's what you were wondering. I see them as heralds who came to prepare the world for His coming."

Michael paused. "What happened back there? You turned deathly white."

"I was remembering," she said.

"Remembering what?"

Catherine pulled off her gloves, exposed her perspiring hands to the cold air. "When I was little," she said quietly, "I stuttered whenever I was nervous or scared. It went away as I got older, but when we first moved to Southern California, when I was ten years old and a new pupil at Our Lady of Grace School, I still had the problem. My mother had informed the school about it, but I guess someone forgot to tell Sister Immaculata, the fifth-grade teacher who, unfortunately, also stuttered. It happened on my first day."

Catherine raked her fingers through her short platinum hair. Her words came out on little puffs of breath. "We were learning about the explorers and I was terrified Sister was going to call on me." She shook her head, remembering. "And of course she did. The lesson was about Vasco Da Gama, but when Sister said his name, it came out V-Vasco D-Da G-Gama. So when she asked me a question and I stuttered out the answer, 'V-Vasco D-Da G-Gama,' the class roared with laughter. Sister accused me of mocking her. She made me stand on a stool and face the class. She hung a sign around my neck that said 'miscreant.' She said I was to stand there until I had learned some respect, and then she resumed teaching the class.

"The kids giggled and whispered about me. I started to cry. And then I realized that I had to go to the bathroom. I was terrified of speaking up. So I tried to hold it. After a while, I couldn't, and it started to trickle down my legs. The kids howled with laughter. And then the laughter died and they were silent, which was even worse because I knew they were feeling my shame. Sister accused me of doing it on purpose. She hauled me off the stool, calling me a filthy little girl, and dragged me to the principal's office."

Catherine plucked at the fringe of her muffler. Aware of Michael's eyes on her, she continued in a quiet voice: "The school nurse took care of me while the principal called my parents. My mother was away at a seminar at the time, but my father was home—well, he was at the college where he taught. Since it was morning, he said he would come for me at the lunch hour. So I sat in the principal's office, my rinsed-out panties in a plastic bag in my lap, waiting for my father to fetch me.

"Lunchtime came and went. And then the afternoon. They telephoned my father again, leaving a message for him. And then school was out and the kids all went home. And then the teachers went home, and finally the custodians were washing the floors.

"The school nurse drove me home. My father was there. He said he had forgotten. He never even asked what happened. He went back into his study and that was that."

Catherine stood up, inspected the film of ice in the birdbath. Inside the church, Mass was starting. "The Church was everything to my father, Michael," she said. "He was something of a mystic. He never should have had a child, he wasn't meant to be a parent."

"So the Church meant more to your father than you did, and you're mad at him for that."

She spun around. "*God* meant more to him than I did! Michael, I didn't curse God because of Father McKinney or the way my mother died. I cursed God because my father loved Him more than he loved me. You know that he wouldn't have left *God* sitting in the principal's office with wet underpants!"

She reached out and touched the ice in the birdbath, splintering it. "The kids at school were awful to me after that. You can imagine the names they had for me. If it hadn't been for Danno—"

"And you never told your mother about it?"

Catherine returned to the bench. "How could I? She worshipped my father . . . and when he died I was so full of anger because we had never resolved it. I always kept waiting for when I was older, more mature, so I could talk to him about it, clear things up. But then he got himself killed and it *was* my mother's fault, because she kept writing books that upset the Church and drove my father away!"

"And because of that you took up your mother's work—the same work that drove him away, ultimately to his death."

She gave him a startled look. "You think I took the scrolls as some perverse way of punishing my father?"

"He is the one you're mad at, isn't he? He is the one you can't forgive?"

Catherine stared down at her hands. She said softly, "They accused him of being a spy, Michael, and he didn't even deny it. He didn't lift a finger in his own defense. He let them put a hood over his head and execute him. When I went to the airport to claim his remains, I wanted to rip the lid off the coffin and demand that he tell me why he never came for me that day. I needed to know if it was because I meant so little to him."

"You're mad at him for getting killed?"

"We had unfinished business," she said. "He copped out." Catherine rose from the bench, began to put her gloves back on. "And that is why I can't walk into that church with you, Michael. It was *his* Church and *his* God. I want no part of it. I shouldn't have come. But you go in, Michael, you belong in there. I have work to do."

He watched her walk away down the street, back toward Mrs. O'Toole's and the fifth scroll.

The Fifth Scroll

FIRST, WE MUST *die*.

Just as Osiris, the Good Shepherd, did. In order to achieve a state of grace, we were required to undergo the same death and birth as the savior did, for only through death and rebirth could we achieve eternal life.

This was what the priestesses of the Temple of Isis preached.

In Alexandria, the followers of Isis, Queen of Heaven, outnumbered the followers of every other god. And I recall that in Antioch, the worshippers of Isis were more numerous than any other religion.

I became involved with Isis, the Savior Goddess, when I offered my services at the hospital attached to the temple. Although I still had my inheritance, I wanted to work, and the nursing sisters had much to teach me in the field of midwifery, while I was able to share with them secrets I had learned in Persia and India. Often, during the course of my duties at the hospital, I helped take care of the sick and I sat at the bedsides of the dying.

And this was how I came to observe the many ways in which people die.

I observed that there are those who approach death with dignity and calm, and those who become restless and frightened. There are those who treat it as sleep, those who welcome death, those who anticipate terror, and those who are full of questions. As I watched them close their eyes and expire their final breath, I watched for the departure of the soul.

Osiris is called the Resurrected One, and his story was by now a familiar one, for he lived thousands of years ago. His birth was prophesied by a star, his mother was a virgin, wisemen and shepherds paid homage at his cradle. As with Krishna and the Righteous One, Osiris was taken as a baby to a distant land to escape the slaughter of innocents by a jealous king. Upon the death of Osiris, the sun stood still in the sky and the earth was covered in darkness. And then the earth shook, as it had when Tammuz and Krishna died. Osiris then descended into the underworld, arising after three days, reborn in life.

The followers of Isis believe that those who have undergone the ritual death and birth of Osiris will themselves be resurrected. And so when Mira, the High Priestess, invited me to take part in the great Mystery, I accepted.

Here, the initiates enter a period of fasting and ritual cleansing, and are then trained in a high form of meditation, which results in a mystical union with the Supreme. As with Tammuz and Hermes, we were led into a subterranean chamber beneath the temple, the symbolic underworld, where we were dressed in white shrouds and given a drink from the cup of death. We then "died" through contemplation, and communicated with the spirits of the dead—and with God. After three days, we were led out to the sunlight and baptized with wine, symbol of the uterine blood, and the congregation greeted us with embraces and kisses, for we had been reborn. We joined the others in a communal meal of bread and wine, which symbolize the body and blood of Osiris. And now we were permitted to read the ancient scripture, which was written more than two thousand years ago: a prophecy which says, "Rejoice O people of this time, the Son of Man will make his name for all eternity." The sacred text tells of a king about to be born, who is called Redeemer, and who comes to deliver Egypt from strife and chaos. I wondered: Is this the Righteous One ? Is it perhaps Krishna, or Mithra? Or Hermes? For I had learned by now that many saviors are called Redeemer, many are the virgin-born sons of a god, and all, it seems, are born only to die for the world's sins.

Mira said the prophecy refers to one who is yet to come.

I learned many things in Alexandria, not the least of which was what I had also learned in Persia and India: that there is no death, only eternal life—this, as I have told you, is the third of the Immutable

Truths. And I learned more, Perpetua, in this enlightened city of Egypt. For example, the writings of Epicurus tell us that peace of mind is attained through control of desire and the elimination of fear. Epicurus instructs us to remind ourselves that there is nothing to fear from God, there is nothing to fear in death. I expand upon this basic wisdom with what I learned in the East and what I have already told you: that there is nothing to fear from God because we are made of God; and there is nothing to fear in death because we return to God.

To the teachings of Epicurus, who said that good can be attained through forgiveness, I add this revelation from Isis: that forgiveness is the first step of the threefold path that leads us back to the birth-soul.

Forgiveness, Perpetua, is the fourth of the great Truths.

But what I learned from Isis was a very profound form of forgiveness. It is not simply the absolving of an enemy, or one who has done us wrong. Forgiveness, in order for it to lead to enlightenment, must encompass all those things which disturb the tranquillity of our soul.

For the Fourth Truth, Perpetua, that will lead you back to your birth-soul and to the Gift, you must forgive those who have hurt you, but you must also forgive the barking dog that robs you of sleep, forgive the heat of summer, the cold of winter; forgive the ingrown toenail, the torn sandal, the flea that bites; forgive the flatness of the wine, the dust in your house, the cranky child, wrinkles, gray hair, a missing comb; forgive rising prices, a forgotten birthday, the crowd in the market, the nosy neighbor, a lost wager, a disappointment, a nightmare, an insult, bread gone stale, the fishbone in the stew.

And these are only the beginning. Such forgiveness must be practiced daily and with sincerity. And when this has become a daily and comfortable habit, then the next Truth can be put into practice.

It was from Isis also that I learned the fifth Truth, but I did not see it at the time. To fully grasp the revelations that I had experienced during my death and rebirth in Alexandria, I would have to travel many miles across the sea, to a distant land of mist that I had heard of only in legend.

When Cornelius Severus announced the end of his sojourn in Alexandria, I asked if I might accompany his retinue. For I had not found the Righteous One in Egypt, I had not yet been able to ask him my question. But although I had no reason to believe I would find him

in the land of mists, I knew that I must continue my search for him.
And so we headed north, to the land of the Shape-Shifters.

DAY TWELVE

SATURDAY
DECEMBER 25, 1999

"Miss Garibaldi? Hello? Are you awake, dear?"

Catherine went to the door but didn't open it. "Yes, Mrs. O'Toole?"

"I was just wondering, dear, if you will be joining us for Christmas dinner later. I need to know how many table settings we'll have to have."

"I don't think so, Mrs. O'Toole," Catherine said. The house was already filled with the rich smells of Christmas cooking. "Thank you for inviting me, but I really don't think I'm up to it."

"That's all right, my dear. I'll bring a plate up to you. Will your brother be joining us?"

Your brother. Michael. He had gone to midnight Mass last night, and then to daybreak Mass this morning. Now he was at the third Christmas service. "Yes," she said through the door. "He told me this morning he was looking forward to it." Those hadn't been his exact words. "Mrs. O'Toole might find it suspicious if we both stayed in our rooms and didn't accept her invitation," was what he had really said. Catherine knew that Michael was feeling guilty about his freedom to move about while she was a prisoner in her room.

After Mrs. O'Toole left, Catherine returned to the table where the fifth scroll, in alarming condition, was laid out. She looked at the last words she had read, "*We are made of God . . . we return to God. . . .*" She hardly recalled reading the words; she had begun translating and, at some point during the night, while Michael was at church celebrating the birth of Jesus, Catherine had ceased seeing words on papyrus but images instead—images that had seemed so real that, for a while, she had felt as if she were there in Alexandria with Sabina.

And the ancient savior-gods of long ago.

She went to the window and looked out. The street was quiet; last night there had been carolers, and the whole block had been lit up with Christmas lights. This morning she had heard the other guests leave the house for their various churches. Mrs. O'Toole and her sister had attended the midnight Mass with Michael; Catherine had heard them come in at 1:30 A.M., inviting Michael to a glass of sherry to celebrate. Voices through walls, scenes viewed through windows.

She saw Michael on the sidewalk below. Bundled up against the cold, with the black hat and muffler, and long black coat he had purchased the day before on Wisconsin Avenue, he cut an arresting figure.

"*You have to forgive your father for not coming for you that day. . . .*"

And what about you, Michael? Why don't you forgive that sixteen-year-old boy for not saving an old man's life? How long are we both going to go on punishing ourselves, burdened by our guilt?

She was near the end of the fifth scroll. After that, there was only one left. And when that was translated, and if it contained no further clues to lead them to the seventh, then it would all be over. And she and Michael would say good-bye.

When she heard a sudden, staccato knocking at her door, she thought it was Mrs. O'Toole. But it was Michael. Catherine let him in, quickly closing the door behind him. The cold from outside was still on him, like an invisible blanket.

"Turn on the TV," he said, shrugging out of his coat. "Hurry."

"What—?"

"I just happened to see it downstairs, as I was passing through the living room."

Catherine flipped through the channels which were showing the usual Christmas programs, until she came to a midday news break.

There was her picture on the screen again; she was almost getting used to it. And the photograph she had taken of the Jesus fragment, also a familiar sight. "What is it this time?" she said impatiently.

Michael pulled off his hat and gloves, and turned up the volume on the TV. ". . . radiocarbon testing was performed at the Institut Technologique in Paris, and at the same time paleographers in Germany and England have been independently examining the fragment using a handwriting analysis called paleography. According to the carbon dating, the papyrus is placed around the year one hundred A.D., and handwriting analysis confirms this date."

"This is wonderful news!" Catherine said.

But Michael held up a cautionary hand.

"Infrared analysis of the fragment," the news anchor continued, "has revealed earlier writing underneath, writing that was washed off but which can be read through infrared. It is a bill of sale which has been dated to the reign of Claudius Caesar. . . ."

"That's not unusual," Catherine said. "Papyrus was often used over and over because it was so expensive."

"However," the newscaster said, "infrared spectrometry revealed something else that had been washed off the fragment, a stamp bearing a museum catalog number. . . ." The picture on the screen switched to a close-up of a faded circle containing the words *Musee d'Antiquites* 4.11.45, faintly seen. "It has been confirmed that this papyrus was part of a collection stolen three years ago from the Museum of Antiquities. . . ."

Catherine frowned. "Stolen!"

A scientist in Denver was being interviewed: "Our lab received a minute portion of the fragment," she said. "We removed particles of the ink and examined them under an electron microscope. We found that the ink contained anatase, titanium dioxide, which wasn't invented until the 1920s. However, since it is possible for an ancient document to contain a minute trace of anatase, we submitted the ink to particle induced X-ray emission and found massive quantities of anatase, which means the ink is of contemporary manufacture."

A film clip came on next, showing an unhappy-looking man speaking before a bank of microphones, and in the lower right corner of the TV screen: *Cairo National Television, from an earlier tele-*

cast. The man was speaking in Arabic, and the American newscaster was saying, "Mr. Nicholas Papazian came forth late last night with a confession that has shocked the world. The Sinai Scrolls, he said, were his creation, made in a small room at the back of his antiquities shop in Cairo. He created the take scrolls, he said, at the request of Dr. Catherine Alexander."

Catherine gasped. "I've never even met the man!"

"Mr. Papazian," the anchor said, "has a history of making and selling forged documents, being most well known for the so-called Pontius Pilate Letter, which was sold at auction fifteen years ago for a record price of ten million dollars, only to be discovered shortly afterward to have been a forgery. Mr. Papazian spent six years in prison, after admitting to the crime, and his license to sell and export antiquities was revoked by the Egyptian government."

"I've heard of this man," Catherine said. "It isn't just Papazian, it's his whole family. They're one of the biggest underground sources for illegal artifacts in the world. The man is obscenely rich and hides his criminal activities behind a facade of newfound respectability!"

"So what's going on?" Michael said. "Why is he saying you paid him to forge the scrolls? An even bigger question is why? Why would he admit to such a crime if he didn't do it?"

"For enough money he would probably admit to anything. Havers has to be behind this. But how did they do it? Michael, I was there when Hungerford's men found the fragment. And I found the basket with the scrolls in it. Believe me, it hadn't been placed there recently, that basket was firmly embedded in the soil."

Catherine moved closer to the TV set, squinting at the picture of the fragment, shown in the upper right corner of the screen. "If I could get hard copy of this. . . ."

"No problem," Michael said, reaching for his coat. "If this news broke in Egypt last night, then it's likely to be in this morning's papers. I'll be right back."

He didn't have to go far, the Saturday paper was downstairs in the living room, having been gone through by the six guests currently staying at Mrs. O'Toole's establishment.

The story was on the front page, complete with photographs of Catherine, Mr. Papazian, the dig site, and the fragment. And a headline that shouted, FAKE!

"If Havers is behind this," Michael said, "what does he gain?"

Catherine studied the picture of the fragment. "Wait a minute . . . ," she said. She took the newspaper to the table, held it under the light.

"What is it?"

Opening the blue gym bag, she carefully brought out the book that had been protecting the scrolls, unwrapped it, and peeled back the front cover to expose the first leaf of papyrus, the lower half that had been torn from the fragment. She placed the newspaper next to it. "Look at this," she murmured.

Michael bent close. "What am I looking for?"

"The fragment in the picture. Notice the bottom edge. Compare it to the top edge of this leaf."

He looked at one and then the other. "They don't match."

"Michael, this fragment," she said, pointing to the newspaper photo, "isn't the fragment I left behind in my tent."

"A replacement?"

"Those scientists weren't lying! They *did* examine a forgery! Not the document I left behind, the papyrus Hungerford's men found, but a substitute!"

"You mean Papazian replicated it, a deliberate forgery, and then claimed you paid him for it. Then where's the real fragment?"

"Who knows? The switch could have been done at a very high level—maybe Mr. Sayeed is in on it. Or maybe officials in the Egyptian government aren't aware that a switch took place. Papazian could have paid some underling to do the switch for him."

"For Havers?"

"Yes. . . ."

"It's going to be hard to prove. Unless you come out of hiding and tell them what you suspect."

"I have a better idea," she said suddenly, going back to her gym bag and pulling out her datebook. "Before I left the Sinai, I sent a fragment of the papyrus to a friend in Zurich. Hans Schuller, he works at a carbon dating lab!" She flipped through the pages until she found a phone number. "No one knew about it," she said as she went to the phone. "I asked him not to say anything. I knew I could trust him. . . ."

"You're calling him now?"

"I'm trying the lab first."

"It's Christmas day."

She heard the line at the other end ring a few times, then she hung up. "You're right."

"Do you have his home phone number?"

"No, but I'm sure I can get it through information."

Her conversation with Schuller, five minutes later, was brief. "Yes, Hans," she said. "I'm sure that must be it. Lost in the mail. These things happen. What?" She glanced at Michael. "Where *am* I?"

She quickly hung up. "Someone got to him."

"But how could they have known about Schuller?"

"I must have said something about him to Danno, that night in the apartment. Havers's men would have heard it." She ran her hand across the back of her neck, rotated her head and shoulders. She was suddenly very weary. "Michael, you go downstairs and join the others for Christmas dinner."

"No, I'll stay with you."

"Mrs. O'Toole would be disappointed. And someone might get suspicious. Things are happening so fast—"

"Hey," he said softly, placing his hands on her shoulders. "It's going to be all right. No one can find us here. And it's all going to be over soon."

And then you and I will part. "I'm going to keep working on the scrolls. The sooner we get to the end, the better."

"Are you sure you're going to be okay?"

"Don't worry, Michael," she said. "As furious as I am, there is nothing Miles Havers could do or say that would make me do something rash."

JULIUS PLACED THE call from a phone booth at a small shopping center on the Pacific Coast Highway.

"I would like to leave a message for a guest who will be checking in," he said quickly, keeping his eye on the traffic. "I'll have to spell the name for you. . . ."

While he spoke, he removed the newspaper that he had tucked under his arm and placed it on the small tray beneath the telephone. Even now, hours after first seeing the headline, he still felt the shock of it. Fake! How could the scrolls be fake? He had seen them himself; he could swear they were genuine. Catherine knew her specialty; she would have known if they were forgeries.

"Would you mind repeating that back to me?" he said into the phone. Then, satisfied that the person at the other end had accurately taken his message, Julius hung up and looked at his watch. Camilla Williams at *Eye Witness News* had assured him that the broadcast would take place tomorrow—on the network. That had been his only condition to the interview, that it air on network television and not just locally.

By this time tomorrow, this whole terrible ordeal would be over. Catherine would learn the unpleasant truth—that Sabina never finished her story, that there was no seventh scroll—and they would be back together again, resuming their normal lives.

All he could do now was wait. And pray that Catherine stayed where she was, hidden and silent, and not do something rash that would give her whereabouts away.

CORNELIUS SEVERUS WENT to meet with the leader of the Britons in Chichester. . . .

"*Who!*" Catherine said out loud, on the verge of screaming. "Give me the name of the leader of the Britons! Was it Cunobelinus?" Cunobelinus would place Sabina in Britain during the reign of Claudius, almost certainly making the Righteous One Jesus.

Catherine slumped back in her chair and threw down her pen. It was all so frustrating.

What was worse, Catherine was getting near the end of the fifth scroll. And scroll six, from what she could see, was not very long. Sabina had very little chance left to identify the years in which she lived.

Rising from the table, Catherine stretched and looked out the window. There were no stars to be seen; the forecast was for snow. She looked at the time. It was eleven o'clock. Mrs. O'Toole's house was silent, as everyone slept after a day of sherry and Christmas carols.

Catherine had seen Michael only briefly, on his way up to bed, when he had stopped in to see how she was doing. Unfortunately, tomorrow was Sunday, so even the computer store would be closed, as would libraries and any other institutions that might offer Internet access. Monday, he had said. They would find a way to get safely back online on Monday, and do searches on the new names Catherine had gleaned from Sabina's years in Britain.

Looking at the clock again, and realizing that it was eight in the evening in California, she had a sudden wish to call Julius. But she resisted. Instead, she turned on the TV to see if the evening news had any developments to report.

She was not surprised to see Miles Havers's face come on the screen.

Havers's trademark smile was filled with moral concern, as he said, "All I can say is that I am enormously embarrassed, because Catherine Alexander duped me along with everyone else! I feel personally responsible for all the hopes that were raised about the scrolls' containing certain religious information. My offer of fifty million dollars put some sort of validation of authenticity on the scrolls, leading many people to believe they were real. For this I apologize."

"So that's your game," she murmured. "That announcement yesterday, about secretly negotiating for the purchase of the scrolls, was to make sure you'd be interviewed today. To make yourself look like a victim and me look like a criminal."

"Dr. Alexander, of course," he continued, "is a name well known in certain scholarly circles because of her mother, Nina Alexander, who was censured by the Vatican for anti-Church teachings. Not just on one occasion but on several occasions, until finally her position at a Catholic college was terminated. You might recall," he said, smiling at the host, with whom he was having a friendly in-studio chat, "that Nina Alexander claimed to have found proof that women should be pope." He laughed softly, and the interviewer smiled, too, at the absurdity of this. "A psychologist friend of mine has theorized that Catherine Alexander perpetrated this forgery as a way of vindicating her mother, and I think proof of that is the fact that she slipped the word diakonos into the scrolls, ostensibly to prove that women should be priests."

"How dare you," Catherine said to the TV set.

"Mr. Havers, what do you think of this latest development, that Mr. Papazian in Cairo has amended his statement?"

Catherine frowned. Papazian had changed his statement? Had she missed something since the midday news?

"Frankly, I'm not surprised, Jack, that it was really Daniel

Stevenson who actually arranged for the forgery. After all, we're talking about a man who believed the Aztecs came from Martians!"

Catherine stared at the TV screen. Bastard!

Snatching up the newspaper, she quickly thumbed through the business section, scanning the ads for online services. She found Galaxy BBS in Baltimore, offering service within an hour. She gave them her credit card number, which she had written in her date- book before leaving the card in San Francisco.

As promised, service was activated an hour later, and as she entered IRC, she prayed that #Hawksbill was open. But it was Christmas night, and if everyone was with their families, then #Hawksbill wouldn't even exit. She might open #janet again, but there would be little chance of anyone from #Hawksbill even being aware of it. She knew it was risky to go online again. She didn't care. Danno . . . Her mother . . .

She typed /list, hit Enter, and curled her hands into tight fists. *Please . . . please be there . . .*

There it was, #Hawksbill. But there was only one person in the channel. When she logged in she saw that it was Jean-Luc, sitting there all alone with the @ in front of his name, as if he were waiting, on this lonely Christmas night, for someone to drop in. Catherine logged in as Janet.

[Jean-Luc] Merry Christmas, Janet.
<Janet> Merry Christmas
[Jean-Luc] You shouldn't be here. Too dangerous.
<Janet> Has anyone joined you all day?
[Jean-Luc] No. All busy with families.
<Janet> Are you alone?

Catherine waited.

<Janet> Jean-Luc: are you alone?
[Jean-Luc] Yes.
<Janet> Where are you?
[Jean-Luc] against Hawksbill rules
<Janet> You know who I am. I get to know who you are.

Another silence while she waited.

[Jean-Luc] Just a friend. . . .
<Janet> Are you a man or a woman?

As Catherine waited for the reply, she listened to the quiet house and the still night outside, the sky pregnant with snow clouds, blanketing the world in silence and peace. She felt as if she and Jean-Luc were the only two people on earth, faceless, ageless, sexless, just pure thought and electrons, two bodiless persons joining in a space that didn't exist. She didn't even know where in the world "Jean-Luc" was sending from. He or she could be in China, or just across the street. Yet there was something strangely intimate about the moment.

[Jean-Luc] u shouldn't have logged on. Dangerous
<Janet> I had to. Defend Barrett
<Janet> Jean-Luc: have you seen tv?
[Jean-Luc] yes >:-[
<Janet> Barrett DID NOT FORGE TFIE SCROLLS. Dr. Alexander did not forge them. *the scrolls are real* And she was not in communication with Miles Havers for fifty million dollars. He has never contacted her.
[Jean-Luc] Is Havers the Bad Guy?

She stared at the screen. *Is Havers the bad guy?* Translated: Did Havers murder Daniel?

<Janet> Havers is accusing Barrett
<Janet> Havers is accusing Daniel Stevenson of forgery. This is because Daniel is not alive to defend himself. You have to believe it. You have to tell everyone
[Jean-Luc] Janet: is Miles Havers Bad Guy?

She hesitated.

[Jean-Luc] Repeat: is he Bad Guy after dr Alexander?
<Janet> I cant say
[Jean-Luc] You have the sympathy of the Net but Miles Havers is a

powerful man <Janet> I'm afraid.

Catherine watched the screen. The cursor kept blinking, and time dragged. Why wasn't he saying anything? She was tempted to find out Jean-Luc's real identity. She knew she could do it by typing in a command that would disclose his IP address. A little detective work would lead her right to him. Or her.

Catherine typed */whois jean-luc* and held her hand over the Enter key.

But then:

```
[Jean-Luc] Janet: we will do what we can
<SERVER> Jean-Luc has left this channel
/leave
File>Exit
Dialer>Bye
NO CARRIER
```

"MAY I ASK, Reverend Bradshaw, how you came by that photocopy?"

They were sitting in the Oval Office, the President not looking pleased about this late-night interruption. But his visitor was a man with political clout. "I am not at liberty to divulge that, Mr. President. But I had it translated, which is why I called for this emergency meeting on Christmas night."

"And what does the translation say?"

"The so-called savior this papyrus refers to is not our Lord but some animal-headed pagan idol. In short, sir, it is blasphemy. It is the Devil's work. To say that Jesus was only one of many is to diminish Him! To imply that He's just part of a *string* of saviors—" The Reverend had to pause to compose himself. "This implies, Mr. President, that Jesus was an imitator! That His followers borrowed from heathen religions and manufactured their own! These scrolls invalidate Christianity altogether—"

He picked up one of the photographs. "Look at this scroll, sir. Let me tell you what it says. I read from the translation." He settled glasses on his nose. "'Mars was born to a virgin mother and laid in a manger. He was called Redeemer and he died for the sins of mankind.'" Bradshaw yanked off his glasses. "Mars! A stone idol worshipped by godless pagans!"

"I would appreciate it if you came to the point, Reverend."

"Mr. President, everyone knows you to be a God-fearing man and that you would not allow such an obscenity' to continue." Placing a bundle of newspapers and magazines on the coffee table, he held up a tabloid with a headline that read: JESUS WASN'T THE FIRST! "Mr. President, we cannot allow this filth to be loosed upon the American people! Chaos will ensue, and a new age of lawlessness and immorality will dawn! America will become the new Sodom, I promise."

The President cast a distasteful glance at the tabloid. "What are you asking I do, Reverend?"

"That you not give the scrolls to the Egyptians for them to put on public display. Burn them, Mr. President."

"Didn't you see the news this morning? Apparently the scrolls are fake."

"If they are fake, sir, then why is that woman still running with them? I tell you, Mr. President, that this fake story is a ploy on the part of the Egyptian government to gain possession of the scrolls. Once they have them, they will declare the scrolls to be genuine and put them on public display. And I promise you that the public display of those scrolls will spell the certain demise of Christianity!"

"I appreciate your concern, Reverend Bradshaw. But we don't even have the scrolls yet."

"But you have photographs of them."

The President smiled. "Do you possess information that I don't?"

"Mr. President, in all due respect, this is no time for word-dancing. I have it on good authority that this government is in possession of those photographs. And I implore you, sir, as a fellow Christian, to step up this government's efforts to obtain those scrolls."

"This government," the President said, rising to indicate that the meeting was over, "is doing what is necessary and through proper protocol. And in any event, nothing will be done until we know for certain what the scrolls say."

EIGHT MILES OUTSIDE of Washington, in a cluster of buildings totaling 2,500,000 square feet in the middle of 258 acres, where etched into the wall of the main lobby is the biblical verse from John:

"And ye shall know the truth and the truth shall make you free"—the headquarters of the Central Intelligence Agency, where no public tours are held—a team of experts was hard at work in a basement laboratory where the lights had not been turned off since they first went on in 1977.

The team was translating the Sabina scrolls, using photographs from the Santa Barbara Police Department, and the Duke University Logos software.

Their directive: to report at once to the President anything in the scrolls' contents that might affect America's fragile diplomatic alliance with Egypt.

One of the team members, a man who was almost as proficient in ancient Greek as he was in English, read a line in one of the last photographs.

He said, "Oh my God. . . ."

The Fifth Scroll

"BEWARE THE SHAPE-SHIFTERS," *Claudia warned me when I arrived in Britain. She spoke in whispers about the Hyperboreans who live in the north, the fabled Arimaspi who rule a cloud-covered kingdom on top of the earth. She cautioned me about "wee folk" and seal-women, and cats that steal the breath from a baby's lips.*

Claudia was the wife of the centurion who was in charge of this outpost, and I saw how she had fallen under the spell of this strange, misty land. I had come to this country with some foreboding, for it was so alien, and yet I found that I, too, soon loved the wind and the rain and the fog, the bewitching oak groves alive with spirits and fairies, and the mists over the plains, the great sweeping vistas of green for as far as the eye could see.

It was here, Perpetua, where I had not expected it, that my heart found a mate. I fell in love.

Although I started a small group of The Way in my home, with a weekly reading of Maria's epistle, and a sermon about the Righteous One and his message of peace and the victory over death, enjoining one and all to share in the bread and wine of communal joy, I was still seeking answers. Back in Antioch, and in my travels, I had of course heard of the god Aesculapius. Who has not? But I had never set foot in one of his temples. Because this was a military frontier, the first buildings to be erected were the garrisons and the hospitals. The Temple of Aesculapius, although humble, was magnificent by frontier standards.

Over the doorway are these words: First do no harm.

And this I later learned is the first rule of the physicians of Aesculapius, who was himself born of a god to a virgin mother.

It was in the temple of Aesculapius that I fell in love.

Philos was a handsome man, with beautiful eyes and a fine nose. He had a passion for knowledge, and he was a gentle healer. We fell in love and married there, in that misty isle, handsome Philos whose love was balm to my pain and my grief for I could never forget the slaughter of my family back in Antioch. When I told him of the Righteous One, and that I was seeking him to ask him a question, Philos understood, and he said he would help me search.

For Britain, it turned out, was also a land of ancient savior gods.

. . .

DAY THIRTEEN

S omething woke Erica.

She didn't know what at first. The luminous numbers on her clock read 3:00 a.m. She listened again to the silence. Then she rolled her head to the side, and saw that Miles wasn't in bed.

Again.

Over the years, whenever he had been involved in an important transaction, or wrestling with a new software code, he would go with little sleep. But it seemed to Erica that the number of nights she had found him absent from their bed was more than usual lately.

At first she had thought it was because of the antitrust suit the Justice Department was promising to launch to stop the release of Dianuba 2000. Twenty-five million copies of the software had already been shipped worldwide, with everyone waiting for the word: will it be released on January 1 or not? But Miles didn't seem at all concerned about it

Then she thought about the startling press announcement he had made two nights ago, about the scrolls. She had had no idea he had been interested in obtaining them, that he had been in secret negotiations with the fugitive Dr. Alexander. The FBI had been here until late, questioning Miles. And then to find out that the scrolls were fake!

He must be so disappointed, Erica thought as she got out of bed and slipped into her robe. She would coax him back to bed, find a way to console him.

"GOT HER!" TEDDY exclaimed. "Alexander signed up with a local bulletin board in Baltimore. Galaxy BBS. They offer a gateway to the Internet."

Havers came over. They had been at it ever since the computer monitoring Catherine Alexander's credit card account had set off an alarm, several hours earlier, alerting them to a transaction.

"How quickly can you get into their system, Mr. Yamaguchi?"

"Depends. Gotta locate her IP address," Teddy said, his fingers already flying on the keyboard, "put a flag on it, install the tracer software. . . ."

"Get into the subscriber files. Maybe Alexander listed the number she'll be calling from."

"It would make our job a lot easier—Hey! Check this out!"

Miles looked at the screen. Galaxy BBS in Baltimore was operating on Scimitar software. "Talk about making our job easier," Teddy said. He had helped write the security code for Scimitar.

Havers looked at his watch. It was five o'clock in the morning on the East Coast. "Get on it. With luck, she'll log on once more before disconnecting service."

While Teddy got to work hacking into the Galaxy system, Miles left the computer room, stepping out into the hall as he pulled the cellular phone from the pocket of his bathrobe, punching in a pager number. He couldn't resist a secret smile.

His plan had worked. By counting on the fact that Catherine Alexander wouldn't tolerate having her mother's name dragged through the mud, or her friend Daniel being called a forger, and counting also on the fact that she would react the same way she had a few days ago, when negative public opinion had driven her to seek assistance on the Internet, Miles had forced Catherine to rashly attempt another log-on. He decided that his "insurance"—hiring Papazian days ago to forge a fragment and switch it with the real one—had paid off. Because this time, he knew, he had her.

"Sorry, Mr. Havers," Teddy called through the open door. "Dr. Alexander didn't list a Baltimore phone number. She gave Galaxy her Santa Monica number. Smart chick."

Smart chick, indeed, Miles thought, as Titus answered at the other end.

Making sure Teddy couldn't hear, Havers said into the phone, "The Baltimore area. I don't care how you get rid of her and the priest, just be sure you get the scrolls and that computer."

Erica, who had been about to come around the corner, stopped and slowly backed away down the hall. . . .

Monitoring GALAXY BBS
IP address 204.16.78.101
»Nbosc has logged on, 8:02 am
»MrySpncer has logged on, 8:03 am
»Cbalarezo has logged on, 8:03 am
»roberts007 has logged on, 8:05 am
«Nbosc has logged off, 8:07 am
»LtChab has logged on, 8:07 am
»kharvey has logged on, 8:10 am

Miles took his eyes off the computer screen to look at his watch. It was now eight o'clock in the morning in Baltimore. Catherine Alexander still hadn't logged on. The line to Seattle was open, with Titus ready to give orders to his agents.

"MICHAEL! OPEN UP. It's me."

He opened the door, shirtless, with a towel around his neck, his jaw smeared with shaving cream.

Catherine slipped into his room. "Turn on your television. Hurry!"

"What is it?"

"It's Julius." She turned the set on and flipped the channels until she found a morning news station. "He called a press conference early this morning."

Michael watched as Dr. Julius Voss came on, sitting in his office at Freers Institute, surrounded by reporters. At the bottom of the screen it said: *Taped earlier at 7:08* A.M. *Pacific Time.* "So, Dr. Voss," the interviewer was saying, "why did you finally agree to this conference? You have thus far been refusing to comment."

Catherine couldn't believe how tired he looked. There were dark shadows under his eyes, his jacket looked as if he had slept in it. And his black beard seemed to have more shades of gray in it than she recalled.

"I just want to say that," he turned to the camera, "Catherine, if you're listening, please give up this madness. Come home. I need you. I can't do the Meritites project by myself. We have always worked well together. *Do you remember the first time?*"

"Meritites!" Michael said. "Isn't Meritites the mummy he worked on last year?"

"He's trying to tell me something." Do you remember the first time. . . .

Catherine went to the phone and dialed information. She hung up and placed a call to the Halekulani Hotel in Honolulu, asked if there was a message for Mrs. Meritites.

She put her hand over the phone and said to Michael, "The reference to our first time—I don't think he meant working together. Yes? This is Mrs. Meritites. I was wondering if you have a message for me?" She waited. "You do? Read it to me, please."

She hung up and quickly scribbled on a piece of paper, handing it to Michael.

"Thomas of Monmouth," he read. "Who's he?"

"The message was: You'll find what you need at Greensville Abbey. Ask for Thomas of Monmouth."

"Where's Greensville Abbey?"

"I don't know. Either Julius assumed I'm familiar with it, or I didn't get the entire message." She headed for the door. "But I know of a way we can find Greensville Abbey in less than a minute."

By the time Michael arrived at her room, wearing a shirt, his jaw wiped clean, Catherine had booted up the computer. She double-clicked on the Galaxy icon, pulled down Dialer and clicked on Login.

Monitoring GALAXY BBS
IP address 204.16.78.101
»george has logged on, 8:15 am
«MrySpncer has logged off, 8:16 am
»joe has logged on, 8:16 am

Suddenly: *Beep! Beep! Beep! Beep!*

The names of log-ons had stopped scrolling and a message was superimposed across the screen:

Starting Phone Trace Sequence. . . .

Miles reached for the phone.

The car phone rang, the driver picked it up. "Yes, Mr. Perez," he said. He listened for instructions, then he hung up.

"She's on the computer," he said to his partner. "They're tracing the call now."

Catherine said, "We'll find a listing of abbeys on the Web—What's this?"

An icon was flashing at the top of the screen: *Check E-mail*

"Someone sent you a message," Michael said.

"Who?" Pulling down File, she clicked on Check Mail.

Please Enter Password for
joe@mail.galaxy.com

Catherine typed in the password and clicked on OK.

Resolving address for 'mail.galaxy.com'
Logging into POP server

Phone Trace Sequence Waiting. . . .

"Tracing her now," Miles said, when a map of Washington, D.C., appeared on the screen. He watched blue lines connecting dots—signals flying to switching stations, zipping along the city map like lightning.

Titus waited at the other end of the line.

"She's in D.C.," Havers said, as he watched the connections jump from point to point. "Street address is coming up now. . . ."

A message appeared on Catherine's monitor:

You Have New Mail :)))

She clicked on Mailbox, and then on New Messages. Michael leaned over her shoulder, to get a closer look at the screen. "Who is it from?"

Catherine frowned. "The sender isn't identified." She double-clicked and the message appeared.

"Here's the address," Havers said into the phone. "She's on N Street, Georgetown."

Return-Path: <anyone@dianuba.com>
Date: Sun, 26 Dec 1999 6:15:47
From: anyone@dianuba.com
To: joe@galaxy.com Subject: urgent
He has found you.

THE FIFTH SCROLL

CORNELIUS SEVERUS WENT *to meet with the leader of the Britons in Chichester, and Philos went with him. While they were gone Claudia confessed to me that she had been attending secret Druidic rites.*

I had already met Druids, and learned that they worshipped a sky god named Myrddin. They esteem nothing more sacred than the mistletoe, which in their language means all-heal. They do not have temples or shrines as we know them, but practice their rites in nature, revering the oak, upon which mistletoe breeds.

I had heard stories of a sacred place on the southern plains, called Myrddin's Stones, which are said to have fallen from the sky and came to rest in a circle. The power of these "hanging stones, " as they are called, is beyond estimation. We were told that these stones are a mystery and possess a healing against all ailments.

I wanted to see them, but by now I had a child, our son, Pindar, and I wondered if I should undertake such a journey with an infant. And then I heard of a Druid god named Hesus, whom they call Savior and Redeemer. And I knew that I had to visit the stone circle on the southern plains.

Hesus was a carpenter and his symbol the tree; he was crucified with a lamb, symbol of his innocence, to redeem humankind's sins. He died, descended into the underworld, and was resurrected. His followers told me that he lived thousands of years ago, when the earth was young.

And so it was here, Perpetua, that I learned the fifth of the seven great Truths and which, after forgiveness, is the second step of the way back to enlightenment.

This revelation did not come to me all at once, but over time, and I learned it as I saw how the Druids respected nature. In witnessing their sacred rites, I saw the truth behind the teachings of Aesculapius. For when he said, Do no harm, he meant the same as the Druids believe, that to remain spiritually pure we must understand our place in Creation.

It means this: to be a respecter of all persons, of all life, of everything the Creator created.

These are the rules to live by: Let the animal go its way. Do not divert the river's course. Leave the egg in the nest; the honey in the comb. Cultivate enough to eat, then let the earth rest. Steal not, lie not, kill not; be faithful to family and friends; honor nature and Her bounty. Let the other person pass by in peace.

This is the fifth of the great Truths, and the second step toward redeeming our birth-soul and the Gift. The first step is forgiveness, the second is respect.

And the sixth Truth, which is the third step that leads to enlightenment and the Gift, was revealed to me in a yet stranger and more distant land, and following again upon tragedy.

DAY FOURTEEN

MONDAY
DECEMBER 27, 1999

A s the train pulled into the station, Catherine opened her eyes
upon a magical winter wonderland.

She had fallen asleep with her head on Michael's shoulder, his
arms around her. She straightened up now and looked out as the
Greensville Station rolled into view, where thick snow lay everywhere.

Their flight from Mrs. O'Toole's had been swift. They had read
the e-message—*He has found you*—and five minutes later were hurrying out of the bed and breakfast by way of a secret entrance Mrs.
O'Toole had shown them. Created during the Civil War, it tunneled
into the house next door, which was currently undergoing restoration, and out back, so that anyone watching Mrs. O'Toole's place
wouldn't know they had left. They had only had time to grab the blue
gym bag with the scrolls, the laptop, and Michael's black satchel. The
rest of their things they had had to leave behind.

At a cybercafe called Bagels & Bytes they had bought thirty minutes
of Net time and found Greensville Abbey.

Catherine and Michael had stayed on the move after that, watching
their backs, staying alert. By the time they reached the station for the
overnight train to Vermont, they were sure they had not been followed.

As they disembarked now, stepping out into frosty morning air, their feet crunching over snow, Michael paused to sweep an errant strand of hair from Catherine's face. "Are you okay?" he said.

She nodded. "And you?"

He looked up and down the platform, rubbing his hands together. When his eyes came back to hers, by the way he looked at her, she knew that he was remembering their flight through the night, huddled in a seat near the end of the train car, watching lights and snow and homes lit for Christmas rush by. And then he had taken her into his arms and held her until she had fallen asleep.

"I'll go see about getting to the abbey," he said.

Catherine went into the station and bought a newspaper. She opened out the front page, with big letters saying, FAKE OR REAL? There were two photographs of the Jesus fragment now, side by side: the original one that had been running in the papers since the day after Danno's death, and the one that had come out yesterday, the fragment which the Egyptian Minister of Culture had ostensibly removed from Dr. Alexander's tent.

According to the story, experts were starting to contest the forgery charge due to the fact that close comparison of the two photographs revealed that they might not be the same fragment.

Catherine had no doubt that Havers knew this would happen, making the scrolls valuable once more and therefore worthy of his private collection. The brief accusation of forgery had only been to flush her out. And it had worked.

He wasn't going to trick her again.

"We're in luck," Michael said. "One of the passengers on the train lives in Greensville, five miles beyond the abbey. He was in D.C. for Christmas and he left his car here at the station. He's offered us a lift."

"MAN!" MICHAEL SAID as they trudged through the snow along the lane toward the abbey. "I am not used to winters like this anymore!"

Catherine glanced back over her shoulder, toward the road where the Greensville man had dropped them off. No one was following them.

Catherine had no idea who had sent the mysterious electronic message, but she had silently thanked him or her all through the long overnight train ride.

Had it been Jean-Luc?

Night before last, she had almost entered */whois Jean-Luc.* She wished now that she had.

Deep in the Green Mountains and surrounded by woodlands, the abbey was home to a congregation of Benedictine nuns who, according to the Greensville resident who had given Catherine and Michael a ride, were only semicontemplative because they allowed guests to stay at the abbey.

Catherine heard singing up ahead through the trees, coming from behind a high stone wall. Heavenly singing, she thought, as she and Michael found themselves facing a tall, solid wood gate with a small grate at eye-level, a panel covering it on the other side. There was a bell beside the gate.

As Catherine took in the stone spires and turrets glimpsed just over the top of the wall, she wondered who Thomas of Monmouth was, how Julius had found him, and what information he was supposed to possess.

Michael tugged on the bell-pull and the old-fashioned bell swung on a hinge, creating a sharp, clanging sound. They waited.

The singing inside continued. He rang again.

Finally someone came, a small woman who walked so swiftly that her black veils fluttered bird-like around her. She didn't speak as she led the visitors down the stone path, up some icy steps, and into a reception room that was as silent as a church and smelled of lemon oil.

She vanished through a door set within an Elizabethan archway, and a moment later another sister appeared.

She introduced herself as Mother Elizabeth, plainly the abbey's superior because of the ring of keys and an enormous wooden rosary clacking at her waist.

"We rarely get visitors at this time of the year," the abbess explained. "People like to spend Christmas with their families. Men are never admitted as guests, although of course, Father," she said with a smile at Michael, "priests are welcome."

She was elderly, but in an ageless sort of way, Catherine thought, her face barely lined, her eyes sharp and clear. With no hair showing, and her hands hidden in the deep sleeves of her black habit, it was even more difficult to guess her age. Even her voice, smooth, unbroken, seemed to belong to a much younger woman. "How may I help you?"

"We're looking for someone," Michael said.

"Or some *thing*," Catherine added. "We think it might be a document or a manuscript. No one is named Thomas of Monmouth these days, are they?"

"Indeed not," the mother superior said cheerfully. "So you've come to see Thomas! We're very proud of our Monmouth document. It's in excellent condition, with the most beautiful illuminations. No one has asked to look at it in years. It would be my pleasure to show it to you. Please, come this way."

They followed her down quiet halls where statues of sad-eyed saints stood in silent mystery, and into a book-lined library where a cozy fire burned against the winter day. When they saw large, unopened cartons stacked in one corner, containing brand-new computer hardware, the abbess said: "A donation to the abbey. What need we have of such a thing I don't know. Not to keep it, of course, would insult the generous giver. However we're going to have to find someone to put it together for us."

Michael surveyed the boxes. "That's top-of-the-line equipment," he said. "Even comes with Dianuba 2000 already installed. I'll be glad to set it up for you, if you'd like."

Mother Elizabeth unlocked a cabinet and brought out a large leather portfolio which, when she opened it out on a table, proved to contain a single sheet of parchment, yellowed but well preserved, the ink still dark and, as Mother Elizabeth had promised, the colors of the illuminated border and capital letters breathtakingly bright and alive.

The document appeared to have once been a page in a book. A small typed label identified it as having been written by Thomas of Monmouth in the twelfth century. "Please," the abbess said. "Feel free to look at it."

Catherine read out loud, slowly translating as she went: ". . . on the Kalends of June, and when the hour had come, the Romans invaded the Stanhengues, or Hanging Stones, hoping to catch Uther"—she ran her finger under the Latin text—"*dux bel-lorum . . .*"

"Dux bellorum. Leader of warriors," Michael murmured. "Uther?" He looked at the abbess. *"Arthur?"*

"That's what we like to think," she said with a smile. "You know how it is with legends, so many facts, all twisted up and mixed in with fiction. Wouldn't it be wonderful if this was Arthurian?" She went to the door. "I'll leave you two to read the document, Father. And, please," she gestured to the room at large, "help yourself to anything here. We're proud of our library."

After the abbess was gone, Catherine resumed translating: ". . . warrior-leader of the Britons, and set upon the Druids that were gathered there. It was a terrible slaughter that day among the circle of stones. The Romans slit the throats of all of them, numbering over five hundred. Included among them were children and women. The wife of the Roman commander, Cornelius Severus, was there among them, and it was to his great grief that he discovered that he had murdered his own wife who, unbeknownst to him, was attending the Druid rite. She was called Sabina Fabianus and she left behind six books of sorcery and alchemy, which were subsequently buried with the High Priestess Valeria, in the holy place."

"Wait a minute," Michael said. "Sabina wasn't married to Cornelius Severus."

"No," Catherine said, "but the story is bound to get twisted over the centuries. Thomas is writing nearly a thousand years after the incident. We know that Sabina went to Stonehenge to witness a Druid rite. And we do have only six books."

"Who is Valeria?"

"Probably a Druid priestess."

"Could the burial be referring to the well in the Sinai? Is the skeleton Valeria?"

"Perhaps. . . ."

"What does the rest of it say?"

Catherine read the last line. *"Of the seventh book, told of in legend, there is no knowledge, for it was never written."* She looked at Michael. "Do you suppose that's true? That the seventh scroll is only a legend?"

"Thomas of Monmouth got some of the other facts wrong, this could be an error, too. How does he know the seventh scroll was never written? If it's spoken of in legend, it must have existed."

"Lots of legends are just that, legend, and never really happened."

"Catherine, do you really think Sabina died there at Stonehenge?"

"I don't know," she said thoughtfully. "We still have one scroll to go." But Catherine had already noticed, without even opening it out, that the sixth scroll was very short. But the Sabina who dictated the scrolls was in her eighties, whereas the Sabina in Britain was at the most around thirty.

As there was no transportation back to the train station, and the sky looked threatening, the abbess offered them lodgings for the night. While Michael joined the sisters in the chapel for nones, the afternoon canonical hour, Catherine took a walk on the abbey's considerable acreage, following gravel paths that had been swept of snow, and explored among the stone buildings and sheds that had been built two hundred years ago to resemble a Gothic monastery.

She heard joyful singing coming from the chapel, sailing on the air as if on wings: *"Laudate Dominum omnes gentes; laudate eum omnes populi. . . ."* Angels indeed, she thought, rejoicing above the treetops.

Catherine peered into the abbey's gift shop, which was closed now but which in the spring and summer sold maple syrup harvested from the abbey's own trees, and beautiful samplers stitched by the sisters. There were no magazines in the gift shop, no newspapers. The abbess had explained that they didn't even have a television at the abbey. She allowed herself a small radio in her office, but it was only for emergencies and weather reports. Otherwise, the sisters didn't allow the world or any news of the world through their high wall.

The abbess clearly hadn't heard of Catherine Alexander, or the Sinai scrolls. She didn't even seem to be concerned that a new millennium lay just four days away.

Night crept slowly across the forest, drawing a dark blanket over the world. As Catherine headed back to the main building, she heard the nuns singing again, and she imagined Michael with them, replenishing his soul after weeks of spiritual starvation. This would be vespers, she thought, recalling her Catholic years.

Dinner was served in a dining room that had originally been designed to hold many more people. Now Catherine saw the community for the first time, a handful of elderly nuns in the habits of a bygone era, practicing observances and rituals established centuries ago. As she ate the hearty soup and solid plain bread, Catherine tried to watch the sisters without being obvious. The meal was conducted in total silence; a gesture brought the salt down the table, a soft rap of the knuckles summoned the water pitcher. What were they thinking, she wondered, as they smiled shyly at her. Did they ever give any thought to the world beyond their high walls; did they ever think about the life they had left behind so many years ago, when they were girls and had given up everything for the adoration of Jesus Christ? Was there a single regret among any of them?

How would they react to Sabina's pantheon of savior-gods that came before Jesus?

Catherine didn't join the sisters for compline, but retired instead to the library, to study Thomas of Monmouth's document once more. She wanted to begin reading the sixth scroll, to find out what happened to Sabina at Stonehenge. But the papyrus was in bad condition; she would need to take her time opening it out and laying it under a lamp for lengthy study, and she didn't want someone walking in on her.

As she sat by the cozy fire, hearing the distant singing, Catherine pictured the old women she had seen in the dining room and tried to fit them to the pure, angelic voices she heard. They lived their entire lives in cloistered silence, appearing to be unwanted, forgotten women, and yet their voices—it was as if their hearts and spirits were actually rising from their throats, there was such joy, as the man from Greensville had said, in their singing.

This was what they lived for, Catherine realized. This small band of outmoded nuns, keeping rites and rituals that were falling before the march of progress, with no new young members, no novices to carry on the traditions long after these devout sisters were gone—they lived for their faith, they needed nothing more. And the ecstasy of their faith could be heard in their voices.

When a lace curtain drifted across the window, Catherine realized she had been staring out at the night. And then she saw that the lace wasn't a curtain at all, but snow, gently falling. She watched it drift down, as if in no hurry, choosing places to deposit flakes. Some of them, Catherine saw, landed on the diamond-shaped panes and melted there. Snow, Catherine thought, with a faint smile.

And then she frowned. *Snow . . .*

When Michael and the abbess returned, the hour seemed far later than it really was. The sisters were all heading off to their cells; they would be awakened in the middle of the night to gather in the chapel for matins.

"We always keep the guest rooms in readiness," the abbess said as she led Catherine and Michael along a drafty corridor where small votive candles flickered at the feet of statues. "But we have no visitors right now, just you two. I hope the pipes aren't frozen. I'll have one of the sisters bring you some hot water, just in case. We breakfast at dawn, right after prime. You are both welcome to join us," she looked at Catherine, "for both the meal and the service. Good night, sleep well."

"Frozen pipes," Michael said with a shudder as they paused outside Catherine's room. They had with them the few items they had managed to flee Mrs. O'Toole's with: the blue gym bag, Michael's black satchel, pangamot sticks, the laptop computer. "Catherine, don't worry about old Thomas of Monmouth. Like you said, he was writing a thousand years after the fact, and got a lot of the details wrong. Sabina couldn't have died at Stonehenge. There *has* to be a seventh scroll. And we're going to find it."

"Michael," she said after a moment, searching his face. "When we were walking up the lane toward the abbey today, you made a comment about the snow. And then just now, you commented about frozen pipes. Aren't you used to winters like this, living in Chicago?"

He stared at her for a protracted moment. Then he said, "No. I'm not."

"But you *are* from Chicago?"

He paused. "I grew up there."

"I don't understand. Don't you live there now?"

Another pause. "No."

"How long ago did you leave?"

"Eighteen years ago," he said. "I left in 1981."

"Eighteen years! But why did you tell me—Michael, you *are* a priest, aren't you?"

He suddenly looked very unhappy. "Yes, I'm a priest."

"Then where have you been—" She suddenly stopped. Her eyes widened. "Oh my God," she whispered. "Oh my dear God, no!"

"Catherine—"

She took a step back.

"Michael, no. Tell me I'm wrong."

"Let me explain."

"You're from the Vatican."

"Catherine, let's go inside and talk."

"Tell me, Michael. Are you from the Vatican?"

He started to say something, then thought for a moment, and finally said, "Yes."

She started to tremble. "But why? I mean—Michael, the day we met at the Isis Hotel, it *was* a coincidence, wasn't it?"

"Catherine—"

"Answer me."

"No, it wasn't a coincidence."

She felt the floor lurch beneath her feet, as if she were on Atlantis again and sinking rapidly. "When I first saw you at the computer in the manager's office, you already . . . *knew who I was?*"

"Yes."

"Bastard!" And she slapped him hard across the face. "I can't believe I fell for it! All those lies you told me, I believed every one of them!"

"I never lied."

"No—" She struggled for control. "You just never told the truth! But it's okay because you were acting under orders, right? And that's a priest's first responsibility, obedience to the Church."

"Please let me explain," he said, reaching for her.

She fell back. "Don't touch me. The minute I met you I didn't trust you. I should have kept mistrusting you. My God, the things I've told you, that I've never told anyone. I bared my soul to you! And all the times I was frightened, and I thought you were the one person I could count on—when the whole world was against me, I knew that at least I had someone. And now I don't even have you!"

Her voice rang in the corridor. Michael glanced at the doorway, where the abbess had gone. "Catherine, let's go inside and talk, please."

Her expression suddenly turned hard. "Which office is it?"

"Office?"

"In the Vatican, which office sent you?"

"That doesn't—"

"Just tell me." Tears rose in her eyes. *"Which office?"*

"I don't see why that's important."

She compressed her lips and narrowed her eyes at him. "There's a reason why you're not telling me, isn't there? Why won't you tell me?"

She closed her eyes and said softly, "Oh my God. You work for the office that destroyed my mother."

"Catherine, I am not directly attached to the Congregation—"

"The Inquisition, Michael! Call it the Inquisition, because that's what it is! And you work for them!"

"I was sent by them, there's a difference. Another priest was supposed to go, but he fell ill. They searched their records and found out that I was on vacation in Israel. I was the closest to you. That's all. I'm not an Inquisitor, Catherine, I'm not Torquemada. I just happened to be in the right place at the wrong time."

"And that makes it all right?" she cried.

"Look, I don't blame you for being mad—"

"What were you supposed to do? Take the scrolls from me? Or just sweet-talk me until you got all the information you were after?"

"At first," he said quietly, "I was sent just to report on rumors of a possible Christian papyrus fragment. The Vatican is always on the alert for news of scrolls, especially in that region."

"How did they find out?"

He ran a hand over his hair. "I don't know. Probably when Hungerford tried to make his secret deal. I think he contacted some-one in Cairo, who then contacted Havers. And then that same person probably got in touch with the Vatican in the hopes of starting a bidding war. I wasn't given the details, Catherine, and it wasn't my intention to keep my assignment a secret from you. When I reported from the Isis Hotel that first night, they asked me if you would be friendly toward the Church and I had to tell them no."

"So they told you to be a spy."

"No, I was called back to the Vatican. They were going to send someone else. And then you disappeared and Mr. Mylonas told me about the package that had come for you and he was distressed over what to do with it."

"So you used Danno's Christmas present as a ploy."

"I followed you, Catherine, because I wanted to know what was in the scrolls. I had a personal interest, I told you that. And I was going to tell you everything, I even came close several times. But when we were in the motel that first night, I called Cardinal Lefevre, I told him what had happened. He said to stay with you and not divulge my true purpose.

Catherine, I was instructed to work in secret. It was not my idea."

"No," she said bitterly. "It wasn't your idea, but it was your doing."

She looked at Michael, into eyes she had once thought so clear and honest, and she started to tremble again, her tears threatening to fall. "So you stayed with me all this time because you were ordered to?"

"Because I wanted to," he said softly.

"And what was *their* purpose? So that I would lead you to the seventh scroll?"

"No. To see that you didn't come to any harm."

Her eyes widened. "You were my *bodyguardP*"

"Yes."

"You could have just taken the scrolls while I was asleep. Why didn't you?"

"Because we had no proof that they were Christian. If they weren't, then the Church had no right to them, and they were, after all, the property of the Egyptian government."

"And if we were to find proof that they were Christian scrolls, then what?"

"I don't know. I was merely to report."

"Why didn't the all-powerful Vatican help us when we needed it?"

"They did, where it was feasible. But officially, the Vatican wasn't involved. It has to do with diplomacy and stepping on toes. The whole thing got very delicate when the Egyptian government appealed directly to the White House."

"So when *did* they help us?"

"My credit card, for instance. It occurred to me that we could be traced through the car I rented at LAX. So I informed Cardinal Lefevre, and he arranged for the record to be erased from the rental agency's computer."

"If they were helping us, then why didn't you feed them the information and let them do the searches for us? They could have found Tymbos."

"Again, they couldn't be directly involved. You had stolen something from the Egyptian government, it wouldn't have looked good for the Vatican to be aiding and abetting you."

"Yes," she said bitterly, "bad PR. So they waited while I did the donkey work."

"I did some of it," he said quietly.

"And what were you supposed to do when I found the seventh scroll? Take it from me?"

He shook his head. "Just to report."

"Do they know we're here?"

"I haven't contacted the Vatican in four days. And I don't intend to."

"Is that supposed to make me feel better? Do you have any idea how I do feel right now? I feel used, Michael. I feel dirty. And worse than that, I feel betrayed!"

"I'm sorry," he said again, his eyes full of pain.

She held out her hand. "Give me the computer."

"Catherine—"

"It's mine. Give it to me."

When he turned the laptop over to her, she said, "You're not staying with me. I don't care where you go—back to your parish in Chicago, I'm sure they miss you. *But you are not staying with me.*"

She turned her back, went inside, and slammed the door on him.

Michael stared at the closed door for a long moment, torn between breaking it down and just walking away.

He had known this moment must come; he was surprised it hadn't happened sooner, considering their days and nights together. As he stared at the door he thought of his dream—not the one about the robbery, but the other, the newer one: Catherine in white, leading him up the steps of a temple, inviting him to go inside. Each time, in the dream, he had refused to go farther. And, waking up, he hadn't been able to sort out his emotions, to grasp what it was he felt in the dream—only a strong resistance to going into the temple with her.

But now he saw with stunning clarity his reason for holding back: it wasn't that he didn't want to go into the temple, it was that he was *afraid* to.

Afraid of what?

Of what might lie beyond.

And now he knew something else. In the dreams it was getting harder and harder to resist going inside. But soon, he knew, he was going to have to cross that decisive threshold. And although he didn't know why, he knew he must never let that happen.

WHEN CATHERINE HEARD a quiet knock, she looked at her watch. It had been half an hour since she had closed the door on Michael—thirty minutes of trying not to cry, trying not to let his betrayal make her forget her purpose. "Go away, please," she said.

But it was the abbess. "Dr. Alexander. You have a visitor."

Catherine opened the door, and when she saw Julius standing there, she flew into his arms. "Julius! God, I've missed you!" she said, holding tightly to him. *Michael. . . the Inquisition . . .*

The abbess discreetly cleared her throat.

"Mother Superior," Catherine said, "this is Dr. Voss, my fiance."

The abbess offered him a dubious smile. "I suppose you will be requiring accommodations, too?"

Catherine said, "If it's not too much trouble . . . ?"

"I'll put Dr. Voss down at the end, on the *other* side of Father Garibaldi," she added pointedly.

Drawing Julius inside, Catherine closed the door, and said, "You don't know how happy I am to see you!"

But he was staring at her hair. "What did you do!" he said, reaching out to touch the short, platinum cut.

"Is it awful?"

"It's . . . different!"

They kissed for a long moment, and when they drew apart, Julius said with a smile, "I guess this isn't appropriate behavior for an abbey."

She filled her eyes with the sight of him, his handsome bearded face and dark, soulful eyes. "I'm so glad you're here, Julius." Everything was going to be all right now. Michael—She would forget him. Let him go back to the Inquisitors, Julius was here now.

"It's been a nightmare, Catherine. Reading about you in the newspaper, not knowing if you were all right. I thought I was going to go insane."

She drew away, wiped the tears from her cheeks. "Julius, I read the Thomas of Monmouth document. How on earth did you find it?"

When he told her, she laughed. "I spent hundreds of hours on the Internet and all I had to do was see Rabbi Goldman!"

He surveyed her Spartan quarters, the laptop computer on the bed, his gym bag with a nightgown trailing from it, and on the table, what appeared to be his book, *The Body in the Bog,* but which he knew was really the scrolls. "I wish we could go right now," he said, shaking his head at how she must have been living these past two weeks. "But I guess we should wait until morning."

"We can't leave, Julius, not until we see where Sabina leads us next. It might take a few days for this last scroll, but we'll be safe here, no one will find us."

"Catherine, we're not staying here," he said. "We're going home."

She gave him a puzzled look. "Home! Why would I go home?"

"Because Thomas wrote that Sabina died in Britain, that there is no seventh scroll. There's no point in continuing to search for it."

"But . . . I thought you sent me here so that I could continue my search, not to end it. Julius, Thomas of Monmouth could be wrong."

"I'm not asking you to end your search. Listen," he said, taking her by the shoulders. "I helped you because I wanted to demonstrate that I'm on your side." He smiled gently, his voice softening. "I really am sorry for that last night at my house. I must have sounded like a self-righteous prig."

"No, just the man of conscience I fell in love with."

"And the second reason I told you about the Thomas document was so that you could see for yourself that there is no seventh scroll."

"I won't know that until I've finished translating number six."

"All right," he said with a smile. "If you want to believe there is a seventh, I'm not going to argue. But you *can* come home, you don't have to stay in hiding anymore. I have it all arranged."

She frowned. "Arranged? What do you mean?"

"You know that I'm acquainted with officials in the department of antiquities in Cairo. I've discussed the situation with them and they are amenable to working out an arrangement whereby they will drop charges against you *and* you can continue to work on the scrolls. It will have to be in Cairo, of course, and under their supervision. But you will be safe, no one will be after you."

"Julius, I can't work under anyone's supervision."

"It's the only way they'll drop the charges."

"And how does this help me get to the seventh scroll?"

"You will have help, other experts analyzing the scrolls."

She frowned. Other experts? Help? And then she thought: Maybe it was time to accept help. No more running or hiding, being afraid of getting caught, stealing time on the Internet, wondering whom to trust—

"What about my dig?" she said. "Will I be allowed to go back to it?"

"I'm afraid that won't be possible."

"Why not?"

"They've suspended your permit to dig. At least until you've cleared yourself."

She sighed. "I don't blame them. I did break their laws."

"Will you do it? Will you turn the scrolls over to the Egyptians?" She thought for a moment, "Let me consider it," she said. "I might agree."

"Good—"

"Under one condition."

"What's that?"

"That they allow me to start a new dig."

"A new dig?"

"On the well. I want to know who is buried down there, Julius. And see if there's perhaps more papyrus, or something that will tell us—"

But he was shaking his head. "That won't be possible."

"Why not? If I cooperate and turn over the scrolls—"

"They're filling in the well."

She stared at him. "They're *what!*"

"They've declared the well unsafe and they've ordered it to be filled in and then sealed."

"Julius," she said in disbelief. "No!"

"Catherine, they examined the part of the skeleton that is exposed and they've deemed it of no historical worth."

"No historical worth! Julius, that woman might have been an actual Christian priestess! There could be tremendous history buried down there with her!" Catherine narrowed her eyes. "I know what this is all about. The Egyptian government is getting outside pressure to cover the whole thing up." *The Vatican. Michael . . .*

"Catherine, that's nonsense."

She stepped away from him. "It isn't nonsense. This is exactly what I told you would happen. They're covering up the body of the woman who was buried with the scrolls. A woman who was buried alive, Julius. Her hands and wrists bound while she was lowered into a well—*alive.* And if I turn the scrolls over to the Egyptians, or to the Vatican, or to anyone, they'll vanish and never be heard of again, and that poor woman will have suffered a terrible martyrdom for nothing! And damn you, Julius, for not seeing that!"

He gave her a startled look. "Catherine—"

She took another step back, away from his reaching hand. "I'm glad you told me all this, Julius," she said in a tight voice. "Because if there was any doubt in my mind about continuing what I'm doing, it's gone. Now my quest for the seventh scroll is not only for my mother and Daniel, but for that poor woman in the well, and for Sabina and Perpetua and Aemelia, and for anyone else who wants to hear the message of the scrolls. Yes, I've broken rules, Julius. I've broken laws, I've managed to get everybody mad at me, and I've probably lost you, as well. But I can't stop. Not now."

"Catherine, please don't do this."

"Go home, Julius. Go back to your safe institution and your rules and your ethics, and leave me alone." She wanted to add, Take Father Michael Garibaldi with you.

Julius's look turned dark. "If this is the way you want it, all right. But if I walk out of here now, it's for good. I won't come back into your life again. I promise."

She held the door open, and when he went out, she closed it and locked it, and then, turning her back on Julius and Michael, she drew in a deep, fortifying breath and prepared herself to read the final scroll.

THE SIXTH SCROLL

THERE WAS A *terrible slaughter at the stone-circle.*

We were a peaceful gathering, wishing nothing more than to honor the magic of that enchanted place and to observe the miracle of the summer solstice, when the sun appeared directly upon the altar.

It was the Britons who attacked us, for we were mostly Romans, albeit women and children. Many died that day, but all would have perished had it not been for the timely arrival of Cornelius Severus and his legion. My friend Claudia died upon a British spear.

And then finally, Perpetua, the day came when Cornelius Severus said that he was going to the colony of Agrippina, known as Colonia, on the Rhine. He asked Philos, my husband, to join his party, for Severus did not wish to undertake such a journey without a physician. Although the memory of my lost baby, years ago in Antioch, made me very protective of our son, I was curious to see the land of the Germans, for I had heard they worship a savior god who was executed on a tree.

Because Philos was cautious, we did not travel together in the event that the three of us should perish at once. Among Cornelius Severus's six ships, I was on one, Philos another, and our son with his nursemaid on a third.

For days there was only the sound of the ships' sails, the oars dipping into the water, the creaking of the boards. All was calm. We kept our eyes sharp for the northern pirates who infested those seas, raiding the Gallic coast and plundering the peaceful communities there. But we encountered no pirates; instead we were attacked by an enemy far more formidable.

We saw dark clouds gathering upon the horizon, swiftly. Before we could be prepared, the storm was upon us. From every side blew squalls, and the waves rose higher and higher, blotting out all visibility and making it impossible for the helmsmen to steer. Many passengers, unfamiliar with the sea and frightened, got in the way of the sailors. Soon, sea met sky in a great watery maelstrom, and we were blown off course by a southerly gale. This tempest drove our frail vessels over the rocky sea and scattered our ships until we could see one another no more. We saw ahead islands with jagged cliffs, and the captain warned of treacherous shoals beneath the water. We saw men swept overboard, the masts splintered, the rigging came down, we were tossed about, many of us on the deck, on our knees praying while the sailors bailed and worked to keep the torrential waters out. We had to lighten the ship. Over the side went provisions, cargo, and our baggage. Horses were jettisoned; we heard their screams as they plunged into the roiling sea.

Although we had lightened the ship, the joints continued to leak and the holds became deluged by the waves. We had long since lost sight of our sister ships, until finally we glimpsed one through the storm: she was on fire, a blazing inferno on a raging sea. She broke up on a reef and went down, all hands and passengers perishing with her.

It was the ship that had been carrying Philos.

And then our own ship was carried by some malevolent force toward the rocky headlands. As I saw a great mountain of water rising up over our vessel and plunging down, to send us all to a certain watery grave, I recalled the prophecy of the fortune-teller the night I was born, when she came to our house and foretold of "a mountain made of water, when the sea turned into the sky."

My last thought, as the ship went down, was for my son.

DAY FIFTEEN

As dawn broke over the desert, unrolling a great golden blanket across the cold, sleeping world, Erica guided the four-wheel-drive along the rugged track. She had no proof that Coyote Man would be out here, but his family and the police had searched everywhere else. And when he had brought her to Cloud Mesa over a week ago, he had confided in Erica that few knew of this secret place.

At the time, she had been touched, and impressed, that the high priest of the Antelope Clan would share such a secret with her, a non-Native American, and a woman. But now, as she maneuvered her vehicle along the narrow incline, hugging the jagged wall of the mesa as the plain dropped away below, she wondered if perhaps there had been a purpose to his unexpected confidence after all.

When she reached the top, she killed the engine and looked around. She knew that Coyote Man would have come up here to pray in the hope of coaxing Solstice Kachina back from the underworld.

She found the shaman sitting cross-legged on a rocky ledge at the edge of the mesa, facing the east. His long white hair was unbraided and streaming in the wind. He was naked, his body covered with clay.

And he was dead.

SISTER GABRIEL MOVED as quickly as her nearly eighty years would allow, declaring that in the history of the abbey she had never heard such a ferocious ringing of the gate bell.

"Patience," she murmured. "I'm coming. Patience, please!"

She felt the slap of biting dawn air on her face as she delivered herself into the snow-blanketed courtyard. Sliding back the panel over the small grate, she peered out. The world was still cast in semi-darkness; she could make out three or four men flapping their arms in the cold. *"Benedicite,"* she murmured.

One of them thrust something toward her face. "FBI, ma'am," he said in a deep voice. "We need to come inside. Unlock the gate, please."

She saw that it was his identification. Agent Strickland.

"What is this in regard to?" she asked.

"We'd like to talk to your superior if we may, ma'am."

"I'm sorry, but you have to state your business. It is against our rules to allow—"

"We have reason to believe a wanted criminal is hiding somewhere on these premises."

"Merciful heaven." Sister Gabriel heard footsteps behind her, crunching through the snow. And then she heard the abbess's voice. "What is it, sister? Who rang the bell?"

"It's the police. They're looking for someone."

The abbess frowned. "Pardon me, gentlemen," she said, taking Sister Gabriel's place at the grate. "Whom is it you are seeking?"

He held up a photograph, barely discernible in the early dawn light. "Have you seen this woman?"

The abbess peered long and hard at the photograph. Then, crossing herself, she said, "What has this woman done?"

"She's wanted in connection with two murders—"

"Murders!" The two nuns crossed themselves again.

"May we come in, please?"

The two women whispered to each other for a moment, then the superior said, "Do you have a search warrant, officer?"

The men shifted on the other side of the gate. "Ma'am," Agent Strickland said. "It's very cold out here and we just want to ask Dr. Alexander some questions. We aren't here to arrest her."

More whispering, and then Sister Gabriel hurried back into the cloister.

"Very well," the abbess said, drawing back the heavy bolt and opening the gate. "But only you, please. We normally do not admit men onto these premises. More than one of you will upset the tranquillity of our house." Strickland motioned for his companions to stay behind.

"I'm awfully sorry, ma'am," he said, as he followed her toward the abbey. "I hate to disturb you and the sisters, but I have to follow orders. We've been looking for this woman for two weeks. You must have heard about it on the news."

"We don't listen to the outside news here, Mr. Strickland." When they delivered themselves into the warmth of the vestibule, the abbess saw that Agent Strickland was a portly man in his fifties, with a ruddy complexion and the sufferingly patient air of a man who has been at his job too long.

She held out her hand. "May I see your identification, please?"

He handed it to her.

"You won't mind, Agent Strickland," she said, "if I make a telephone call to the FBI office in Montpelier to verify your identity?"

He sighed. "Be my guest."

Five minutes later, the abbess was leading him down the corridor of the currently unoccupied guest wing where Michael, Catherine, and Dr. Voss had been given rooms the night before.

She paused before Catherine's door, then knocked softly and said, "Dr. Alexander? Are you awake? You have a visitor."

They listened for a response.

The abbess knocked a little louder. "Dr. Alexander? Are you in there?"

Strickland looked around. "Is there another exit?"

"No."

"Could she be visiting the john, I mean bathroom?"

"These rooms were equipped with private baths in the 1950s."

He looked back over his shoulder. "This is the only way in or out?"

"If Dr. Alexander had left we would have seen her." The abbess knocked again. "Dr. Alexander, are you all right, my dear?"

"Unlock it," Strickland said, adding, "please."

The abbess removed the keys from her belt and opened the door. They saw clothes and toiletries piled on a chair, the bed rumpled, and there was a laptop computer on the small desk, the screen dark. The window was open, cold wind blowing in.

"Oh dear," the abbess said, crossing the room to look out. "Dr. Alexander must have gone out this way. She'll freeze out there!"

"Left in something of a hurry," Strickland said, walking around the small room. "Seems to me someone warned her we were here." He flashed a smile at the abbess, who ignored it. "Is this everything she had with her?"

The abbess wrung her hands as she looked over the things. She saw Dr. Alexander's blue gym bag on the floor beneath the desk. "Yes," she said. "I believe this is everything."

He looked out at the snow, and the forest beyond. "Her clothes still here, even her shoes," he said. "She won't get far. We'll pick her up."

The Sixth Scroll

I DO NOT *know how I survived, or how I got to shore. But when I awoke I was on a pebbly beach and a thin sun was shining on me.*

Scattered along the shore were the bodies of people I had traveled with, and also dead horses, pigs, and dogs. I walked the length and breadth of that beach for Wo days and a night, and found no one else alive. I looked out over the many islands that were scattered along this coast, and I wondered how many others of our party were in this same position. I tried to seek the means with which to light a fire and make a signal, and likewise I remained watchful for a smoke signal from the distant islands.

I never saw any.

By the time Freyda's clan found me, I was weak and delirious with fever. It took months for them to nurse me back to health, and by then it was winter. I was fed and kept warm and dry in the house of a woman who seemed to welcome my company. But I rarely spoke, for I was numb with shock. It was as if everything inside me had perished with my husband and son, and my dear friends Severus and his wife.

When the snows melted and the sowing and planting began and the men struck out to hunt, my faculties slowly returned. I asked to be taken to the Romans. Because we did not speak the same tongue, Freyda managed to communicate to me through gestures and diagrams drawn in the earth that we were far from any Roman outpost and that,

Barbara Wood

at the moment, a hostile tribe ranged between us and the Roman frontier. The clan would not risk their safety for me, and they would not let me go alone. So I had to stay with them, and wait.

Freyda was the clan's wise-woman, for Germanic men regard women as possessing prophetic powers and they are often consulted and their counsel is listened to. I gradually learned Frey da's tongue, just as I had once learned Satvinder's, and Freyda taught me about her people. And in this way I learned about Odin, their savior god.

Months passed, and then a second year, and every day I went down to the water's edge to scan the sea. I would imagine a Roman trireme coming into view, and it would be flying the colors of Cornelius Severus; I would hear a familiar voice call out, and see Philos on the deck, holding Pindar, both waving to me. When visitors came to the village, I asked them if Romans were searching for a woman. But they had nothing to tell me. Philos was dead, I knew, and so I was a widow. And surely Pindar could not have survived the storm. So I was child-less as well, for the second time in my life.

For a long time my grief and my pain were so constant and so real that it was as if they were part of my flesh, and that I would never know anything but pain and grief again. The seasons came and went, and I stayed with the clan—for the hostile tribes surrounding us kept me from leaving them, and prevented any of Frey da's people from escorting me to the frontier where her son, and the other half of the clan, lived. I could not understand how Freyda could live for so long separated from her family and those she loved. She told me that it was fate, and she accepted it. As for my anger and bitterness over the loss of Pindar and Philos, Freyda said this: "It is over. Accept it, for other-wise you will never know peace. "

I kept my faith in The Way in that savage land, just as I had carried it from Antioch to India, from Alexandria to Britain, and I shared it with the others. Since Freyda was the clan's saga-teller, from her I learned how to spin out a story that kept listeners in thrall over many nights. I told them of the Righteous One; I repeated his sayings to them and his parables. I told them of his miracles and his healings. And the most wondrous miracle of all: how he himself had over-come death. They in turn told me of Odin, the savior god who was sacrificed upon a tree, dying from a spear wound to the side, and

340

from where he descended to the under-realm for three days before ascending to the plane of the gods.

And in this way did I gradually come to understand another great truth.

You will remember, Perpetua, that in Britain I had received an insight into the fifth mystery: and this is Do no harm, the first tenet of the god Aesculapius. But I was to see in the Rhineland that this rule was practiced also among Freyda's people who, I came to learn, bear a great respect for nature. In hindsight I saw also that this truth was part of the creed of Tammuz and Zoroaster, Buddha and Krishna, Hermes, Isis, and the Righteous One, that it was not unique to Aesculapius, that it was not a new discipline. For all religions say this: Respect creation around you, for it comes from the Creator. Cause no unhappiness. Let no war be fought in your name. Practice kindness. Above all: respect as you would be respected.

But it was during my solitude in the forests that I experienced another revelation, the revelation of the sixth Truth, which is the third and final step of the threefold path to enlightenment.

Fear, anger, bitterness, mistrust, hatred, envy, jealousy—these block the Light that we are born with. But by embracing the third step, which is acceptance, then we cast off fear and the doors are unlocked to admit the light. I remembered the teachings of Epicurus, who taught that good is attained through forgiveness. He said something else: that evil can be endured by acceptance. Evil takes the shape of all of life's ills—sadness, grief, anger, pain, hatred, the desire for revenge. When I finally embraced the rule of acceptance, I felt my anger and grief melt away. I faced the awful tragedy that had befallen me and I said in all sincerity: it was to be so and I accept it.

With acceptance, Perpetua, we complete the threefold steps that take us back to the birth-soul: forgiveness, respect, acceptance. And these lead us to the Seventh Truth—which proves the first six, and brings the Gift. But the Seventh was not revealed to me here, and not at this time.

The day came when word reached us of fierce fighting among the tribes to the west, and that the enemy of the clan had been vanquished. Freyda spread the sacred rune stones upon a white cloth and read the good omens there. We were free at last, she declared, to move closer to the frontier, where the other half of the clan had been separated from the main body by war, and then kept apart by hostilities.

There, Freyda was united with her son again. And there, in that wild forest, I was fated to meet Segimund—my beautiful, brave, godlike Segimund. . . .

DAY SIXTEEN

A s Miles Havers was about to open Daniel Stevenson's laptop, his private line rang. A phone call he had been waiting for.

"Sorry to have left it to the last minute, Miles," the caller said. "But you know how it is. I had to make it look like I studied the case and gave it a great deal of consideration."

"No problem," Miles said to his friend, who was calling from Washington, D.C. "I understand."

"Of course the Justice Department will drop the suit against your company and Dianuba 2000 can be launched on January first."

"Thanks, Toby. I owe you one. Give my love to Sandi and the kids. Happy New Year."

"Same to you," said Toby Jackson, the first African American to hold the office of Attorney General, and the third of the three survivors of Miles's combat unit who had used tiger-power to get to the top.

As Miles returned to Daniel Stevenson's computer, he decided that rich was definitely good. Otherwise he never would have been able to make a certain FBI agent an offer he couldn't refuse. Miles imagined that Agent Strickland was halfway to Brazil by now.

Rich bought other things as well. Without money, Miles couldn't

343

also have had as many men watching Dr. Julius Voss as he had, with one of them reporting the instant Voss made his fatal error: buying a ticket to Montpelier, Vermont, and arranging for a rental car at the other end. The carelessness must have been because Voss expected his trail to end at the abbey, that it would be all over and it didn't matter if he wasn't careful. Maybe he even went to bring his fiancee home. Whatever, it hadn't worked.

But some good had come of Voss's three-thousand-mile journey: Havers finally got Stevenson's laptop.

Now he was in his gray and burgundy office, with the door double-locked and the surveillance camera monitoring the hall in case Erica should come by. When he booted up and the screen brightened, Miles surveyed the files on the desktop, to see if there was anything significant. After opening a few, he realized that Stevenson had used the laptop mostly for laboratory conferencing, his software included Virtual Imaging, which had enabled him to superimpose designs over videos transmitted from elsewhere. When Miles saw the Mayan frescoes superimposed over Minoan art, he felt a grudging admiration for Stevenson. Maybe he hadn't been such a crackpot after all. Too bad he had got in the way.

Miles stared at the well-used computer. Strickland had said the laptop was plugged into the wall when they found it, and there was a half-finished cup of coffee next to it, plus a legal pad and pencil and some scribbled notes. Catherine Alexander had clearly been working at the computer before she was interrupted.

When Miles saw the e-mail icon, he decided to open it, out of curiosity. He was surprised to see that there was a message in the mailbox; he had thought Alexander was being careful not to communicate through the Net. He clicked on it and read: *He has found you.*

Havers frowned. The date and time were three mornings ago, when he had located Catherine through Galaxy BBS. Titus had reported that she wasn't at the D.C. address on N Street, that a Mrs. O'Toole said they had checked out. As Miles stared at the message, he realized someone had tipped them off.

When he saw the electronic address—*anyone@dianuba.com*—he snorted. The snitch had even used Dianuba Network, the one that came with Scimitar software.

Returning to the desktop, Miles scanned the icons for a utilities program. Double-clicking on PCTools, he was relieved to see that Stevenson had installed "undelete" software. Miles hadn't wanted to load an undelete program and risk erasing files.

Clicking on Undelete, he entered the root directory by typing *c:\>* then he checked the subdirectories for files that had been deleted, opening and closing them quickly. Mostly, he found, they were correspondence and articles that Stevenson had submitted to publications. And all were dated weeks ago. Havers was looking for a deleted file with a specific date and time.

When he came to subdirectory *tmbX52*, he clicked on it and found that one file had been deleted:

Tymbos.exe Date deleted: Dec. 28, 1999 Time deleted: 6:48 am

When Agent Strickland had arrived at the abbey.

Havers pictured the scenario: one of the nuns warning Catherine Alexander, she jumps out of bed, boots up the computer, deletes the most important file, then climbs out the window just as Strickland and the abbess get there.

"Clever girl," Miles murmured as he clicked on the file. "But not clever enough."

A new box appeared on the screen:

File: ?ymbos.exe
Size: 94800
Path: d:\tmbX52
Modified Date/Time: 12/21/1999   10:00   am
Deleted Date/Time: 12/28/1999 6:48 am
First Cluster: 30248
Condition: Good
Protected by: DOS

The first letter of this file name was destroyed by DOS. Please enter the new first letter. ?ymbos.exe

Since Miles had no idea what *_ymbos* was, he typed in the letter *B,* then clicked on OK.

Now the screen read: Bymbos.exe. Recovered.

He had the deleted file.

Two minutes later the file was downloaded and Miles had a printout.

He frowned at what he saw. It appeared to be a daily worksheet of some sort, which Alexander had accessed every day, adding new information, rearranging notes, configuring Greek letters in an infinitesimal variety of sequences. She appeared to have been trying to decipher a puzzle. None of it made any sense to him.

He scanned the next few pages. It looked as if she had been trying to find out what Tymbos was. There were notations: *Not found through Lycos, InfoSeek, UniCom, WebCrawler, Dianuba. . . .*

Then he came to the end: *"Tymbos, a mythical land supposedly along the trade route to Sheba. King Tymbos should be read King of Tymbos."*

Miles stared at the last two words. King of Tymbos.

At the end of the Jesus Fragment it had read, "take it to King—"

This was the king!

He read the last of her notes: *"Sheba was thought to be the ancient name for Ethiopia. Is Tymbos in Africa?"*

Miles quickly reached for the phone to get Teddy. It shouldn't be too difficult to find out if any Americans had landed in Addis Ababa in the last couple of days. This was almost too good to be true!

But his hand paused over the telephone.

He went back to the laptop, accessed the word processing program, and created a new file, labeling it *Havers.* Then he saved it to the hard drive, putting it into the *tmbX52* subdirectory, and logged off. Locating File Manager on the desktop, he clicked on the icon, scanned the list of subdirectories, found *tmbX52,* opened it to *havers.exe,* pulled down File, and clicked on Delete.

A new box, labeled *Delete,* appeared, and the options listed were:

0 Normal Delete
0 Wipe Delete
0 DQD Wipe Delete

Havers was familiar with these functions: Normal Delete meant an ordinary DOS deletion, which deleted the file but left the data on the disk so that it was possible to retrieve later. Wipe Delete, however, wrote zeroes over the data so that the file couldn't be recovered. And DOD, Department of Defense, wrote over deleted file clusters *three times* so that it was impossible to get the file back in any way. Stevenson's software had Department of Defense capabilities, and yet, for some reason, Catherine Alexander had chosen Normal Delete. Why?

Havers's frown deepened. He looked again at the date and time on the deleted Tymbos file—6:48 a.m. And he realized it meant nothing. Alexander could have changed the time on the computer, deleted the file, and then changed the time back. So the deletion could have occurred at any hour—probably long before the FBI even got there.

If Catherine Alexander had faked the time on the deleted file, chosen Normal Delete so that the file was not in fact lost, and then staged a last minute getaway, "accidentally" leaving the computer behind, it meant only one thing: she had *wanted* him to find this file!

To make him think that Tymbos, if there even was a Tymbos, was in Africa.

Annoyed with himself—how could he have fallen for such a transparent trick?—he went back through the files and searched for the journal Stevenson had mentioned, the journal in which he named his murderer. It wasn't there. This was one file, Miles was certain, that Catherine Alexander had done a DOD wipe on. But not, he would wager, before she had downloaded it onto a floppy.

So she had bested him again. She still had the scrolls and the incriminating journal, and now he had no idea where she was.

The FBI had questioned the abbess and Father Garibaldi. Both claimed not to know where Alexander had vanished to. And there were no clues left behind, except for the laptop, which he now knew was useless.

As he got up and paced, trying to figure out which way to go next, a warning signal sounded on his monitor, alerting him to a transmission coming over the dedicated fax machine downstairs. Miles got down there just as the machine finished spewing out the message. He saw that it was the last translation from Papazian in Cairo, with a note at the bottom demanding more money.

Miles ignored the last part.

The translation was of the only photograph Miles had from the sixth scroll. It had taken Papazian longer to translate than the rest because of the poor condition of the papyrus, and also because the photograph itself was blurry. Catherine Alexander must have rushed toward the end, after photographing so many panels of text, and gotten sloppy. The photograph was marked on the back: *sixth scroll, page 12 of total 13.*

It was the second to the last page of the Sabina story. Which meant that time was almost out. If there were no clues here, then Catherine Alexander had won.

Havers quickly scanned the sheet. He stopped in the middle, hardly believing his luck as his eyes fixed on two words: *Aquae Grani.*

What was that? A town? *Maybe where Catherine Alexander has gone.*

Returning to his personal computer, he accessed the encyclopedia that was built into Scimitar software, clicked on Search, typed in Aquae Grani and hit Enter.

"Well, what do you know," he said a moment later, smiling. There was even a picture.

The Sixth Scroll

OUR NEW PERMANENT *home was at Aquae Grani, and Freyda,
now the matriarchal head of the united clan, came to me one day,
saying that because I was still young and of childbearing age, I must be
married, for I needed a protector. But as I was not a virgin, she said,
no man would want me.*

*She had asked her son, Segimund, who was a widower and childless,
if he would take me. He had barely noticed me, for his thoughts were
on uniting the tribes and recapturing the lands the Romans had wrested
from his family. But as it was his mother's wish, he agreed to it.*

*How was I to respond, dear Perpetua, for I still held out hope
of being rescued. But Freyda was right; an unmarried woman of
childbearing age could cause trouble among the men. And since my
survival depended upon staying with the clan, and since I had noted
that Segimund was rarely there, I agreed to the marriage.*

*Among the Germans, it is not the bride who brings the dower,
but the husband. And it is tradition to give a horse and bridle, a
shield and a sword, for these symbolize the wife's dedication to her
husband's heroism, and remind her that she shares her husband's
hard work and peril. The shield and sword, Freyda told me, pass
eventually to the wife's daughters, and then to her granddaughters.
But I had no intention of having children by Segimund and neither,
it seemed, did he, for on our wedding day there was a great feast and
much drunkenness, and that night when I went to Freyda's timber*

house, I waited for a husband who never came.

I continued to live in Freyda's dwelling, and rarely saw Segimund after that.

Because they were a tribe expelled from their ancestral lands, they were now homeless petitioners for a safe place of exile, and Segimund was their leader. I watched him at council meetings, and he made great speeches. He said: "Just as heaven belongs to the gods, the earth belongs to man. And tenantless land can and will be occupied!"

He traveled through dangerous territory to meet with the Roman governor, presenting the tribe's petition. The governor, we heard, offered to strike a private deal with Segimund, to keep the peace, offering land to Segimund but to no one else.

And my husband, we were told, said to the governor, "We may have no where to live but we can find somewhere to die!"

He returned to us and began to gather the other tribes together to fight the Romans once more. Segimund heartened his warriors by reminding them that in every battle the eye is conquered first.

I had never seen war before. May I never see it again, dear Perpetua.

In the forests they fought, and it was a terrible sight, for the wives and mothers waited at the edge of the battle, crying out to the men to fight bravely. With their cries, and the cries of their children, the men were heartened and fought more fiercely, and when I saw the bravery of Segimund and his men, I felt a strange change taking place in my heart. They were fighting Romans, and yet suddenly my desire was for Freyda's people to win. I had been with them for three years; they had saved my life and taken me in. And Segimund in battle was a sight to behold, with his long red-gold hair and arms of iron and the courage of a god. He stood head and shoulders over the shorter Romans, and spears and arrows seemed to go right through him, as if he were enchanted. When the battle began to go badly for his men, as they had been driven into the marshes, the women rushed in, baring their breasts, to remind their sons and husbands of the fate that awaited them if the battle was lost— slavery in Rome. And this time I joined them, Perpetua, with cries and shouts loud enough for Segimund to hear. Our warriors were heart- ened and made a new push against the legions.

The soldiers of Rome fought valiantly, but they had no women to spur them on, no children to remind them of why they fought. They were paid warriors, not men who were fighting for their homes, their family honor.

And so the Germans were victorious. And Segimund was a hero.

When it was over, we women rushed in and carried out the dead, to give them honorable burials. The wounded men came to their wives and mothers, to bare their injuries and have them treated; neither the women shrink from the sight of the blood, Perpetua, nor do the men hide their wounds in shame. I showed the women how to wrap a better bandage than they knew, which Satvinder had taught me, and herbs to stem infection. And they trained me in their way of stitching wounds, with a thorn and thread.

I treated Segimund's injuries, as was my right as his wife, and he praised me for my bravery at the edge of the battle.

We made love that night for the first time.

And when, weeks later, I felt the new life stirring within me, Segimund's child, I knew that my own life in the civilized world had come to an end and a new one was beginning. I embraced Segimund and his family as my family. I accepted the new name they had given me, and gave myself completely to Segimund and his world.

My only regret was that I had failed to find the Righteous One, and I thought then that I never would.

In that, Perpetua, I was wrong.

DAY SEVENTEEN

THURSDAY
DECEMBER 30, 1999

"Aquae grani?" the concierge at the Detmolderhof had said. "That would be Aachen. The ancient Romans went there for their health."

And so, after visiting the Teutoburg Forest in the north, Catherine had come to Germany's westernmost town, on Holland's border, Charlemagne's Aix-la-Chapelle, a modern city with a medieval heart. And at the center of that heart, a stunning cathedral.

As she stood in a cobblestone street built twelve centuries ago, the December wind whistling past her, Catherine gazed up at Gothic spires that rose to the winter sky, she scanned the curious dome and the stained-glass windows that appeared to be five stories tall—an old, stately, timeless monument to God—and she felt something tugging at her, daring her to cross the street and go up the steps to the massive, carved doors. She recalled the church in Washington, when she had gone with Michael for midnight Mass, only to turn away at the steps. But Catherine knew there would be no turning away now.

Did Sabina visit this spot? she wondered. Did Freyda's clan camp where the cathedral now stands; were they perhaps buried here—Freyda, Sabina, Segimund—beneath this hallowed, Christian ground?

Catherine was suddenly afraid. Of what she might find. Of what she might *not* find.

Her feet had a will of their own, they carried her over the forbidden threshold, a threshold she had vowed thirteen years ago never to cross again, and suddenly she was inside, feeling the winds of time rush forward to seize her, to pull her in, deeper and deeper into the vast, echoing stone church. Catherine crossed into the Octagon and when she looked up, she was suddenly overcome by a wave of awe so devastating that her breath caught.

Overhead, suspended on a long chain from the center of the dome, was a colossal gilded copper chandelier, and surrounding it, like awestruck spectators themselves, were arches upon arches, in twos and threes, supported by Corinthian columns atop yet more columns and more arches, all rising up like a marble wedding cake to a magnificent domed ceiling where white-robed saints and apostles marched in royal splendor against a gold background. Other details registered on Catherine's spellbound brain: the tall stained-glass windows admitting rainbows of light into the chancel, spilling upon the golden shrine containing Charlemagne's remains. The high altar, faced with gold, illustrating scenes from Christ's passion; and the ornate wooden boxes with velvet curtains: the confessionals. At the base of one of the Gothic piers, a sloe-eyed Virgin gazed down with such unutterable compassion that Catherine was overcome with emotion.

She put a hand to the stone wall, to steady herself. It was all rushing back too quickly, a kaleidoscope of images, sensation, memories: her first Holy Communion in her little bride's dress, and her father in the sacristy doorway, proudly aiming the camera to capture the exact moment the Host touched his daughter's tongue; Confirmation—the oil on the forehead, the gentle tap on the cheek to remind her that she was now a soldier of Christ; all the Sundays and holy days, the feasts and the fasts, the rosaries and novenas—twenty-three years of devout Catholicism rushing toward her and crashing over her before she had time to save herself.

It was far worse than the Atlantis island sinking. Because this time Catherine knew there was no escape. With her eyes riveted to the sad countenance of the medieval Virgin, standing eternal vigilance in the

Gothic sanctuary, Catherine heard a prayer begin to sing in her mind, it had been her favorite, long ago. . . .

Hail, Holy Queen, Mother of Mercy, hail, our Life, our Sweetness, and our Hope. To thee do we cry, poor banished children of Eve; to thee do we send tip our sighs, mourning and weeping in this vale of tears. Turn, then, most gracious Advocate, thine eyes of mercy toward us; and after this exile—

The precious words released a torrent of memories: of little girls placing flowers at the feet of the white marble Mary in front of Our Lady of Grace Church; of Catherine kneeling between her parents, safe and secure and filled with happiness because the church was so beautiful, and the priest in his pulpit assuring everyone that God loved them unconditionally.

The memories kept coming, wave after wave of them—the feeling after leaving the confessional, so clean and light and absolved; the sensation of the Eucharist in the mouth, and reveling in the knowledge that, through this act, she was joined back through the ages to Jesus Himself.

Sabina's words whispered in her mind: *The first lesson the Righteous One preached was the blessedness of forgiveness. . . .*

Oh Julius! Catherine thought. I am so sorry. You were only following your conscience. You were doing what you thought right. I saw it as a betrayal of me, and I was wrong.

Danno. It was because of me that you were murdered. It was my fault.

Mother, I should have told Father McKinney to leave the moment I saw him come into your hospital room. I could have insisted upon another priest. And I should have apologized for the terrible things I said to you when Daddy died. It wasn't your doing.

Daddy . . .

Forgiveness leads us back to the birth-soul. . . .

Daddy, you were born in the wrong century, into the wrong culture. You couldn't help what you were. You fell in love with a woman who was too strong for you. You continued to love her, even though you had to retreat from her. And the accidental daughter who wasn't planned, as strong-minded as her mother. You retreated further and further into your books and Catholic mysticism until finally you had to flee to another country to find yourself again. Why did you allow them to accuse you of spying? Why did you go so meekly to a martyr's death? Oh Daddy, I am so sorry. Forgive me, I just didn't understand.

And . . .

O Mary, conceived without stain, pray for us who fly to thee. Refuge of sinners, Mother of those who are in agony. . . .

And . . .

Holy Mary. *Pray for us.*

Holy Mother of God. *Pray for us.*

Holy Virgin—

And, Daddy . . . *I forgive you.*

Catherine suddenly experienced a sensation of incredible lightness, as if she were being lifted up. For one giddy moment she didn't feel the stone floor beneath her feet; she was weightless, without body or form, and she felt, for an instant, inexplicable joy.

And then the stone floor was beneath her again, she was back in her body. And when she saw a tall, dark figure standing in the shadow of an archway, she thought he was an apparition, the product of her overwhelmed mind. But then he stepped into the light and she saw that he was real.

She wasn't surprised that Michael had found her. She imagined the abbess would have told him how she had left the abbey. He was, after all, a priest. Although he wasn't dressed like one now, just as Catherine had exchanged the nun's habit for new clothes purchased in Detmold.

He approached her holding out his hands in a gesture of surrender. "Don't worry," he said softly, "I haven't told anyone where you are."

She hadn't thought he would. She knew he was here on his own, not acting under Vatican orders but impelled by something within himself, just as something inside *her* had set her on Sabina's trail, bringing her here.

They met under a stone archway that led to the chapel housing Charlemagne's marble throne; Michael spoke softly, out of the hearing of the few others visiting the cathedral. "You gave us a scare when the FBI arrived and it looked as if you had fled through the snow in your nightgown."

"The FBI?" she said. "How did they find us?"

"Havers probably," Michael said, searching her face. "I wouldn't be surprised if he worked a deal with them. The abbess said you left the computer behind. You must have really left in a hurry."

She still felt light-headed, and wondered if the brief ecstasy of moments ago—was it an epiphany?—had really happened. "I was gone long before the FBI arrived," she said. "I thought that if Havers got the computer he would be satisfied for a while. I even created a phony file, assuming he would find it, and that it would throw him off the trail. With luck he's on his way to Ethiopia. . . ."

"What made you leave in the middle of the night, Catherine? Was it because of me?"

She reached up and touched his cheek. "I'm sorry I slapped you, Michael. I shouldn't have done that. But I was just so shocked and so hurt."

"I don't blame you. I'm sorry I made you so mad that you left in the middle of the night in all that snow."

"It wasn't because of you—well, not completely. It was that e-mail message we received in Washington," she said. "I realized it wouldn't be long before Havers picked up our trail again. And when I read the beginning of the sixth scroll, and found out that Sabina had gone to Germany, I decided not to waste any more time. So I arranged my room at the abbey to make it appear that I had only just departed. How did you find me?"

"The abbess told me you used the abbey's library to find out where a German hero named Arminius had lived. She told me how she helped you to escape, sending for a taxi in Greensville to take you to the airport. After that, I had no trouble finding out about an American nun who had visited the Arminius monument, and who had then asked about Roman baths in the west."

"But how did you know you would find me *here,* in the cathedral?"

"I didn't. I came in here for myself."

He fell silent and seemed to study her. She noticed that the blue in his eyes was darker, a somber blue, she thought, as if they were absorbing the melancholy shadows that crouched in the corners where Carolingian arches met Gothic nave. Or possibly it was because his soul was closer to the surface in this monumental house of God, as if he were almost naked and she could see more clearly the deep passions which Father Michael Garibaldi needed constantly to restrain. Pangamot won't help you here, she wanted to say Here you have to face the past that is haunting you.

"Why did *you* come in here?" he asked quietly.

She wanted to tell him. She wanted him to explain what had just happened. She shook her head.

"I understand," he said. And Catherine had the feeling that he really did understand, that she didn't need to try to find words to explain what had happened. When Michael reached up and brushed his fingers across her cheek, she realized he had wiped away a tear. Had it been there all along, while they were talking, evidence of the extraordinary experience she had just had?

"Have you found anything here in Aachen relating to Sabina?"

She shook her head. "And I don't know where to look next."

"Have you finished the sixth scroll?"

"I have one page left."

She felt his hand on her elbow. "Shall we read it?"

WHEN CATHERINE HAD arrived at Aachen that morning, after the train ride from Detmold, she had checked into the modest Wilferterhof on the Marktplatz. Michael followed her back there now, and while she went upstairs to wait, he went to the desk to arrange for a room for himself.

The hotel was in the center of the city, next to the medieval town gate, and from the window Catherine could see narrow, cobblestoned streets where thirteenth-century buildings seemed to lean in toward one another. There were no cars, only the occasional bicycle, and Catherine thought that if she ignored the blue jeans and windbreakers, she could imagine she was back in the Middle Ages.

I'm shifting in time, she thought. *I've been cut loose from what anchored me to the twentieth century. . . .* Now she would go back to the ancient days, because she was going to read Sabina's story—the final page.

Michael knocked on the door and came in, once again, she noticed, filling the small room with his size and presence. Was this their last hour together? she wondered. After the final page of the sixth scroll, there would be nothing left to keep them together, and Michael would return to the Vatican, while she went . . .

Where? *Where will I go after this?*

Catherine read the final page of scroll six, while Michael listened.

"That was five decades ago, dear Perpetua and Aemelia, when I bore my first child to Segimund. After that, I gave birth to eight more sons and daughters, and saw the birth of twenty-six grandchildren and seven great-grandchildren. We buried Freyda in her favorite meadow countless harvests ago, and I took her place as the head of the clan, for Freyda had taught me the sagas, and I continued to tell them around the fires at night, along with my own story, which everyone claimed was mythical. And I told them also about the Righteous One.

"On the day that Ingomar, my oldest son by Segimund, received his first shield and spear as a sign of manhood, I thought of Pindar, my son by Philos, and the other child, lost long ago during the religious riots in Antioch. My only regret was that in all those years I was never able to convert my family to The Way, which I believed to be the true faith.

"I was not to know that it would be here at last, in these wild forests, that I would learn the seventh great Truth, and the answer to the question I had carried in my heart from Antioch so many years ago—the one question I yearned to ask the Righteous One.

"Tragedy struck a third time, for they are all gone now, dear Perpetua. Segimund, our sons and daughters, Ingomar, the whole clan, they were wiped out in a single instant. How long have I been here with you? Then you must add to that the time I spent wandering in the forest and you will know how long ago they were all killed. A month, perhaps longer. It was a surprise attack, we had no idea they were coming, the invaders from the north. We were unprepared. Our men fought bravely, but we were outnumbered.

"Some of us fled into the woods and hid. I was alone, separated from the others, and I was afraid of—"

Catherine stopped reading. Night silence rushed in behind her words. Finally she looked up from the papyrus. "That's it," she said softly. "That's all we have of Sabina's story."

She went to Michael, put her hand on his arm. "I'm sorry," she whispered. She knew he had hoped for a personal message, words of guidance, maybe even another reference to Jesus.

"I am, too," he said, "but for your sake, Catherine, not mine. I

359

wanted you to find the last scroll." He stepped closer. "And I truly am sorry for having deceived you—"

She placed her fingertips on his mouth. "It's all right," she said. "I'm no longer angry. I knew that you did what you had to do. But . . ."

"But?"

"I *am* disappointed. I was hoping for more details from Sabina. I want to see what she sees. I want to see *her.* Michael, I've been trying to imagine what she looks like, I've tried to conjure up her image, but I can't."

He took Catherine by the hand and led her to the mirror over the dresser. "This is why you haven't been able to see Sabina," he said. "You've been looking through her eyes."

Catherine gave him an astonished look. "How do you know this?"

When he didn't reply, she turned and faced him. "You've seen her, haven't you? You've seen Sabina."

"I've seen her in my dreams."

"But why does she reveal herself to you and not to me? Why are *you* having the visions?"

"I don't know, but I can tell you I don't want them."

"What do you see in the dreams, Michael? Share it with me. Help me to see."

"It's always the same: she wants to lead me somewhere. I don't know exactly where, but I fight it."

"Why do you fight it?"

"Because in the dream Sabina has your face. And where you are going I cannot follow. And I have *my* destiny, Catherine—"

"That's no reason. Why don't you follow her into the temple?"

"Because I'm afraid."

"There's nothing to fear," she said softly. "Next time you have the dream, don't fight it. Go with her."

When Michael took Catherine's hand and pressed it to his lips, she looked into his blue eyes and allowed herself to swim into them, to explore the darker currents she had glimpsed there. She felt his warm lips pressed into her palm; she saw his pupils flare, saw the turbulence she had been seeking. Michael's buried passion.

"In the cathedral before you came in," she said, "I finally forgave my father. You were right. It was what I had to do. And I forgave Julius, too."

"Julius! For what?"

"For—" She stopped. She had been about to say, For letting me down. And suddenly she understood what she hadn't seen before: that when Julius had refused to go along with her, and then had come to the abbey to take her home, she had seen it as *another* betrayal. Catherine had not been aware of it until this moment—that she had been drawn to Julius because he was so like her father.

"And it is what you have to do," she said. "You need to forgive the sixteen-year-old boy you once were, forgive him for not preventing a senseless murder."

"Oh Catherine," he said, turning away from her. "That's not it. It's not me I need to forgive. Don't you understand? *I'm* not the problem." He faced her. "It's *him! He's* the one I resent, he's the one I can't forgive!"

Catherine knew who he was talking about. Not the punk who did the killing, but the old man behind the counter.

"He just stood there," Michael said in a voice filled with pain. "Like a dumb creature, he just stood there pleading with his eyes for me to do something. And when I didn't move, his look changed. He saw that I was a coward. And his eyes were filled with disgust. The punk shot him, grabbed the money, and ran, and in the instant the bullet hit him in the chest, the old man gave me a look of such utter scorn that I hated him. I hated him for knowing I was a coward, I hated him for accusing me with his dying eyes. And God help me, I hate him still!"

His words rang up to the raftered ceiling, echoing. And then silence rushed in. When Catherine saw the tears rising in his eyes, she stepped up to him and said, "Forgive him, Michael—"

"Forgive him for what?" he cried. "For seeing the truth? Catherine, I iwa coward. And God knows I've been trying ever since to make up for that cowardice!"

"And running from the priesthood is a solution? Michael, maybe this is the second chance you've been praying for. This is the test. But if you leave the priesthood you will have lost. God still loves you, you told me that yourself."

"You don't believe in God."

"No, but I believe in forgiveness. Sabina was right, forgiveness liberates us, it makes us see clearly. Forgive the old man, Michael, and you will see that you must stay in the priesthood."

"Forgive the old man the way you've forgiven your father?"

"Yes."

"So now you're back in the Church? You're a Catholic again?"

"Well, no—"

"You see? It isn't that simple, Catherine! Just to forgive is not enough."

"Michael, I don't believe in God. But you do!"

"And I don't believe in my worthiness to serve God. So we're right back where we started."

"No we aren't. This time we're fighting in the same arena, fighting the same opponents."

He took her by the shoulders. "You would fight for me?"

"Yes—"

And suddenly he was kissing her hard on the mouth.

Catherine flung her arms around his neck as he drew her to him, enveloping her in a strong embrace, holding her tightly, the kiss deepening, intensifying.

He reached behind her head, cradled the vulnerable nape of her neck, driving his fingers up into the silky platinum hair.

Catherine unbuttoned his shirt and pushed it off his shoulders, drawing the sleeves down, letting it drop to the floor. She explored his chest, ran her fingers over firm muscles. When she touched the scab on his left biceps, she remembered. "Does it hurt?" she whispered.

"No."

She kissed the wound where the bullet had grazed him, two weeks and two lifetimes ago.

He traced his fingertips over her face, following them with his eyes as if memorizing every curve and line, every lash and pore. He kissed her again, in the long, slow, and achingly tender kiss of a man who had wanted this for a long time but was afraid to hurry, afraid to bring it all to an end.

There was no asking or wondering *if,* no stopping to weigh the consequences. They both knew they were no longer who they were when all this had started.

Michael carried Catherine to the bed. He kissed her tenderly as he lowered her onto the quilt. Their pulses raced but their bodies moved slowly, seeking answers, and finding them at last in each other.

CATHERINE AWOKE AND gazed for a moment at the ceiling. Then she looked at Michael, slumbering gently at her side. The sky was dark beyond the window, but with a hint of fading that meant dawn was not far off.

She touched Michael's face and tears came to her eyes. It had been so beautiful, and so special. Whatever might come after this, she knew they would always have this night, and Aachen and the cathedral.

She returned her gaze to the ceiling, where she noticed a curious water-stain pattern in the plaster, indicating that, at some time, a pipe had leaked. And as her head began to clear, she remembered that she had had a dream. What was it about?

It had something to do with—

She felt her heart begin to race.

The dream!

Catherine drew in a sharp breath. *The dream!*

Tymbos!

She knew where the seventh scroll was.

FINAL DAY

When Catherine entered the room, Michael turned from the window and watched her as she came inside and closed the door.

She remained standing there, still in her coat, hugging a small package to her chest. "Hi," she said.

"Hi."

She saw how the bright morning sunshine spilled over his broad shoulders. He was wearing a pale blue chambray shirt tucked into new blue jeans. No cassock, no Roman collar. She wondered when he was going to be a priest again. "I wasn't sure you would be here," she said.

He smiled. "Why not? Because of last night?"

"How do you feel?"

"How I feel is"—he came toward her—"I love you, Catherine."

"Do you?"

"Why not? It doesn't mean that I love God any less. If anything, my love for you helps strengthen my love for Him." He stood close to her, smiling with his mouth, but his eyes held a serious expression. "But what about you? Any regrets?"

"Oh no . . . ," she whispered.

"Catherine, please believe me when I say that I don't regret one

365

minute of last night. I don't regret one minute of these past two weeks with you."

"But you're going to do years of penance."

His smile deepened. "Maybe."

"You're going to remember me as the wicked woman who caused your downfall."

He took her face into his hands and said gently, "Are you aware that you always put words into other people's mouths?"

"I always have been a control freak."

"My God, you are beautiful," he whispered, caressing her with his eyes.

"Michael, have I . . . ?"

"Have you what?"

"The priesthood. Have I made you want to quit?"

"If I decide to leave, it w ill be because of events that happened long ago. If anything, you have made me face the fact that the only way I shall find peace is to forgive."

He fell silent, and his silence was more eloquent than poetry, for what it was telling her w'as that he was remembering last night, just as she too was remembering: not merely their physical coming together, for although it had been beautiful, something more had occurred between them, something that transcended love and romance and words of passion. Michael had held her and whispered in her ear, and when he had been unable to go further, Catherine had then whispered to him until they had spun a vision together that only they could see, their shared dream.

If they never had another moment, if today should see the end of their journey together, they would always have last night, and whispers in the dark.

"Tonight is New Year's Eve," she said softly, watching his lips, wanting him to kiss her, and yet afraid he would. Last night w'as last night—rare, special, beautiful. But she knew that today had to be different. "Tomorrow is the start of the new' millennium," she said. "Michael, I know where the seventh scroll is."

Shedding her coat and placing the package on the bed, she said, "I noticed yesterday a religious bookstore across from the cathedral. I thought I might find what we needed there."

She opened the traveling bag the abbess had given her and brought out the yellow legal pad on which she had been writing her translation. "Before I left the abbey," she said excitedly, "I copied down the Thomas of Monmouth document. Something about it has been bothering me ever since we first read it."

He folded his arms. "Well of course, all those errors."

"But are they really errors? Think about it, Michael. When you break the document down, you see that Thomas actually has all the right facts, he's just put them together wrong. And it's been nagging me ever since. It came to me during the night." She paused. There had been something else in the dream—something strange and cryptic. She shook her head. It was gone now. "Look." She opened the legal pad and spread the single page out in the light pouring through the window.

"Let's say this is *our* Sabina. We know she went to Stonehenge, that much is true. She wasn't married to Cornelius Severus, but she was in his entourage. Now then, as for the other facts." Catherine pointed to the line that read: *She left behind six books on alchemy and sorcery, which were subsequently buried with the High Priestess, Valeria, in the holy place.*

"Six books involving alchemy and sorcery," Catherine continued. "That is also somewhat true. Now here—Valeria. First let's take the word *Priestess,*'" Catherine said, "and change it to deaconess." She scratched it out and wrote above it. "And the six books. Make that *one* book."

Michael said, "But it still doesn't make sense."

"It makes sense if you add one missing piece to the puzzle, then it all falls into place."

"And what's that?"

"Tymbos," she said with a triumphant smile.

"But he isn't mentioned here."

"Not he, Michael, *it*. We've been trying too hard to find Tymbos—the kings, the anagrams, making it harder for ourselves than we needed to when it was right there all along! And that's what came to me in my sleep. Michael, *tymbos* is Greek for *grave!*"

"Grave!"

"Here where it reads 'were buried with' insert the Greek word for grave—" Catherine wrote furiously, scratching out and substituting words, until she had a whole new sentence that read:

Sabina left behind six books on alchemy and sorcery, one of which was subsequently taken to tymbos by the Deaconess Valeria.

"And Perpetua," Michael said in amazement, "typical of the Christians of her era, added the word king to make more of a puzzle of it—take it to the king, take it to the Kingdom."

"The Kingdom of God," Catherine said.

Michael frowned. "Buried in a holy place. . . ."

"No, not a holy place, Michael, it says *the* holy place."

"What holy place would that be?"

"If you were a Christian living two thousand years ago, what would you consider *the* holy place?"

"I can think of three, actually."

"Me, too," she said, "which is why I decided to try the religious bookstore near the cathedral. It was a long shot, but . . ." She went to the bed, picked up the package, tore off the wrapper, and handed it to Michael.

He looked at the title. "It's in German."

"The man in the bookstore translated the title for me. *Early Christian Martyrs.* Turn to page thirty-two."

He flipped the pages. "Valeria," he read. "I assume this says, 'died circa 142 A.D.'" He looked at Catherine. "The date fits but I still don't see . . ."

"Further down the page. Keep reading."

Among the German words two in Latin jumped out: Aemelius Valerius. *"Tochter,"* Michael read. "Daughter?"

"She was the daughter of Aemelius Valerius. Michael, she would have been Aemelia Valeria! Roman women were called by either their last name or their first name, depending."

"And apparently she was known as Valeria to her family and friends."

"But Perpetua called her Aemelia! And that's why we weren't able to find her in all of our searches. Michael, the seventh scroll was buried with Aemelia in *the* holy place!"

BECAUSE HE WAS downstairs in his private museum, the most secure spot on his vast estate, Miles couldn't see the sunlight. But he could *feel* the morning as he waited for the message at the other end of the scrambled phone line.

Guests had already begun to arrive for the big New Year's Eve bash; their vibes, Miles would swear, were penetrating the two-foot-thick concrete walls surrounding his precious collections. He sensed the energy', the excitement and hopes and fears of the first of the over one thousand people who were going to descend upon Casa Havers for twelve hours of revelry and millennial madness.

Miles had worked it out so that his guests weren't going to have to settle for just one midnight, but a string of them, starting with Sydney, Australia. He was managing the miracle through a series of enormous TV screens set up around the house and grounds, bringing live coverage of New Year's Eve events from cities that preceded New Mexico in the march toward the date line: Sydney, Bombay, Rome, London, New York. The champagne would be flowing, the barbecues flaring, the music booming out to the Sangre de Cristo Mountains.

It was a good time to be alive. And rich.

"Hello?" he said into the phone. "Yes, I can hear you. What's the report?"

He jotted the information on a pad of paper: *Catherine Alexander . . . six o'clock flight out of Frankfurt.*

"Where to?" he asked.

And when he heard the response, he knew that Dr. Alexander had figured out the whereabouts of the seventh scroll.

He hung up and dialed another party, who was waiting for the call. . . .

ELEVEN P.M. AND THE countdown to midnight had begun.

"He's a friend," Michael said as they jumped out of the taxi near St. Peter's Square. "He's been following the news, and when I told him about my involvement with you—" He took Catherine's hand as they ran through the stalled bumper-to-bumper traffic, through the cacophony of blaring horns and shouting motorists, and hundreds of blinding headlights.

Michael was in his cassock again, having changed at Frankfurt Airport. And the friend he was referring to was a fellow seminarian from Chicago, now attached to the office of Vatican archaeology.

They plunged into the formidable crowds congesting St. Peter's Square. Nearly everyone was holding a light of some sort—candle, lantern, flashlight—so that faces were illuminated like an enormous painting by Georges de la Tour. As they pushed through, Michael's priestly attire parting the way for them, Catherine glimpsed faces: male and female, young and old, expressing the range of human emotion from stark fear to ecstatic joy. Some were weeping, others laughing; but many wore anxious, stony expressions as all eyes were trained upon the papal balcony, waiting for the white-clad successor to St. Peter to appear.

They were stopped several times by Rome police and Swiss Guards; a few authoritative words from Michael got them through. They met Father Sebastian at the Arco delle Campane, on the left side of the basilica. He led them across a courtyard that was deserted because of wooden barricades and the conspicuous presence of the Swiss Guard, under another archway, around a corner and through a doorway with a sign that read UFFICIO SCAVI—Office of Excavations.

"For a Roman Christian," Catherine had said back in Aachen. "There can only be one *the* holy place—where St. Peter was buried." Aemelia Valeria must be *here,* and so, they hoped, was the seventh scroll.

Once inside the office, with the door closed, Michael introduced Catherine to his old friend. "Father Sebastian was actually the one who was supposed to have gone down to the Sinai and check out reports of a Jesus fragment."

"But I had the flu," the other priest, a small man with thick glasses and a slight stoop, said—apologetically, Catherine thought, and somewhat wistfully, as if he regretted having missed out on such an adventure.

He produced a ring of keys. "We have to hurry," he said. "At midnight they're going to open the doors and commence a thirty- day showing of St. Peter's bones. Half the population of the world will be down there!"

He led them past desks littered with correspondence, manila files, memos, and pieces of pottery and statuary, to a side door that opened upon a narrow corridor with stairs going down. "We'll be seen if we go through the church," Father Sebastian explained, his voice edged with excitement. Catherine wondered how much Michael had told him. She looked at her watch. They had to hurry. Once the public was allowed down into the Grottoes, they would lose their chance to open Aemelia's tomb.

For that was what they had decided they must do. And they had to be fast. Once Michael's superiors found out about Aemelia, Catherine knew the scroll would be lost forever.

The Sacred Grottoes was actually a long, low-ceilinged chamber beneath St. Peter's, broken up into small chapels containing the crypts of popes and royalty: a tenth-century German emperor was buried here, as were Hadrian IV, the only English pope, Queen Christina of Sweden, and James II of England.

As they hurried through, their footsteps echoing on the marble floor, Sebastian explained: "It was in 1939 that the Roman necropolis was discovered. Workers digging out an extension for the burial chapel of Pope Pius XI came across a wall that wasn't supposed to be there. When it was determined that the wall was sixteen hundred years old, archaeologists were brought in to excavate."

While he spoke, he led them past small pews, modest altars, and elaborate sarcophagi, until they came to a spectacular chapel with a blue and gold vaulted ceiling and individual prie-dieux facing the crypt of Pope Clementine. As Sebastian searched among his keys for the one to an unmarked door set in the elaborately decorated wall, his hands shaking with excitement, he said, "The archaeologists made amazing discoveries! For one thing, the bones of the holy martyr himself, who was crucified upside down on this very spot, in Caligula's circus." He added, "St. Peter," in a reverential tone.

Catherine looked back the way they had come, through the shadows, wondering if anyone had followed them here.

Hurry, she mentally urged Father Sebastian. Hurry, hurry. . . .

Sebastian found the key, turned it in the lock. "The circus is gone now, of course," the priest continued in a voice edged with urgency, "but we know it was here and archaeologists have evidence of it. Anyway, a long tradition—watch your step here," he lifted the hem of his cassock and led the way with a flashlight, "tradition says that the body of Peter was claimed by his followers and secretly buried, right here. Three hundred years later, during the reign of Constantine, there was still the original shrine on this spot, and it was here that the emperor built his new basilica. So, when bones were found . . ."

Catherine already knew the story. Both of her parents had believed that the human remains housed beneath the great altar of St. Peter's belonged to the blessed martyr himself. Although, as an archaeologist, she was trained to be skeptical, Catherine was familiar enough with the ancient Christians' obsession with relics to agree that the bones were most likely those of the apostle.

"When Constantine decided to build a large basilica in the fourth century," Sebastian continued, leading them into a formidable darkness filled with the smells of dust and decay, "'Vatican Hill was much smaller than it is now. So he constructed a series of retaining walls and filled in the spaces in between, to broaden the hill. What Constantine effectively did was to bury this ancient city of the dead. Look," Sebastian said in a hushed tone as he swept his flashlight on the ceiling high overhead. "What you are looking at is the *underside* of the floor of St. Peter's. Seventeen hundred years ago we would have been looking at open sky."

Catherine stared in amazement as they proceeded to walk down what seemed to be an actual street, passing courtyards and fountains along the way, and facades of enormous Roman mausolea created to resemble houses, complete with thresholds, doorways, windows, and, in some instances, stairways leading up to a roof that was now incorporated in the foundation of the church above. As they peered through windows and doorways, Catherine had the curious feeling of peeping into private homes.

It was all optical illusion, a city of the dead created to look like a real city, and as they walked along narrow streets with blind alleys, past frescoes intended to look like meadows and open spaces, Catherine was reminded of the Minotaur's Maze.

"All these tombs were cleared out years ago," Sebastian said, now whispering as they walked past dark, silent "houses," his flashlight briefly capturing a playful dolphin, a vase of flowers, a flock of birds—all beautifully painted by artists long dead. The darkness around them was so deep and terrifying, that Catherine sought Michael's hand and stayed close to him.

"There are many more tombs," Sebastian said, "stretching under the whole length of St. Peter's, but they can't be excavated because it would undermine the foundation of the basilica."

Catherine sensed the mighty Renaissance church overhead, pressing down. . . .

Shining his light into a columbarium containing many niches for funerary urns, Father Sebastian said, "You can see the gradual change from paganism to Christianity. The farther away from the burial place of St. Peter, the more urns and references to the old gods we find."

He stepped inside a tomb, with Michael and Catherine following, and trained his light on the vaulted ceiling to illuminate a golden mosaic depicting Christ as Apollo riding the Sun chariot, the sun's rays emanating from his head. "Evidence of the transition," Father Sebastian said.

As Catherine gazed up at the recognizable face of Jesus, but with the sun's rays crowning his head as he commanded the chariot, she thought of Sabina's many savior gods.

They passed more tombs, and Catherine noticed that the majority of the graves seemed to belong to women. Tacitus, writing two thousand years ago, had called the new faith "a religion of women and slaves." And as they passed more and more women—- even another Aemelia, although her last name was Gorgonio—Catherine found herself silently asking once again: When did the men take over?

As they plunged deeper under the basilica, and the atmosphere grew mustier, with the darkness opening only briefly when Father Sebastian's flashlight passed through, closing quickly behind the intruders to plant a solid black wall behind them, a phrase suddenly went through Catherine's mind: *On the final day the dead shall rise. . . .*

She felt the back of her neck prickle as she imagined, on the stroke of midnight, all these stone lids sliding open, moldering corpses sitting up, climbing out of their tombs. And the bones of St. Peter, would they rearticulate themselves into a complete skeleton, enabling him to rise up and walk?

"What was that?" she said suddenly.

Michael looked at her. His face was cast in a supernatural glow. "What was what?"

"I thought—" She brushed the air in front of her face. "Never mind."

They continued on, down another street. Catherine could almost feel the press of humanity overhead, the millions of people—

Then she heard the singing, soft at first, but growing, like a groundswell. It had begun at one edge of the crowd and was now being carried from person to person, as the multitude in the square, with their lamps and flames, lifted their voices to the star-splashed sky: "Ave Mari-ia . . ."

It must be close to midnight, Catherine thought. She was almost afraid to ask. "Father Sebastian, are you sure the tomb of Aemelia Valeria is here?"

"Oh yes. One of our nicer ones, too."

"A-ave, ave-e dominus, dominus tecum."

"And," he announced with a sweep of his flashlight, "here it is!"

It was actually a building, two stories tall, that might have appeared on the streets of ancient Rome. The exterior was painted red, with a magnificent triangular pediment supported by Doric columns. The interior walls, done in white stucco, were imbedded with niches shaped like scallop shells and painted with delicate flowers, ivy, and birds. One beautiful niche framed a painting of Venus rising from the sea, with stucco dolphins frolicking in plaster surf at her feet. The place had the feel of someone's elegant living room.

"Those niches," Sebastian said softly, playing his flashlight beam over the walls, suddenly illuminating astonishing examples of Roman art, "held cremation urns. So this was once a pagan tomb. At some point, however, the family was converted to Christianity. We think it was due to this lady."

He swiveled the beam onto a breathtaking fresco of a family scene, in the center of which was an *orante*—the representation of the deceased person in an attitude of prayer, the symbol of salvation. Beneath the figure a name was written: Aemelia Valeria.

The crowd above continued to sing: *"Benedictus tu in mulieri-bus. . . ."*

Catherine stepped closer, to examine the fresco. The deaconess was dressed in white robes, her arms held out, her eyes heavenward. Aemelia had been a beautiful woman, with her hair elaborately styled in tiers upon her head, the height of noble fashion in the Roman Empire.

"Et benedictus fructus ventris tui . . . Jesus."

A leader of the early Church, Catherine thought. A Christian priestess. Was the seventh scroll buried with her? And was it going to contain proof that women, not men, were the heirs to Jesus' authority?

"And here is how we know this is a Christian tomb," Father Sebastian said. "Aemelia's sarcophagus. We believe she was the first in the family not to be cremated."

"Was it opened?" Catherine whispered. She stepped up to it, placed her hands on the finely carved marble.

"Oh no. Only the pagan graves were opened. And all the urns, which of course were pagan, have gone into museums."

Catherine saw words etched into the lid of the sarcophagus: *dormit in pace*—sleep in peace; and *anima dulcis Aemelia*—sweet-souled Aemelia.

Catherine looked at Michael. There was an intensity to his face that made her think: he, too, is wondering if the final scroll is here. For if it was, then it meant that it contained a volatile message indeed, for it was only under threat of persecution that Aemelia was to take it to her grave with her. And her persecution could mean only one thing: that those who persecuted her did not like what was written on the scroll.

"All right," Michael said. "Let's find a way to open it."

TEN TIME ZONES away, Miles Havers excused himself from the fete going on at his Santa Fe estate, and left his guests to go down to his private museum and wait for a phone call from Rome.

"SANCTA MARIA, ORA pro nobis—"

The singing stopped and they heard a sudden roar overhead. "What's that?" Michael said.

Father Sebastian looked up. "I believe His Holiness has just appeared on the balcony."

And then suddenly blinding lights came on, flooding the mausoleum. Catherine cried out as a tall, gaunt apparition materialized— Cardinal Lefevre in a black cassock with red piping, red buttons, wide red grosgrain sash, and red skull cap on sparse hair. An enormous gold cross suspended from a gold chain lay dramatically on his chest.

Catherine cast a sharp look at Michael. He said, "Hey, I didn't—"

"No, Dr. Alexander," Cardinal Lefevre said, his voice reverberating in the subterranean sepulcher. "Father Garibaldi did not inform me that you would be coming here. In fact," he cast Michael an admonishing look, "I have not heard from Father Garibaldi in several days."

"*Someone* helped you," Catherine said. "Who?"

"I received a phone call. A tip, as you Americans would say."

Catherine sized up the four young men accompanying him—the Cohors Helvetica—Swiss Guard, established five hundred years ago to protect the Pope and the Vatican. Although their pikes and halberds, the Shakespearean ruffed collars, doublets and striped breeches, and conquistador-style helmets made them appear to be purely ceremonial, Catherine knew that these expertly trained young men discreetly carried tear gas canisters, antipersonnel grenades, and automatic firearms. She knew also that they had sworn to serve the reigning Pope and his successors at risk, if necessary, to their own life and limb.

"Dr. Alexander, please believe me when I tell you that we are your friends," Lefevre said.

"I remember seeing your name," she said, "at the bottom of a letter to my mother."

"An unfortunate episode, Doctor. One which I had truly wished to avoid."

"You're going to take the scroll from Aemelia's sarcophagus, aren't you?"

"If it is a Christian document, yes, because it belongs to the Church."

"It belongs to the world. And I am going to see to it that the world reads what is written in that scroll."

"Dr. Alexander, I know that you see me as an enemy. But I am not. I am here to prevent chaos. Unleash proof of a thousand messiahs and you weaken the influence of Jesus. Do this, and you rip the power base out from under the Church. If you topple the Catholic Church, you topple national economies."

"So the Church is just a big corporation. This is all about business."

"Of course," Lefevre said. "A priest is a businessman in a way. People are born with dark places in their souls, Dr. Alexander. We sell them lightbulbs."

"Who told you I was here? Miles Havers?"

"Mr. Havers and the Church see eye to eye, Dr. Alexander. We do not wish the scrolls to be made public, Mr. Havers has the same desire."

WHILE MILES'S AND Erica's guests, spread around the estate, sipping drinks in the rays of the setting sun, watched the many indoor and outdoor TV screens and prepared to mark a simultaneous countdown with the people in St. Peter's Square, Erica looked around for her husband. It was about to turn midnight in Rome. Where was Miles?

THE GROUP DOWN in the tombs heard the multitude in the square above begin the midnight countdown: *"Died!"*

"Forgive me, Your Eminence," Michael said. "But we are going to open this sarcophagus." He glanced at the four Swiss Guards.

ON THE TELEVISION screens around the Havers estate, the millions gathered at St. Peter's cried out in one voice: *"Died!"* And as Erica went through the house, she heard her guests echo merrily: "Ten!" It was their third millennial countdown since noon and they were well into the spirit of it.

"Nove!"
Lefevre gestured to two of the guards. They laid aside their pikestaffs and approached the sarcophagus.

"Nine!"
Erica arrived at the museum downstairs. "Miles? Are you in here?"

"Otto!"
Michael and Father Sebastian repositioned themselves at the side of the sarcophagus, and with the help of the two young guardsmen, while Cardinal Lefevre intoned a prayer for the dead, they began to push.

"Eight!"
Erica pushed open the door and looked in. "Miles, darling?"

"Sette!"
"Okay," Michael said. "Let's push together, on my mark!"

"Seven!"
Erica searched the museum, its treasures softly illuminated. "Miles?"

377

"Sei!"

The lid of the sarcophagus wasn't budging.

"Six!"

Erica walked past the treasures her husband had collected over the years and saw the cabinet in the corner. It was new, she had never seen it before.

"Cinque!"

Catherine watched Michael's broad back as it strained with the exertion of pushing against the lid of the sarcophagus, sealed nearly two thousand years ago. She held her breath as she waited for the lid to move.

"Five!"

Erica decided that the cabinet must have been created to house a new treasure. She wondered what was inside.

"Quattro!"

"Okay," Michael said. "Once more! Put everything into it this time!"

"Four!"

Erica reached out. The cabinet was unlocked. She seized the small ivory knob and started to open the door.

"Tre!"

The lid of the sarcophagus created a loud scraping sound as it finally slid an inch.

"Three!"

Miles came out of his office at the other end of the museum, cellular phone in hand. He saw Erica, opening the cabinet.

"Due!"

The sarcophagus lid scraped another inch, and then another, until there was an opening wide enough for flashlights.

"Two!"
"Erica!" Miles said, starting toward her. "Don't—"

"Uno!"
Catherine looked inside Aemelia's sarcophagus.
"Buon Anno!"

"One!"
Erica found herself staring at the Solstice Kachina.
"Happy New Year!"

THERE WAS A tremendous, deafening roar overhead. The eight down in the Scavi looked up. They listened and waited, expecting the walls of the tomb, the ceiling, the massive basilica to come crashing down around them.

Nothing happened. No trumpets or angels, no earthquakes or upheavals. Just a single moment of silence as the world held its collective breath.

And then they heard cheering and shouting, and cries of jubilation pouring from hundreds of thousands of throats.

Cardinal Lefevre released a sigh of relief and said to his companions, "It would seem we shall not be witnessing the apocalypse this millennium."

"The millennium isn't over," Catherine said, adding, "Your Eminence." She definitely did not like this man. "Not until the end of the year two thousand. That's the true end of the century, isn't it?"

He sent her a cryptic smile. "Indeed, so, Doctor," he said. "Then we must wait another three-hundred and sixty-five days before we know if this is the age prophesied."

He went to the sarcophagus and looked in.

"Ora pro nobis!" he whispered, crossing himself. For there was nothing in Aemelia Valeria's coffin—no scroll, no skeleton, not even any ashes.

"I would speculate," Lefevre said in a tone that Catherine couldn't identify—was he disappointed or secretly triumphant?— "that this tomb was plundered ages ago. Perhaps before Constantine ordered this necropolis to be filled in." He sighed. Again, Catherine wondered: with relief or chagrin? "It has been, as you Americans say, a wild goose chase."

Catherine looked around the tomb, now brightly illuminated; she searched the niches, the corners, even the frescoes—there was nowhere a scroll could be hidden. She looked again inside the sarcophagus. It appeared almost new. No one had been buried in it.

Then where was Aemelia?

"Dr. Alexander, may we have the scrolls now?"

"They're in a safe place."

He waited.

"They're in a locker at the airport."

"Which airport?" When she didn't reply, he held out his hand. "May I have the key to the locker?"

But she shook her head. "I'm not the one to make that decision. I'll turn the scrolls over to the United Nations. You can all fight over them after that."

His eyes flickered. "Very well." He turned to Michael. "I must join His Holiness now. Father Garibaldi, we will talk in the next few days?"

"Yes, Your Eminence."

They turned and began to file out, a procession through the streets of the dead, shadows moving along walls like a funerary procession of long ago, sad and somber, indeed a parade of mourners. Michael discreetly took Catherine's hand. He sent her a look of deep regret and apology.

When they emerged into the night air, surrounded by millions of cheering people, Catherine looked across the square to the papal balcony, where a man in white was signing a benediction over the ecstatic throng. Her eyes sparkled with tears and anger as she said, "It was all for nothing, Michael. Danno dying. You and I running for our lives. All meaningless. I had even started to believe what Sabina said. I actually started to fall for it. I even went so far as to forgive my father. And what did it get me?"

"Maybe it doesn't work like that."

And what happened in Aachen—their night of love, and the revelation they had experienced together in shared whispers. How could she and Michael have been led so far only to have it end in disappointment? What cruel joke was this?

"Michael," she said. "Stay in the priesthood. It's where you belong."

He seized her wrist. "And you?" he said, passion just beneath the surface, barely controlled. "Where do you belong?"

"Well, I don't have a dig to return to," she said bitterly. "I'll probably never be allowed to dig again. And I don't have a lover to go back to. I certainly don't have a best friend waiting for me. But I do know one thing, Michael. If it consumes the rest of my life, I am going to see to it that Miles Havers pays for Danno's death."

THE NEW MILLENNIUM

The condo had a strange feel to it.

Although Catherine had come and gone from this place many times over the years, often returning after an absence of months, this was the first homecoming that made her feel as if she were walking into a stranger's house.

The weekly cleaning service had kept it spotless, giving it a sterile, unlived-in feel. The only thing not orderly was the pile of newspapers and mail on the dining room table. Her answering machine listed thirty messages.

The unraveled threads of her life.

Somehow, she was going to have to find focus again, and rebuild. There was no question that she and Julius could reconstruct their shattered relationship after all this. And Michael—somehow she was going to have to live with loving him, knowing that she could never see him again. But the first thing she planned to do was to drive to Santa Barbara and talk to the police, tell them what happened. She wouldn't mention Miles Havers's involvement in Danno's death. They wouldn't believe her.

His picture had been on the front page of that morning's newspaper, along with photographs of crowds overwhelming computer stores in Singapore, Sydney, New York. The caption read: "All over the world people arc snapping up the new Dianuba 2000 software in a buying frenzy that has eclipsed the madness that heralded Microsoft's Windows 95 four and a half years ago."

Let him savor his victory for now, Catherine thought. She would bide her time.

As she started for the kitchen, she saw a small package at the top of the pile of mail. Plain brown wrapper. No return address. American stamps. In the lower left corner, in red ink: URGENT

She opened it and found a small book. There was no letter or note, no inscription inside to tell her whom it was from or why they had sent it.

And then she saw the title: SACRE GROTTE Y SCAVI SOTTO SAN PIETRO—*The Sacred Grottoes & Excavations Beneath St. Peter's.* Published by the Vatican's own publishing house: Libreria Editrice Vaticana. Publication date, 1953.

The text was in Italian, but the black-and-white photos brought back painful memories of four days ago, although the excavations of the necropolis weren't as far along in these pictures as they were now. She frowned. Why had this been sent to her? And by whom?

She looked at the wrapper again. Then she saw the postmark, barely discernible over the stamps.

Vermont.

She read the date. It had been mailed a week ago. The day, in fact, that she had left the abbey.

Opening the book again, she went through it more carefully, past the pictures of Christ as Apollo and the orante of Aemelia Valeria, until, near the end, she came upon a group photo of a team of archaeologists. Bringing it into better light, she squinted at the seven tiny faces. None was familiar. Then she read the names. Again, all unfamiliar to her. Except—

Gertrude Majors.

Catherine frowned. Where had she heard that name before?

A voice came back: "I'm Mother Mary Elizabeth now, but before I joined the order back in 1966 I was—"

"Oh my God," Catherine whispered. She realized that she was gazing at the face of the abbess, as she had appeared forty-six years ago, *when she had been an archaeologist excavating the tombs beneath St. Peter's.*

Catherine ran to the phone. Michael had been ordered to a retreat at a Cistercian monastery. Saint Somebody-or-other. Just outside of Toronto.

Sainte Solange!

She called information, and three minutes later was dialing the number of the monastery.

"I'd like to speak to Father Michael Garibaldi, please. It's urgent."

It took him forever to get to the phone.

"Michael," she said excitedly. "The seventh scroll does exist, and this time I do know where it is!"

MILES QUICKLY PUT a call through to Titus. "She's made the error that I've been expecting," he said. "Dr. Alexander forgot that her phone might still be tapped. I knew that if the seventh scroll did exist, she would eventually find it. And apparently she has—Greensville Abbey in Vermont. How quickly can you have someone there?" He smiled. "Excellent. I'll be waiting for your call."

CATHERINE KNEW THEY were following her.

She had realized too late that she should have called Michael from a pay phone. Whoever had been chasing her for the past three weeks— Miles Havers, the FBI, the Vatican—was most likely still watching her, still had a tap on her phone. But she couldn't stop now. She had to keep going.

As she felt the 747 begin its descent, she looked at the week-old magazine in her lap, and its headline: IS THE WORLD ABOUT TO END? The world hadn't ended after all when the clocked ticked over on midnight, four days ago, but millennium fever was building again as people realized that the two thousand years had not in fact ended on December 31, 1999, but rather would end on December 31, 2000.

She felt the 747 shudder.

Looking out the window at the cloud cover below, Catherine decided she must be somewhere over New York. She closed her eyes and mentally counted off the miles, silently urging the aircraft to go faster, faster. . . .

"YES," THE ABBESS said, "I was one of the archaeologists who excavated the necropolis beneath St. Peter's."

Catherine and Michael were in the library at the abbey, the January
sunlight pouring through the leaded windows. The two had met at the
Montpelier airport and taken a rental car to the abbey. The abbess had
greeted them with no trace of surprise.

"I knew you would come back," she said, "once you saw the book.
I didn't tell you about the seventh scroll before because I wasn't sure I
was supposed to."

"Supposed to?" Michael said.

"Forgive me, Father, this will sound strange I'm sure. But I had
no intention of taking anything from the Scavi. I had never stolen
anything before, and certainly not an artifact from an archaeological
site. I've always deplored plundering of that sort. But I came under an
inexplicable influence. When I saw the scroll, tucked in an urn in a
niche, I couldn't help myself. All I could think was that if I didn't take
it, the scroll would get damaged or stolen by an unscrupulous collector. I felt almost like a guardian of the scroll."

"Mother Superior," Catherine said. "Do you know why Aemelia
wasn't buried in her tomb?"

The abbess closed her eyes and crossed herself, whispering, "God
forgive me."

Catherine exchanged a look with Michael.

"The urn which contained the scroll," the abbess said, "also
contained ashes."

Mother Elizabeth regarded her visitors with infinite sadness. "I
disposed of those ashes, as if they were rubbish. God forgive me, God
forgive me. I didn't know. I thought they were pagan."

Michael's voice was somber as he said, "Aemelia's family had
her cremated? Even though they had created a Christian sarcophagus for her?"

"Maybe," Catherine said, "it was the authorities who forced them
to do it. Maybe the persecutions had begun."

"When I brought the scroll home and translated it," the abbess
continued, "and I thought I had come upon a lost gospel, I became
obsessed with finding the first part—I had no idea that six scrolls

preceded it. I spent twenty years searching for anything that might lead me to more, and that was when I found out about the Thomas of Monmouth Manuscript. It was here, in the abbey's archives, and when I came and read it, I realized that the manuscript contained errors, and I became even more determined to find out who the author of this scroll was. I ended up staying here."

She wrung her hands. "My conscience was deeply troubled. I realized I had mistakenly disposed of the ashes of a Christian. I was very devout when I was young, and conceited in my religion. I thought it was all right to treat the remains of a pagan with disrespect."

She looked at Michael. "I am sorry, Father, for lying to you with my silence. When you and Dr. Alexander arrived, I was quite taken aback. I had not heard the news, I had no idea you possessed Sabina's story. I needed to pray upon it, I needed to ask God to guide me."

She turned to Catherine. "When you came to me that night, after you had spoken with Dr. Voss, and you said you needed to leave, that you were in danger, I knew I had to help you. And I almost told you about the seventh scroll then, but something made me hold back."

"It's a good thing you did," Michael said. "Because the FBI would have confiscated it."

"Yes," she said, "and when those hooligans did come looking for Dr. Alexander, it became clear to me what I had to do. And so I mailed the book."

"Is it here now?" Catherine said. "Is the seventh scroll here?"

"Yes. You may read it if you wish."

"Mother Superior," Catherine asked, "is it the end of Sabina's story?"

The abbess smiled. "You can decide that for yourself."

It was still in scroll form, the ends of the papyrus attached to two rollers. And they saw in amazement something they had not expected to find: at the bottom of the last panel, the signatures of Sabina and Perpetua.

The sixth scroll had ended with, *"and I was afraid of,"* and so the seventh scroll began, *"this dark and fearsome realm. Although I had lived most of my life in the forest, I had never been alone, but always with the family. Now I was alone, running for my life, with scenes of slaughter fresh before my eyes, and suddenly the woods were no longer a friendly place. The spirits and ghosts who dwelled there, although they were the gods of my husband's people, I saw now as malevolent beings and I was terrified. But worse than this was my despair at having never converted my family to The Way. This terrible pain filled me as I plunged deeper into the forest, the low-hanging branches cutting my arms and face, and I thought about all those evenings around the fire when I had told the family about the Righteous One and they did not listen. A dread filled my heart, for my beloved Segimund and our children had died not knowing of eternal life. And I would never see them again. I wept so bitterly that my tears turned to ice on my cheeks.*

When I could go no farther, I lay down in the snow, praying that wild beasts did not consume my body. And when I was near death, I sent out a prayer to the Righteous One. And after a while I sensed a presence in the forest. I looked up and saw a man, coming through the trees. I saw by his dress and the ax that he carried that he was a woodsman, but I wondered where his house could be, since he was a stranger to me and I knew these woods.

And when he called me by name, not my German name but Sabina, I wondered who he might be. When he lifted me up out of the snow, I told him of my tremendous despair, that my family was lost to me forever, and he said, Believe.

I said, Believe what, Master?

He said, "My father's house has many rooms." And he passed a hand over my eyes and I saw a vision—Segimund and the family, not dead with their blood running crimson in the white snow, but in our village, with the fires burning and venison on the spit and mead in the cups. They were blissful, the earth was plentiful, and the sun was shining. And I knew that this was their abode for eternity, because this was what they had believed.

I understood then what the preacher in the marketplace of Antioch, so many years ago, had meant when he said, "The Righteous One instructed us, Be not afraid, only believe. And go thy way, for as thou hast believed, so be it done unto thee."

I asked, "Are you the Righteous One?"

He said, "I am who you have been seeking all these years." Suddenly my eyes filled with light, and I saw that he was the Righteous One, whom I had met so many years ago by the Sea of Salt. I asked: "Why could I not find you?"

He said: "But you did. For everywhere you traveled, I was there. Tetyou did not see me."

And I knew this was true, for I have seen the Righteous One in his many guises in many lands; there is proof of his existence in temples around the world, and in the hearts of myriad believers. And since I knew this was true, then I knew that all else which he told me was true, the Seven Truths which he had revealed to me in his many temples under his many names: That we are not alone; That we are divine; That we are eternal; That we return to the Source in eternal life when we die; That forgiveness is the first step back; That respect is the second step; That acceptance is the third; And that a messenger is sent periodically to teach each generation these truths, starting with the first, which is that we are not alone. . . .

He said it is a circle that is never broken. It begins with the Creator and ends with the Messenger. And when we have entered into this circle, following the Seven Truths to enlightenment, then is the Gift given to us.

And the Gift from the Creator is this: That faith creates. As you believe, so shall it be. And when I realized this, then I knew that all my dear friends, and all the people who shared the journey of my life but who did not embrace The Way, were not gone forever but continued to live, and are alive now, dear Perpetua, dwelling within their own faiths—the followers of Tammuz and Zoroaster, of Mithra and Krishna, of Osiris and Isis and Odin—they have all joined their gods in the blissful kingdoms of those gods.

I asked the Righteous One the question that had burdened my heart ever since followers of other faiths blamed the people of The Way for pestilence in Antioch. When my family was slaughtered, my heart had cried, Why ? For, if we were the true faith, then how could we perish while those of other beliefs thrived ? So I asked him: "Which is the true faith?"

And he replied, "They all are."

And I knew this was true.

I asked him: "Willyou come again?"

He said: "I have come before and I will come again. I shall come back as many times as I must. Each time humanity needs to be reminded of the truths, I will return."

"How will we know you?"

"By my signs. I will return as a king and as a peasant. I will be born in Arabia many years hence; and a thousand years hence I will be born in a distant land as yet unnamed. I will appear in a building as tall as a mountain, I will appear in a cave deep in the earth. I will appear as all things to all people, for I am a personal savior as well as the savior of humankind."

He returns to each of us in different ways. Some might not recognize him because he will not be in corporeal form, to some he will appear as a prophet, or as a god familiar to them. And to yet others he might appear as an ancestor, or an angel, perhaps simply as a sign in the sky. And he will tell you this: that we are all the children, the sons and daughters, of God. We are born from eternal life and to that eternal life we shall return, and whatever we believe of that Kingdom, so shall it be.

And he told me this, too: that the world ends for all of us, not in one great cataclysmic millennial event, but to each of us in a separate and individual moment. The Second Coming is not a particular day or hour, it is not a universal event but a private one, a moment of personal epiphany, marking the moment of our own true belief

Dear Perpetua, you tell me that a scouting party found me and brought me to the garrison. You thought I was dead, and then you felt my pulse and saw me breathe. I believe perhaps I was dead, but that I was allowed to come back one last time, to bring this message to the world.

Catherine gently unfurled the brittle papyrus, trying to keep it from breaking apart.

She began to read the last panel.

AS MILES STOOD up from his desk, he was startled to see Erica standing in the doorway. He hadn't heard her coming. Even now, she stood there staring at him, not saying anything.

"Darling," he said, going toward her, "you're not still upset about the kachina, are you? I told you, I didn't know what it was when I bought it. And I did give it back to the Pueblo, didn't I?" She came into the office and looked around for a moment. Then she said, "Do you remember when we had only been married for a few years, we were broke and you were struggling to write computer programs in our garage?"

"Of course I do. Those were the best—"

"You had a friend, a young man named Solly. The two of you used to talk about your dreams of owning a computer company. And then one day Solly showed you a revolutionary new software program he had designed, one that he was certain was going to make a lot of money. You both talked long into the night, I recall, and Solly went home at dawn. And then next night he was killed in a freak accident—he was electrocuted in his bathtub. The police said a radio had fallen in."

"Why are you bringing this up now, Erica?"

"You went for a walk that evening, you never said where. And then you had Solly's new software and you told me you had bought it from him."

"Is there a point to this?"

"I know what you've been doing, that you've been after those scrolls. Miles, I overheard—" Her voice broke. She drew in a breath, fought for composure. "I overheard you tell someone to get rid of Dr. Alexander."

"You misunderstood—"

She held up a hand. "Don't insult me with another lie. I have proof, Miles, of what you have been up to. Teddy has told me everything."

"Teddy!"

"It was because of him Dr. Alexander got away from you. He told me he sent her a message through e-mail, warning her. He said you broke the rules, that you caused someone harm."

"Hacker ethics! An oxymoron. Erica—"

The phone rang then, and when Miles started for it, Erica said, "Don't pick it up. It isn't the call you're waiting for. It isn't Titus."

He narrowed his eyes. "What are you talking about?"

"Titus didn't send anyone to Vermont. He and I had a talk and he has decided to terminate his contract with you."

"Why are you doing this?"

"It's for Solly and Coyote Man and whoever else has fallen victim to your lust for power."

"So you're going to turn me over to the police?"

She shook her head. "You'll never be convicted. You have too much money and too many powerful friends. I'm going to let the world judge you and sentence you, Miles. I'm going to tell about Solly."

"And then what?"

She held up the manila envelope she had been carrying, and brought out the photographs and Papazian's translations. "I found these in your office," she said. "I am going to use them to find my way back. I am going to continue on the spiritual path Coyote Man helped get me started on, I am going to find myself again. And maybe . . She hesitated. "In time . . . I shall find it within me to forgive you."

Remember the words of the preacher from the marketplace, when he said, "Seek and ye shall find, knock and it shall be opened to you." For what he was saying was this: Believe and it will be.

This was what the Righteous One meant when he said, "My father's house is many mansions." And He prepares one for each of us, Perpetua, according to how we believe.

Remember this too: We are born believing, and we must find the way back to the birth-soul. And when we do, we receive the Gift, which is this: faith creates.

I taught my children that wonderful things awaited them in the afterlife. Children die so young, they have not had the time to develop faith, and so we must give it to them. I draw comfort now, knowing that when three of my precious little ones were taken from me, and perhaps Pindar as well, if he died in that storm, they closed their eyes believing in my wondrous stories, and so that is where they are now, living in joy, waiting for me.

I leave you, Perpetua, with this final prophecy: as the Messenger came before, he will come again to reveal to future generations the Seven Truths and the way back to the birth-soul. The messenger will be high-born or low-born, man or woman, friend or stranger. Be watchful, and listen.

And finally, Perpetua, the most wonderful news of all—

"What's that?" the abbess said suddenly, looking in the direction of her office, which was off the library.

"It's the signal on your modem," Michael said. "You have a call coming through."

Not yet accustomed to the new computer system that had been

donated to the abbey and that Michael had set up over a week ago, Mother Elizabeth had to be shown how to route the call through the computer so that she could view the caller on the screen.

"It's for you, Dr. Alexander," she said when she came out of her office a moment later. "Your fiance."

Before leaving Santa Monica, Catherine had called Julius to tell him that Thomas of Monmouth was wrong, that the seventh scroll *did* exist, and where. He was calling now from the Sinai; his image filled the computer screen as he said, "Catherine, there is something you have to see!"

When she looked at the monitor, she was not surprised to glimpse Mr. Sayeed, Culture Minister for the Egyptian Antiquities Organization, standing in the background with a scowl on his face. Mr. Mylonas from the Isis Hotel was there as well, waving at the camera. Samir, Catherine's site supervisor, who had helped her to escape, was there, too.

The tents were gone, nearly all traces of Catherine's encampment erased. She could just make out her excavation site, roped off with warning signs to keep out. And in the distance, where Hungerford's men had blasted up the Jesus fragment twenty-three days ago—

Julius was standing beside the well. It was covered with a tarp anchored by stones. "Catherine," he said, his image flickering on the computer screen, "when I came to the abbey that first night to ask you to come home, to tell you that there wasn't a seventh scroll, and you refused, and then the next morning we found you gone, I realized that never in all my life had I felt as strongly about something—a belief, or a cause—as you did about the scrolls, I had never been willing to sacrifice myself for something. In that moment I envied you, Catherine. I had always lived by the rules, playing it safe, never willing to take a risk. But what you did, while I didn't agree with it, filled me with such admiration for you that I decided it was time for me to do something as well. So I came to Egypt, I sought out Samir, got some loyal workers to help me, and I went down into the well."

He made a gesture, and whoever was handling the video camera, panned over. "I uncovered what the authorities had covered up," Julius said, "and then I began to excavate out the rest of the skeleton."

"You broke the rules," Catherine said.

He smiled jubilantly. "Every rule I could think of!"

She moved closer to the screen. "What did you find?"

Lifting the protective tarp that covered the mouth of the well, Julius clicked on a high-beam flashlight and lowered it on a rope down the shaft. Catherine watched as the stone walls were illuminated layer by layer, until the beam widened at the bottom and shone on the bones of—skeletons.

Two—not one.

Just then, in the distance, they heard the abbey's gate bell ringing. "I know who this is," the abbess said with a sigh. "I received a call earlier. I refused to take it. Now I have some explaining to do."

"The first body," Julius continued as Mother Elizabeth left her office, "the one you discovered, is a woman. She appears to have been put in the well with her hands and feet bound, most likely while she was alive. But the second skeleton is male, his wrists aren't bound, and he doesn't appear to have been thrown down the well, although he is somewhat lying on top of her."

The picture quality was poor, but Catherine could see the gentle draping of the arm over the smaller skeleton, the protective way the male skeleton was curved against the back of the female. "Lovers," Catherine murmured.

"My theory is, he followed her down into the well and stayed with her while she died. And then either couldn't or didn't want to leave."

"And are they connected to the scrolls, Julius?"

"Beyond a doubt. The male seems to have draped a cloak over himself and the woman, and over the basket as well. I examined fibers from the skeletons and from the basket under an electron microscope. They are an exact match."

Catherine felt her throat tighten at the sight of the fragile, naked bones. "I wonder who they were."

"I don't know that we'll ever find that out for certain."

As she gazed down at the frail, pale skull at the bottom of the well, Catherine thought: Was she the last of the deaconesses? Was this the last Christian priestess?

"There's something else," Julius said.

SISTER GABRIEL MOVED cautiously along the icy path. In all her years with the order, she could not recall a winter that had seen so many visitors at the abbey.

"Benedicite," she murmured to the distinguished caller. "Come this way, please. Watch your step."

Mother Elizabeth, having heard the gate bell, met Cardinal Lefevre in the reception room.

Julius turned away from the camera and fairly raced over the sand, giving his cameraman a run. He arrived at a table standing under a canopy. "I found these pieces in the well, Cathy," he said excitedly. "Look!"

The camera zoomed in on pieces of pottery. "Israelite!" Catherine said.

"If not proof," Julius said, "then a start anyway, toward proving that Moses and Miriam came this way! Proving that you were right!"

"Julius!" she cried. "I *love* you!"

He nodded and smiled. *"Mazel tov,* Cathy." And the screen went dark.

She remained at the computer for a long moment, before she finally broke away and looked at Michael.

"WE HAVE A visitor," the abbess said as she entered the library a few minutes later. Catherine and Michael, who were also just coming back into the library, were not surprised to see Lefevre.

His look, sharp and disapproving, went straight to Michael. "The monsignor at Sainte Solange had instructions to inform me, Father Garibaldi, should you ever receive a communication from Dr. Alexander. It is fortunate that I was in Washington, D.C., at the time. However," he added, scowling at the abbess, "the telephone call I made to this abbey went unheeded."

"You would have told Mother Elizabeth to give the scroll to you," Catherine said. "And she would have had to comply."

He looked at Catherine. "Mother Elizabeth told me she gave you the scroll." He held out a hand. "May I have it?"

"No."

"I am prepared to, how should we say it, purchase the scroll from you."

"I don't want the Vatican's money."

"I do not offer money." He paused, thoughtfully tapping the gold cross on his chest. "We could try force, I suppose. But that would only make you a martyr and the Church a villain. So I will strike a bargain with you. What I offer, Dr. Alexander, is total restoration of your mother's reputation and reburial in Christian ground."

The room fell silent; the clock over the fireplace ticked softly.

Catherine stared at him, a veiled expression in her eyes.

"I see that you weren't expecting that," Lefevre said. "So it comes down to this—which is more important to you, Dr. Alexander, the scroll or your mother?"

"Why do you care so much about this scroll?" she asked. "When the United Nations turns the other six over to the Egyptian government . . . or, tell me, do the other six scrolls even exist anymore?" She nodded. "I see. And the photographs I took, have they also vanished?" She regarded his cryptic expression. "So . . . they never existed, and these past three weeks never happened. What do you intend to do with the seventh scroll? Destroy it, too?"

"What is your decision, Doctor?"

Catherine said, *"Full* restoration of my mother's reputation and standing in the Church. *And* reburial next to my father."

"As soon as I return to Rome I shall get the process started." She regarded him for a moment longer, then she said, "Come this way." She turned abruptly and went into the mother superior's office, where the seventh scroll lay on the desk.

Catherine wordlessly picked it up and handed it to him.

"Your translation as well, Dr. Alexander."

She gave him the yellow pad.

He flashed a victorious smile. "You have made a wise decision, Dr. Alexander."

"Two things Sabina taught us," Catherine said, "is to accept and to believe. I accept my mother's death. And nothing on earth, not even you, Your Eminence, can turn back the clock and change the way she died. My mother believed she would join my father. I believe it, too."

"I am glad you have made peace with the past."

"You don't understand. What I am saying, Your Eminence, is this." And she stepped aside so that he could see the computer screen.

Upon which was displayed a scanned image of the seventh scroll.

"I've already entered the English translation," Catherine added. "Are you familiar with this new software?" It was Dianuba 2000. Designed to connect the world's one hundred million Internet users in a simultaneous instant.

Lefevre's expression darkened. "Who will believe you? Without the other six scrolls," he gestured toward the monitor, "this is worthless."

"It's enough. People will see *this* scroll, at least, and my translation of the other six. They'll know this is real." Catherine reached out, poised her finger over the Global Transmit key.

Lefevre spoke quickly: "Do this and you destroy Christianity!"

"I *validate* Christianity."

"All those messiahs—you will weaken Jesus in the eyes of the world."

"All those messiahs *prove* that Jesus was who He said He was." She glanced at Michael, and a silent communication passed between them. "Sabina's scrolls have proved to me that He did exist, and that His word is truth."

"If you do this," Lefevre said, "then you cancel our agreement. I will no longer be bound to act in your mother's behalf."

"That doesn't matter anymore," she said.

"For the love of God," he began, "don't—"

"I do it," she said, "precisely *for* the love of God."

Lefevre moved so quickly she was caught off guard. "I can't permit it," he cried, holding her wrists in a surprisingly strong grip.

Michael jumped forward.

"No!" Catherine said to him.

But then suddenly Mother Elizabeth was pushing through, and before anyone realized what she was doing, she hit the keyboard precisely on target and in the next instant—

Sabina's testament flew out into cyberspace.

Greek and English words scrolled up the screen so fast that they were a blur, spinning off onto the Internet to fly to millions of terminals all over the world. The four gathered in Mother Superior's office didn't speak as they watched, mesmerized, the lines of text zip up the screen, scrolling as if on invisible rollers, the letters vanishing onto unseen lines, to race around the globe—words spoken long ago in a marketplace shooting out to receptive eyes and ears faster than any mind could comprehend, the names of ancients gods and their virgin mothers, stories of crucifixions and resurrections, of Christian priestesses and universal saviors, and beliefs written in many tongues, read now in a new tongue by the followers of new gods and new gospels.

Lefevre made a move to shut the machine down, but Michael blocked him. Lefevre leveled his gaze at him. "This is no longer your concern, Father Garibaldi. Need I remind you that disciplinary action is currently pending against you? Don't weaken your case further. I have suggested leniency so far, but if you don't step aside—"

"Your Eminence," Michael said, looming tall over the older man, "for a long time I was so wrapped up in myself that I could no longer hear God. I had convinced myself that He hadn't called me, that I had entered the priesthood for the wrong reasons. I didn't understand. But now I do. Being a priest, Your Eminence, isn't about piety or obeying the rules. It's about spreading a message of faith and hope. And I know now that this is my calling, what God sent me to do."

"I was the one who sent you to the Sinai!"

Michael smiled and shook his head. "No, Your Eminence, it wasn't you."

Michael stepped aside, knowing it was too late for Lefevre to intervene. And as they looked at the monitor, with the abbess crossing herself, a look of new peace illuminating her face, and Cardinal Lefevre murmuring a desperate prayer, Michael went to stand close to Catherine to watch how finally, near the end, the words began to slow, with the final page of the seventh scroll and Catherine's translation appearing on the screen, handwritten letters blending with digital bits and bytes. . . .

"And now for my own wonderful news. Although my hour draws near, do not grieve for me, dear Perpetua. My body is old and weary and I am ready to go. But my soul is invigorated and eager to enter into the Great Mystery. Last night, the Righteous One came to me in my sleep. He said, 'Do you believe?' And I replied, 'Yes.' He said, 'O woman, great is thy faith. Be it unto thee as thou will it. Stretch forth thine hand and come with me.'

"And so, dear Perpetua, I shall."

EPILOGUE

THEY STOOD BESIDE Nina's new grave, next to her husband's in the Catholic cemetery, while Michael read the prayer: "O God, Creator and Redeemer of all the faithful, grant to the souls of Charles and Nina Alexander, Thy servants departed, the remission of all their sins, that through pious supplications they may obtain that pardon which they have always desired. O God, Who livest and reignest, world without end, may they rest in peace. Amen." Michael closed the prayer book.

"Amen," Catherine echoed.

She felt Julius take her hand. In a few hours he was to board a flight for Cairo; the Egyptian government had invited him to join the excavation of what they were now calling the Well of the Prophetess, a site that, if proven to be where the ancient Hebrews had indeed once camped, would be sacred not only to Jews but to Christians and Muslims as well, attracting new pilgrims and tourists to Egypt. Julius was to oversee the care and analysis of the bones of the two martyrs found in the well, and to supervise the construction of their mauso-leum.

Catherine was not going with him.

As a breeze whispered among the headstones, stirring up leaves and dust, Catherine's eyes met Michael's. She knew that he was remembering their night together in the medieval inn in Aachen when he had held her in his arms and whispered, "We have found the way to the Light. . . ."

While Michael had spoken, Catherine had seen. Sabina's world had finally blossomed behind her eyes, exactly as Michael described it, as it must have been. But when they reached the threshold of the temple, Michael couldn't go in. So she had whispered to him, "Don't be afraid. Take my hand. We shall go in together." Then she had whispered what they were seeing inside the temple, and Michael had seen the vision that he had been afraid of—his own divinity.

As Catherine stepped away from her mother's grave, she saw something roll into her view, tumbling end over end like an autumn leaf. It was papery and yellowed, and she thought for an instant that it was a fragment of papyrus. But then she saw that it was only newspaper that had been out in the sun too long. Brittle, it nearly disintegrated as the breeze slapped it against Nina Alexander's new headstone. Catherine saw the headline: NEW MILLENNIUM STILL TO COME!

People were beginning to realize that the end of the two thousand years had not occurred on December 31, 1999, but would in fact take place on December 31, 2000, nine months from now. And as millennial fever began to swell again, so did people's spiritual hunger and their quest for answers.

Catherine had thought, three months ago, that her involvement with the scrolls had ended with their global transmission from the abbey: downloaded from the Internet by those who were curious, and then gaining in popularity through word of mouth, Sabina's scrolls had been copied and passed along, reproduced, e-mailed, sent around the world many times—now they were being read by millions. But people were asking questions, they sought answers, interpretations, and reassurances about the scrolls' message and authenticity. So Catherine knew her work was not yet finished, that she couldn't return to the Sinai with Julius. She also finally understood the meaning of the cryptic dream she had experienced at the inn in Aachen.

The first part of the dream had revealed to her that tymbos meant "grave," but there had been a second part which she had been unable to decipher, a curious vision in which she saw the whole world—continents and oceans, cities and wildernesses—turn gray, and then white, and then pink and green and gold, and then gray again; she saw leaves fall, turn to dust, vanish, then burst forth on green branches—all the seasons occurring at once. In a flash, nature had died and then been reborn before her eyes. She hadn't known at the time what this signified. But later, at the abbey, as she had read the final scroll, the prophetic meaning of the dream had come to her: that the ancient cycle of faith and believing was about to start again. It was time for the Messenger to return.

"Good-bye, Cathy," Julius said now as he kissed her softly on the lips. He paused to delve into her eyes, he saw her purpose shining there, and the difficult road that lay before her. The scrolls were being attacked and discredited from all sides, their message ridiculed, their ancient author vilified. Someone had to defend them, and spread their universal message of faith. "I will always love you," he murmured.

"God go with you, Julius," Catherine said, and she watched him walk to where his car was parked, spring sunlight guiding his way. Then she turned to Michael, who was waiting for her.

Their work together was about to begin.

ACKNOWLEDGMENTS

It is a fact that this book would not even exist if it had not been for the support and willing assistance of the following people, to whom I truly cannot say a big enough Thank You:

Lieutenant Rick Albee (retired) of the Riverside Police Department for patiently explaining the workings (and human mentality) inside a police station and for providing some interesting tips.

The staff of the Lordston Corporation, for sharing generously, and at a frantic moment's notice, their expertise in technical wizardry and computer know-how.

Fredi Friedman, my editor, who saw the same "vision" I did, and whose encouragement, advice, and guidance were always so spot on it's uncanny.

Carlos, for taking me by the hand and leading me onto the Internet, turning me into a happily addicted cyberjunkie.

Sharon, for providing me with the NIV Study Bible, with astoundingly auspicious timing!

Acknowledgments

My husband, Walt, of course, as always, whose patience throughout the entire writing process never ceases to amaze me.

Finally, Harvey Klinger, a dear friend who also happens to be my agent—the best in the world (every single author on the face of this planet should be so lucky).

Love to you all!

CPSIA information can be obtained at www.ICGtesting.com
Printed in the USA
BVOW08s0848060515

399232BV00002B/55

31192021231913